THE SPANISH HOLIDAY PROPOSAL

BY
ROBIN GIANNA

THE RESCUE DOC'S CHRISTMAS MIRACLE

BY
AMALIE BERLIN

MILLS &
BOON

Christmas in Manhattan

All the drama of the ER,
all the magic of Christmas!

A festive welcome to Manhattan Mercy ER—a stone's throw from Central Park in the heart of New York City. Its reputation for top-notch healthcare is eclipsed only by the reputation of the illustrious, wealthy Davenport family and the other dedicated staff who work there!

With snow about to blanket New York over Christmas, ER Chief Charles Davenport makes sure his team is ready for the drama and the challenge…but when it comes to love, a storm is brewing such as they've never seen before!

Available now:

Sleigh Ride with the Single Dad
by Alison Roberts

A Firefighter in Her Stocking
by Janice Lynn

The Spanish Duke's Holiday Proposal
by Robin Gianna

Aristocratic paramedic Mateo Alves needs a temporary fiancée, but will he be able to let Dr Miranda Davenport go when the holiday is over?

The Rescue Doc's Christmas Miracle
by Amalie Berlin

Risk-taking air ambulance paramedic Penny Davenport has a secret to tell her partner, the cautious, wary Dr Gabriel Jackson—she's pregnant with his child!

And coming soon:

Christmas with the Best Man
by Susan Carlisle

Navy Doc on Her Christmas List
by Amy Ruttan

THE
SPANISH DUKE'S
HOLIDAY PROPOSAL

BY
ROBIN GIANNA

HarperCollins
PUBLISHERS
Since 1817

Published in Great Britain 2017
By Mills & Boon, an imprint of HarperCollins*Publishers*
1 London Bridge Street, London, SE1 9GF

© 2017 Harlequin Books S.A.

Special thanks and acknowledgement are given to Robin Gianna
for her contribution to the Christmas in Manhattan series.

ISBN: 978-0-263-92674-3

Our policy is to use papers that are natural, renewable and recyclable
products and made from wood grown in sustainable forests. The logging
and manufacturing processes conform to the legal environmental
regulations of the country of origin.

Printed and bound in Spain
by CPI, Barcelona

Dear Reader,

It's always a pleasure to get to work with other authors on a continuity like this one! The Davenport siblings are certainly interesting, with challenging dynamics and a few family struggles, but they all eventually get their happily-ever-afters. :)

I love it that the editors set my story mostly in Spain. I enjoy researching interesting places, and Spain was no exception. One thing that surprised me is that there really *are* a large number of dukedoms in the country!

This is the first book I've written with the fake engagement trope, which was fun.

ER doctor Miranda Davenport agrees to help Mateo with the ruse—partly because her life history has made her a people-pleaser, and also because she knows what it's like to feel as if you might not live up to your family's expectations. Mateo Alves, EMT and member of the Spanish nobility, thinks Miranda is just the woman to stand up to his parents. They're pushing him to move back home, marry, and take over running the family estate, but he wants to keep his life in New York City. Then he finds out that Miranda might be a great doctor, but her toughness and confidence are a veneer she puts on to cover her vulnerabilities—and he's placed her in a situation that reminds her of past pain in her life.

Mateo and Miranda help each other reconcile their pasts and see that the things they've always believed about their roles in their families aren't entirely true. They've both held close to a deep conviction that they've never measured up, and by seeing each other carrying this false belief they learn to let go.

Robin xoxo

I'd like to dedicate this book to wonderful fellow medical author Amalie Berlin, who helped me brainstorm parts of this story and was always there when I needed to wail about the struggles I had pulling it together. Thanks for always being there, Amalie! xoxo

A big thanks to Dr Meta Carroll for helping me with the medical scenes in this book, per usual! Meta, you are the best! xoxo

After completing a degree in journalism, then working in advertising and mothering her kids, **Robin Gianna** had what she calls her 'awakening'. She decided she wanted to write the romance novels she'd loved since her teens, and now enjoys pushing her characters towards their own happily-ever-afters. When she's not writing, Robin's life is filled with a happily messy kitchen, a needy garden, a wonderful husband, three great kids, a drooling bulldog and one grouchy Siamese cat.

Books by Robin Gianna

Mills & Boon Medical Romance

Visit the Author Profile page
at millsandboon.co.uk for more titles.

CHAPTER ONE

FOR HEAVEN'S SAKE, can't you go any faster?

Since it was obvious the massive traffic jam made that impossible, Miranda Davenport bit her lip to keep from exclaiming exactly that. Her cab driver seemed as frustrated as she was, not being able to move more than a few feet at a time as the minutes ticked by, and no amount of impatience by either one of them was going to help her get to the hospital sooner. Even from several blocks away, the blue and red strobe-like flashes from multiple emergency vehicles covered the street, jammed so heavily with cars that could only inch along every five minutes or so.

"Subway tunnel collapse must be bad. Hope it isn't a terrorist attack," her cab driver said.

"Yeah. Me, too." The thought of the subway tunnel collapse being done by terrorists made Miranda shiver, but she also knew that sometimes things like that happened from structural decay, and prayed that was the case this time. She also prayed there wouldn't be too many casualties, and she clenched her teeth with impatience because it might be critically important for her to get to the hospital ASAP. Excruciatingly long minutes ticked by until she couldn't stand sitting there any longer.

"Listen, I think I'm going to get out and walk from here." It was still quite a few blocks to the hospital and her trek home had proved that winter had decided to arrive in New York City with a vengeance. But sitting here barely moving felt torturous when the Manhattan Mercy ER might well be swamped with patients, and they'd called her back, anticipating the worst.

"Hang on a few more minutes, lady. Let me see what I can do."

Like so many of the drivers whose vehicles filled the street, her cabbie honked his horn, and Miranda nearly clamped her hands to her ears at the cacophony. Growing up in Chicago then living in New York City for the past thirteen years meant the sound of car horns usually faded into the background. But after being stuck in the middle of this traffic mess for the past half-hour, it was starting to give her the mother of all headaches. Or maybe her headache was from not enough sleep after the twelve-hour shift she'd just worked in the ER, not expecting a catastrophe to bring her back before she was even home.

The cab managed to move a couple feet before the driver laid on the horn again, and Miranda knew the poor guy was going to be creeping along in this traffic for a long time. "Sorry, but I've got to get to the hospital. Thanks for bringing me this far. Here's extra for your trouble." Never having had that "extra" in her younger life was something she'd never forget, and even after all this time it felt good to be able to share the wealth. She shoved a fold of cash through the window to the front seat, then opened her door to exit right in the middle of the street. Not that dodging between stopped cars to the sidewalk brought any risk to life and limb at that moment.

The frigid air sneaking down her neck felt practically sub-zero, and she grabbed her coat collar, ducked her head down against the wind, and hurried toward the hospital. Good thing she had on the comfortable shoes she always wore to work, and her strides ate up the pavement fairly quickly until she came to the dust particles filling the air. Then she stared in shock at the yawning hole where the pavement had collapsed in the street, the subway tracks clearly visible below. Her heart tripped into double-time as she watched numerous firefighters and paramedics running in and out of the tunnel. Then she yanked herself out of her shocked stupor, moving closer to see if she could assist.

"You have any patients that need help?" she shouted above the chaos. "I'm—"

"You need to move to the other side of the street!" a paramedic yelled back. "It's not safe here."

"I'm an ER doctor, heading to the hospital. Wondering if you need any help here."

"No. We're doing okay. Thanks, but you need to move on."

"Can you tell me how many injured the hospital might be dealing with?"

"Right now, looks like not a lot. The collapse was only in a small area, and not many people were waiting for the train there." He swiped a grimy gloved hand against his forehead. "Unless something else happens, we're hoping for minimal victims. Right now we're focusing on shoring up the tunnel as we search to see who else might be down there."

The air Miranda sucked into her lungs in cautious relief was cold and full of the nasty dust, and she coughed. "Okay. Good luck, and be careful in there."

She pulled her scarf up over her mouth and moved away from the hole to hurry on to the hospital, only to be stopped by police officers who were setting up orange barriers on the sidewalk, insisting she cross over to the other side of the street.

About to argue and tell them her mission, she decided to just do as they asked. There were hardly any pedestrians on the other sidewalk to impede her progress, so she'd be able to walk faster anyway. As she moved across the barricaded street, a sound caught her ears. Something that sounded like someone crying out in the distance, and she stopped, straining to hear. Another faint cry had her heart pumping faster, and she hurried around the barricade in the street to see what was making the sound, abruptly stopping at the sight. Had no one seen this other, small collapse in the pavement? Dust swirled up from a virtual stepping stone of concrete and asphalt, leading down into the darkness.

Had the first responders been so focused on the large collapse that they hadn't discovered it yet? Did they know someone was in there?

She swung around to get the attention of one of the police officers, but they'd moved too far away to hear her. Heart beating in triple-time, she windmilled her arms to get the attention of the firefighters and paramedics, but in the midst of everything going on, nobody noticed a lone woman in a black coat waving at them. It probably didn't help that this hole was a good block away from them now.

Would she lose precious time trying to get help? Her heart jerked at the thought of going down into that tunnel, but she had to do something, right? Whoever was in there might be injured, and surely the paramedics would see this small hole any minute. The question was, would they arrive too late, when she was there right now?

Miranda battled down the fear that rose in her throat as she fished in her purse for the small but bright flashlight she always kept there. Stumbling a little, she picked her way through chunks of asphalt and concrete as quickly as she could, leaning over to place her free hand on the jagged lumps to steady herself as she descended beneath the street. The farther down she went, the harder her heart pounded, finally leaving the light of day completely behind her as she headed into the flat darkness.

She peered through the dark, fighting a slightly panicky feeling of claustrophobia. But she was here now, and she'd never forgive herself for being cowardly and climbing back up when, for all she knew, someone could be dying down here.

"Hello? Anyone there? Are you okay? Do you need help?"

A moan and a shout she couldn't understand came back, which sent adrenaline surging through her blood.

"Hang on! I'm a doctor. I can help if you're hurt."

No answer this time. Moving through the rubble wasn't easy, and she felt beyond frustrated at how hard it was to see through the fine silt filling the tunnel beneath the street, swirling up as occasional small bits of rubble fell from the ceiling. Where were the victims in this mess, and how far inside could they be?

The dust made it hard to breathe, and she coughed, pulling the scarf looped around her neck up to cover her mouth again. Not to mention that she was short of breath from the worry of who might be trapped and if she could help at all. And, oh, yeah, the idea that the whole street might come crashing down was just a tad unnerving. She tripped a few times, until a second beam of light from farther inside the tunnel slashed across her, illuminating the way a little more.

"What the hell are you doing in here? Get out!"

Taken aback by the angry male voice, Miranda stopped in her tracks for a second and didn't answer. Then she gathered her wits and sent her own flashlight toward the voice as she fired back, "I'm here to see if I can help."

"Not if this tunnel collapses on you. Get out of here. Right now. Can't you see it's dangerous down here? There's only one injured person, and I'm taking care of him. Last thing I need is someone else getting hurt through her own stupidity."

Anger joined the adrenaline heating her veins. Who did this guy think he was? Being told what to do was something she'd hated for years, let alone when it was coming from some hero wannabe. She moved forward again, trying to see through the dust and rubble.

"There's nothing stupid about helping injured people. Where...?" Her flashlight finally landed on two men. One was on the ground, bleeding from his forehead and lying awkwardly on one arm. Even with the lack of light, his pallor told her he was going into shock. The other man was crouched over him, his fingers on the man's neck, apparently trying to get his pulse rate.

"I'm not going to say it again—you need to leave! For all I know, this could be the work of terrorists, with a chemical attack to follow. I've got this guy, and responders will be here any minute."

The thought of a chemical attack sent a shiver down Miranda's back, for both herself and anyone else nearby, but she wasn't going to leave until she knew survivors were taken care of. "Have you seen anyone besides this victim?"

He yanked off his coat, completely ignoring her question. His tone changed so completely when he spoke to the man, its gentle quietness surprised her. "I'm going to move you so I can look at your arm. Try to relax, and don't help, okay?" He slowly rolled the victim to his back with extreme care, wadding his coat up under the man's feet to elevate them, obviously knowing how to treat someone going into shock. Then in one fluid movement he pulled his shirt over his head before ripping it into pieces, pressing one section against the man's forehead. "You hold this against your head wound while I look at your arm."

"My dog," the man said on a moan. "Do you see my dog?"

"Remember? I said I'll look for him after I check you out. And I will, but it's not going to do your dog any favors to have you go into shock, is it?"

The patient nodded in response. Miranda finally reached them and crouched down. "I'm a doctor. I can help."

The bossy man paused to look up at her, his eyes meeting hers in an intense stare before he gave her a quick nod. "All right. Hold his arm steady as I get this off." He pulled a knife from his coat pocket, flipped open the blade, then began quickly and efficiently cutting away the victim's coat sleeve.

"Got it." She briefly flashed her light over the victim's arm, noting the navy-blue sleeve was dark with what was probably blood. She put her flashlight down on the rubble, trying to direct the light toward the man's arm, before she reached to gently but firmly hold it in place as the rest of the sleeve was cut away.

He paused in his cutting to clamp his flashlight between his teeth so he could use both hands and see at the same time he worked, which made Miranda look more carefully at his shadowed and dirty face. His ridiculously handsome face, which she now realized with a start she'd seen before, and that always made her take an involuntary second and third look. A face that belonged to an EMT she'd often seen in the hospital, bringing in patients.

Trying to remember his name, she was filled with a short rush of relief that she wasn't alone in this place, trying to deal with this serious injury before figuring out how to get him to the hospital. That the man working on the patient knew what he was doing, and that they could work together as a team.

The way he was leaning over the patient made it hard to see the man, so she stared at the medic's head instead, tipped downward as he cut away the cloth. She knew his short hair was normally black, but right now gray powder covered both it and his dark brows. More of the silt filtered down onto all three of them, and she swallowed hard, shoving down the fear that skittered down her back again at the thought of being buried alive.

The last of the coat and clothing was cut off, and they were both finally able to see the jaggedly ripped and bleeding flesh of the victim's forearm. While she couldn't see the bone beneath it, there was no doubt this was a compound fracture. Which meant the bleeding had to be stopped and the arm stabilized while trying not to jar the broken pieces in the process.

The medic's eyes met hers, and what she saw there telegraphed loud and clear that he knew as well as she did that if the bones got moved the wrong way, they risked an artery being torn, which would turn a bad situation worse.

He took the flashlight from his teeth and tucked it under his chin. "You still got his arm steady? I'm going to wrap it."

"Yes. You can let go. I have a book in my purse. We can use it as a splint."

He glanced up, his intense eyes meeting hers again. "I have a magazine folded in my coat pocket. I'll use both to stabilize the arm after I get the bleeding stopped, so leave the book, then go."

Ignoring his comment the way he'd ignored hers earlier, she watched him carefully lay a piece of his shirt on top of the bleeding wound, then lift his hand, apparently planning to press down on it.

"Don't do that, you'll dislodge the bones!" she said. "We need to be as careful as possible not to cause further damage. Putting pressure on it isn't a good idea. A tourniquet is a better option to try first."

"I realize that a lowly EMT knows little compared to you, Dr. Davenport," he drawled, emphasizing the word *doctor* as he continued to work quickly, wrapping a strip of torn shirt around either end of the cloth bandage. "But I know a lot more about field medicine than you do and I have the technique down pat."

Surprise that he knew her name was quickly replaced by serious annoyance as his nearly amused tone started to really tick her off. She opened her mouth to retort that an ER doctor was fully trained in all kinds of emergencies. Until that emotion and her words dried up fast as she watched the remarkable efficiency and competency he showed as he tied off a makeshift tourniquet, then held the victim's legs up with one arm as he grabbed his now filthy coat from the ground to pull out a magazine.

All right, she had to admit it, but not to this autocratic male. While she worked hard to be the best doctor she could be, this guy had her beat when it came to this kind of emergency, working without all kinds of medical supplies and the equipment she always had available at her fingertips.

"This is probably going to hurt, so hang on," he said to the patient. "You doing okay?"

"O-Okay," the man said on a gasp that turned into a groan as the medic slowly and carefully straightened his arm. He then curved the magazine beneath the man's elbow.

"Can you—?"

"Yes." She reached to cup her hands underneath to hold it in place as he worked to secure it with strips of his shirt. The patient moaned, and Miranda leaned closer. "I'm sorry, sir. I know it hurts, but the hospital's close by. As soon as we get the wound secured, we'll get you out of here. You're going to be fine, and getting meds to help with the pain really soon."

"Where's that book?" the medic asked, never pausing as he knotted the strips and reached for another.

"Here." With one hand, she slid her bag from her shoulder and reached in to fish out the book. "I'll place it under his wrist when you're done."

A quick nod as he finished up with the magazine, then suddenly lifted his eyes to hers. The quick grin he sent, along with a smile in that brown gaze, took her totally by surprise, and for some ridiculous reason made her heart beat little harder. Apparently helping him had taken her off his list of highly irritating things. For the moment, at least.

"I'm sorry, I should know, but what's your name?" she heard herself ask, suddenly needing to know.

"Mateo Alves. This is John, and his dog, Benny, ran in here after the collapse, which is why John came down here in the first place. He's a fast one for a shorty dog, but I'll find him. And I already know you're Miranda Davenport. I'd say it's nice to meet you, except you shouldn't have come in here to begin with."

"Too bad. There's nothing falling now, so we're probably safe." She knew she sounded a little breathless, which was probably due to the silt in the air and not at all to the fact that she'd fantasized about the über-handsome EMT more than once in the ER. During those times, they'd all been busy treating patients, so there hadn't been time to spend more than a brief moment staring at him, and now wasn't a good time either. Except she found that, for what felt like a long moment of connection between them, she was staring at him anyway.

"Yeah, well, that could change in one second."

She glanced up, gulping at that reality. To cover her worries, she threw out a tart response. "Aren't you going to admit that both of us working on John's arm has been faster than you doing it alone, and better for him?"

"Maybe." Another quick flash of teeth.

"I'm going to put the book under his forearm now."

"Wait. I want to cover the wound better first."

Her rapt attention on his handsome features was interrupted when he frowned and paused in his work on the wrist splint. She looked down and saw that he'd used every scrap of fabric from his torn shirt.

"Give me your scarf."

"Oh. That's a good idea," she said, wishing she'd thought of it. She slipped it from her neck and handed it to him. "And I can cut the bottoms off my pants, too, if we need them."

That flash of grin. "What do you think, John? How often do you have a woman offering to rip her clothes off for you?"

"Not often enough." A weak smile accompanied his words, then disappeared again. "My dog. My Benny. I haven't heard him bark."

"Probably too scared to bark. But I have a surefire way to call dogs—you'll see. Right now, though, we have to get you out of here without jostling your arm any more than necessary. Dr. Davenport?"

"Yes?"

"I'm afraid I'm going to have to take you up on the offer of your pants. Don't worry, I won't cut any above your knees." That sexy smile again. "But that fabric is a lot better than my jeans to finish securing the splint, since I'm going to use your scarf as a sling to keep it still."

"That makes sense." Of course he'd need a sling, and she thrashed herself that it hadn't occurred to her. Thank God none of her siblings or father could see her. She'd spent the last thirteen years trying to make them proud of her, to earn their respect, and right now she felt totally inept.

She reached for the knife and pushed the point into the knit material. It went in easily, even as she inwardly cringed at the thought of accidentally jabbing herself in her own calf. And being that kind of wimp proved even more that Mateo was absolutely right—he was definitely better at this field medicine stuff than she was, and she vowed to study it again, maybe even go on some runs with the EMTs to refresh her skills.

But not with Mateo Alves. She'd find someone whose sexy face and body wouldn't distract her from her training mission.

"Careful. Don't cut yourself."

"I know how to use a knife."

"Do you cut clothes off yourself on a regular basis? Pretty sure that's harder than cutting a sandwich."

"Funny." She struggled to move the knife down through the pants leg without gouging herself in the process, and as she did so heard an impatient sound come from Mateo.

"Let me."

"I'm doing fine."

"Yeah? Well, every second is time John isn't at the hospital for pain meds and treatment, and we're all still down here."

"There hasn't been any debris for a while. Right?" She paused in her cutting to look up at the dark tunnel ceiling again, wishing he'd stop pointing out the possibility of impending collapse.

A snorting *humph* was his only response as he tugged the knife from her hand and took over, getting it through the cloth in mere seconds, then hacking it off from around her knee before tearing it into strips. For some reason, having the blade so close to her skin didn't worry her when it was Mateo doing the cutting. Maybe it was because the touch of his fingers on her skin as he moved them down her leg distracted her from being scared. "Rule number one is to get the hell out of any collapsed building ASAP. Which you're going to do right now, to get a crew down here with a stretcher. I'm surprised someone hasn't already come in here."

"Okay." She knew he was right, that trying to move John, even with his injury splinted and in a sling, would be painful and dangerous if he had to try to walk, especially after all the blood he'd lost. "I'll be right back."

"Back?" His focus was on finishing tying the last strip over the book then fashioning a sling from her scarf, but his scowl was most definitely directly at her. "Don't be stupid. Just tell them where we are."

And again he was right. Why she was feeling this weird need to actually see both of them make it out, she didn't know. But she wasn't needed here, and might well be needed at the hospital. "Okay," she repeated as she stood, ridiculously feeling a need to brush some of the powdery dirt from her coat. "Since I definitely am not stupid, I'll see you at—"

"Anybody in here?"

Miranda sagged in relief at the voices and the sight of two bobbing flashlights.

"Back here! About thirty feet. Bring a stretcher," Mateo called. "Just one victim. No access to the subway platform. He came in because he was trying to get his dog out."

"Got a stretcher right outside." In mere moments two medics were there, Mateo helping them get John settled on the stretcher as he shared details of the patient's condition and treatment. They wore full gear—reflective coats, hard hats, gloves, and various tools dangled from their belts. Which made Miranda wonder, for the first time, why Mateo was in street clothes. Or, actually, at that moment, very few clothes, with his shirt destroyed and his coat still off, and she found herself staring at his wide, muscled chest and broad shoulders.

"Are you off duty?" she asked.

"Yes. I was on my way to the main collapse when I saw John run in after Benny, then get hit by a chunk of concrete."

"My little dog…" The two men picked up the stretcher, ready to carry him out, and John's words were bitten off as he moaned.

"You get out of here too, Mateo," one of the rescuers said. "You're not equipped. I'll send some guys in to check for anyone else, just in case, but the good news is that it looks like a structural collapse, nothing else. We've got plenty of crew on the scene and if no one else is in here, that means everyone's out and clear both places. So you can go on home."

"I have make sure a certain stubborn doctor gets to the hospital first."

"Tough job you have," one said, laughing, as they made their way toward daylight.

Miranda bent to casually retrieve her purse and flashlight from the ground, not wanting to show him how eager she was to get the heck out of there now that John was taken care of. Not wanting him to see how she'd been staring at his beautiful body. "You know, I'm not stubborn. It just seemed like I should help if I could, just like you did."

"It's my job to run into harm's way when necessary. Don't think that's in your job description. Come on."

He slid the filthy coat back on over his naked torso, then reached for her elbow. As they stepped over chunks of concrete, Miranda suddenly longed to be outside in the cold air and out of the dark gloom. Which she wouldn't admit to Mateo for the world. "You don't need to hold me up. I'm perfectly capable—"

"I just want to get outside, and if you fall and gash open your head we'll be stuck in here all that much longer."

"I'm sorry if I've made the situation more difficult," she said, her stomach churning a little that he seemed to still think she'd done exactly that, and what did that make her? A pain in the neck, that's what, just like her step-mother had told her for years. "I should have thought it through better and gotten a firefighter instead of coming in here myself."

"Yes, you should've. But I have to admire how brave you are. And you were a big help, even though I hate to admit it."

Even in the darkness she could see the smile in his eyes, which put a warm little glow in her chest and had her smiling back.

"That's much better than telling me I'm annoying and stubborn," she said. "You—"

A deep, ground-shaking rumble was followed instantly by sharp cracks and the thud of chunks of concrete hitting the ground. Miranda gasped, instinctively covering her head with her arms, as though that flimsy barrier could protect her in any way, when a heavy weight slammed straight into her.

CHAPTER TWO

MATEO'S HARD BODY took her down like a football line-backer, as he somehow managed to wrap his arms around her before they hit the earth. The sharp pebbles they landed on stabbed and scraped her one bare leg, a bigger chunk of concrete jabbed into her ribs, and her face landed on the hard pillow of Mateo's muscled forearm before sliding off it into a pile of silty debris.

His weight smashed her down so hard she couldn't get her mouth clear to breathe, and his body jerked at the same time as he grunted loudly in her ear. Lifting her head half an inch to suck in a chokingly dusty breath, she twisted and pushed at him, blinded by the dirt in her eyes, which sent tears streaming down her cheeks. "Get off! Can't breathe…"

He didn't move, and she jabbed her elbow into his ribs, which sent another low grunt into her ear. "Hold still a minute," he said. "I just took a boulder for you and you're trying to hurt me more?"

"What?" His weight lifted slightly off her, and she twisted around fully to lie on her back, sucking in deep breaths as she stared up at his grim face. Her hands decided on their own to grab at him, landing inside his coat on his shoulders, clinging, pulling him close. Somehow, she wriggled enough to move her spine off whatever was currently lodged there.

"You okay?"

"I— I'm okay." She realized that was true, she was fine, possibly only because she had a two-hundred-pound blanket of bone and muscle covering her. "You?"

"Bleeding, but okay. And see? Seems to be all finished," he said in a ridiculously calm voice. He lifted his gaze to scan the tunnel. "Let's give this a few more seconds to make sure it's done, then we'll get the hell out of here."

Light silt still showering down in intermittent swishes mingled with his heavy breaths against her lips, and her own fast breathing against his. Their eyes met and held, and she was suddenly acutely aware of the feel of his skin against her palms, the strength of his muscles, the movement of his naked chest against her. The grip she had on his warm shoulders loosened, and her hands moved down his pectorals, smoothing across the soft hair covering them before she realized with dismay what she was doing. Making herself let go, she curled her fingers into her palms to keep from touching him again. Fought the peculiar combination of sensations swirling around her belly that didn't seem connected to the fear that had consumed her just moments before.

She pulled in another deep breath. What in the world? The two of them were lying in a collapsed tunnel, for heaven's sake, and it was long past time to get safe.

"I'm... I'm ready," she said unsteadily. "To leave."

"Finally?" His lips curved just a little. "Let's go."

His big body lifted from hers, and his hands grasped her waist, effortlessly swinging her to her feet. His arm wrapped around her shoulders as they moved quickly out of the tunnel toward the light. Miranda blinked at the brightness of the sky—how had it seemed so gray and gloomy before? The fresh, cold air filled her lungs, sharp and stinging and wonderful. Trembling a little now that the whole thing was over, she tried not to think about how bad it could have turned out, and turned to see Mateo watching her with an odd expression on his face.

"You sure you're okay?"

Probably, she looked pale and shaken, her pretense of bravery through the situation now shot to heck. "Yes, okay. Thanks for, you know, crushing me with your body so I didn't get crushed worse by flying debris."

"You're welcome. Except I didn't completely succeed. Your coat is torn."

She followed his gaze to the large rip in the shoulder seam of her coat, and couldn't help the little dismayed sound that came from her lips. "Oh, no! I just bought this last month! Must have happened when you tackled me."

"Better a torn coat than a broken head. Which you would have deserved for not leaving when I asked you to."

"Not even I deserve a broken head."

That statement made his lips quirk as he reached out to brush his finger across her dusty eyelids. "You'd better get washed up."

"Me? You look like a gray-haired old man right now." Which couldn't be further from the truth, since no old man had the kind of wide, muscular chest that was mostly bare right in front of her, or flat, rippling abs, or such a chiseled jaw. And because she couldn't stop looking at him and was enjoying their banter far too much, she forced herself to look away up the sidewalk, pretending to focus on all the emergency equipment and personnel. Then her peripheral vision caught bright red drops of blood splattering on the sidewalk behind his feet.

Wide-eyed, she jerked her attention back to him. "You're bleeding! Oh, my God."

"I can tell it's just a scrape. Maybe a gouge, too, but nothing worse than that."

"Take off your coat so I can see."

"I'll freeze."

"Better to freeze than die from blood loss." She pushed at the shoulders of his open coat and, shaking his head and grumbling, he finally slid it off. She turned him around, then stared in dismay at the swollen, raw scrape and shallow puncture wound that was the source of the drops of blood. "For heaven's sake, you really did take a boulder for me!"

"I'll live."

"Does it hurt anywhere else?" She ran her hands across his shoulders and back, wiping off the dusty debris from when he'd had his coat off earlier, looking for other injuries that might not be obvious. "I feel just terrible that I was pushing and jabbing you to get off me when you really were hurt."

"Like I said, just a scrape. And I'm tough."

He tried to turn around, but she stopped him. "And you call me stubborn! Just be still a minute." With her scarf gone, the best she could do to staunch the trickle of blood was a pathetic wad of tissue she scrounged from her coat pocket, pressing it firmly against the bruised indentation as her left hand continued to roam his hard contours and smooth skin.

Abruptly and without warning, he surprised her by turning, her hands moving along with him, and the sight of that manly chest and the feel of his skin and soft hair on her palms had her mesmerized again, touching him the same way she'd touched his back, slowly and thoroughly, though there was clearly no injury on this side of his body.

"You about finished examining me, Doctor?"

Oh, my God. His low rumble made her realize exactly what she'd been doing. Dropping the tissue and yanking her hands back like she'd touched a hot furnace, horrified that she'd practically been fondling the man, she stared up at amused brown eyes.

"I'm sorry… I didn't mean to, you know, run my hands all over you like that, I was just, um, checking for more injuries, but you seem…" She cleared her throat, utterly mortified. "Fine."

He gave her a slow smile that said he knew exactly why she'd been touching him, which had been way too softly and leisurely to be considered a medical necessity. Heat flooded her face because, yes, the man was very, very fine and she'd just made an utter fool of herself.

Beyond relieved that he slid his coat back on, she wished with all her heart that he'd button it up, too, so she wouldn't have to keep finding other things to look at. Like his gorgeous face.

"Thanks for the first aid." He reached out to gently smooth a finger down her dirty cheek. "You're a mess. Do you live nearby?"

"No, I live in Brooklyn. But I'll go to the hospital and use the showers there."

"Be careful walking—looks like some of the sidewalk has heaved in the collapse."

He turned and, astonishingly, it looked like he was about to head back inside the collapsed street they'd just come from. "What are you doing?"

"I've got to find John's dog."

"What? Surely you're not going back in there! Or at least get the safety equipment and hard hat on before you do."

"Unless he somehow got out, it won't take long. The

space beyond where John was injured ends just another thirty-five feet or so back."

And with that, he disappeared, leaving her with her hands clutched to her chest and her mouth gaping open after him.

What should she do now? Go on to the hospital like she didn't know the crazy man had gone back into harm's way? Go tell the first responders that one of their men was insane? She felt bad about John's poor dog and understood why he'd gone back in for it, but what if the whole ceiling collapsed and neither one of them survived? He should have gotten help before going back in to look for him, and protected himself somehow.

She stood there with various horrible scenarios running through her mind, each worse than the last, making her feel a little woozy. After several minutes ticked by she decided, nearly hyperventilating, that she had to tell someone so that he wouldn't be in there alone, knocked unconscious by a slab of concrete or buried under a shower of rubble, and just as she was about to rush to one of the fire trucks, an even more dusty Mateo trudged up out of the wreckage. A small dog was tucked into the crook of his elbow like a football, and Miranda wasn't sure if she wanted to laugh or yell at him.

She planted her hands on her hips and sucked in a shaky breath. "Are you out of your mind? You had me worried to death!"

"Unnecessary. But when a beautiful woman worries about me, it's appreciated nonetheless." He held up what she could now see was a rather chubby dachshund that was probably brown, though it was hard to tell for sure. "Benny likes it, too, don't you, buddy?" Mateo scratched beneath the dog's chin, who managed to feebly wag his tail despite his ordeal.

Miranda smoothed her hand across the pup's back, smearing the dust around, and her fear and desire to yell at Mateo faded into a smile of her own. "He's so cute. John will be very glad. How in the world did you find him?"

He stuck two fingers into his mouth, and the shrill whistle was so loud it made Benny squirm and Miranda cover her ears.

"Oh, my gosh! That would make me run instead of come to you. And you do realize your hands are filthy."

"Eating a little dirt is good for one's immune system, which you surely know, Dr. Davenport."

"Yes. Well, I already ate my quota of dirt for the day." Aware of a ridiculous desire to just stand there and talk with him for hours, filthy and cold or not, she managed to remember that she had to see if the hospital had a big patient load after the collapse. "Gotta go. You want me to find John and tell him? What are you going to do with the dog?"

"Take him home. I'll call the hospital and have them tell John, and he can find someone to come pick him up."

"That's...nice of you." In spite of her best intentions, her eyes kept wandering from the dog to Mateo's naked chest beneath his coat, remembering how his skin and body had felt, and she decided she'd better get out of there before he could see exactly what she was thinking. "Well..."

Fixated as she was on his handsome face and beautiful physique, she didn't even hear the chime of her cellphone announcing a text until his finger pointed to her purse. "That your phone?"

"Oh! Yes. Thanks." Lord, had he noticed her distractedly, ridiculously, staring at his body? Again? She quickly fished in her bag and read the message. "The hospital says they don't need me. That there aren't too many injured, they're sure it wasn't a terrorist event, and everything's under control. So that's good news."

"It is."

She lifted her eyes to his brown ones, and something about the way he was looking at her made her chest suddenly feel oddly buoyant. The thought of going to her apartment and being all alone for the rest of the day pushed that air right back out, but she shook it off. When she wasn't working, didn't she spend most of her time alone anyway?

"Well, good luck with the dog and all." She cleared her throat. "See you at the hospital sometime."

She turned away from that mesmerizing brown gaze and started walking, then realized she'd have to rethink her route, since the subway she usually rode might be out of commission. She pulled up the subway updates on her phone to check which ones were running and which weren't, when a large, dirty hand rested on her forearm to stop her in her tracks.

"So where are you going?" Mateo asked.

"Brooklyn. My subway might be open but if not, I'll just take a taxi."

"In this mess? It'll take you hours."

And wasn't that the truth? The clogged-up traffic looked even worse than when she'd left the taxi. "Then I'll go to the hospital after all."

"Do you have a friend or boyfriend who lives close enough to walk to their place?"

"No boyfriend, and most of my family live on the Upper East Side."

"I live just a couple of blocks from here. You might as well come with me and Benny and get cleaned up there. I probably have pants that'll fit you that you could wear home."

She'd hardly be surprised if a man as hunky as Mateo Alves had clothes women had left at his place, but she wasn't about to wear any of them. "Thanks, but no. I'll be fine."

"Suit yourself. Walking ten blocks to the hospital, covered with dirt, wearing a torn coat and pants with one bare leg exposed in this cold, is going to feel very uncomfortable." An indifferent shrug made her wonder why he was even asking. "And if you can ride the subway, people will think you're homeless and want to sit far away from the strangely dusty woman with ripped clothes. Or offer you money."

She had to laugh at that, but as she looked down at herself, she realized he was right. Not to mention that her leg already felt a little numb from the cold wind. And what if she ran into someone she knew, or a former patient, and had to answer a gazillion questions and have people think she was crazy to run into a collapsed tunnel, just like Mateo had?

She thought about how her sister Penny always accused her of doing everything in her life as safely as possible, and today she'd proved that wasn't always true. And taking Mateo up on his offer would definitely not be the quiet, boring route either, would it?

"Fine." Her pulse quickened as she agreed. "I appreciate it."

"I have a secret reason for asking, you realize."

Her heart lurched at the wicked glint that suddenly appeared in his eyes, and a whole lot of possibilities swirled through her head. Was she out of her mind to actually go with him? Her eyes glued to his, she breathlessly asked, "What?"

"Benny can't be returned in his current condition." He

held out the little dog. "I'm hoping you'll take him in the shower with you to get him washed up as well."

Miranda felt warm from head to toe as she shoved her arms into the oversized white robe Mateo had given her before her shower. She had a bad feeling that the heat pumping from her pores was from more than just the hot shower. That it might have something to do with feeling embarrassed that she was naked in Mateo Alves's bathroom, and that she'd been thinking thoughts that should not have formed in her brain at all.

Thoughts of Mateo coming into the small space while she was in the shower, which of course would be horrifying and creepy in real life. But in her fantasy world, safe behind a locked bathroom door? Very, very exciting. And what woman wouldn't think about that for at least a second, when the man was the most gorgeous male specimen she'd ever laid eyes on?

Not to mention that there was something about him that made her feel utterly safe. Had even felt absurdly safe in that tunnel with debris showering down on them, which was ridiculous. His body, big though it was, couldn't have fully shielded her if the entire street had collapsed on them. But that he'd thrown himself on her to protect her the best he could made her feel a little warm glow, even though she knew it was part of his job and he'd been angry with her for even being there in the first place.

She stared into the mirror and finger-combed her damp hair, glad she'd decided to cut it into a bob a couple of years ago. With her work schedule it was easier to take care of now, and after today's crazy events it would have been a tangled mess if it had been longer. She shook her head at the sudden wish that she had more than just lipstick, making a mental note to put some makeup in her purse for next time.

As though there'd be another time she'd rush into danger, be yelled at by the world's most handsome paramedic, then insistently brought to his home to get cleaned up. No, this was a once-in-a-lifetime moment, and she needed to get her clothes dried fast and get out of there before she embarrassed herself again by ogling him. Before he remembered he'd been annoyed about her getting in his way today. The kind of annoyance she'd gotten all too used to once Vanessa Davenport had grudgingly allowed her to live with her father and half-siblings.

"Thanks again for your robe," she said as she walked into his small but comfortable living room, tying the attached terrycloth belt of the over-large robe even tighter. She stared at him lounging on his sofa and licked her dry lips, trying to sound calm and normal instead of absurdly nervous. Which was obviously a ridiculous way for a mature woman to feel, but boyfriends had been few and far between in her life, mostly because she'd quickly learned that none of them had been interested in her, just in her name and the Davenport money and connections. "Are my...are my clothes almost dry?"

"They need maybe ten more minutes." Unfolding his body from the deep leather sofa, he moved toward the bathroom with Benny, now wrapped in a towel to keep the dust from getting everywhere, tucked under his arm again. "I hope you left some hot water for us."

Her mouth went even dryer. "You're...going to shower? Now?"

Dark eyebrows lifted at her as he paused. "Do you object to me using my own shower? I believe I'm covered in even more silt than you were. And I can't exactly pass

Benny on in his current state, since you refused to take him in with you."

"Of course I don't object." Which was a lie, because she really wanted to say, *Yes! I'd really rather you wait to take off your clothes until after I'm gone!* "And I didn't refuse, you said you'd take care of washing him."

"Because I'm an excellent dog washer, and I suspect you don't have much experience with canines."

It was true, but the way he said it seemed to imply he thought she was a prima donna or something. "You sure do claim to be excellent at everything. And I'm sure I could handle washing a little dog."

"I have no doubt you handle all kinds of things with aplomb, Dr. Davenport." That quick grin of his flashed before he disappeared into the only bedroom.

Apparently, she'd fooled him pretty well, because there was only one thing she was really good at, and that was being a doctor. Something she'd worked hard to do, trying to live up to the Davenport name. The family she only sort of belonged to, and would probably never be worthy of.

The sound of the bathroom door clicking behind him sent Miranda to perch on the end of the sofa, looking around his small apartment. His decor could be described as minimalist, but the furniture was obviously expensive, and the few pieces of art unusual and eclectic. Not posters from a cheap store but beautifully framed originals hung on the walls, and several excellent sculptures were placed on the modern tables.

She ran her finger across a bronze with fluid lines. Interesting and unexpected that an EMT would have the financial resources for art like this. Maybe he was the kind of man who bought very little, but when he did, it was only the best.

Pondering the man, she absently picked up a magazine, surprised to see that it was about horses and horse-breeding, and flicked through the photos of beautiful animals, hoping for a distraction from her nerves. Until the sound of the shower put a completely different image in her head. Picturing a naked, muscular Mateo with water streaming down the dark hair on his chest shortened her breath and did other things to her body that embarrassed her all over again, reminding her of exactly how she'd felt in that tunnel when he'd been lying on top of her.

Lord, this was ridiculous. What in the world was wrong with her? She was twenty-nine years old, for heaven's sake, and a doctor who'd seen plenty of naked men in her career. Naked men were in her life every day!

Except Mateo wasn't a patient, and she couldn't remember a single man she'd ever known, patient or otherwise, who'd been even close to as gorgeous as he was.

She blew out a breath, and just as she was about to go to the small laundry closet to check on her clothes and throw them on, damp or not, a loud knock sounded at the door to his apartment.

She stared, frozen. Should she answer? The distant sound of the shower told her Mateo wasn't even close to being done, and if she hadn't been there, he wouldn't be answering anyway, right? Besides, what if it was a girlfriend or something? How could she explain being in his apartment in his robe? Then she remembered it might be whoever was coming to get Benny, and decided she'd better answer before they left, assuming no one was home. She moved toward the door as a man's voice boomed through it.

"Mateo! Are you there?"

To Miranda's surprise, she heard the keypad beep just before the doorknob turned. The door opened to reveal an older couple, probably in their early sixties. The petite woman had dark hair with streaks of gray, coiffed into an elegant chignon, and the man was tall and unusually slender. He held a cane and was walking slowly, a step behind the woman as they came into the apartment. Both stared at her with raised eyebrows as their gazes took in her wet hair and the fact that she was standing there naked except for Mateo's robe.

The embarrassment she'd felt before flamed another hundred degrees, and if there'd been anywhere she could have run, she would have torn right out of there.

"Is Mateo here?" the woman asked, her eyes remarkably cold-looking for being a warm, velvety brown.

"Um, yes. He's…he's in the shower. See, there was an accident today, part of the subway tunnel collapsed, you might have seen it on the news, or gotten stuck in all the traffic? So I went to help and Mateo was in there rescuing a man and his dog, and we got all dirty, and then…" Her voice faded away. Lord, she must sound like a raving lunatic. "Um, come in. I'm sure he'll be out in—"

"Mother. Father. What are you doing here? I thought you'd already left for home."

Miranda turned to see Mateo standing in the doorway to his bedroom, and what little breath she had left backed up in her lungs. Because he was wearing a towel around his waist and nothing else, with a sheen of water droplets in relief on his wide shoulders and athletic chest, a few dripping down the dark hair on his taut stomach just as she'd visualized earlier. Only even better.

She gulped. Obviously, he'd heard voices and hadn't taken the time to fully dry off, and between the vision in front of her and her embarrassment that these two people were his *parents*, she thought she just might go into a swoon.

"Our plane is ready to go, but we decided to come here before we left, hoping to convince you to come home with us now, instead of waiting. But apparently you are otherwise engaged."

His mother turned those cold eyes to Miranda, and they reminded her so much of the way her stepmother had always looked at her, it made her heart constrict oddly. Made her feel as unwelcome as she had in her teens when she'd first shown up at the Davenport mansion, which was absurd. She didn't even know these people, but she couldn't help feeling like she'd somehow shoved herself somewhere she was unwelcome anyway.

Mateo folded his arms across his damp chest, his features stony. "I told you I'd be coming home soon. And I will."

"It must be very soon. There are things we need to address right away. You are the heir now!" His father pulled a sheaf of papers from his coat pocket and held them out to Mateo, his hand shaking with what looked to be a tremor as he did so. "Your mother and I are trying to manage until you arrive, but it is difficult for us to attend to everything. Too many people are relying on me, on you, to be ignored."

Miranda looked from Mateo to his parents, and back. What in the world were they talking about? Unlike his mother, his father's attention was focused exclusively on Mateo, who made no effort to introduce her to them. Which shouldn't have bothered her, except it made her feel even more like the lowly interloper that Vanessa Davenport had clearly viewed her as thirteen years ago. And still did.

"I understand. I'll let you know when I'm going to arrive, which I promise will be in just a few days." Mateo's biceps bulged as he lifted his arm to squeeze the back of his neck, his expression grim. A now clean, tail-wagging Benny ran from the bedroom to stand next to Mateo's feet, looking up at him adoringly as Mateo dropped his arm back to his side. "However, as you can see, I'm rather busy right now."

"You have a dog? In this ridiculously tiny apartment you insist on living in?" his mother asked in an incredulous voice.

"It's not my dog."

A man of few words. Miranda had to wonder about the odd exchange between Mateo and his parents, with him obviously not wanting to share anything about the events of the day. It was also obvious they weren't going to be sharing warm and fuzzy hugs. She knew how it felt to have a strained relationship with your own family, and hoped it didn't bother him the way her own situation always had.

"Well. We will see you at home, then, and look forward to your arrival."

His mother's eyes rested on Miranda one more time before she turned and swept out into the hallway without another word, her husband slowly following. It struck Miranda that their bearing was remarkably regal, their clothes obviously expensive. It was somehow surprising that these two unusually elegant people had a son whose chosen profession was that of a paramedic. But as she watched Mateo move to close the door behind them, it struck her that there was something intangibly noble about his bearing too.

He turned, his face impassive. "Sorry about that. Probably your clothes are ready."

His words reminded her that she was still standing there in his robe, otherwise naked, and that he was practically naked, too. She found herself staring again at the beyond sexy contours of his torso, the beautiful golden shade of his skin, and the dark hair covering his pectorals and hard stomach, which she knew felt soft to the touch. Jerking her eyes up to his didn't help the breathless feeling that came over her, as they only managed to land on his chiseled jaw and the beautiful shape of his unsmiling mouth, and her own lips parted to suck in a much-needed breath.

What was it about Mateo Alves that had her feeling so peculiarly stirred up and uncomfortable and embarrassingly aroused whenever he was near?

One hand lifted to clutch her robe tighter to her throat before he turned to get her clothes from his small laundry closet. Eyeing the wound on his back as he opened the dryer, she nearly offered to bandage it for him in case it started bleeding again, but decided she needed to keep her hands off his body. Getting dressed and out of there as soon as possible was the best plan, and she practically snatched the warm clothes he brought from the dryer.

"There are a pair of women's sweatpants on my bed for you. It's the best I could do."

"Anything is better than walking down the street with only one pants leg," she said, feeling a little strange about wearing pants that had presumably belonged to a lover of his, but she didn't have much choice. "I'll get dressed, then out of your hair."

Finally respectably covered up, she swiped on a little lipstick, still feeling oddly jittery as she went back to his living room.

"Thanks again for letting me get pulled together here. I guess I'll see you around the hospital sometime."

"Are you feeling all right?" The way he was carefully looking at her made her wonder what she was seeing. "Not stressed or odd about having concrete showering down on you, wondering if it was going to get worse? It's okay if you do. Even after regularly being in harm's way, plenty of people suffer emotional aftereffects from it."

"Well, as you pointed out, it's pretty much my own fault for going in there to begin with. Makes you think about how quickly things can happen, doesn't it? I see the results of bad accidents in the hospital every day, but somehow I never think about it happening to me."

"So next time promise you'll stay put and get someone trained in search and rescue."

"I'm hoping there's no 'next time.' But I can't promise— I took an oath to help sick or injured people, and if I have to put myself in harm's way, I'm going to do it."

"Yep, a very stubborn woman." A small smile curved his lips even as he shook his head in exasperation. "Just be sure to take care of yourself, and if you start to have bad dreams or flashbacks, talk to someone about it."

"Don't worry, I really am fine. But thanks." Maybe he thought she sounded stubborn and brave, but the truth was, she fervently hoped she never came across another situation like that in her life. "I do have vacation time coming up this week. I'm planning to get out of the city, do something fun."

"Like what?"

"Still figuring that out." The main reason to go away was so she didn't have to be at the big Thanksgiving family gathering at the Davenports'. She shoved her hand toward his, and his warm one engulfed hers. "Goodbye, and thanks again."

The way she rushed out of his apartment probably made him wonder if she really did have some post-traumatic stress going on, but she couldn't worry about that. She had enough to worry about.

Like what she was going to do with her week off, and why she'd had a sudden, astonishing urge to ask Mateo Alves to join her.

CHAPTER THREE

THE CHILD'S PIERCING shrieks would have unnerved even the most hardened EMT, and Mateo stepped up the pace to get her into the ER fast. Based on what the father had told him when he'd picked the wailing child up off the sidewalk, it seemed unlikely she had an internal injury. No blood, no visible head injury, no misshapen limb told him it probably wasn't extremely serious. But because he couldn't know for sure, that's why they were heading to the hospital—to check out the possibilities then go from there.

The anxious father had agitatedly told him the story of how the three-year-old girl had been sitting on his shoulders as they'd walked through the crowds. The dad hadn't expected his daughter to suddenly lunge sideways to get a better look at a toy store's glittering Christmas window display, and he'd lost his grip on her legs.

"I just couldn't catch her all the way, you know?" the father repeated as Mateo and the other EMT lifted the stretcher out of the ambulance. "I partially broke her fall to the sidewalk, but I'm so scared she might be really hurt."

"I know it's scary," Mateo said in a calm voice he hoped would keep the poor guy from hyperventilating.

"But Manhattan Mercy's ER docs are the best so, whatever's going on, they'll figure it out. Try not to worry."

The man nodded and gulped in some air, and Mateo turned to his patient. "Almost there, Emily," he said, giving the girl an encouraging smile. "Soon the doctors will figure out why you're hurting and get you something for your pain, okay?"

"What do you think is wrong?" the girl's father asked. Apparently, Mateo's attempts to reassure him weren't working. His voice was panicky, and his knuckles were white as he hung onto the gurney Mateo propelled through the ER's doorway. "It...it didn't look like she hit her head, but I couldn't tell for sure, you know?"

"Her vital signs are normal, other than an accelerated heart rate, probably caused by pain. I'm guessing it's not anything major, but we'll have the doctor take a look." Hopefully, whoever the doctor was would do a better job calming the dad than he'd managed to accomplish.

A nurse sent them to an exam room, and when a white-coated doctor with chin-length brown hair appeared in Mateo's peripheral vision, he knew it was Miranda Davenport before he'd even looked up. As if he'd somehow sensed it was her, and how strange was that? Also strange that he couldn't help the smile that formed on his face just from seeing her again.

"Hi," Miranda said with a sweet smile as she came to lean over the child and give her a comforting pat. "What's going on?"

"Three-year-old girl fell from her dad's shoulders onto the sidewalk." Mateo began his report as he unbuckled her from the gurney. Being careful to not jostle her, he gently moved her to the bed. "Ambulatory at the scene. Heart rate one twenty, BP ninety over fifty. Her name is Emily, and this is her father."

"What do you think, Doctor?"

The man's anxious eyes stared at Miranda, and Mateo decided that the professional but still warm smile she gave him would have had anyone breathing slightly easier. "We're about to find out," Miranda said as she turned that smile to Emily. "I know you're hurting, but can you be brave for me? Just like the princess here always is?"

Miranda tapped the sticker of a glittery cartoon princess she had attached to her name badge, and, remarkably, the child nodded and hiccupped as her crying lessened a little.

"Wow, you really are brave, like her! So, can you tell me where you hurt?"

The child waved her left hand toward the right side of her body, and Miranda moved her hands gently over Emily's head, then her arms and torso. Her careful fingers slowly went to touch Emily's neck, and Mateo instantly saw the swelling forming there. The child shrieked again, and Miranda lifted her head, her gaze meeting Mateo's for a long moment before moving on to the child's father.

"It looks like she has a fractured clavicle. See the bulge here on her collar bone? That might not sound like good news since she's hurting so much, but it's a comparatively simple injury that will heal well on its own. We'll get her pain meds right away to make her comfortable, then an X-ray to confirm the diagnosis. But I'm sure that's what the problem is."

That smile, her quick diagnosis, her ability to calm the child and her father, and the utter confidence illuminating her amazing blue eyes, all wrapped up in what Mateo knew was a hell of an attractive body, were one irresistible package.

"Thank God it's nothing super-bad," Emily's father said, swiping his hand across his brow. "What can you do for it? My wife is probably gonna kill me. I really need to know what to tell her when she calls me back."

"We'll get her a sling called a clavicle strap to keep her arm and shoulder from moving as it heals. And you can tell your wife that it's very common for young children to fracture their clavicles, sometimes even from a simple fall in their own homes. So she's actually a pretty tough cookie, aren't you, Emily?"

The child sniffled between whimpering cries and nodded as Miranda pulled one of the princess stickers from her coat pocket and handed it to Emily. "I hope this will always remind you how brave you were today. Your mom and dad should be proud of you."

Another nod, and as Emily even managed to smile through her sniffles this time, Mateo realized that Miranda had a special gift for soothing little ones.

"You don't put a cast or anything on it?" the father asked.

"If the two ends of the broken clavicle are in the same state, I promise it will heal on its own." Miranda sent the man another encouraging smile before giving instructions to the nurse about not moving Emily's arm or shoulder, and what pain medication to give her.

Mateo's job was done here, and though he would have liked to stay a little longer to watch Miranda work her magic, he figured he should get the ambulance back to the station. He pushed the gurney from the room, but as he passed Miranda in the hallway, she paused in typing her instructions into the computer chart and turned to look at him.

"Busy day?"

"Not too bad. No collapsed tunnels with crazy doctors running inside."

"Or dusty dogs to deal with." Her lips curved. "Did John's family come and get Benny?"

"Yes. My apartment seemed quiet after the little guy was gone."

"So getting a dog might be on your to-do list?"

"Probably not." He had other things on that list. Like being forced to move back home when he didn't want to, despite being needed there, and the guilt of his feelings about all that gnawed at his gut. He couldn't tell his parents he didn't deserve to step into his brother's shoes to take over the family's estate full-time. That his not being there for Emilio, for not doing more to help him, might be part of the reason he wasn't alive anymore. That memories of his laughter and jokes, of their closeness and all they'd done together their whole lives, were a constant ache every moment he was back in Spain.

The weight of all that hung heavily on his shoulders, as it had for the past six months, and he didn't know what he was going to do about it. Didn't know how he could convince his parents that it would be fine for him to be home just a few months of the year, when they expected him to be there full-time now that Emilio was gone.

As he stared at Miranda's pretty face and smiling eyes and thought about the disapproving looks his parents had given her, a radical idea struck him, slowly forming fully in his mind. And the more he thought about it, the more he liked it.

Yes, it just might be brilliant, and actually work. But would she possibly agree? He had no idea. But what he did know? Trying to persuade her just became the number one thing on that to-do list.

By the end of the day, Mateo had become convinced that the idea that had developed in his head earlier was the perfect solution to his problem. If Miranda was willing to go along with it, that was.

After all, what did he have to lose by asking her? He definitely couldn't suggest it to one of the women he casually dated, because they might read more into it than he wanted them to. But since he and Miranda barely knew one another, he couldn't imagine she'd read his proposal the wrong way. Plus, she was a Davenport. Someone from a wealthy and powerful family wouldn't think his lineage was a big deal and because of that, she'd be unlikely to get excited about it, like the women back at home always had. Women who wanted nothing more than to snag a wealthy duke, live a lavish lifestyle, and lord it over everyone who worked for his family, like his sister-in-law had.

Which was just one of the reasons he liked living anonymously in a big city like New York. He could date women for a short time who didn't want anything from him. No long-term commitments offered or expected, and that's how he wanted to keep it.

Miranda had said she didn't have a boyfriend, which he found incredibly surprising, but was more than glad about. She had also said that she'd like to get out of the city for a week or so. Get away from work and the challenges of getting to her apartment while the subway was being repaired. Away from memories of the tunnel collapse and how scary he knew that had to have been for her, even though she'd put on a brave front.

He thought about that again while he waited around for her shift to end. Frustrated with her as he'd been at that moment, now that she was safe and it was over with he had to admire that she'd run in there to help. Search and rescue had been his passion since his days in the Spanish military, but she lived her life on the receiving end of casualties in the ER. Without a doubt, lots of physicians would have waited for the rescue crews to bring out any injured before they got to work taking care of them.

He leaned against the wall of the hospital corridor, his gaze on Miranda standing farther down the hall, talking to the doctor taking over her patients. Did she always take this long to tie up loose ends after her shift was over? He glanced at his watch, impressed that, unlike some of the docs in the hospital who ran out the door the second their shift was over, she obviously wanted to make sure everyone was taken care of before she left.

Restlessly squeezing the back of his neck, he wondered if there was any way she'd agree to his proposal. If she said no, he'd just be in the same situation he was in now, right? But maybe he'd get lucky and she'd say yes, which would solve his problem at least in the short term. At the same time, he'd get to look at her pretty face and enjoy her lively mind during the time they spent together.

He'd always taken a second and third look at her whenever he'd brought in a patient, never dreaming he'd have her lush body beneath his the way it had been in the tunnel, or her nearly naked in his apartment. The memories of how both those things had made his blood pump hard and his breath get short had him turning to look somewhere other than at her before his body reacted all over again.

Miranda finally headed to the locker room and emerged just a few minutes later. Mateo pushed off the wall and moved toward her, watching as her slender fingers slowly buttoned her coat. She looked deep in thought about something, and he wondered if her brain was working overtime about her patients, or if something else was on her mind.

"Miranda."

She turned, and her amazing blue eyes that had shone through the darkness in that tunnel lifted to his in surprise. "What are you doing here? I thought your shift ended quite a while ago."

"It did. I came to see if you'd like to join me for coffee. A little thank-you for doing such a great job with Emily this afternoon."

"Oh. Well." Her tongue moistened her lips, and he found himself fixating again on how soft and full they were. "I was just doing my job, you know."

"Yes, but you do it very well." She looked so wide-eyed and shocked he couldn't help but tease her a little. "It's just coffee, Miranda. Surely your time in my apartment showed you I'm not a big, bad wolf."

A nervous little laugh left those pretty lips. "No. I mean, yes, I know. Of course, I'd love some coffee."

"Good. How about we go to the coffee house two blocks down? Pardon me for saying so, but the stuff they serve in the hospital is swill."

Another laugh, but this time it was a real one. "I don't mind it. But I suspect those of European heritage are a little more picky than those of us raised in Chicago."

He felt his eyebrows rise. He'd seen the Davenport mansion, and it was in one of the most exclusive areas in New York City. "Chicago? What do you mean? I know you live in Brooklyn now, but didn't you grow up on the Upper East Side?"

"Long story."

He wished he hadn't said anything, because the smile on her face instantly disappeared, and he hoped he hadn't ruined his chances of her going along with his proposal before he'd even had a chance to ask. He grasped her elbow and headed toward the revolving back door. "Come on. It's been a long day for both of us. I don't know about you, but I need a double shot of espresso, *pronto*."

"Espresso pronto sounds like exactly the drink I need

right now." The twinkle in her beautiful eyes was new to him, as she'd been so serious during their previous interactions. But he liked it. A lot. "Let's go."

A somewhat private corner table was open, and Mateo steered them there, glad he could ask his important question without anyone overhearing. After some general hospital talk and conversation about the continuing traffic mess from the tunnel collapse, Mateo drew a breath.

It was show time.

"I have something I'd like to talk with you about," he said. "To ask you."

"All right." She looked a little concerned about that, and he wondered what his expression was, forcing himself to relax. Not a big deal, right? Nothing to stress about. She'd either give him a yes or no, and he'd go from there.

"You met my parents yesterday," he said. "They—"

"Actually, I didn't meet them," she interrupted. "You didn't introduce me."

He stared at her, then realized that was true. Their stopping by his apartment unannounced, lambasting him and trying to drag him home right then and there, had upset him so much he'd completely forgotten his manners.

"I'm very sorry. That was rude of me. I was frustrated at the situation, which is what I want to talk to you about."

Her eyes met his, serious again. She sat quietly, sipping her coffee, and something about her expression and the caring way she was looking at him helped him relax.

"I've heard your family described as New York royalty. My family is a little like yours. We have a dukedom in Spain. In Catalonia, about an hour from Barcelona."

"A...what? A dukedom?"

"Sí." He had to smile at her incredulous expression. "I know you may think I'm making up a story, but it's true. You're welcome to look us up on the internet. You'll see my father, Rafael Alves; my mother, Ana Alves; and myself listed under the Duchy of Pinero, living at the Castillo de Adelaide Fernanda. My brother, Emilio, is listed as well." Just saying his name made Mateo's chest constrict with pain and disbelief. It was probably even worse for his parents since Emilio had been the favorite, golden son, which was another reason Mateo could never take his place.

"Wow. That's real royalty, not the fake kind the Davenports enjoy." Her palm pressed against her cheek as she stared at him. "I wondered what in the world your father was saying about you being an heir or something. What made you move to New York, if you had a cushy life of back home?"

Cushy life. If only she knew the difficult dynamics of their family. "I served in the Spanish army for four years, and discovered there my love for search and rescue. For field medicine. Being part of a team. Working as an EMT is a little like that, and I enjoy the anonymity of a big city like New York."

He wouldn't go into all the reasons he'd wanted to leave home, which included despising his brother's cheating, social-climbing wife and Emilio's private pain because of it. Somehow, for as long as possible, he had to avoid being thrust back into that world. Did part of him feel bad about that attitude? Hell, yeah. He also felt horrible that his father's health continued to decline. He had to find some kind of compromise where he could be there for his parents while still living most of the year here. Away from painful memories he didn't want to be reminded of every day.

"But they want you to go back home." She said it as a statement, not a question, which wasn't a surprise, since she'd heard his parents insisting he go back right away.

"Yes. My father is ill and handed over his responsibilities to my brother a few years ago. Then, six months ago, Emilio died in an accident. I became the heir and they believe it's my responsibility to run the estate."

"Oh, Mateo, I'm so sorry. I know how hard it is to lose someone you love."

She placed her warm palm on top of his as her eyes filled with a deep compassion. Remarkable, really, how a blue that intense could be warm and soft and brilliant all at the same time. Normally, he didn't want others' sympathy, but hers felt genuine and so full of caring for a man she barely knew that he found himself soaking it in, despite himself.

"Yes, it's been…hard. And just as hard is the thought that I have to leave my life here. We have many managers at the estate who are good at what they do. If I'm there only part-time, I believe that will be enough."

"You grew up there. Why don't you want to move back?"

"I like my job here. And there are reasons that I've been somewhat isolated from my family for a long time." Despite the question and the way her eyes focused on him in a way that showed she cared, he didn't want to go into them right then. "My father's illness puts pressure on me to step into his shoes, the way Emilio did. While I know that I have to take over for him in some capacity, I'm not going to move back to Spain full-time. I'm confident my parents will come to see that all will be okay when I'm there only part of the year. But I need some time to make that happen, for them to understand that. And that's where you come in."

"Me?"

"Yes, you." He smiled at her expression of startled surprise. "You'd said you have some vacation time and want to get out of the city for a while. I know that, as a Davenport, you have the means to travel anywhere you want, any time. But I can show you the beautiful area of Spain where my family has lived for centuries, have some fun riding our horses. Tour Catalonia and the Pyrenees. At the same time, you can help me accomplish an important goal by doing me a huge favor."

"Goal? Huge favor?" Those intense blue eyes had widened even further, and Mateo drew a fortifying breath, because her saying yes to his proposal suddenly felt much more important than it had an hour ago.

"I'd like for you to pose as my fiancée. My parents won't like me planning to marry an American who doesn't share their culture. I'll tell them you have a contract with the hospital, and can't possibly leave there for another year. You saw their disapproving expressions when you were at my apartment. I'm confident that our faking an engagement would buy me extra time and get them more used to the idea that I'll only be there a few times a year. Please, Miranda?" His heart sped up as he held her hand between his. "Will you pretend to want to marry me?"

Miranda realized her mouth had sagged open and stayed that way for a very long moment. Managing to finally close it, she stared at Mateo in utter astonishment, unable to find her voice. But who wouldn't be in total shock at his unbelievable proposal?

Pretend to be his fiancée? A fake engagement to keep his parents from insisting he move back right away, while the two of them, two people who barely knew one another, spent vacation time together in Spain? It was the most unbelievable, outrageous thing anyone had ever asked her to do.

And also crazily, absurdly, tempting.

The man was utterly gorgeous. The kind of man any

woman would love to spend time with. She'd seen he was caring, too, the way he'd run into the tunnel to help John, and had even put himself in danger again to go back and find Benny. Then today he'd been so good with little Emily, and the synchronized way they'd worked together had been remarkable and impressive.

But all that was a far cry from spending a week with him. And pretending to be engaged, for heaven's sake! Impossible.

"I'm just… I…" She gulped. "I don't even know you, really. That would be too strange, pretending we're, you know, a couple. And going on a trip together. I'm sorry, but I can't."

"I can tell you that it wouldn't be hard for me to pretend to want to spend time with you, because I genuinely do. I know we'd have a good time adventuring together while we're there." He gave her a crooked smile as he squeezed her hand, speaking softly. "When was the last time you did something crazy, Miranda? Just threw caution to the wind? That's what I just did, asking you to pretend to be engaged to me. What do you say? Good or not so good, it will be a true adventure for just a week, right? When we get back, you'll go back to your regular life, as I will, taking with us some enjoyable memories."

When was the last time you did something crazy, Miranda? His words echoed in her head. Her sister Penny lived her life as a daredevil, and had often asked Miranda that question, wondering why she was okay with her life being pretty mundane outside the excitement of the ER. She could just see Penny rolling her eyes at her hesitation, which was part of what had motivated Miranda to be bold and go to Mateo's after the tunnel collapse. How often had her sister challenged her to come along on one of her adventures? Each time she'd refused, Penny had run off without her, shaking her head and grinning, to climb some mountain or abseil from a helicopter or drive a dirt bike on a race course.

When *was* the last time she'd done something crazy? Probably when she'd been sixteen years old, and had gone to see Hugo Davenport, which was a long time ago now. Mostly, she'd lived her life carefully. Sensibly. Studying hard to become a doctor, to try to fit into the Davenport family at least a little. To make them proud of her. She'd excelled at school, and now she mostly worked, still proving herself.

If she'd been looking in a mirror, she could easily see *dull and dutiful* practically tattooed on her forehead.

So wasn't she due for something crazy? Something illogical and inappropriate and completely mad? Something ultra-exciting to do with her week off? After all, when she travelled with her family, she still sometimes felt like the outsider she'd always been. And most of her friends had boyfriends or husbands, and didn't want to vacation without them. So that left Miranda vacationing alone, as she often did.

As she'd planned to do this week. Because she knew that Vanessa Davenport only had a place setting for her at their Thanksgiving table because she was obligated to. And even though Miranda loved her siblings, and knew they cared about her, holidays always reminded her that she didn't really belong the way everyone else did. Having travel plans had become her MO in recent years to avoid that.

Suddenly, the thought of another trip all by her lonesome felt unbearable. Could she really do it? Do something insane and use her vacation time to travel with Mateo? Maybe it would be a disaster, or maybe it would be wonderful, but, no matter which, it would be something she'd never done before, right? Something not careful and sensible and dutiful. And if it turned out to be awkward, it was only one week out of her life. Seven days.

At the same time, she'd be helping Mateo with his problem, and never mind that her friends would tell her she was just being a people-pleaser as usual, which was a learned behavior she'd been trying to work on.

No, Mateo was obviously disconnected from his family, and didn't she know all about feeling that way? The pain he felt over his brother's loss? She had the power to help him during this difficult time. And she couldn't help the thought that, maybe, if she told Vanessa afterwards that she'd been briefly "engaged" to the heir of a dukedom, the woman might actually be slightly impressed.

And how pathetic was it that something like that would even cross her mind?

She drew a breath then stared at the incredibly handsome man sitting there, smiling encouragingly. "This is... this is the most outrageous thing anyone's ever suggested to me," Miranda said, and the reality of exactly how outrageous it was made her start to laugh. "But I find that, somehow, I can't resist. So my answer is yes, Mateo Alves. Yes, I will go to Spain with you and pretend we're going to get married."

CHAPTER FOUR

MIRANDA WASN'T NEW to flying in a private jet, since the Davenport family often used theirs, and she'd occasionally joined them. So it clearly wasn't the plane departing at night that was making her stomach jump up and down and her heart feel all fluttery.

No, it was the close proximity of the über-sexy man sitting across from her, his deep brown eyes focused on her during the entire take-off. It was the peculiar feeling that, despite the strangeness of the situation, it somehow felt oddly right, too. During the taxi ride to the airport and while they'd been waiting on the tarmac for clearance, he'd talked with her about his work and the ways it intersected with hers. Had shared an amusing story from his childhood that had made her laugh, putting her at ease. He had been an utter gentleman as he took pains to make sure she was comfortable on the plane. He was so proud and regal in his bearing, it struck her that she should have realized he was different from most of the EMTs who brought the injured and ill into Manhattan Mercy's ER.

Her eyes met his and the way he smiled at her had her smiling back, and at the same time her stomach felt oddly squishy, as though she'd known this man for years instead of days.

"Miranda."

His voice made her start. Probably because she'd been fixated on his handsome features and brown eyes and charismatic smile. "Yes?"

"A very small part of me feels a little guilty to have asked you to participate in the charade we are playing. But most of me is very happy that you've agreed to come with me, and I hope you know that. I'm looking forward to spending time with you, and this isn't just about my situation with my parents. So, for all those reasons, thanks for coming with me."

"No need to thank me. I came because I wanted to." And she had. Even when she'd been shocked at his proposal, deep inside she'd wanted to say yes the moment he'd asked, despite the self-protective part of her telling her she shouldn't.

Swatting down those insecure misgivings, she let the excitement of this adventure bubble up in her chest. It overflowed into a big smile she couldn't have stopped even if she'd wanted to.

"We'll be served a late meal soon, then you should try to get some sleep. I'm sure you know that, with the time change, traveling overnight is always best, arriving in the morning refreshed and ready to go."

"I'll try to sleep, but have to confess I'm not good at that."

"Not good at sleeping? What, are you in reality an android?" The corners of his lips tipped up as he raised his eyebrows. "Is this why you seem to always be at the hospital, working?"

She laughed. "No, I'm very human. I just mean I'm not good at sleeping on planes and in cars and such. I just get restless and start thinking too much and then I can't sleep."

"I hope you're not thinking too hard, and worrying,

about how our week is going to go. I'll do my best to make it less awkward when dealing with my parents, and show you Catalonia when we're not with them. I can't imagine you not loving it there."

If he felt that way, why was he so determined not to return? "I'm not worrying." Well, truthfully, now that she was actually on this plane with him, she couldn't help but hear, again, those whispers that reminded her she wasn't good enough for a man like Mateo Alves. But it wasn't real, right? So she didn't have to be concerned about not measuring up.

He reached into the pocket of his sport coat, and she stared when he held out what was obviously a small jewelry box, wrapped in light blue paper with a silver ribbon. She looked up to see him giving her an encouraging smile. "Go on, open it."

Oh my gosh. Her breath catching, she carefully tore the paper and lifted open the lid to expose a ring. A ring that held a pale blue stone at its center, surrounded by small white diamonds.

"I…" Miranda swallowed and tried again. "I assume this is a ring you'd like me to wear to convince your parents that we really are engaged?"

"I hope you like it. I got the blue diamond for you to wear because it reminded me of your eyes. Though no stone could look anywhere near as vivid and beautiful."

Her heart oddly fluttered at the seeming sincerity of his words and expression, though at the same time she knew they were probably just the practiced words of a man very good at charming women. "Well, it certainly is…pretty. I'll take good care of it for you."

"Thank you. I had no idea that I'd have to search for a jeweler that would allow me to return a ring. I'd assumed that if the woman said no, that would be a given."

"Well, now you know for up the road when you're asking a woman to marry you for real."

"Trust me, that's never going to happen."

The light amusement on his face disappeared and he turned to look out the window, seeming to concentrate on the gray clouds swirling around the plane. Feeling even more awkward now, Miranda sat there wondering what to do with the ring. Should she put it on, so it was safe on her hand? Or wait until they were about to meet his parents? A part of her wanted to put the dazzling ring on her finger just to see what it would look like there, but that felt too weird. Not that the whole situation wasn't weird. What if everyone at his estate, and not just his parents, took one look at her wearing that and knew she was nowhere near good enough to be a duchess one day? Fake or not, the thought sent a feeling of panic through her lungs that made it hard to breathe.

She swallowed hard and stuck the box in her purse just as Mateo turned to her with another smile that banished his somber look. "One note of warning when it comes to the ring. We have quite a few animals at the castillo, both inside and in the barns. One mischievous Siamese cat we had named Tup Tim was always sneaking onto my mother's dressing table and taking off with any jewelry she'd put there as she was changing.

"Once he stole a diamond bracelet that had belonged to my grandmother, and all of us chased Tup Tim out of the house, all around the grounds, then into the barn, where he ran up to stand on a high beam, triumphantly staring down at us with the bracelet dangling from his mouth. I had to shimmy up a pole and stagger across the beam like a tightrope walker, finally cornering him and retrieving it, and getting bitten for my efforts. He was not happy to lose his prize, but my mother was very pleased with me when I got it back. She never left jewelry on her dressing table again."

The amusing story was just what she'd needed to relax. Had he somehow known?

"That is really funny—I can just picture the scene."

"There was a lot of anxiety on the part of various staff and stable workers as everyone tried to grab the cat, with my mother shouting orders at everyone. I was glad to be the one who succeeded."

Something about the way he'd said his mother had been pleased with him made her wonder if that had been in short supply in his life. She wanted to ask, but decided it wasn't the right time to delve further into the Alves family dynamics. "I promise not to leave the ring out anywhere, though I admit I'd like to see you tightrope walking."

"Other than getting bitten, I thought it was quite an adventure. I ended up practicing walking along that beam as fast as I could whenever nobody was around to scold me. Turned out to be a good thing. Learning how to do that has come in handy plenty of times during various rescues, believe me."

His flashing grin made her chest feel buoyant all over again. Yes, Penny had been right. Doing something crazy had been the best decision she'd made in a long time. Miranda leaned back in her seat and gave herself up to the pleasure of being on this beautiful plane with smart, gorgeous, and amusing Mateo Alves as her surprise companion for a whole week of adventure she knew would be like nothing she'd ever done before. Nothing serious. Nothing to worry about. Just seven days to enjoy some no-strings fun.

The drive to the family estate was about forty-five minutes from the airport, and now that Miranda was past feeling a little concerned at the speed with which Mateo pushed the sports car through the open, winding roads, she was enjoying every second of the drive. It was more than clear that Mateo was a confident, excellent driver, which allowed her to sit back and soak up the incredible views. Valleys, still green in November, stretched far to the mountains in the distance, only to disappear as the road wound through forested areas with gold, orange, and red leaves clinging to the trees. Farms dotted the landscape, with cattle, pigs, and sheep grazing between long, ancient-looking stone walls. Picturesque towns came and went, each with at least one church featuring a tall bell tower that reached toward the sky.

"I can't believe how beautiful it is!" Miranda exclaimed again, pointing at the mountains rising behind a distant valley, snow visible at the peaks, with the bluest of lakes shimmering in front of it. "The colors take my breath away."

"At this time of year, you won't see all the flowers that Spaniards like to grow everywhere but, yes. The fall color and green valleys are still pretty. Have you not been to Spain before?"

"No. I haven't been to Europe at all."

"What?" Stunned eyes flicked her way before he returned them to the curving road in front of them. "How is that possible? Surely the Davenports travel all over the world."

Miranda struggled with how much to say about her life, explaining when and how she'd come to live with the Davenports, but decided to settle on a basic answer. Going into the strange, sad, and upsetting truth of her past, and the rest of her family's, would put a damper on the drive she was enjoying more than she could remember enjoying anything in a long time.

"Well, I was in college, then medical school, which takes a lot of time and focus, you know? Then I went on a few medical missions to Africa and Central America before working at Manhattan Mercy. I do go on vacation but they tend to be short breaks."

"I respect the single-minded focus and dedication it takes to become a doctor. And that you worked on medical missions says good things about you, Miranda."

The admiring smile he gave her made her tummy get squishy and she could feel herself blush. "Not really. Just another way to use the skills I'd learned." And to hone them more in a place where the Davenport reputation wouldn't hang over everything she did, making her nervous that she might let the whole family down if she made some mistake. Which probably meant that working overseas had been more selfish than altruistic.

"So." She moved the subject to him, because she'd wondered a lot about who he really was since the moment they'd met. "Did you ever think about going to medical school?"

"Honestly? Yes. For just a short time." His voice held an odd tone—a smile tinged with maybe bitterness? "Since I planned to leave Spain, my parents would have appreciated that occupation much more. Something better to tell friends and family about why I was going to the U.S. I realized, though, that while I like the medical aspect of my job, my time in the army showed me that search and rescue is in my blood. Which they never understood. But I came to see that I had to live my life for me, not for them."

She could tell that figuring that out had been a major struggle for him, and part of why she was on this trip to begin with. "Lots of people never find their calling. It's wonderful that you found yours."

"It is. And I thank you for helping me keep living my life as I want to. At least, as much as that will be possible. And now we are finally here. Welcome to the Castillo de Adelaide Fernanda."

A keypad was imbedded in a tall stone wall that seemed to surround the entire front of the property, and Mateo leaned out his window to punch in some numbers. Ornate iron gates probably ten feet high slowly swung inward as Mateo nosed the car through, then up a sloping, curved driveway, and Miranda couldn't contain a gasp at what lay at the top of the hill.

A huge, obviously very old stone house with a terracotta tiled roof sat nestled on lush green grass, looking nearly as though it was a natural part of the landscape. Other buildings made of stone or wood in various sizes could be seen not too far away, some surrounded by trees and others completely stark. Forests and fields seemed to stretch forever, with long stone walls dividing the spaces, and Miranda turned to stare at Mateo.

"Is...is all this your family's? It looks like it goes on for miles!"

"The estate is about one hundred and twenty-five hectares, which translates to about three hundred acres. We have livestock, farmland, and an equestrian center where show horses are bred and sometimes shown. The horses were always a big part of my and Emilio's lives when we were growing up, but when my father became too ill to manage the estate, they became my brother's passion. I...don't know what's going to happen with that part of the business now that he's not here to run it anymore. It's one of the things I'll have to talk with my parents about."

She looked at his profile, unable to read his impassive expression. "A lot of things to figure out, I'm sure. I'm sorry this is going to be a difficult trip for you."

He didn't respond, and she had to wonder if the mere act of driving through those iron gates had brought home to him full force the challenges he'd have to deal with on this visit. Since he didn't seem to want to go into that right now, Miranda made small talk about the amazing views until he stopped the car in a wide, circular turnaround in front of the house.

"We'll go inside and see where my mother has decided to put her house guest. I didn't tell her who my guest was—we get to surprise everyone."

"You didn't warn your parents ahead of time that it's the woman from your apartment, and that we're...er... engaged?"

"What was the point of having them stew about it in advance and be ready with protests? The military tactic of surprising the enemy is always a good strategy."

"Your parents aren't the enemy, Mateo. Remember that they've had a hard time of it recently, too."

"Believe me, I remind myself of that every day. And, no, not the enemy, but hostile to my chosen way of life? Yes." He turned his dark, shadowed eyes to her as they walked up stone steps to the massive arched wooden door decorated with a large, evergreen wreath with pine cones and a red bow. "But I know they don't understand, and are dealing with their own struggles. I plan to tread lightly, I promise."

Mateo swung open the huge door, and the moment they stepped inside, a plump, friendly woman came rushing up, exclaiming in Spanish as she wrapped her arms around him in a big hug.

"*Hola*, Paula! It's good to see you." Smiling, he hugged her back, and Miranda was struck by the joyous way he was being greeted by this woman compared to his mother's interactions with him in his apartment in New York. "I'd like you to meet Dr. Miranda Davenport. Miranda doesn't speak Spanish, so we'll stick to English, hmm?"

"*Sí, sí!* It is very nice to meet you, Dr. Davenport. Please come in." To Miranda's astonishment, Paula gave her a quick, motherly hug, too, and she wasn't sure what to do, finally giving her a hesitant hug back. Another stark contrast. Vanessa Davenport hadn't hugged her in her life, and being embraced by this woman felt uncomfortable yet oddly nice at the same time, bringing back long-ago memories of her own mother's love. "The guest house is all ready for you. Alfonso will get your luggage."

"Thank you. What I've seen of the place so far is beautiful, and I'm looking forward to my visit."

"Mr. Mateo will show you around as soon as you're settled. I have some breakfast waiting for you—after your long trip through the night, you must be hungry, *sí*?"

Right on cue, Miranda's stomach growled. "Oh, dear!" The way Paula chuckled kept her from feeling bad about that. "I didn't even know I was hungry until you mentioned it. Thank you."

She glanced at Mateo's face, and was surprised to see a scowl there, which made her flush scarlet. Had she embarrassed him?

"Paula, I don't want you to call me Mr. Mateo. You've called me Mateo my whole life."

"I must!" Paula looked shocked. "You are the heir now! You are owed that respect."

"But…" Mateo looked like he wanted to keep arguing, but sighed instead. "All right. Are Mother and Father having breakfast?"

"No. They left for a doctor appointment in Barcelona. I expect them to be gone most of the day but back to dine with you tonight."

Miranda's core relaxed a little at this news. She hadn't

even realized her belly had been tensely knotted about meeting Mateo's parents, and how they'd react to their "news." Based on what she'd seen so far, and what Mateo had said, it wouldn't be with happy, open arms, the way Paula had greeted them. But she was here to support him, right? Help him smooth the way with his family as they all moved into a new reality now that their son and brother was dead.

"Isn't Barcelona pretty far?" Miranda asked in a low tone as they were ushered back to the kitchen. "Your dad doesn't have a doctor that's close by?"

"The local doctor practiced for years, and didn't retire until he was well into his seventies. But now we have no one, and even though Barcelona is only about an hour away, it isn't very convenient for all the people who live and work on the various estates around here."

The kitchen was huge; ancient and modern at the same time. Arched stone walls and doorways met intricately tiled floors, and the cabinetry was a dark cherry wood. A cheerful fire in a large stone fireplace at one end warmed the space, as did homey touches like copper pans on the walls, a verdigris teakettle on the big, modern stove, and colorful plates and cups lined across a large wooden hutch.

"Sit, sit. I have made all your favorites, Mr. Mateo."

His lips twisted as he shook his head, guiding them to sit at the long table while Paula moved to the stove. "How am I going to get her to stop calling me that?"

"If I had to guess, you're not. Just go with it. If you're not home all that often, it'll just be here in Spain that you are 'Mr. Mateo.' Unless you'd like me to tell the other EMTs and staff at the hospital to use it when speaking to you."

"Funny."

His tight lips relaxed into a small smile, and she was

glad she'd made the joke. She gazed around at the large expanse of the kitchen, awed at how beautiful and comfortable it was. "Your home is incredible, Mateo. And I know I've barely seen any of it yet."

"It is beautiful. I admit I've taken its beauty for granted all my life. It feels strange to be here without Emilio, though. He and I wreaked a lot of havoc in this room, and the whole house, over the years."

He stared out the wide window overlooking pastureland, and Miranda's heart squeezed at the pain etched on his face. "I know how that feels. But over time the memories become ones that make you smile more than those that bring you pain."

"I know."

He turned back to her and reached for her hand, and she gave it a little squeeze before she realized he'd doubtless been giving Paula hints about their "relationship." She tugged it loose to tuck both hands in her lap. "Why is the house called the Castillo de Adelaide Fernanda?"

"Named after a great-great-, however many greats, grandmother. I'll give you a full tour after you've rested, since I know you didn't get much sleep on the plane."

"I admit I'm a little sleepy." The words sent a sudden, deep fatigue through her bones, and had her covering an unexpected yawn, which made Mateo chuckle. "Oh, dear. I'm sorry. But you put that idea in my head."

"And once you have a good meal by Paula in your stomach, you will need a nap for sure. Then when you're feeling energetic again? A little adventuring this afternoon. If you'll join me, Miranda?"

His dark, brooding eyes met hers. The man who'd seemed like he wanted nothing more than a fun adventure with her was gone, replaced by this grim-looking stranger, and her stomach bunched in knots at the reality of the situation.

Mateo was dealing with grief over the loss of his beloved brother. Also his parents' lack of appreciation and their expectations, along with those of everyone who worked here. All that was tangled up with the life he'd made for himself in New York. She understood well those kinds of awful and overwhelming feelings, and how they could affect every aspect of your life if you let them.

Then there was Paula, obviously delighted over their engagement and Mateo being the heir now, having no idea he didn't want to be, or that their relationship wasn't real. When Miranda had agreed to the fake engagement, it had seemed like such a harmless thing. Something to tell his parents to help him smooth over his wanting to stay mostly in New York. But seeing Paula's happiness drove a nasty pang of guilt straight into Miranda's gut.

Was this charade really a huge mistake, and had she done more harm than good by agreeing to it?

CHAPTER FIVE

MATEO PAUSED ON his way to the guest house, which was perched on a part of the property that overlooked the valley, below where the estate's sheep roamed. He breathed in the brisk November air and stared across the golden pastures, memories of his childhood flooding his mind and heart. Good memories of times spent with his brother, with the animals and the horses. Not so good memories of his parents always putting Emilio first, pandering to his every need as the future Duke, even when he hadn't wanted them to.

Now that he was here, he was filled with confusion about exactly what his mission needed to be.

He knew that living here full-time was the last thing he wanted to do. Flooded with constant reminders that his brother would never be here again. Being a disappointment to his parents, where they expected things from him he couldn't give. Accepting a bride of their choice, complete with providing grandchildren, which was never going to happen.

Being married at all had never been on his list of life goals. The girls and women of his youth here in Catalonia, and at college, had all seemed to care about the same things his sister-in-law cared about. Money and prestige and titles and power, and who would want to be saddled with that kind of woman? A fate worse than death, as far as he was concerned.

Or, maybe, a fate that led to one's death.

The thought made Mateo's chest ache. When he'd agreed to his brother's pleas to keep the kind of woman he was married to a secret from their parents, he'd had no idea what he was promising. That the burden of a secret like that could lead to terrible consequences.

He rubbed his hands over his eyes. Tried to remind himself that he didn't know for sure if that's why his brother had become more and more reckless. Regardless, he should have been here for him. Supported him and advised him, instead of living his life hiding far away in New York, where he could turn a blind eye to how bad things had gotten.

The same with his father's illness. Showing up once every couple of years hadn't been much help with his father's ongoing deterioration, but his excuse was that he'd known Emilio had been all the support they needed.

So, now they wanted to believe Mateo was good enough to take Emilio's place, when it had always been more than clear he never had been? Never would be?

No. There was a better solution that would be right for everyone, including his parents. He just had to figure out exactly what that was.

The depressing thoughts clouded his mind and threatened to put a damper on the afternoon he wanted to enjoy with Miranda. Why Emilio had loved the woman their parents had chosen for him, Mateo had no clue. Even more now that he'd met a woman like Miranda Davenport. Growing up privileged hadn't spoiled her—if anything, it must have been part of what had molded her into the strong, driven woman she was today. In fact, Miranda was the kind of woman who might change even the most hard-ened bachelor's mind when it came to ideas on marriage.

The thought startled him, and he wondered why his mind insisted on going to strange places. Must be from the stress of being home again, and he shook the discom-fort from his shoulders to walk up the few stone steps and knock on the door.

No answer. He glanced at his watch to be sure it was 2 p.m., which was the time they'd agreed on. About to knock a second time, the door swung open with a sleepy-looking Miranda standing there in a robe, looking em-barrassed.

"*Buenas tardes*, Dr. Davenport."

"Oh, I'm so sorry!" She ran her fingers through mussed brown hair. "I was so sound asleep I must have slept through my alarm. Come in."

She opened the door wider, and every uneasy thought Mateo had had moments ago evaporated. As his gaze touched her soft-looking hair, her full lips and slumber-ous eyes, all he could think about was the same thing that had filled his brain—and body—the last time he'd seen her wearing a robe. Thoughts of reaching for her and tan-gling his own fingers in her hair, of kissing that tempting mouth and sliding off that robe to touch her soft skin and see where it all might lead.

He forced his attention to the window, and cleared his throat. "We don't have to go out this afternoon if you're too tired."

Maybe that was a better plan. Keeping his distance for now probably made sense, since he'd been having trouble thinking of her as just a friend. A woman who was helping him out with a problem, someone to enjoy spending time with as he showed her the country of his birth.

Not a woman to have mind-blowing sex with, a tempting thought that kept appearing foremost in his mind whenever he saw her, despite telling himself he shouldn't be thinking about her that way. Not when she was his guest, and had agreed to a friendly trip, not a quick affair.

"No, I'm ready. I slept well, obviously." Her lips curved in a sweet smile. "Give me five minutes to get dressed."

It felt impossible to not watch her run up the stone steps, her slender, shapely legs and bare feet making her seem very much like any other woman, and not the skilled and accomplished doctor she was.

No, not like any other woman. Something about her attracted him, drew him in, in a way he couldn't remember happening before. Minutes ticked by as he was trying to figure out exactly why, when she trotted down again to sit on the bottom step and shove on walking boots.

"This house is like a small version of your big house. So old, yet so warm and inviting. I can't believe even this space is all decorated for Christmas."

Mateo looked around at the evergreen boughs and gold ribbon wrapping the bannister, the candles circled with greenery and pinecones, the Christmas tree in the corner covered in gilded balls, and breathed in the scent. Memories from his childhood rushed back, and he was glad all of them were pleasant ones.

"My mother loves to decorate for Christmas. Has for as long as I can remember. She's often had numerous holiday parties and church gatherings, too, which the priest always appreciates. Even winter barn parties with friends in the horse business. Christmas is always a big thing at the Castillo de Adelaide Fernanda."

Miranda didn't answer, seeming to fiercely concentrate on lacing her boots, which made him wonder about Christmas at the Davenport house. "What about your family? Is Christmas a big deal?"

"Depends on who you ask, I suppose." That seemed like an odd answer, but before he could ask her what she meant, she stood and ran her hand along the stone wall. "Tell me about this guest house. Is it the same age as the main one?"

"Yes. About three hundred years old, give or take a few."

"It must be something special to not only be a part of that, but to be a member of the nobility."

"Special? I think you already know how I feel about my family obligations, Miranda." He didn't want to talk about that right now. About the deep pain and guilt he felt over Emilio's death. The reality that he wasn't the man his brother had been. The man his parents had always trusted to be there. "Is your coat in the closet? I'd like to get going so we have all afternoon before we have to be back. I suggest we take today for one of your must-sees while you're here—the sacred mountain of Montserrat. What do you think?"

"I think I'm up for anything you suggest." Finally, he got a smile, which managed to make him smile, too. "Especially since I didn't have time to grab a travel guide and research what all you have to see and do here in Catalonia, and have no idea what Montserrat is."

"You have a travel guide, and that is me."

"Which makes me very lucky, I'm sure."

"I believe I'm the lucky one to get to show you around." He helped her slip on her coat, knowing that was beyond true. "I hope you'll be impressed and amazed by what we're going to see, Dr. Davenport."

"Those words fill me with breathless anticipation, Mr. Alves."

Twinkling blue eyes had his hand sliding down her

arm to grasp her hand, because it just felt right. "Then let's get going."

The ride in the car was filled with conversation about the places they passed, and at other times a silence so comfortable it struck him as unusual for two people who didn't really know one another.

For probably the twentieth time, Mateo turned to look at the woman sitting in the passenger seat, anticipation welling in his chest at what her reaction might be to seeing Monserrat. He still remembered the first time his nanny had brought him and Emilio to this place. They'd been amazed by the soaring rocky crags and the thrill of riding the cable car up to see the amazing monastery nestled in the stone, looking almost as though it had simply grown there.

"Those mountains are incredible!" Miranda exclaimed, staring upward as he parked, then came around to her side to open her door. "I can't believe the shape of the stone, almost like a giant hand dribbled wet sand into spires, and they all stuck together that way."

"Wet sand fused into a mountain. I like that description—very apt. Just wait until you see how we're going to get up the mountain to see the basilica." He reached for her hand because he'd enjoyed holding it the first time, and why not? This trip might have a serious agenda, but he fully planned to enjoy the company of this smart and beautiful woman who had been surprising him since he'd first asked for her help. Since the moment she'd run into that tunnel.

"I hope it's not rappelling, like my sister Penny does. I'd probably faint, then fall to my death."

"No rappelling, promise. And falling to one's death only happens here maybe once a month."

She playfully swatted his arm and he started to laugh.

With her hand tucked into the crook of his elbow, he found himself unable to keep from glancing into her smiling eyes as they moved toward the funicular.

Whenever he'd seen her in the hospital, she'd been all business, working efficiently, and not one of the docs who joked around sometimes with the staff and medics that came and went. When she'd come into that tunnel collapse, how unnerved she'd been afterward had surprised him, though it shouldn't have. Most people would be freaked out to have rubble falling on their heads, but, then, most people wouldn't have run in like that either. Angry as he'd been at her, and, yes, worried about her, he had to admire that she'd come to help even though he now knew she'd been scared the whole time. She didn't strike him as an act first, think later kind of person, so he had to assume she'd decided she had to go in there regardless of the risk, and that impressed the hell out of him, though he wasn't about to admit that to her.

"We're going to take the—"

He quit talking because she'd stopped dead, yanking him to a halt as she did. "Please don't tell me we're going to get in that yellow thing and go up into the sky."

"Well, we're not going up into the sky, we're going to see the basilica and museum at the monastery up there, and the Black Virgin of Montserrat. But, yes, we're getting in the funicular to do that."

"Oh, my gosh." The blue eyes staring up at him were no longer smiling, they looked beyond worried. Even panicked. "I don't know. I'm sorry, Mateo, but I don't know. I never thought I had a fear of heights, but looking at that thing now has me freaking out."

"Miranda." He turned her to him and tugged her close against him. "I would never suggest you do something that frightens you. So of course we may just stay down here, and go somewhere else if you want. But if you can face your fear the way you did in the subway tunnel, I can promise you that seeing the basilica, the Black Virgin, and the incredible views will make you glad you did."

She pressed her hands against his chest and stared at him, her eyes still wide, but looking a little less panicked now. "I'm being silly, aren't I?"

"Not silly. You know as well as I do that lots of people have a fear of heights. But I can tell you that I'm an expert at that rappelling you don't want to do. So if the cable car gets stuck, I'll hold you in my arms like Tarzan with Jane, and we'll still make it down."

She managed a weak laugh. "I can't say that really reassures me."

"It should. I really have rescued a number of people that way, whether it was on a mountainside or a building or from a helicopter while I was in the military. But the odds of having to do that fall into the slim-to-none category, as I've never heard of the cable car getting stuck. I'm as sure as I can possibly be that it's completely safe."

"All right." A steely look of determination came to her face that reminded him of how she'd looked in the tunnel when he'd told her to leave. "Let's do it. And I apologize in advance if I hyperventilate or hold on to you too tightly."

"I can handle either scenario." He hoped she didn't hyperventilate, but her holding on to him? Now, that he'd be more than fine with. "And I'll do what I can to make you feel more comfortable."

With that promise, he wrapped one arm around her shoulders while holding her hand with the other. Miranda squeezed it hard and, as the cable car jerked to a start, pinched her eyes shut. Mateo had to grin at her cutely scrunched-up face. Soon, though, her worried expression wasn't funny at all as the slight sway of the cable car and the chilly breeze touching their skin seemed to ratchet up her panic big time.

"Oh, God, Mateo. I don't think I can do this."

Looking like she might actually cry, she practically cut off the circulation in his hand as she gulped in breaths. "Damn it, Miranda. I feel terrible that this is making you miserable."

"I... I can do it."

"You can. You *are* doing it. Look upward at the clouds instead of down. I think that one looks a little like Benny, don't you? Except not as fat."

As he'd hoped, giving her something to think about besides how high they were seemed to calm her slightly. "Definitely not as fat." She sucked in a breath and pointed at another cloud formation. "That one looks a little like the beautiful Christmas tree in the guest house, doesn't it?"

That she was trying so hard to act brave and composed when she obviously didn't feel that way tugged at his heart. Just like when he'd realized later that the show of confidence and determination in the tunnel had been an act.

Miranda was the kind of woman who donned a persona of perfection, acting the way she expected others wanted and expected her to, even if it made her suffer.

"It does look a lot like a Christmas tree, doesn't it?" He grasped her chin and gently turned her face toward him, and the obvious anxiety there sent a sharp stab of guilt into his chest. "We'll be on solid ground soon, Miranda. Hang in there for just a few more minutes, okay?"

He pressed his cheek to hers, cupping her face in his hand as he held her close. "Just close your eyes. Think about wonderful, beautiful things you enjoy. What are those things?"

"Puppies and kittens," she whispered against his skin. "Babies. Snow. Walking in nature. Cake. Especially cake."

"Now you're talking." He smiled, hearing her relax a little, feeling the tenseness in her neck and arms fade. "What kind of cake?"

"Chocolate. Rich chocolate with chocolate icing, too, but really any kind of cake makes me happy."

"Good to know. It's also good that you like to walk in nature, because that's our next excursion, no scary heights involved. And see?" The funicular squeaked and jerked as it swung into the terminal, and Mateo found himself pressing a lingering kiss to her warm cheek before pulling back. "Here we are, safely on the mountain. You made it! And I think going down won't be as scary."

Her hands slowly slid from his shoulders as she opened her eyes and looked around. With a deep breath, her gaze turned to his. "I'm so sorry I was such a baby. Thank you for helping me get through it."

"You weren't a baby, you were expressing genuine fear, and we all have things we're afraid of, don't we? Believe me, I saw lots of men break down during training exercises in the military, even when they knew they weren't in real danger but were scared anyway. Human nature, right?"

"Right. Thank you for…for not judging me."

Did the woman often feel like she was being judged? He couldn't imagine that, considering her stellar reputation at the hospital. Then again, he knew first-hand what it felt like to be judged by people close to you.

He held her hand as they exited the car, and some of his guilt faded when a genuine smile lit her face as they walked along the wide path, looking at the scenery surrounding them.

"This is breathtaking! The mountains are like none

I've ever seen before. And the monastery looks like it's almost part of the rock, you know?" Her grip on his hand loosened, and that blue gaze turned to his, a look of awe sliding over her face. "The engineering that had to go into that funicular is incredible. I wonder how they built it?"

"Impressive engineering, yes. But since it was done with modern equipment, to me, it's not as incredible as getting the monastery built. You said you haven't traveled in Europe so you haven't seen the many fortresses built high on mountains to keep the population safer from marauders, and make it easier to see enemies coming. You should plan to do a European tour soon. Even growing up here, I still marvel every time I see one of them."

"I had some chances to travel with my family, but knew I had to concentrate on college and medical school instead. All that didn't come as naturally to me as it did to my siblings, you know? They're all superstars in their own ways."

She seemed utterly serious, which Mateo couldn't believe. He might not know the Davenports personally, but being around Miranda for mere hours showed she wasn't just smart, she had street-smarts and people-smarts that not everyone with a high IQ possessed.

"I might not know you well, Miranda, but you seem like a superstar to me."

Her face turned pink and she gave him a shy smile. "Thanks, but you obviously don't know my siblings very well. And wasn't I just about to have a panic attack on the way up here?"

"Irrelevant to being a superstar. And even though you were scared, you handled it just fine."

"I think it's because you made me feel safer. Just like in the tunnel. So thank you for that. Sometimes...well, there have been a few times in my life when feeling safe was hard to come by."

The almost shy look of gratitude on her face bothered him. What had he done for her other than hold her close and tell her it would be okay? What exactly did she mean by not feeling safe at times? Did no one she knew support her?

"No thanks necessary." His voice came out a little gruff. "I'm glad I could help. So now that we're here, I can't wait for you to see why you made the effort."

The tour of the basilica and museum seemed to fascinate Miranda, and her pleasure at seeing them made him smile too. How long had it been since he'd been up here? Too long, as his parents had pointed out, and the now familiar guilt of all that pressed on his chest.

He shook off those thoughts, wanting to enjoy being alone with Miranda for the short time he had. "Quite a few monks still live here at the Montserrat Abbey, though I doubt if we'll see them. And right over here is the Black Virgin. One story says she was brought here during an eighth-century invasion for protection. She lay in hiding until being rediscovered about two hundred years later. Today, many people come to pay homage to her."

"Oh, she's so beautiful!" Miranda breathed as she looked at the statue. "I've never seen anything like this. What is she made of?"

"It's said she was carved from wood in Jerusalem. Apparently her dark color is from hundreds of years of candles being burned in front of her, though she has been painted black more than once over the centuries. Many have reported miracles after being here."

"There was a time I didn't believe in miracles, but then one happened to me. And this place is so amazing, who knows?"

"Indeed. Who knows?" Personally, Mateo didn't believe in miracles, though he'd never tell his deeply Catholic mother that. "What miracle happened to you?"

Her smile grew a little stiff. "Not important. Silly of me to say that, really. It wasn't really a miracle. So now where do we go?"

"It's possible to climb to the cave where the Black Virgin was hidden, but that's very strenuous. We should probably just explore the area a little more then head back, to give you time to rest before having to pretend to be my adoring fiancée."

"Adoring? I don't remember that being part of our deal."

"Ah, my mother may get frustrated with me, but I think she'd expect my fiancée to think I'm wonderful."

She chuckled, obviously knowing he was teasing. But, truthfully, he was a little worried how his parents would react to his pretend engagement. Being surprised and not happy that she was an American was a given. But would they be cool with her, or possibly rude? They certainly hadn't been very cordial to her at his apartment.

His parents were normally polite, but the loss of their beloved elder son had hit them both hard. He knew they were still grieving deeply, and worried about his father's health. Weren't they all? That pain and worry, combined with feeling stressed over the future of the dukedom, had taken their toll, eating away at their innate decorum.

He sighed. If only this plan with Miranda would make his parents decide they wanted him to be there only part of the time anyway. Choosing a bride—pretending to choose—who they wouldn't deem suitable for the future Duke would hopefully give them second thoughts about their insistence that he come back permanently. He might not be able to ignore the guilt gnawing at his gut, but thinking about living here full-time made his stomach churn.

No point in fighting that argument with himself all over again. The week with Miranda here posing as his fiancée would unfold as it would, and he'd figure out the next steps as they went along.

Thankfully, their trip down the funicular didn't seem to stress Miranda as much as coming up had, and they talked like old friends on the drive back. Mateo was struck all over again at the odd connection he felt with her. Maybe it had something to do with the ruse, but he didn't think so. He'd felt that way during the very first hours they'd spent together during and after the tunnel collapse. A mysterious chemistry that just happened sometimes, he supposed, but he couldn't remember feeling so utterly relaxed and happy to be with someone, even as the dreaded first meeting with his parents loomed over them.

"Here we are, with plenty of time for you to rest before dinner." He drove straight up to the guest house. "Thank you for joining me, and for not hating me for putting you through the funicular."

"It's good for me to face my fears. Maybe that's the big lesson I'm going to get from this trip."

"I hope it won't be full of fears for you to overcome, Miranda. That it will be more about adventure and having fun together." The truth of that struck him as he remembered how scared and vulnerable she'd looked, and how protective it had made him feel. As much as he wanted her here to help him with his family problems, he knew that, even more, he wanted to help her feel more confident and appreciated, which seemed to be lacking in her life for some inexplicable reason.

With that goal now forefront in his mind, he nudged

her into the guest house, slipped off her coat, and pressed a kiss to her forehead, wishing he could kiss her for real. "Get some rest. I'll be back at seven to take you to the house."

"Okay."

That uncomfortable look slipped onto her face again, and it made his chest tighten. He knew then that he had to somehow try to smooth the rough edges off the meeting with his parents ahead of time. Let them know they had to be on their best behavior without actually telling them about the engagement, because he had a feeling that if they had too much time to think about it before they met her, they'd be so upset they'd forget their manners entirely.

"They're not ogres, Miranda. It will be fine, I promise."

"I know. I'm being silly. Again. It's not even a real engagement, anyway, so there's no reason them being upset should bother me."

"Right. See you in a bit." He gave her a smile and a quick hug to hopefully reassure her before heading to the house to find his parents.

"Paula. Are Mother and Father here?"

"They got back from the doctor's about an hour ago, and are having coffee in the front room."

Seeing them sitting like they always did in their favorite chairs made him feel a warm familiarity, at the same time the knife edge of guilt stabbed his gut. His mother was reading, but his father just stared out the window.

Something about seeing them here at home was different than when they'd been in New York, and the knife twisted deeper. How had he not noticed how thin his father had gotten? How pallid and frail? Even his hair, which had always been thick and difficult to tame, seemed thinner and more gray. But grief as well as illness could age a person, and it struck him that both his parents looked about ten years older than they had at his brother's funeral.

Mateo's throat tightened, and he had to swallow before he could speak. "Madre. Padre. How did the doctor appointment go?"

"Mateo!" His mother stood and wrapped her arms around him and he held her close for a long moment, trying to remember the last time he'd done that. "Paula told us you and your friend were here, and had gone out for a bit."

"Yes, we went to Montserrat. I haven't been there for a long time."

"You haven't been home at all for a long time, other than for your brother's funeral."

And here they were, straight to familiar criticism. He bit back a negative response, instead walking to his father's chair and crouching down to grasp his bony hands. "How are you feeling?"

"Not bad."

Mateo knew his father's pride demanded that he be stoic, and he was never sure how to handle that. Whether or not he should leave it at that, or ask specific questions about his father's difficulty sleeping, or if his co-ordination was worsening, or if he was scared at the ways his body functions were deteriorating.

"Any new medications or therapies they want to try?"

"They want him to try a new medicine for his tremor, and see if it will also help him walk better," his mother answered.

Mateo nodded, making a mental note to look later at what they'd given him. He gently squeezed his father's hands, then stood. "Well, as you know, my…friend is here with me. Thank you, Madre, for having the guest house looking so beautiful. Your special Christmas touches are everywhere, which Miranda appreciates."

A smile banished the seriousness and disapproval he'd come to expect from her. "I'm glad. What time are you bringing her here?"

"Paula told me seven. Is that right?"

"Yes. We look forward to it. But remember, Mateo."

Her stern expression back, he had a feeling he knew what was coming. "Remember what?"

"We have important things to talk about privately. So be sure to leave us with plenty of time to do that before you go back to the States."

He glanced at his father, who was just looking at him with those scarily sunken eyes. When he turned back to his frowning mother, his gut tightened as he realized all over again how complicated this situation really was. How hard it was going to be to find a solution that made everyone reasonably happy. "I won't forget. And I hope that, despite that upcoming conversation, you'll be cordial and welcoming to Miranda. See you in a few hours."

CHAPTER SIX

MIRANDA CURLED HER fingers into her palms, the ring on her finger feeling strangely uncomfortable. She stared at the huge, heavy wood front door of Mateo's family home, awed by it all over again. Small evergreen trees covered with twinkling lights sat in decorative concrete pots that at each side of the wide stone porch, and the whole house looked like something out of a travel magazine during the holidays.

The door opened before they reached it, with Paula standing there, all smiles. "Welcome! Come in! Your parents are expecting you in the blue salon for drinks and appetizers before dinner."

"Thanks, Paula." Mateo took Miranda's hand and thumbed the ring as they walked into his parents' house. The feel of his hand holding hers might have eased her discomfort about their upcoming big "announcement" to his parents if he hadn't been wearing a slightly grim expression. "Thank you for wearing this. I appreciate it."

And how strange had it felt slipping it on? It wasn't as though she'd ever been in a school play to hone the minimum of acting skills required for this charade. At the same time, though, she couldn't deny that wearing such a gorgeous ring would be nice under different circumstances. Like a real engagement to someone she loved, and thinking about this deception had her feeling nervous and uncomfortable all over again. Was it wrong of her—and of Mateo—to be deceiving his parents this way?

Butterflies flapped around in Miranda's belly, even though she knew it didn't make sense, since she'd known all along why she was on this trip in the first place. And she'd already met Mateo's parents, right? Or sort of met them. While wearing Mateo's robe. With him naked in the other room.

Heat flooded her cheeks to join her nervous jitters. It seemed only a few hours ago she'd been so happy she'd agreed to come to Spain with Mateo. Now? Now she knew that *crazy* was exactly that—what had she been thinking?

"Are you ready?"

"I'm... Honestly, I don't know." She looked around the amazing old house, with its stone walls, fine carpets, and gorgeous furniture. Decorated even more lavishly for Christmas than the guest house, and she felt more out of place than when she'd first moved in with the Davenports as a teen. "I feel uncomfortable. I'm not sure I'll be able to act like we're engaged, to convince your parents that we really are."

"Then I'll be sure to do something to make you feel more convincing, hmm?"

She stared up into his dark eyes, filled with an impish teasing that had banished his frown. What that "something" might be had her worrying even more as he led her into a beautifully appointed room. A stunning Christmas tree so tall it touched the high ceiling was loaded with small white lights, gorgeous and unusual ornaments, and silver tinsel. Several surfaces in the room featured golden angels and heavy candles set in loops of evergreen that smelled wonderful.

The long, wide room they entered, filled with two settees and comfortable-looking chairs, was empty of humans, which had Miranda drawing a deep breath of relief. Maybe his parents weren't coming after all. The second that hope came to mind, she chided herself for the ridiculous thought. Getting together with them and making their big announcement was the whole point of the evening, and the entire trip, wasn't it?

"How about a drink? A cocktail or a glass of wine?"

"Wine, please. White." With any luck, maybe a little alcohol would calm her nerves, because right now they were jangling so much she thought Mateo might actually hear them.

He didn't let go of her hand until they'd walked to a well-stocked bar made of what looked like carved mahogany. After pouring wine into two crystal glasses, his dark gaze lifted to hers, so intense she wondered what he might be seeing on her face.

Then, to her utter shock, his hands cupped her face and he kissed her. Not a chaste kiss either—it was a full onslaught of heat that stole her breath and ignited a flame deep inside her quivering belly. The light scent of his cologne filled her nose and a tingle swept from her head to her toes as they curled in her shoes. The surprise of it faded as quickly as the kiss had begun, his mouth moving on hers so slowly, so expertly her heart pounded hard as she leaned into him. Her hands lifted to his wide shoulders and her head tipped involuntarily to one side, wanting more of the hot, delicious taste of him.

Just as she was sinking so deeply into the kiss she felt dizzy from it, he lifted his head. Barely able to open her eyes, she met his heated gaze, dark and alive, only to see it slide right past her one second later.

"Ah, Madre. Padre. I'm sorry, I didn't see you come in," Mateo said smoothly, not seeming at all embarrassed.

Dazed, Miranda spun to see his parents standing just inside the room, and horror froze her veins. First they'd seen her fresh from the shower, then kissing Mateo like she wanted to devour him whole. She was positive that's what it had looked like, because that's exactly how she'd felt. Good Lord, they probably thought she was a sex addict or something.

For a wild second, she wondered if that might be true, considering her embarrassing reaction to Mateo's kiss.

His parents both stood motionless, staring. Then with deep frowns they slowly moved toward the two settees set across from one another. A coffee table was placed between the couches, and Paula was currently putting plates on it, piled high with several kinds of food.

"You told us you were bringing a guest. We thought it was one of your old friends from here." And it was more than obvious that his mother was not at all pleased that it wasn't.

"Why would you assume that?"

"Because of our new situation. Your obligations."

Mateo didn't respond to that comment, but she could see him working to seem relaxed. Miranda tried hard to shore up indifference, remind herself she was here to help Mateo and not win a popularity contest, but couldn't help but feel that familiar hollow in her gut. The one she'd felt when she'd first shown up at the Davenport home to face Vanessa Davenport's hostility. That she felt every time she was at a family event she was supposed to pretend to be a part of, despite Vanessa's dislike.

"I don't see what our…difficulties have to do with Miranda. And I wanted it to be a surprise." He cupped Miranda's waist as he turned to her with an adoring smile on his face so convincing it was startling. The man should receive an acting award. "I was horribly amiss in not introducing you the last time you met. Miranda, I'd like you to meet my parents, Rafael and Ana. Mother and Father, I'd like you to meet my fiancée, Dr. Miranda Davenport."

"Fiancée?" Ana sank into the sofa, her face blanching so much that Miranda worried she might faint. "What?"

"I know this comes as a shock." Mateo tugged her closer. She wondered if he'd sensed that her legs felt a little wobbly, and she definitely needed the support. "Miranda and I met at a tunnel collapse, rescuing a man together. And it was love at first sight, wasn't it, *querida*?"

His smile was wide and coaxing, and she wanted to say, *Not exactly. I believe you yelled and cursed at me.* But she'd come here to help Mateo, though the way his mother was looking at her, like an unwelcome rodent that had found its way into their home, made her suddenly wish with all her heart that she'd never agreed to this.

"Yes, Mateo is a very special man." She choked out the words, though they should have been easy to say since she knew it was true. Giving him the adoring gaze he was giving her might be even harder, but she tried, forcing her lips to curve into a stiff smile. "He swept me off my feet. Literally."

Mateo chuckled and pressed his mouth to her temple, sliding it to her ear. "Nicely done," he whispered. "Thank you for letting me kiss you."

Her chest deflated a little, and she instantly berated herself for feeling disappointed at his words. Hadn't she realized almost immediately that he'd only kissed her because they had an audience? Why would it hurt her feelings to hear him confirm it?

"I can't believe you didn't discuss this with us first." His father focused his attention on Mateo as though Miranda wasn't even there. "If you had stayed here, where you belong, we wouldn't be so distant from one another.

Why you had to move to New York is still a mystery to us. And to be an EMT when you could have chosen a dozen other careers here in Spain!"

"I chose to be an EMT because that's the path that called to me. As did New York City. I could be anyone there, not treated differently because of who I am. Surely you understand that."

"Yet you are part of this family, whether you like it or not. You must take on your responsibilities now that you are the heir." His father's voice quavered. "And marriage is a big decision. We would have liked to participate in that."

"I understand that." Miranda could see he was taking time to choose his words carefully. "I know Emilio was comfortable with you deciding who he should marry. But I'm a grown man who wants to decide on my own if, who, and when I'll marry."

"Camilla is a lovely girl, Mateo, and Emilio was very happy with her," Ana protested. "You would do well to have a bride as lovely a person as she is. You have a responsibility to marry someone who understands our culture. Who is one of us."

Miranda's gut clenched at their total dismissal of her. Even though their engagement was fake, she couldn't deny it felt horrible to be an interloper yet again. Someone utterly unwelcome to the matriarch of the house. Hadn't she spent years trying to come to terms with that? Being faced with it again, however temporarily, made her want to run from the room and never come back.

Maybe Mateo sensed she was about to flee because his grip on her tightened. His jaw ticked and he seemed to take a moment to draw breath before he spoke again. "I do have a bride who is not only a lovely person, she's a physician as well. I would appreciate it if you would welcome her—the first woman I have ever brought here."

"You should have warned us," Ana said sharply. "An American is not a suitable bride for you, as you well know."

"Perhaps in your view," Mateo said in a remarkably calm voice, considering the twitch Miranda could see in his jaw. "But I believe that the people who live here would welcome a beautiful, intelligent and accomplished woman as their duchess, don't you?"

Miranda stared up at him, wondering how he managed to sound so relaxed when his parents were attacking him. She also wondered about the glib compliments falling from his lips. Had she ever been called those things by anyone?

"The people who live here value our long heritage, Mateo. Something an outsider would not understand," Rafael said.

"You are being very selfish here, Mateo." Ana narrowed her eyes at him before sliding them toward Miranda. "An unwelcome shock like this is not good for your father's health. What is so hard about accepting your duties here? Your brother never hesitated to take on the role when asked. And yet you act like it's a burden to even come home briefly to visit."

"I'm fully aware of Father's health, and my duties. The pain we all feel over losing Emilio. I'm sorry to be such a grave disappointment to both of you."

"You are not a disappointment, Mateo." Frowning, his mother waved her hand. "It's just that…we are having a party here tomorrow to celebrate your coming home. I would prefer not to announce this…engagement yet. Give you some time to think more about it."

"There's nothing to think about." Mateo's voice had

become hard now, and the look he was giving them would have had most people quaking in their shoes. "Miranda and I are engaged to be married, which I want announced to the world. In addition to that, I would appreciate some civility and manners toward her, which so far have been sorely lacking from you."

His parents glanced at one another, each huffing out a frustrated breath as they seemed to realize how unpleasant they'd been. "Our apologies, Dr. Davenport. This is…a very big surprise, but we certainly want all our guests to feel welcome here. Please sit down and have something to eat."

The thought of trying to swallow anything make Miranda choke. They wanted her to feel welcome? That wasn't going to happen because to say she was most definitely *not* welcome would be an understatement. And the way they spoke to Mateo? Anger on his behalf tightened her chest. She knew all too well how it felt to be talked to as though you're an outsider by someone who was supposedly family. If she didn't get out of there, she might say something she'd regret.

"Please call me Miranda," she said, drawing in a calming breath. "It's very nice to meet you. But I'm afraid I can't stay to eat at the moment. The…the busy day and traveling has left me feeling a little unwell. I'm sorry, but I'll have to visit with you a little later. Excuse me."

She pulled from Mateo's grasp and practically ran from the room. It wasn't a lie that she didn't feel well. Her stomach roiled as she hurried through the huge French doors at the back of the house that opened to a patio, and beyond to a garden that even in November was appealing.

The brisk air felt wonderful on her hot cheeks, and she gratefully gulped in large breaths of it. The moon hanging above the carefully trimmed hedges and shrubs lining the stone paths was barely larger than a sliver, but it cast enough light for her to see where she was going.

She'd wanted an adventure. Wanted to see more of Spain. Wanted to spend a little time with interesting and attractive Mateo Alves. But not anymore. Not when they'd said loud and clear how they felt about her being there.

Maybe she should just go home. Or somewhere else. Get on a train to Italy or France, or a plane to somewhere warm, before going back to cold and gray New York. Avoiding Thanksgiving with her family so she didn't have to feel like an outsider hadn't worked out so well, had it? She'd ended up feeling exactly the same way, worse even, in someone else's home.

Mateo could find some other solution to his problems with his family. She felt bad for him—she did. But she'd done what she'd promised, right? She'd posed as his fiancée, and now she could leave if she wanted to. Maybe he could still leverage that into the extra time he wanted to let his parents know he wasn't moving back permanently, and, wow, she sure understood now why he didn't want to.

A shiver racked her, and she wrapped her arms around herself, realizing she'd been in such a hurry to get away from the smothering situation in the house that she hadn't grabbed her coat. About to turn back, she felt warm wool drape over her shoulders and big hands holding it there. She didn't have to turn to know it was her own coat and Mateo's hands.

"I'm so sorry, Miranda." His fierce voice rumbled in her ear. "I knew they wouldn't be happy, but their behavior was worse than I expected. I apologize for the way they acted."

"It's okay."

"No, it's not okay. I'm trying to excuse them because they're frustrated with me that I moved away, now leaving our estate without anyone to manage it full-time. They're worried about my father's health problems, and I admit he looks more frail than I'd realized. And they're still struggling with the pain of my brother's death, their favorite son. I hope you understand that it's all a very heavy weight on them."

"Favorite son?" Miranda stared, then realized he was utterly serious. "Why would you say that? They want you to come back to your home. To take your brother's place."

"Only because he's gone. Believe me, there was no doubt they considered their elder son to be their best son. They insisted he serve only one year in the Spanish army because they needed him here. He was always a huge support to both of them. Whereas they were happy for me to serve four years, and I'm thankful for that. It helped me find my calling, which is one of the reasons I don't want to move back here permanently."

"Is your father too ill to take on the responsibilities of the estate again for at least a little while?"

"Unfortunately, yes." He sighed, and the deep pain in his eyes was obvious. "He was diagnosed with Parkinson's six years ago. You can see he speaks and moves slowly, and suffers from a tremor. He's diabetic as well. So it made sense for him to relinquish his responsibilities to Emilio. Except they insisted he marry as soon as possible, and chose his wife for him. As they've wanted to do for me, but I have no intention of ever getting married."

"No? You told me that on the plane, but I wasn't sure you meant it." Somehow, it didn't surprise her, though. Even when he was being charming and wonderful, there was a part of him that seemed closed off. That he didn't care to share. She wondered why, and even as she did so, that part of her brain that was self-protective started whispering again. Reminding her that she didn't really know him, that he didn't do long-term relationships, and that falling for him would be the worst idea ever. "Why not?"

"Even if it had ever crossed my mind, the way women always acted when they knew my lineage made it impossible to know if they liked me or my title. And if I ever did marry someday, it certainly wouldn't be someone of my parents' choosing. My brother's marriage definitely convinced me not to."

"It wasn't good? He didn't love her?"

"He actually cared for her very much." A bitter laugh came from his lips. "But Camilla cares only for herself, what she can buy with our family's money, and spending time with the wealthy Spaniards she's met through Emilio and my parents. She enjoys the company of men greatly, and hurt my brother deeply with her numerous affairs. I never told him that I was one of her targets before I moved to New York, but he knew about plenty of others."

"That's horrible! Why do your parents think she's so wonderful, then?"

"Emilio insisted that I not tell them, to let them continue to believe that the woman they'd chosen for their son was a paragon of virtue and a devoted wife. Which was probably a mistake on my part." He stared off toward the trees before heaving a sigh. "Anyway, I don't know how they've been able to turn a blind eye to her shallowness, though I suspect it's because they don't want to know."

The Alves family didn't have as many skeletons in the closet—or out of it—as the Davenports, but they certainly had their share. Maybe every family did.

"Listen, I get why you wanted me to come, with your parents putting pressure on you to marry someone they like, and come back here when you don't want to. But now that you've introduced me as your fiancée and they were obviously unhappy about it, I think I should leave. Maybe you can use that to play into your not coming back for a while or something. You'll have to figure that out, but I just… It's too uncomfortable for me to stay."

"Is that why you practically ran from the room? I hope you know it has nothing to do with you—it's because of their grief, and their anger with me. Please don't take it personally."

Please don't take it personally. Isn't that what her father had always told her? It was hard not to take it personally, though, when you knew that, inside, someone greatly disliked you, even when they tried not to show it.

"I'm afraid that's impossible."

"Why? My parents don't even know the real you, so why would you care what they think?" The concerned brown eyes looking down at her seemed genuinely perplexed. Probably because self-confidence practically oozed from the man.

"I… Nothing." Sharing her sad, strange and shocking life history wasn't something she enjoyed doing. Lots of people in New York and elsewhere still remembered the scandal, but if they didn't, the last thing she wanted to do was talk about it.

"Miranda." His hands cupped her cheeks as they had before, reminding her of that searing kiss. "I'd like to know why you would let my parents' attitude mean anything to you."

She stared into his eyes, and the warmth and obvious caring there, so astonishingly sincere despite having known the man only a matter of days, somehow made her want to talk about it after all. Help him understand why she needed to leave, and not be angry with her about it.

"Everyone believed that the famous Davenport family was close-knit and perfect. And to some degree they are. My brothers and sister are all close to one another, and to…to Hugo and Vanessa. Until a huge scandal rocked the Davenports' world."

"What kind of scandal?"

"Me," she whispered. "I was the scandal."

"What do you mean?"

"I grew up in Chicago with a single mom. Well, I did meet Hugo a few times, then I guess he was worried that contact between us might hurt the rest of his family, and he couldn't allow that to happen. That it wouldn't be fair to his other children and wife if they knew about me, so we didn't have any more contact."

"That makes me think less of Hugo Davenport."

"I think he was in a difficult situation. He'd made a mistake having an affair with my mother, with me as the result. He had to put his wife and family first."

"And his reputation. I think you're giving him too much credit, Miranda."

Maybe. She'd chosen not to judge him, perhaps because her mother had always insisted she shouldn't. Had told her he was a good man, and that she was the one who insisted his responsibilities were to his other family.

"So what happened?"

"My mother died when I was sixteen, and I was all alone. I didn't know what I was going to do, but she'd always shown me where her important papers were, like her will, so of course I had to go through it, to see what was there."

Talking about it felt like she'd ripped open a scab from a painful wound that still hadn't fully healed. Even thirteen years later, the memories of how horrible all that had been brought tears to her eyes. Memories of feeling so lost and alone, missing her sweet, wonderful mother, and having no idea what her future might bring other than foster homes and poverty. Filled with hopelessness and a feeling of despair, wondering if she should even make the effort to endure it.

"Ah, Miranda." His hands moved from her cheeks to her back beneath her open coat, tugging her closer against the warmth of his hard body. "What a terrible thing for you to have to go through."

She nodded, letting her forehead rest against his chest, lingering there. It felt nice, and she realized it had been a long time since she'd allowed herself to really lean on someone else.

"In her papers, I found a letter she'd written to me, telling me that if anything ever happened to her, I should contact Hugo Davenport, and she gave me his phone number and address." She lifted her gaze back to his warm one. "At first, he was shocked to hear from me. Then even more shocked when we both found out money he'd instructed his accountant give to us every month for my support had been embezzled by the guy. My mother had had no idea he'd been sending money. So I had almost no financial resources."

"What? That's unbelievable!" He stared and shook his head. "So he finally stepped up? Acknowledged you?"

"He did. I became Hugo Davenport's daughter, and a member of the Davenport family. But not before someone leaked the news, much to the media's delight and my shame."

"Your shame? Your father's shame, not yours."

"I suppose, though it didn't feel that way. The whole family was not only shocked and humiliated that their father had had an affair that was now very publicly out in the open, but that a child had been conceived as a result. I give my father credit, though. He could have just financially supported me, but instead he insisted I live with all of them. It was a little rocky at first, as you can imagine." And was that an understatement, or what? An emotional and physical upheaval for everyone in the house. "No one was sure how to deal with the person responsible for all the turmoil and embarrassment in their lives at that moment. A sister they'd never known about, a new-found daughter, a girl who was the result of your husband's infidelity."

"Dios mio," Mateo murmured. "I can't imagine. Were they unkind to you?"

"Not exactly. Distant, at first. You can guess that it felt beyond awkward, living there with all these people I didn't even know. I... I missed my mom so much." She swallowed down the tears that threatened even after all these years. "From the beginning, Charles was very kind to me. Eventually, as we spent time together, my brothers and sister accepted me, and I'm so grateful that we're close now. Especially Penny and me. Hugo went out of his way to be nice and supportive, I suppose to make up for all the years he wasn't there."

"As well he should have."

His tone was so dark and grim it made her smile a little. "I know the way he dealt with it before wasn't perfect. But his taking me in, his caring, was like a miracle. There were some dark days after my mom died, and I thought I'd be alone forever. I thought my life was over. But him wanting me to know my siblings and for them to know me was a wonderful gift. I'm coming to believe that, in spite of what I know about Hugo and Vanessa's relationship and his infidelity, good marriages do exist. That someday I might be able to find a man who loves me. A husband who will always be there for me and a family that is truly and completely my own."

"I'm surprised that you still believe that's possible, after all you've been through."

"There are a lot of times I'm not sure who I am or what I'm worth, but I'm learning as I go along."

"Now, that is something I completely understand." His gaze searched hers before he slowly nodded. "Learning things as we go along seems to be part of life, doesn't it?"

"Yeah, it does."

Thankfully, he left it at that. The insecurities she still carried around were private, and not something she liked to talk about.

Seconds ticked by before he spoke again. "You don't go into any detail about your stepmother. How did she feel about you moving in?"

"I'm sure you can guess the answer." Her lips twisted, and her stomach did, too, because even now her resentment toward Miranda was very clear. "Vanessa hated that my father insisted I come there to live. And I get that, you know? Probably every time she looked at me, it was like a slap in her face. A reminder that her husband had cheated on her."

"Again, though, it wasn't your fault."

"She tried, I think. And I tried. I tried so hard to be a model house guest. Which is how I felt for a long time, you know? To feel like a real member of the family was impossible. No matter what I did, I was the trespasser who wasn't truly welcomed by everyone in the house. Who wasn't quite a real Davenport." She forced a smile, figuring she should just stop talking now. Knowing she had to be boring Mateo with her sad story. "Anyway. I'm sorry, but I don't want to be that unwelcome person here, too, even if it's just for a short time. Maybe that's childish of me. But I think it's best if I just go somewhere else for the rest of my vacation, and not make your parents miserable."

CHAPTER SEVEN

THE VULNERABILITY, THE little-girl-lost look he'd glimpsed back in the tunnel and again on the funicular was clear in Miranda's eyes. It tugged at Mateo's heart the way it had then, and at the same time guilt tightened inside him. It seemed like he had an awful lot to feel guilty about these days, and he had to wonder if maybe that said something about the way he'd been living his life. If maybe he should figure out what changes he needed to make to fix it.

No one seeing her work at the hospital, the picture of calm confidence, would guess at the insecurity that lay behind her professional mask. And that her mask had slipped because of the situation he'd placed her in here, reminding her of her difficult adolescence, made him feel angry and remorseful and determined to make it up to her.

"Miranda, I wish my parents had behaved differently. That you weren't feeling the way you are now. All I can say is that I think you're absolutely perfect, and anyone who doesn't see you for who you are, appreciate you for who you are, is a fool."

"Thank you. That's… That's a very sweet thing for you to say. And in case you don't know it, that's true for you, too."

Her words and expression loosened the band of guilt in his chest. Even in the darkness, he could see that the eyes looking up at him looked less forlorn. Shining with the amazing blue that startled him nearly every time he looked into them, and he found himself reaching for her before he'd even thought about it. Pulling her close, and as he did so, her lips parted. He wasn't sure what his intention had been, but seeing the look on her face gave him a very clear idea of exactly what he wanted to do now.

"It's not sweet. It's just true." And he lowered his head to kiss her.

"Your parents aren't out here now," she whispered, her breath feathering against his lips before his mouth connected with hers. "There's no need to kiss me."

"Believe me, I do need to kiss you. I've been thinking of little else since I kissed you before. From the moment I saw you standing here in the moonlight."

And because it was true, he did, wanting to taste again the soft lips he'd barely been able to pull back from when his parents had come into the room. For a long moment she stood there motionless, a little stiff, seeming to absorb what was happening between them, until he could feel her finally melt against him. A gasp left her mouth and swirled into his and she wrapped her arms around his neck and kissed him back. It was so good, so intoxicating, he found himself crushing her close, loving the feel of her lush, full breasts against his chest, the chemistry between them practically igniting the air as he deepened the kiss. Her body fit perfectly with his, and vague thoughts of secretly slipping to one of their rooms and making love with her short-circuited the back of his brain.

No. The thought both aroused and disturbed him. He'd asked her to come here as a friend, to help him. Not to push himself on her while she was feeling vulnerable, stuck at his parents' home with only him for company in the midst of their disapproving attitudes that had disturbed her so much.

He forced himself to pull back and look into the blue of her eyes which, even in the night air, he could tell were focused on him with the same turmoil and uncertainty he felt. Not sure exactly what to say, to explain what had just happened, he dropped his arms.

He couldn't do this. Miranda was doing a favor for him by coming here with him. A bigger favor than he'd even realized, not knowing the lack of belonging and welcome she'd felt in the Davenport home, and now being subject to the same thing here.

Only a special woman who deeply cared about helping others would have agreed to this ruse, knowing his parents would probably be unhappy about their "engagement." What kind of rat would take advantage of her, kissing her and maybe even eventually making love with her, when, as far as he was concerned, their relationship would end as soon as they returned to the States in a week?

She'd admitted she'd like to have a family of her own someday, hadn't she? A husband who would be faithful and a home with children who loved their parents and one another. She hadn't had that growing up with a single mother, and while she now had a taste of that with her Davenport half-siblings, it was clear that having it all, belonging to a family that truly was all hers, was important to her.

And he was a man who could never give her that.

"I'm sorry. I hope you don't think I invited you here to be inappropriate with you. I'm not sure where that came from, but it won't happen again."

Confusion clouded her eyes, and he thrashed himself for being so weak as to kiss her when he shouldn't have. Had he hurt her feelings in the process? Reaching to hold her cold hand, he led the way back inside, not sure what exactly to do when they got there.

"Mateo."

"Yes?" He risked a glance down at her, relieved to see her expression was more normal now and, in fact, held some of the same determination he'd seen on the funicular earlier.

"I'd like to talk with your parents again. Have something to eat with them. It was silly of me to react the way I did. Part of the plan was to be engaged to a woman they wouldn't approve of, right? I'm fine with being that person. Really."

"Are you sure?" He studied her, wondering if keeping her here a few more days would be completely unfair. "I can't promise that my parents will magically be nice to you. In fact, I can guarantee that, right now, they're trying to figure out how to scare you off or change my mind. Stick me with some Catalonian girl who fits their criteria."

"Like I said, I can handle it. I survived moving into the Davenport mansion that was vibrating with disapproval when I was only sixteen, didn't I? If I could do that, I'm sure I can let your parents' dislike roll off my back."

"It didn't roll off twenty minutes ago."

"And I feel embarrassed about that. I'm a grown woman, not a child whose feelings get hurt at the least thing. I was being absurd, and I'm over it."

He looked at her closely, trying to decide the right and fair thing to do that wouldn't upset her any more. "It might still work for you to be angry with me and ditch me. I could play up having a broken heart to keep my parents' matchmaking at bay. Act wild and go out with a different woman every night, mortifying my parents so much they'd be happy to see the back of me returning to the States for a while."

"Would that work?" Her lips quirked. "I have to wonder if that's always been your MO, and everyone's used to it already."

He'd only been partly joking about seeing other women, since that strategy might actually work. But looking at the curve of her lips, the cute way she shook her head at him, he knew Miranda was the woman he wanted to spend time with here. There was something about the way she'd faced her fear on the ride up the mountainside, the way her intelligent mind worked, the way she smiled and laughed, that made the thought of spending time with anyone else seem utterly unappealing.

"Not exactly my MO. My wildness only comes out on occasions that warrant it." And there it came again. That shimmer of awareness, the chemistry that had zinged between them from practically the moment they'd met, was crackling all around them, and he knew he had to cool it before he did something he'd regret.

Like drag her to his room and make love with her all night, forgetting all about the reason they'd come here in the first place.

Mateo breathed deeply and picked up the pace to the house, forcing his mind away from thoughts of hot sex that kept interrupting his good intentions to keep it strictly friendly between them. "So, what's it to be?" he asked, somehow managing to make his voice sound calmly conversational. "I can have the Alves jet ready to fly later tonight or tomorrow morning. Or we can go back and talk to my parents more, setting the tone for this trip and my life. Giving them hints that they shouldn't expect me to move back permanently, at the same time reassuring them that I'm planning to take on at least some of the responsibility they're worried about."

"I'm in," Miranda said firmly. "I just realized with

certainty that I'm not done adventuring here and trying to be at least a little crazy. I can do this. My sister Penny would be proud that I'm not bailing out."

"*Gracias.* I'm proud of you, too." He brought her cold hand to his lips and, after a long moment, forced himself to let go. "Tonight, we'll deal with my parents together. Steel ourselves for the party they'd already planned with a number of friends tomorrow night, which now will be a vehicle to announce our engagement. To try to take our minds off how awful that's going to be, we'll spend tomorrow adventuring again, okay? I think you'll enjoy what I have planned."

"You said that about Montserrat, completely leaving out details of the funicular flying through outer space up the mountain."

"Do you trust me, Miranda?"

Her eyes met his for a long time before she smiled, then said softly, "Yes, Mateo Alves. Yes, I think I do. I do."

"*Bueno.*" His chest felt lighter at her answer, and he couldn't help but drop a soft kiss to her lips one more time. "I promise not to let you down."

Miranda wasn't sure what all the emotions were that swirled around in her chest and belly. Excitement? Yes. Who wouldn't be, getting to spend another glorious afternoon with Mateo in amazing Spain?

But discomfort squiggled its way in there, too. Last night had been so strange, meeting his parents, Mateo upset with them, kissing her breathless, then backing off, clearly regretting that he had, even as he'd asked her to spend today with him.

Which made her regret the kiss, too. The last thing she wanted was to be worryingly attracted to a man who wanted to be "just friends." Except the way her heart fluttered as she combed her hair into the neat bob she kept it in told her that maybe it was too late. But she was no slave to her hormones, right? She could be friends with Mateo, and not want anything else. Couldn't she? A fierce little inner voice told her there was no question about it. The man was way out of her league, and falling for him would just set her up for heartache.

Mateo had refused to tell her what he'd planned for them to do this morning, just advising her to dress warmly and to bring extra layers, which was intriguing. Obviously, they were going to do something outdoors. Hopefully it wasn't anything more daring than hiking this time. She'd loved seeing Montserrat, but thinking about that funicular ride still gave her palpitations, as did anticipating what he had in mind, and whether or not it might include more kissing. Which, of course, it wouldn't, and why was she even thinking about it?

He'd been sure to keep his distance from her the rest of last night, even in front of his parents. No more kissing or touching, just that *I'm so in love with you* look he kept giving her that was impressively convincing. Maybe that look was what kept stirring her all up, even when she'd scolded herself to stop. She knew what this game was about, and deluding herself it could be anything else was just stupid.

Dinner with the Alveses had been awkward at best, but at least they'd been civil toward her. Less civil toward Mateo, which was hard to understand, and made Miranda glad she'd come to support him, no matter how odd and uncomfortable it felt to play this charade. How could they seem to disapprove of him so much? He'd served in the military, helping save lives. Then had honed those and other skills in the U.S., helping more people. And he'd come back as they'd asked, trying to find a balance between how he wanted to live his life and his obligations to family and their role here.

Yet, by the way they spoke to him, you'd think he was living his life as a frivolous playboy, off spending his family's wealth.

The part of her that saw such innate strength in the man told her that seemed impossible. But he'd fully admitted he didn't want to come home, and they'd always been able to rely on Emilio. Was part of the reason for that because he himself believed he didn't measure up to his brother?

She shook her head. It was true she didn't really know him, except that she knew he was good at his job. And it wouldn't be surprising if "playboy" fit into his lifestyle somewhere, since she was positive most women would fall into his arms at the least invitation. Hadn't she been one of them?

To her shock, she had, and the memories of that brought hot color to her face. Thinking bad thoughts at his apartment, then falling into his kisses so deeply she'd nearly forgotten how to breathe. Which was beyond embarrassing, since the first time he'd kissed her, he'd done it for his parents' benefit. And the second time? Who knew what that had been about, but the way he'd instantly backed off had told her loud and clear that it hadn't been because he felt the same pull she did. Maybe it was that playboy thing, and he always kissed any woman he was close to in a dark garden lit by a fingernail moon. And hadn't she learned that playboy types, or men wanting to date her for her Davenport connections, weren't to be trusted? Not with her heart, at least.

This whole thing is a charade, remember, Miranda? she scolded herself. *Not. Real.*

She huffed out a sigh and stepped down the beautifully decorated stairs to find Mateo waiting for her by the front door, as he'd promised, giving her a warm smile. Paula was standing patiently next to him, holding a pair of leather boots and beaming. Her expression helped Miranda relax and smile, too. At least one person in this house seemed to like her, and was happy for Mateo. Too bad her happiness would be dashed in the very near future when they broke off their "engagement."

"We're lucky to have a beautiful day," Mateo said. "Ready to get some fresh air and see more of the beauty of northern Spain?"

"I'm ready. Though I know there's skiing in the Pyrenees, and I'm hoping that you telling me to wear warm layers isn't because you're planning on us doing that, because I don't know how."

"Not today. Though I'm happy to teach you to ski tomorrow, if you like."

"No, thanks. I'm beginning to see that my desire to be adventurous is battling with the wimpy side of me I didn't realize was there." Embarrassingly true. Which was one more reason she was glad she'd agreed to come, despite everything. Definitely past time to push herself out of her cocoon a little more. "Tell me what you have planned, so I can stop worrying. Or start worrying, depending on what it is."

Paula looked up at a chuckling Mateo. "You are taking Dr. Davenport paragliding, yes? Show her the beautiful scenery of the area of my birth? I know that has always been a favorite pastime of yours. She will love it."

"No, Paula. My fiancée is not fond of heights." Mateo's smile flat-lined and he took the boots from the housekeeper's hands. "We'll just be hiking. Thank you for bringing her some boots."

"I am sorry, Mr. Mateo. I... I should have realized,"

Paula said, now looking upset and worried, her smile gone. "I know that it hasn't been very long, and—"

"It's fine, Paula. Are you ready, Miranda?"

He helped her with her coat before leading her to his car, and as they drove in silence she had to wonder about his exchange with Paula. The way he'd interrupted, then dismissed the woman's words seemed very unlike him. Coupled with the expression on his face, which could only be described as grim, and Paula's obvious distress, it was clear something was bothering him.

"We'll be driving through parts of the Parque Nacional de Ordesa y Monte Perdido—our national park. Then hiking some of the beautiful trails. Don't worry." His teeth flashed in a smile, banishing some of the grimness as they drove down the winding road from his parents' estate. "We'll stay in the lower elevations and off the cliffs. It's too late in the season to go on the high roads, which are likely covered in snow. But you'll enjoy the panoramic views and communing with nature, I promise."

"Sounds wonderful. This trip is helping me see that I spend way too much time in the city, and shut inside the busy hospital. Breathing fresh air and having nature all around me sounds like the perfect getaway." Especially with Mateo Alves to look at along with the mountains and valleys. She'd admire him the same way, with a detached appreciation for beauty. She could do that. If she tried hard enough.

"*Bueno*. Paula has packed us a picnic lunch. Hopefully it's warm enough to enjoy it outdoors, but if it's too cold, we'll make it a car picnic, if that's all right with you?"

"So long as we're not hanging up in the sky from a funicular, hang-glider, or ski lift, anything and everything is all right with me."

"I'll put that in my reference notes. Everything is fine

with you except hanging from the sky—does that almost sound like a song lyric to you? I think I'll compose that, and title it 'Miranda in the Sky with Diamonds'." He grinned and reached across the console to tap the ring he'd given her to wear as part of their ruse.

"I think that song's sort of taken. And the diamond isn't really mine."

"All right, how about 'Miranda's eyes are like diamonds the color of the sky.' How's that for romantic?"

"Save it for when your parents are around to hear it. And who knew you had mad skills like song-writing to add to your résumé?" She kept her voice light, fighting down the silly flutter in her tummy when he talked about romance. And why was he? He'd made it clear last night he didn't think of her in that way. Or, at least, didn't want to. Flirting probably just came as naturally to the man as breathing, which she would do well to remember, and not read any meaning into it.

He gave her that grin that made her stomach flutter annoyingly even more, then sent the car through mountain passes at speeds that would have thrilled Penny, but had Miranda clutching her seat and holding her breath. She knew if she asked, he'd slow down, but hadn't she decided that it was past time to live her life a little more on the edge? This trip was certainly accomplishing that in more ways than one.

Mateo told her about the old and charming towns, as well as educating her on the geographic elements they passed. She gazed in wonder, thinking how incredible it would be to live here. She knew Mateo's reasons for moving to New York, but had to admit that the longer she was here, the harder it was for her to imagine he'd planned to leave all this behind forever, until the tragedy of his brother's death was forcing him to modify that plan.

"The hiking trail along the river is the easiest, but still beautiful," Mateo said as the road ended in a parking area. "I figured you weren't up for a long trek up the steepest trails, though the views are incredible from there."

"I appreciate that. I'd probably be sucking wind on a steep trail."

"You definitely need to get out of the hospital more. I see you practically every time I'm there."

"Maybe." It was true, she probably did work too much, but taking extra shifts was one more way to try to prove she was worthy of the Davenport name. Not to mention that dating wasn't high on her list of things to do. She'd learned the hard way that they either didn't like the work hours she kept, or they figured that she was the key to a fortune, and didn't really care for her personally at all. Not trusting a man's attention or words of love to be real was something she'd eventually taken to heart.

Mateo got their gear out of the trunk of the car and set everything on metal benches next to the parking area. Shoving her feet into the hiking boots was a bit of a challenge, but after she got them laced, she stole a look at the man sitting next to her. At his strong jaw, thick black hair, and sensual lips that brought back memories of their searing kisses.

Aside from his obvious sex appeal, she had to wonder if his status as the heir to a dukedom was one of the reasons she found herself so drawn to him? He had family money of his own, and wouldn't be interested in hers. Plus he'd said loud and clear that he wasn't looking for a long-term commitment with any woman. Which made him safe to spend a little time with, right? She didn't have to worry about impressing him in hope of something more.

The thought made her frown. Safe. Impressing others. Was her whole life focused on those two things? Keeping herself safe from heartache and pain? Safe from criticism by accomplishing things people expected of a Davenport? Safe from the hazards of the world, to the point where she wrapped herself in cotton wool to insulate herself?

"You're scowling." He leaned closer, his fingertip smoothing across her forehead. "Are you not wanting to hike? We can just have our picnic here, if you like, then drive some more and see the various views from the road."

"No." Miranda looked into Mateo's eyes, then noticed him shoving the backpack that presumably held their lunch to the end of the bench. Her heart warmed at his consideration—when was the last time she'd spent time with such a sweet and thoughtful man, who seemed to really want to do whatever made her happy and comfortable? "I'm just thinking about the way I've been living my life. Maybe this trip was meant to help me take a look at that in a way I haven't been doing."

"And how have you been living your life, other than working too much?"

"I guess I've been worried too much about trying to impress people. Prove I might be worthy of the Davenport name. Not put myself in situations that might be scary or potentially hurtful. I… Maybe I've been living my life as a coward."

"A coward? Now, there's a word no one would ever use about you, Miranda. Aren't you the woman who braved going into a collapsing tunnel? Who went up the funicular, even though it scared you? Who came on this trip with me after barely knowing me and having no idea how it would go?"

"I guess." His words, along with the admiring smile in his eyes, had her smiling back, even though she tried not to put too much trust into all he was saying. But a warm little glow filled her chest anyway. "Maybe it's being around you that makes me feel more brave than usual, putting myself in situations I normally wouldn't. So thank you for that."

He smiled and gently flicked his warm finger beneath her chin. "So I don't need to feel so guilty about dragging you here to terrify you on the funicular and have to deal with my parents?"

"Like I told you last night, I'm here by choice, and you know what? I'm ready to hit the trail."

"Bueno." He shrugged on the backpack, enfolded her hand in his, and they set off.

The farther they walked, the more Miranda was amazed at the beauty surrounding them. Tall beech trees, maples with a few gold and red leaves left, the beauty of the rocky cliffs and the valley, with trout clearly visible in the glassy river as they trekked beside it.

"This is incredible! I didn't know what to expect, but this is beyond anything I'd imagined. Living in big cities for my whole life, I guess I've forgotten how wonderful it is to enjoy nature and open spaces like this. I feel... I feel at peace here, you know?"

"Do you?" He paused, seeming struck by the comment. "I guess I always did too. Whenever I felt buried by schoolwork, or my family was driving me crazy, I'd come out here."

"How did your family drive you crazy back then? Did you and Emilio have sibling squabbles?"

"Of course." A smile twisted his lips. "But Emilio and I were close, and did a lot of things together. I only got a little jealous when my parents favored him so much, but it wasn't his fault. And honestly? He deserved most of the admiration they gave him."

"How did they favor him?"

"In lots of ways. Hey, look!" He pointed to the sky.

"See the eagles? If you pay attention you might see vultures, too, all looking for their lunch."

It seemed clear he didn't want to keep talking about his brother and the Alves family dynamics. "Wow, that's incredible. I've never seen an eagle before. The way they fly and glide is magnificent, isn't it?"

"There are ways humans can fly here, too, Miranda. Base jumping, hang-gliding, parasailing."

"Um, thanks, but you already know I'll leave the hanging in the sky to the birds. Parasailing and all that looks too dangerous, as far as wimpy me is concerned,"

To her surprise, he suddenly looked somber, instead of amused, at their banter. What had she said to make him look like that?

"This looks like a good place for our lunch break," Mateo said as they walked on in sudden silence. He stopped to gesture at a large, flat rock jutting from the hillside by the path. "Are you hungry?"

"Famished. I can't remember being this hungry before."

The dark eyes staring into hers held an odd expression. Miranda wasn't sure what it was, she only knew that her breathless feeling came back in spades and her heart beat a little faster.

"I can't either, *mi belleza*."

His gaze lingered on hers, and just as she felt she was drowning in it, he turned away to drop the backpack onto the rock. Miranda couldn't believe the containers of foods and sandwiches he pulled out, making her mouth water—or was it Mateo that had done that? Thoughts of kissing his beautiful mouth, tasting him again, suddenly seemed even more appealing than lunch, fool that she was.

With the food laid out, his gaze met hers again before dropping to her mouth. Mesmerized, she felt her lips part in anticipation. His face slowly lowered and his mouth met hers, soft and sweet and delicious.

The sound of voices coming from down the trail jerked Miranda back to reality as their lips parted, and she quickly looked down, pretending to decide on a sandwich. Wow, she needed to get her thoughts back on track. If he wanted a quick affair with her, he'd already be pursuing that, wouldn't he? Instead, he'd backed off each time they'd kissed, or come close to kissing.

Surely she had enough pride not to want a man who didn't particularly want her, didn't she? And she was well aware that a simple kiss on a rock in the middle of nature didn't mean a thing. So why did she keep trying to make it mean something it didn't?

The family passed by, two parents with three children, the youngest looking only three or so years old. They smiled and spoke in Spanish to Mateo, and he answered back.

"I really need to study Spanish," Miranda said as she picked up a sandwich. "It would be helpful when treating Hispanic patients in the hospital."

"It is very helpful. Some of the EMTs even call me to translate if I'm not on a run with them."

"So, was that family envious of all this food?" she asked, trying to bring back the pleasant normalcy they'd been enjoying before, squashing the heat she'd felt vibrating between them. Vibrating from her end at least. But she just couldn't seem to help it.

"They said they'd just enjoyed theirs, so I thankfully didn't feel a need to offer them some."

"Looks like Paula packed enough for them and us, too."

He smiled. "She always fussed over Emilio and me when we were kids. Almost like a second mother to us, you know?"

"How long has she been with your family?"

"As long as I can remember. Raised her own brood, and us, too. All of her adult children now work somewhere on the estate."

"That's really wonderful, having a connection like that."

"I guess it is." He looked at her as though he hadn't thought about that before. "I took it for granted, growing up with it. It's like having a huge, extended family, I suppose. I need to meet with some of them before we go back to New York, talk about the most pressing things that need to be dealt with now that Emilio's gone."

"Are you going to try to address some of it while you're here?"

"I don't know. First, I have to find out if things are in good shape or not so good. So, how's the food?"

Again, a change of subject. Miranda wondered if he didn't want to think about the weight of his family's expectations in running the estate, or the loss of his brother, or both. She was coming to realize even more how many really tough things he had to deal with right now, and she was glad all over again that she'd come, if her being here helped even a little.

"Speaking of family, I haven't told you. I got a message that Charles is engaged."

"Your brother? Is this good news, or bad?"

Trust a man who never wanted to marry to ask that question. "It's wonderful news. He's been very alone since his wife died, spending all his spare time taking care of his twin boys. And he's marrying Grace Forbes, another ER doc you probably know. I'm really happy for both of them."

"Well, if you're happy, I guess that's good."

His expression showed he couldn't really imagine an engagement—a real one—being good.

They ate in silence for a while, listening to the sound of the river gently swirling by and the birds chattering in the trees. Even though he'd changed the subject several times, would it help Mateo if he talked a little more about his brother? Maybe offering him her ear was what a friend should do.

"Your brother," she said quietly. "How did he die?"

"Doing something we both loved to do. That we spent a lot of time doing together."

"How does that make you feel?"

"The way he died was the result of being very reckless. And I have to wonder if I'd been more in touch with him, talked with him about the problems in his life, that might have helped him feel more at peace. I don't know, but I do know that being here makes it feel more real than when I was in New York. It seems impossible that he's not here any more, where everywhere I turn, there are memories of him."

"Oh, Mateo." She wrapped her arms around him and gathered him close. "I'm so sorry that you lost him."

He pulled her close and pressed his cheek to hers. The long, silent connection made her realize it was the first time he'd really talked about it to her. Had accepted comfort from her. And that made anything his parents had to say to her much less important.

Slowly, he eased away. "So am I. For a lot of reasons. But being sorry won't bring him back." He gathered up the remnants of their lunch and stuck them in the backpack. "Ready to move on? There's a waterfall not too much farther on that I know you'll like to see."

Clearly, the subject was again closed. But at least he'd opened up a little, and that was a start.

"A waterfall sounds wonderful." The bleakness, the pain she could see in the depths of his eyes had her reaching to cup his cheek in her palm. "Just remember that I know well how much it hurts to lose someone you loved dearly. That it's the kind of pain that takes years to heal. The pain of losing my mother is still with me, and I have a feeling I'll miss her, miss getting to share important things in my life with her, forever."

He nodded, turning his head to press his mouth against her palm. "Talking with you is making me realize I can't keep just shoving it down and pretending it isn't there, when being home just brings it to the surface anyway. It's time to start dealing with it, I guess. I'm just not sure how."

He tugged her close against him and she lifted her mouth to his, intending the kiss to be comforting, to show she cared and was here for him, a chaste kiss before she pulled back. But his palms came up to her face and he kissed her slowly, sweetly, until one hand slipped into her hair and tilted her head back, deepening the kiss. Making her feel weak in the knees and way too hot in all her clothing layers, and she clutched the heavy coat covering his wide shoulders to keep from melting to the ground.

A piercing shriek, then alarmed shouts came from quite a distance away, sending their lips popping apart and both their heads swiveling toward the sound. There was no sign of anyone on the path, but as the shrieking grew even louder, Mateo took off running. Miranda, her heart pounding and already out of breath from that kiss and from trying to catch up with him, focused on getting to whoever needed help without breaking her neck on the stones and tree roots trying to trip up her feet as she ran.

CHAPTER EIGHT

THE SHRIEKS WERE eerily similar to the way Emily had
sounded after falling from her father's shoulders, and
Mateo knew it must be one of the children that had passed
by earlier, or possibly a different family coming from the
opposite direction. He knew not to panic, but also knew
it could be something serious, and the only way to find
out what they might be dealing with was to get there fast.

Miranda followed him, but he couldn't hear the sound
of her steps anymore. Whatever had happened, he and
Miranda could deal with a medical emergency. And if
it was more than that, if there was some kind of rescue
needed, he always came prepared.

Rounding a curve in the path, he saw the woman they'd
seen before clutching two of the children close to her
sides as she stared down the steep embankment toward
the river, crying out to whoever was below. Mateo ran up
next to her, looking down to see that the man who had
passed them earlier was picking his way down, sliding
at times as he went.

"Hang on!" the man yelled, obviously panicked. "I'm
coming to get you. Don't let go!"

Mateo's chest tightened when he saw the gravity of the
situation. The tiniest child was hanging on with only one
arm to a scrubby, leafless bush growing straight from the

side of the embankment, his feet and other arm dangling and swaying over the river. The water wasn't running fast enough to take the child downstream very quickly, but if he fell? He definitely could suffer a serious injury on the rocks below.

"I've got a rope." Mateo pulled the deceptively thin line from his pocket and moved toward the embankment, working as fast as he could to wrap and secure one end around a sturdy tree.

"Oh, my God, will that hold both of you?" The woman stared up him with wide, terrified eyes.

"Don't worry, it's stronger than it looks." One last wrap, and it was ready. "I'll get the child. Stay where you are," he yelled to the man below, "because you're as likely to fall as he is." He knew too well how true that was. He couldn't count how many times a second person, or more, had lost their footing trying to help someone else.

"Oh, my God, please help them," the mother cried as he unrolled the line and began to rappel down to the boy.

"I'm almost there. I can get him and hand him up to you," the man said, grabbing a root to stop from sliding before staring up at Mateo with wild eyes.

It was never good to have the rescuer as freaked out as the one in danger. "Let me. I'm a search and rescue specialist, and an EMT. You can trust me to get him, I promise. Stay right there."

Doubtless because Mateo had already moved past the man, he stayed there, gripping the root. When he got parallel to the boy, Mateo braced his leg against the rocky embankment, grasped the rope tightly with one hand, then curled his free arm around the child, holding him close to his body.

"I've got you, okay? Don't be scared, and don't look down. Are those your parents up there?"

The boy kept crying, but nodded through his tears, clutching at Mateo's coat.

"Look at them, okay? Wrap your arms around my neck and hold tight. All set? Up we go now."

Mateo wanted to make sure the child didn't look down at the river and get so scared he tried to loosen himself from Mateo's grip. That seemed counterintuitive, but he'd had more than one soldier or patient do exactly that, making it very hard to hold onto them, but at least this little guy probably weighed only thirty or so pounds.

"You stay there," Mateo commanded the father as he pulled himself and the boy up the rope, passing him. He'd learned that sounding firm and authoritative was important in this kind of situation, when people were panicking and not thinking straight. "I'll send it down for you after he's safe. Don't move."

The man nodded, stilling hanging onto the root, and Mateo prayed it would keep holding him for a few more minutes. He looked up to see if the mother was ready to take the boy, or if he'd need to bring him all the way over the ledge. Miranda was standing there, her arms open, reaching instead as the mother kept her other two safely away from the edge.

"Ready for me to hand him over?" Mateo asked as, with one more hard pull, his head rose above the ledge. "Don't try to take him straight from my arms. Let me get his bottom safely sitting before you take over."

"Got it."

Mateo reached to sit the kid on the ledge, and the moment he seemed secure there, Miranda had her arms around the child. She dragged him away from the edge until he was a good four feet from it, and Mateo was surprised to hear him start to cry even harder when the

mother rushed over to him and Miranda and pulled him
into her arms.

Mateo hauled himself up and over the ledge to stand by
the tree. Barely glancing at the howling child, he turned
to look down at the father, knowing Miranda was more
than capable of handling whatever the problem was with
the boy.

"Ready to catch the rope? When you do, pull yourself up with a hand-over-hand movement. On the count
of three—one, two three." Relieved that his first attempt
at tossing the rope went straight to his hands, he and the
man worked together. The guy slowly heaved himself
up, jamming his feet into the rocks for leverage, and at
the same time Mateo helped by pulling on the rope as he
climbed. In a matter of minutes he was scrambling over
the ledge and Mateo grabbed him by the armpits to help
him get to safety. Obviously shaken, he stood and pumped
Mateo's hand.

"Thank you. Thank you so much," he gasped.

"You okay?"

The man nodded, catching his breath, then frowned
when he saw their little boy was still extremely upset. "Is
he hurt?" he asked, looking first at Mateo then at his wife.
"Or is he just still scared?"

Mateo turned to see Miranda, who'd moved far away
from the ledge and was carefully checking the boy. She
was now every inch the calm, medical professional who
would make any worried parent feel better, and not the
sexy, vibrant woman he'd been unable to resist kissing not
long ago. Then he realized she had no idea what the parents were saying and needed to connect them all.

"This is Dr. Davenport, she's an emergency room doctor in the States. She doesn't speak Spanish, but I'll in-
terpret as soon as she finishes her exam. Miranda," he

said, switching to English, "can you tell what's going on? Find anything?"

"One more minute." Miranda carefully wrapped her fingers around the child's arm, and received a scream in response. She glanced up at him, then smiled at the parents. "See the way he's holding his arm close to his tummy? Tell them I'm almost positive this is nursemaid's elbow, which isn't serious. Can you ask if one of them yanked on his arm as he was falling off the path?"

Mateo did as she asked, and, sure enough, they confirmed that the dad had grabbed the boy's arm, trying to pull him up, but he'd slipped from his grasp.

"All right," Miranda said. "Please ask one of the parents to hold him in their lap. I'm going to check it again, then, assuming that's it, I'll pop the radius back into place. You have anything to distract him while I do that?"

If the boy had been a grown man, he'd say that Miranda and her calm, friendly demeanor, gorgeous blue eyes and disheveled hair, which he realized he liked as much as her carefully combed bob, were plenty of distraction on their own. "I have a whistle in my pocket. Let's see if he wants to blow it."

Her smile widened, and he loved the twinkle in her eyes. "That's perfect. Wish I could use a whistle at the hospital, but probably other patients wouldn't appreciate it. Is mom or dad ready?"

Mateo spoke with the parents, and the dad took over the two older ones as the mother held the child close in her arms. Now that he was looking, he could see the boy's arm was hanging limply at his side.

"Now I see why he was holding onto that bush with only one arm. Which was nerve-racking, let me tell you. I thought he might lose his grip and fall before I got there. But don't tell his parents."

"They already know you're a hero, so why keep that a secret?"

"Because heroes are never scared, don't you know that?"

She shook her head and grinned at him before turning to carefully palpate the boy's entire arm, with shrieks that made his parents cringe following each movement.

"Yep, that's definitely it," Miranda said. "Whistle time. Tell the parents to expect a loud scream, then he'll be feeling fine, just a little bruised."

Mateo translated again, and the boy was, thankfully, fascinated by the whistle. As he was blasting everyone's ears, Mateo watched Miranda gently tug on his arm, and even through the whistling he could hear the bone pop back into place. As expected, the boy screamed, the parents exclaimed in distress, then visibly relaxed when the boy's misery quieted to mere sniffles.

"You're good with that whistle, young man," Mateo said, trying to distract all of them now that the worst was over. "You want to keep it?"

He nodded, and when he began to blow it again, his parents laughed, obviously relieved. They thanked both he and Miranda over and over again, the mother giving her a hard hug as Mateo re-rolled his rigging and placed it back in his pocket.

"I bet they're going to hang on to all three of them all the way back to wherever they're parked," Miranda said with a smile as she watched them move down the path. "How scary to see their little one fall over the embankment like that. I wonder what happened?"

"Kids can move fast. One second they're walking on a sidewalk, or in this case a path in the woods, the next they've darted into the street or off the edge. I see it all the time."

"I know. I regularly see the results of kids' impulsiveness in the ER. I guess there's no way to keep everyone safe all the time, is there?"

"No." His chest got that heavy feeling again, as her words sent him back to their earlier conversation. Some accidents—fatal accidents—were incomprehensible. Seemingly impossible. But when they happened, everyone else had to live through the tragedy, wondering what they might have done to prevent it.

"I guess we'd better go back and gather up the picnic stuff before it attracts bears and we have another problem on our hands," Miranda said. "And as I say that, I hope you're going to tell me there aren't really any bears here."

The way her eyes had gone from grinning to questioning and slightly worried brought him out of the dark place he'd gone. "*Ursus arctos*—brown bears—definitely live here. And I'm thankful for that, as there are very few left, and they're an important part of our great wilderness."

"I'm all for brown bears being part of your wilderness, but not if they show up when I'm hiking."

"I can't disagree with that. Let's gather up our stuff and go. I think I've had enough excitement for one day. You?"

"Definitely yes. And by the way, you were amazing. When I saw how fast you rappelled down that embankment, and how calmly you got the boy and brought him back up, I couldn't believe it. You really are an expert at rescuing people, aren't you? They were so lucky to have you close by."

"To have ER doc extraordinaire Miranda Davenport here, too. Diagnosing his injury and fixing it also made them very lucky."

"Anyone at any hospital could have fixed his arm, including you. Not too many could have rescued him the way you did."

The blue eyes looking up at him were utterly serious now, and something about the way she was looking at him gave him an odd sensation. A little uncomfortable at accolades he didn't need to hear—he did what he did because it was his calling. A little bit proud, too, despite not needing that kind of praise. And a little confused at the first thing that came to mind when she'd said all that was that they worked remarkably well together. Both when it came to taking care of patients and when it came to enjoying time together in a way he couldn't quite remember enjoying so much with anyone before.

"We make a good team." He hadn't meant to say it out loud, but there it was, hanging between them. Words that felt bigger and more significant than a simple statement about working together.

"Yeah, we do."

Mateo stared down to see the same confusion in her eyes that swirled through his mind and body. Let his gaze travel to her lush lips, down to the pulse he could see beating in her throat just above her coat collar, and couldn't believe he felt so aroused when he wasn't even touching her and both of them wore heavy clothes covering nearly every inch of their skin.

After each kiss they'd shared, he'd promised himself it would be the last. And yet, at this moment, he wanted to do nothing more than lie down on the hard rock slab they'd picnicked on and kiss her breathless.

Damn. How had this gotten so complicated and confusing? He'd dreaded coming back home, but being with Miranda had made it so much better than he'd imagined it would be. Seeing his home through her eyes, as well as parts of Catalonia he hadn't visited for years, made him feel completely different than he'd expected. Filled him with pleasure and happy memories, and not just the painful ones he'd known he'd have to deal with. It had brought a smile and joy to his heart to spend time with a woman who enjoyed simple pleasures like hiking and picnicking. Kissing and holding each other close.

Much as he knew he shouldn't be doing that kissing and holding, there was something irresistible about Miranda. Maybe it was the combination of sweetness and smarts, of vulnerability and bravery, of caring and giving that was a soul-deep part of her.

Whatever it was, he knew he didn't want the day with her to end with their hike. The enjoyment to be over before they had to deal with going to the party, where he'd have to answer questions he didn't want to answer. Where there'd be hushed conversations about Emilio being gone, and about Mateo not being the kind of man his brother had been. About what would happen now.

He didn't want to think about all that quite yet, and looked down into Miranda's beautiful face. "It's early still. How do you feel about a little tour of part of the estate as I talk to a few managers before we have to get ready for the party? There's probably more to do than I realize, and I should get started scheduling meetings with them now, and not wait."

"I'd love that. It's all so beautiful to see from the guest house. Looking at it up close, learning about all you raise and grow there, about the horses and all the different livestock, would be really interesting."

"*Bueno.* We'll take an hour or so to do a quick tour while I set up times to meet with everyone before we have to get ready for tonight."

"Well, this makes me happy." He could tell from her shining eyes and wide smile that she really meant it, and somehow her excitement had him looking forward to it, too. "I admit I wanted to see more of the place, but didn't know if I'd just be in the way."

"You could never be in the way. Having you with me will make a difficult task easier." *In the way?* That she'd actually say that bothered him. How could such a special woman still carry around those kinds of worries that must stem from her early years at the Davenports?

He reached for her hand and drew her closer. "You'll have to keep your boots on, as trudging through fields will be part of it. And climbing olive trees. And walking across barn beams."

Her chuckle and laughing eyes reached inside him, making him feel grateful all over again that she was here. Knew that having her with him for at least a little of this necessary task would help him get through it. He was sure the various estate managers could handle taking over all the things Emilio wasn't here to do anymore. In fact, they'd probably all prefer to do it themselves, instead of working with him if he tried to fill his brother's shoes.

No way could he come close to doing all the things his brother had accomplished here. And he was sure they all knew he couldn't either, despite what his parents claimed to believe.

"Look at all the olives on these trees! How many acres... er...hectares of olive groves do you have?" Miranda asked as they walked between the rows of trees, now more gnarled-looking than Mateo remembered, on their way to the horse barns.

"Not sure exactly what we have anymore." He'd talked earlier to several of the livestock managers, but hadn't yet spoken to those who took care of the various crops. "But in the past, not a huge number. The olives we grow here have mostly been eaten by everyone living on the estate, with about two thirds of the crop pressed into oil."

"How do you press it?"

"There's a local press that all the nearby orchards use. The harvest is taken to be processed pretty much the same way it's been done for hundreds of years."

"When is it harvested? And how? There's no way you could pick all these tiny olives off the trees—it would take forever."

He chuckled at the way she stared at the trees, reaching to touch the silvery gray leaves and not yet ripe olives before running her hand over the rough bark. "You're such a city girl, with an inquisitive mind. The harvest will be soon. Probably in the next month or two, depending on the weather. They're raked off the tree onto nets."

"What? You rake them off?"

"Yes, and I know from personal experience how hard it is. By the end of the day your shoulders and back muscles are groaning big time." He smiled at the memories of Emilio and himself complaining like mad, even though they both secretly liked the labor of pulling the olives from the trees. "Our parents insisted that Emilio and I do some of the raking, even though most of our friends on neighboring estates never had to. They felt we needed that personal connection with the land, and our home. Be a real part of it all."

Miranda turned to look at him, and he could practically read her mind, because his words struck him exactly the same way.

A personal connection. A real part of it all. Walking across the land of his ancestors, he couldn't deny that, for the past couple days, he'd been filled with powerful memories of his childhood. Happy memories of how much this place had always meant to him, until he'd realized he had to forge his own path away from here. Even the memories of Emilio and himself doing things together brought a smile to his lips, along with the ache of loss.

"And your personal connection to the horses? You told me you and your brother spent a lot of time here."

They'd arrived at the paddock, with a few of their horses inside. One whinnied at them, and as he reached to rub the animal's nose, Mateo's chest filled with some kind of emotion he couldn't quite identify. It had been a long time since he'd ridden a horse, and he suddenly knew he wanted to make that happen before he went back to New York.

"We did. Again, my parents made us do some of the mucking out and feeding. Said we couldn't have just the fun of riding, we had to do some of the work, too."

Miranda moved close to him, pressing her shoulder to his arm. "You love this place, don't you? Admit it."

He could feel her looking at him, and finally turned to meet her serious gaze. How she could see that so clearly, when he hadn't, had refused to, was a mystery.

But she was right.

"I guess I do. I grew up here. It's in my blood, I suppose. But loving the land and the animals and the beauty doesn't mean I belong here any more. My job in New York helps me make a difference in other people's lives."

"Have you thought about how this place makes a difference in people's lives?"

"What do you mean?"

"All the people who work here. Who live here. You said they were like family, didn't you? Without this place, their lives would change completely. They'd all have to find work on other horse farms, other olive farms, other places that raise the livestock you do."

He stared out across the fields. Miranda was right, and

yet it didn't really change anything. "Emilio worked to make sure this whole place ran like a well-oiled machine. Nothing will change with him gone."

Except everything had changed. This place would never be the same without him, and the thought of living here in his brother's big shadow, facing grief and guilt every day, felt unbearable.

"Mateo." She grasped his hands, and just that touch made him feel a little steadier. "Perhaps you need to take a little more time to think about everything. That's what our pretend engagement's really all about anyway, right? To give your parents time to adjust to their new situation without demanding you do exactly what they want. To give yourself time to figure out how you want to handle it."

"I don't need more time to know that I can't take Emilio's place. And, deep inside, I have to believe my parents know that, too."

"Being yourself will always be enough. Remember that."

Her words squeezed his heart, and he folded her in his arms. "You seem to have trouble believing that about yourself, Miranda."

"Yeah, maybe I do," she whispered as she wrapped her arms around his back and held him close. "Maybe that's something we can both work on, hmm?"

"Yeah." He pressed his lips to her warm cheek, calling upon all his strength not to move on to her sweet lips. "And tonight's party will be a good place for us to start."

CHAPTER NINE

"I HOPE THE dresses fit, Miss Miranda," Paula said, showing her to a guest room in the main house for her to change in. "Mr. Mateo wanted you to have several to choose from. He asked me to tell you to wear whichever you like best."

"I admit the dress I brought isn't quite this fancy, but it's adequate, I think."

"Mr. Mateo wanted you to feel comfortable at the party, not worrying about your clothes. He made a special effort to get them for you. Miss Camilla never liked the dresses her husband chose for her, and I know it made him sad."

She looked at the woman in surprise, wondering why she'd mentioned Emilio's widow. "It bothered him?"

A shadow crossed Paula's face. "Yes. But he tried very hard to make Miss Camilla happy."

Miranda felt a flash of anger at the self-centered woman who'd hurt Mateo's brother, and who was part of the reason Mateo had kept such a distance between himself and his family for so long. From the place he'd admitted today that he loved very much. "Were Emilio and Mateo close?"

"Oh, yes. Very close. When they were both home, they

did everything together. Rode the horses, skied, sailed boats, and—"

She abruptly stopped talking, and Miranda prodded, "And?"

"And many other things." Paula moved to the dresses and smoothed the skirts. "So, please, choose whichever dress you like. Just ring if you need me to help you find the one that fits best."

"Thank you, Paula. I'm sure at least one will fit me perfectly. I'll be pleased to wear one, especially since Mateo picked them out."

"I'm so happy that Mr. Mateo has found a wonderful woman he wants to marry," she said, smiling again. "We all wondered if he ever would, and if he'd return home. It's…it's a very happy Christmas celebration here at Castillo de Adelaide Fernanda."

Did she really think so? Surely Paula knew Mateo's parents didn't approve of their engagement. But maybe she figured they'd get over it if Mateo came back to live here. The thought made her feel a little sad that everyone in this beautiful house was going to be disappointed that Mateo—the man they'd seen grow up and who was their new heir—wasn't planning to return to his home full-time at all. Unless he thought more about that decision. After walking around the estate with him today, seeing how he felt about the place, she hoped he would.

"Well, thank you again. I'll see you downstairs."

Paula beamed and nodded, leaving Miranda alone, still battling the melancholy she'd felt after her hours with Mateo that afternoon.

Why were family situations often so difficult? Even though he hadn't said much about it, she knew the loss of Mateo's brother had been hard on him. Add to that the stress of his father's health, his parents' demands, and all the people depending on the estate for their livelihoods, and indirectly depending on Mateo, well, she had a feeling he hadn't fully shared the weight he must be carrying around from it all.

No time to dwell on that now. She took a deep breath as she looked at the beautiful dresses neatly hanging in the closet. Ever since she'd become a Davenport, she'd been blessed to be given glamorous clothing like she'd never seen in her life before that. Wearing them to attend various charitable events and symphonies and Broadway shows never got old, she had to admit. But despite having done that now for thirteen years, having these dresses brought here for her to choose from made her feeling absurdly Cinderella-like.

She wished Vanessa was here to see her as the guest and fiancée of a Spanish duke, and couldn't help but enjoy the vision of how her mouth would fall open. Wished Penny was here to see her doing this crazy thing, too, and couldn't wait to tell her about it. Though that reminded her that the adventure would be over and she'd be back to regular old Miranda, living her boring life and working all the time, very soon.

As she flicked through each dress, she couldn't help but imagine which one Mateo would like best. Which one would be the most flattering. Which one would make Mateo look at her the way she caught him doing sometimes. As though he liked what he saw.

The same way she caught herself looking at him.

She drew another deep breath, wishing she could feel totally confident, without worrying which dress would suit her best. But how could she not feel nervous about it, knowing all the guests would be staring at her even before they announced their fake engagement? Feeling curious about the two of them together? Knowing Mateo would be seeing her in a beautiful dress for the very first time, instead of her usual scrubs, or the jeans she'd worn on their excursions?

With her stomach all jittery, she debated the choices in front of her. Should she go with classic black? The shimmery one in pale gold was made of her favorite fabric, a crepe that hung in beautiful folds. Or would the blue one bring out the color of her eyes, which she knew were her best feature? It was probably the one she liked best, so long as it wasn't so low cut that her full figure didn't threaten to fall out of the bodice.

Turning this way and that in front of the full-length mirror, she smiled at the way the cobwebs of blue and aqua threads shimmered as she moved. She eyed the neckline, and decided that, even though her breasts were slightly on display, it wasn't so overt as to be in poor taste, or a reason for people to talk.

The light caught the diamond on her hand, and as she looked at it, melancholy poked at her again. Such a beautiful ring from a beautiful man. Would she ever have someone like him for real?

With a sigh, she grabbed an exquisitely beaded evening bag that had also been provided by her fairy godmother—or in this case, Mateo—and went down the stairs. Nervous butterflies danced in her belly as she wondered how the evening would go; at the same time anticipation welled in her chest at what Mateo would think of how she looked. And what would he look like dressed in his finery? Droolworthy, without a doubt.

Paula appeared at the base of the stairs, and showed her to the large ballroom where at least three dozen people were already gathered. As she stood in the doorway, her gaze went straight to the most gorgeous man in the room, and her breath caught in her throat.

A perfectly cut tuxedo that had doubtless been tailor made for him enhanced his broad shoulders and regal bearing. One hand held a glass of champagne, the other was tucked in his trouser pocket, elegance and power simply exuding from the man. It struck Miranda that his fellow EMTs would be astounded that the hard-working man usually wearing a uniform and sometimes heavy gear could also look like he'd stepped straight out of a James Bond movie. Calm, capable, and, yes, very, very drool-worthy.

Feeling unable to move, Miranda just stared. She saw him smile and nod to whoever he'd been talking to, then move toward another guest. Maybe he sensed her gawking at him, because he turned and, as their eyes met, she saw him stop dead.

His gaze slowly traveled from her hair to her sparkly shoes, then back up to linger on her breasts before meeting her eyes again. Something about that leisurely perusal made her pulse leap, then flutter even faster as he moved toward her in a relaxed gait that somehow enhanced his graceful sophistication.

When he stopped only inches from her, his hand reached for hers, thumbing the blue diamond ring circling her finger. "You look incredible."

She managed to unstick her tongue from the roof of her mouth. "Thank you. Did you get the dresses because you feared I might wear something to embarrass you?"

"Nothing you could do or wear would ever embarrass me. Even if you wore your hospital scrubs. Though I admit you look even more stunning than you do at work." He smiled, leaning forward to brush his lips against her cheek before speaking softly in her ear. "I know this thing isn't something you've looked forward to. So thank you again for coming. There's not a soul here who won't be dazzled by you."

"You...you look pretty dazzling yourself."

The intimate smile that curved his lips made it hard to breathe, which was further complicated when he closed the small gap between them, pressing his mouth to hers. So softly and sweetly, she closed her eyes and soaked in the sensation, drowned in it, even as the niggle at the back of her mind reminded her he was kissing her to make everyone in the room believe they were in love.

When he drew back, his lips stayed parted, his breath feathering across her moist mouth as their eyes met again. He reached to slide a strand of her hair between his fingers before tucking it behind one ear. "I like your earrings, but I may have to get you blue stones for your ears, too. Of course, your amazing eyes bring the sky into any room you enter."

"There's that romantic, poetic side of you coming out. Who would have guessed?" Her voice was breathy, she knew, but it was the best she could do. The current swirling around them felt like an electrified tornado, holding her close to him.

"Not me. I never knew I had a romantic bent until I met you." He dropped another soft kiss to her mouth. "And speaking of never guessing, who would suspect that Dr. Miranda Davenport was hiding such an incredible body beneath the scrubs she always wears?"

She felt a blush heat her cheeks. "You've seen me out of scrubs."

"Wearing winter street or hiking clothes covering you from neck to toe. Or a thick robe." His voice went lower. "And now I think we should stop talking about seeing you out of scrubs before something happens and I embarrass myself." The crooked grin he gave her somehow managed to be both amused and sexy at the same time, and she forced herself to look away from it, knowing there had to be a number of people here watching them.

"So, now what? We talk with your parents? Mingle?"

"Both. Then, when we can't take it any more, we dance, so I have an excuse to hold you close."

Miranda swallowed hard, and tried to concentrate on the various people Mateo introduced her to. But it all felt so surreal. Standing beside a handsome, elegant man, wearing a beautiful dress and spectacular engagement ring, with him touching her and looking at her like she meant everything to him. The whole fairy tale come to life.

Except it wasn't. None of it was real, not the flirtatious things he'd said, not the kisses and not the engagement. He was playing the part of loving fiancé for his parents and their guests, and that reality made her throat ache and her chest feel a little hollow.

Stupid. She'd known exactly how this would be, hadn't she? Except she hadn't, not really. All the pretending, knowing Mateo didn't really feel that way about her, made her feel a little empty. Made her ask herself if she'd ever have a man in her life who really did love her.

Somehow she managed to keep her end of the bargain. So many introductions and chit-chat for what seemed like forever left Miranda's cheeks aching. Her smile felt frozen on, especially when talking with Mateo's parents, aunts and uncles.

She'd assumed that Rafael and Ana would at least pretend to be happy about their son's engagement, but it seemed like every time Ana looked her way, she scowled instead of smiled. They hadn't even officially announced it yet, and now it seemed that they really might not, probably to give Mateo more time to think about it, as they'd said yesterday. Though it was obvious people had figured it out, as she'd seen and heard the whispers about Mateo's future wife.

Miranda knew she shouldn't be bothered by his parents' attitude. She should try to understand that they were hurting horribly over their son's death, and because of that weren't able to think in a normal way right now. Except Mateo had told her they'd always favored his brother and, watching their distant and cool treatment of him, it was sadly easy to believe.

"Mateo! My handsome brother-in-law. It's been far too long since you've come home."

Miranda knew it was wrong to instantly judge the small blonde with an obviously saccharine smile as she hugged Mateo, giving him the European two-cheek kiss as she did so. Except how could she not? She'd been prejudiced by what Mateo, and Paula, too, had told her about the woman who was obviously his brother Emilio's widow.

"Hello, Camilla." Mateo quickly extricated himself from her grasp and turned to Miranda. She couldn't help but feel impressed at his impassive expression. She knew how he felt about Emilio's wife, but no one would know it. For the first time that night, he introduced her as his fiancée, despite his parents not having made any announcement, and Miranda wondered if it was to keep the woman from making a play for him, as he'd said she'd done in the past.

"Well, well. The woman who finally reined in Mateo Alves. I didn't think I'd ever see the day. It's so very good to meet you." Camilla smiled brightly, but her eyes were even colder than Mateo's mother's, and held something else besides disapproval.

Disdain? Jealousy? Miranda had no idea, but she did know that she disliked the woman instantly.

"Nice to meet you, too." If only to see that Mateo wasn't making things up about the woman. The way she looked at Mateo, then Miranda, showed loud and clear how she felt about him belonging to someone else. Was she the kind of woman who wanted any man she could claim, or did she have a real thing for her late husband's brother?

"When is the big, happy day?"

"We're still finalizing our plans. But don't worry, I'm sure my mother will apprise you of it as soon as we decide." Mateo's arm tightened around Miranda's waist, but his cordial expression didn't change.

"I'm glad to see you're finally stepping up to your duty to your parents. Emilio felt so frustrated, hurt really, that you never came to help."

Miranda cringed at the woman's nasty barb, knowing that had to score a painful, direct hit on Mateo. She glanced up at him, and the tic in his jaw and tightness of his lips showed she was right.

"I don't think I'm the one who hurt him. But do I wish I'd been here for him when things got rough? Yeah. I regret that more than you'll ever know."

He swung away with Miranda still held in the crook of his arm and strode toward the dance floor. She thought about saying something about his exchange with Camilla, but his hard, fierce expression told her that keeping quiet was a better choice.

A headache began to form in both temples, and just as she was considering telling Mateo she'd like to excuse herself for a while he led her onto the dance floor. His arm stayed closed around her as he grasped her hand, but he didn't pull her close. Probably, he was as exhausted by the charade as she was.

"How are you holding up?"

"I was about to ask you the same thing."

"Don't worry about me." The tension around his eyes and in his jaw had her wanting to reach up to somehow smooth it away. "I'm used to people whispering and talking about me. About why I moved away. About why I don't come home often. Bringing you here has greased the gossip wheel, doubtless making everyone's day as they wonder what's going on."

No mention of Camilla and her words. "It doesn't bother you that your parents obviously aren't going to announce our...our engagement?"

He shrugged as he swept her into a turn. "My goal with our engagement was to buy some time. Give my parents a reason to understand why I'm not coming back full-time. We've accomplished that goal, so I don't care about the rest."

She wished she could say the same. Stupid as it was, there was still that tiny part of her that felt a little like she had as a teenager showing up at the Davenport home, barely tolerated by the matriarch.

Another turn took them to the edge of the room, and to her surprise Mateo swept them out the French doors onto a wide stone loggia dimly lit by the lights from the ballroom. The cool air felt good against her cheeks, and it felt wonderful to be away from the crowded room.

They came to a stop next to a wide pillar, and Mateo tipped her chin up, their eyes meeting.

"You didn't answer my earlier question."

"What question?"

"About how you were holding up. Is it bothering you that people are talking about you? That my parents have virtually ignored you?"

She nearly denied it, not wanting him to worry about something so silly when they weren't really a couple. But the brown eyes looking into hers seemed to already see what she was feeling. "It shouldn't, I know. But I can't help feeling a little...uncomfortable about it, you know?"

"I know. After what you told me about your lack of welcome by Vanessa Davenport, I've been worried. I wouldn't have asked you to do this if I'd known. I'm sorry."

"No need to be sorry. Honestly." He looked so concerned, she tried to reassure him. "It's just baggage that I shouldn't still be carrying around with me."

"There's no 'should' or 'shouldn't' when it comes to feelings, Miranda," he said quietly. "We feel how we feel."

She stared up at him, seeing that was true for both of them. And it struck her that observing the way Mateo was dealing with tough issues and feelings of grief and loss had made her think about her own life and how she'd been living it. While all the flirting and kissing didn't mean anything, his confidence in her did. And maybe that meant it was long past the time she should learn to have more confidence in herself.

"I know. But maybe what we're feeling isn't based on reality. Vanessa didn't want me around, but it didn't take long for everyone else to accept me. Maybe it's time I accept myself."

"What about yourself haven't you accepted?"

"That I don't have to keep pushing myself to try to live up to the Davenport name. Maybe I've accomplished that."

"No maybe about it." He tugged her closer. "You're a very special woman in a beautiful, tempting package."

The warm rumble of his voice, the way he was looking at her, sent her thoughts away from her past and her lack of confidence. They made her think about him, and that he was right. That how she felt wasn't something she could control, which was a deep attraction and connection to this man. Could he have been thinking that, too, when he'd talked about feeling what they felt? Was there any way his kisses and touches were more than a show of make-believe?

"I guess that's true," she whispered. She licked her lips, wanting more than anything to kiss him, to explore those feelings squeezing her chest and heating her body even in the crisp November air. But what if that's not what he'd meant at all? What if she embarrassed him, and herself, which would just complicate an already odd situation? What if putting herself at risk like that would be a huge mistake?

Wearing her high heels, his mouth was at her eye level, and she found herself fixated on the shape of it, thinking of how it felt to kiss him, and her own lips involuntarily parted. Heat curled in her belly, and that swirling electricity seemed to charge the air around them all over again. She managed to lift her gaze to his, and the eyes that met hers held a hot flicker of awareness that sent her pulse racing.

His hands tightened on her arms, bringing her close. The slight tic showed in his jaw again, and his eyes slid to her mouth, but he didn't move to kiss her.

She pressed her palms against his hard chest. Feeling the heavy beat of his heart, she suddenly decided to go for it. To use her new-found confidence. To find out exactly what he might be feeling—hadn't doing crazy things been part of her reason to come here?

"So what are you feeling right now?" she asked. Before he had a chance to answer, she shocked herself, finding she couldn't wait to hear his response, sliding her hands up around his neck to kiss him. For a split second his mouth stayed soft until, with a soft groan, he kissed her back. Taking it deeper, hotter, sliding one hand up her back to tangle his fingers in her hair.

Her body melted against his, the kiss spreading fire across her skin and weakening her knees. When his lips separated an inch from hers, she looked up into hungry eyes gone black, both of them breathless.

"What I'm feeling is obvious, isn't it?" he said in a low rumble. "I think you know that I want you, Miranda. That I'm attracted to you in a way I don't remember feeling before. But I can't offer you what you want and need in your life. And it wouldn't be fair to take advantage of you after I've brought you nearly captive into this ruse."

"I'm not captive. And I'm not asking for anything other than for you to kiss me. Unless even that's more than you're willing to offer."

A slow smile curved his lips, even as he looked at her like getting her naked was suddenly all he wanted. "As you've already noticed, kissing you any time, any place, has always been high on my list of offerings, *mi belleza*."

His lips caressed her jaw, moved to the sensitive spot beneath her ear, sending a delicious shiver down her spine. Slowly traveling down her neck, his hot mouth kept going until they rested on the mounds exposed there, his tongue leisurely licking along her neckline making her gasp.

"Your breasts tantalize me, Miranda." His breath whispered across the dampness of her skin. "So beautiful, so soft."

She clutched the back of his head, loving the way he nuzzled the cleft between her breasts, nearly hyperventilating with the sensation of it as his hands moved to her hips and over her buttocks.

"Mateo! Mateo, where are you?"

The distant voice permeated the sexual fog clogging her brain. Miranda opened her eyes as he lifted his head, his eyes glittering into hers. "Shh." He pressed his lips to hers. "My mother. Probably someone important in her world has arrived and she wants me to talk to them. If we're lucky, she won't look out here."

"She'll think even less of me if I'm keeping you away from her guests."

"And you care because?"

Just as they were smiling at one another, his mother's voice calling him got louder, frantic sounding, and Mateo straightened to his full height, a frown dipping between his brows as his arms fell to his sides. "I'd better go and see what's wrong. I'll be back."

"I'll come with you."

In her heels, Miranda couldn't keep up with him as he strode through the ballroom, all the guests moving to make way for him. Across the room, she could see his mother leaning over a large, wingback chair and in it sat Mateo's father, slumped to one side, looking extremely ill.

CHAPTER TEN

"MOVE BACK, PLEASE. Mother, give us some room." Fear tightened Mateo's chest, but he ignored it as best he could, relying on his medical training to address the problem, without letting emotion cloud his perspective. This wouldn't be the first time his father's Parkinson's disease had left the poor man feeling weak and out of it, but it was always alarming, no matter how much they'd all become somewhat used to it.

Mateo crouched next to his father's chair, concentrating on getting his pulse. Trying hard to ignore the way his head was lolled back and the gibberish and strange sentences he was stringing together in a slurred voice that constricted Mateo's gut even more.

"When did he start to feel this way?"

"I'm not sure." His mother stood to the side, clutching her hands together. "I was talking with guests, and haven't been with him for a while. But he was having a bad day to begin with. Felt extra-shaky this morning and couldn't sit very straight. He was feeling anxious about that, with our guests coming tonight."

"What's his pulse?"

Miranda asked the question in a quiet voice as she crouched beside him. He glanced up to see that piercing blue carefully studying his father. "Bradycardia—about fifty. Some arrhythmia."

Sweat prickled his body as he turned back to his father, feeling uneasy about the way he was staring at him, barely blinking. "I think we should get him to bed and give him a dose of his medications. Usually when he's having a bad day, that helps."

"The horses!" Rafael suddenly exclaimed, shakily waving his hand. "There! Don't let them in the house!"

God, he hated that this terrible disease was slowly whittling away at the strong man his father had always been. No matter how many times he experienced it, his father suffering hallucinations because of his disease deeply disturbed Mateo, and his mother, too, and he sucked in a breath, forcing himself to respond in a matter-of-fact tone.

"No horses here, Padre. They're all safe in the stable. Let's get you to bed so you can rest, okay?"

"No! Not leaving." His father was shouting now, looking a little wild-eyed and mulish. "We're waiting for Emilio to get here."

Emilio. Mateo's chest squeezed, wishing with all his heart that could be true. "Emilio's not coming, Father, so you don't need to wait. Let's go so you can get a little rest now." He pinned his gaze on his mother with a message he hoped she read loud and clear. "Get the staff to clear the room. You know he wouldn't want this kind of audience."

She stared at him before jerkily nodding. Instantly, she instructed the staff to move the food to another room, and asked the guests to follow.

"Didn't you say he's diabetic, too?" Miranda asked, a frown dipping deep between her brows. "We should check his blood sugar before you take him to his room. Where is his glucose meter?"

Mateo glanced at her, surprised. "It's not uncommon

for his Parkinson's symptoms to flare up sometimes. A decreased blink rate and hallucinations are all part of that."

"I understand. But shakiness, delirium, and belligerence are all symptoms of hypoglycemia, too, which you know."

Well, damn. Because his father's Parkinson's was such a big concern, both he and his mother had assumed he was just having a bad day. But could Miranda be right? "Paula, can you please get Father's glucose monitor?"

"You think this might be his diabetes?" His mother looked anxiously at Mateo, then her gaze slid to Miranda.

"Not sure. Do you know what he's eaten today?"

"I don't know. We were all busy with the party, and I didn't pay attention like I usually do. Perhaps he didn't…" She stopped talking and turned, obviously distraught, to one of the staff who'd been tending the buffet. "Please bring some food right away."

"Not yet," Miranda said gently, reaching for her hand to try to calm her down. "If it's hypoglycemia, he could easily choke, trying to eat."

His mother stared at Miranda, then nodded as she gripped her hand. "Then what…?"

"We need some regular, granulated sugar, please," Miranda said. "As soon as possible."

"Yes. Do as the doctor says. Right away."

The staff member rushed off, and Miranda wrapped her arm around Ana's shoulders to give her a reassuring hug. The respect in her eyes as she looked at Miranda was beyond good to see. Much as Mateo hated seeing his father feeling so ill and unsteady, maybe the silver lining would be new respect for his pretend bride-to-be.

Paula rushed in with the glucose monitor, and he quickly pricked his father's finger to draw the drop of blood they needed, his father now practically bellowing in protest, yanking his hand back, making it harder to get the test strip in place. In moments, though, the test showed exactly what Miranda had obviously expected.

An extremely low reading practically screamed from the monitor. Miranda's gaze lifted from the test at the same time his did. Their eyes met, and he gave her a smile and a nodding salute.

"Miranda was right. His blood sugar is very low, Mother."

"Oh, dear. This is terrible." She wrung her hands, looking nearly ready to cry. "This is my fault for not attending to him."

"It's not your fault." Mateo reached for her tense hands again, giving them a reassuring squeeze. "We need to set up a system where others in the house are also paying attention to his meals from now on. It isn't fair to you to feel you have to hover over him every time he's supposed to eat, and be the only one checking his blood sugar."

"Thank God you were here to help. To find what was wrong."

His gut clenched at the tears that sprang into his mother's eyes. That she was right made his chest ache. Made him wonder if he could let himself make the same mistake with his parents that he'd made with Emilio. In not being here for him when his brother had needed him most.

He rubbed his hand across his forehead and looked away from his mother's distress. What was he going to do about this complicated problem?

He drew a deep breath before turning back to his mother, explaining what needed to happen now. At the same time, Miranda went to work. He knew it definitely wasn't the way she'd normally take care of hypoglycemia in the hospital. But had he really said in the tunnel that she didn't know anything about field medicine? Her simple but efficient treatment showed he'd been wrong about that as he watched her stick her finger straight into the sugar bowl she'd been given and wipe it directly onto his father's tongue.

She talked soothingly as she slathered on another tea-spoon-sized dollop of sugar, his father no longer protesting but making little smacking sounds as he swallowed. His eyes began to focus and blink more when he stared up at Miranda and Mateo, obviously slowly becoming more alert, though at the same time he clearly was confused by what was going on.

"Feeling a little better?" Miranda asked with a smile.

"What…? I don't… Why?"

"It's all right, Father." Mateo reached for his father's thin hand. "You can't have eaten much today, and got into a little trouble because of that. But your blood sugar is coming up now. You're going to be okay."

His father nodded, obviously feeling a little wiped out, which was hardly a surprise. Mateo stood, helping Miranda up to stand next to him. He kept his arm around her waist as he spoke to his mother, then ordered some food brought to his father. His mother insisted on sitting next to him, poking food into his mouth, and Mateo knew it was because she didn't trust anyone else to do it, feeling guilty that he'd gotten into trouble to begin with.

With everything settled, he finally could turn to look at Miranda's beautiful smile, and he knew it wasn't just gratitude that filled his chest with an overwhelming emotion. The chatter and dishes clanking around them faded as he looked into her warm blue eyes, felt how perfectly her body fit in his arm, and it seemed as though the world was turning on its axis. His breath backed up in his lungs as the truth smacked him square in the solar plexus. As he realized that what he was feeling for Miranda was something he'd never experienced before.

He was teetering dangerously close to loving this amazing woman. He wanted to pull her close and kiss her, but wasn't sure if he should let himself do that. Though he had a feeling there was no way he could resist, since he sure as hell hadn't managed to keep his distance so far. Except she deserved so much more than a man like him, and he battled back the urge to tell her exactly how he was feeling.

The quizzical expression on her face as she looked at him had him wondering what his face looked like, and he swallowed hard, still reeling from his revelation.

"Are you okay?"

He nodded, having no idea if he was okay or not, then somehow managed to speak. "Thank you. You just might have saved my father's life tonight."

Her face went pink. "You would have figured it out."

"Maybe not in time to prevent him from going into a coma. Having experienced my father's Parkinson's symptoms so many times, I was being tunnel-visioned, assuming that was what was happening."

"Easy to do when you're as close to it as you are. I had the advantage of being an impartial observer."

"And an excellent doctor."

"Like you said before, we make a good team."

"Yeah, we really do." The truth of that shocked him. When was the last time he'd felt that way? Once he'd left the army, he'd mostly isolated himself, except when he'd worked on patients with other EMTs. But the more time he spent with Miranda, the more he realized what a truly special woman she was, in so many ways. A woman he was falling way too hard for.

He leaned down to give her a soft kiss, wishing they could go back to what they'd been doing before, which had involved having his lips and tongue kissing her and caressing her beautiful breasts. "I'm going to help my father to his room and keep an eye on him for a little while. I'll find you later?"

"I'll be here."

She'd be there. His chest filled again with a mix of emotions at her words. He knew it was true. Knew that she'd be there for him because that was the kind of woman she was, and he'd never needed her more than at this moment. And yet it was also a reminder that he hadn't done the same for his brother, which was a terrible regret he somehow had to learn to live with.

"Gracias," he said, his voice rough. "I'll see you as soon as I can. And, *mi belleza*? Please plan for us to take up right where we left off."

Each time she walked along the stone paths meandering through the back gardens of the Alves estate, Miranda found it a little more peaceful. The fingernail moon still hung within a thin mist of clouds, surrounded by the kind of twinkling stars she rarely got to see back in the city. The night sky of New York City was lit by millions of city lights, not nature and the universe, and this sight made her heart feel a calmness and serenity she hadn't felt since… well, she couldn't remember ever feeling quite this way.

Mateo had told her the gardens had been there for hundreds of years, carefully tended and refurbished as necessary, full of gorgeous blooms of all kinds during the spring and summer months. She found herself wishing she could see it during other seasons, instead of dormant as it was in November. Found herself wishing she could spend more time with Mateo, too.

Neither of those was going to happen. Yes, he'd said he

wanted to take up where they'd left off an hour or so ago, and just the thought made her feel flushed and breathless. He might have kissed her because he'd wanted to, because he'd wanted *her*, as he'd so excitingly told her, and not because he was trying to convince everyone that their fake engagement was real. But kissing her now, wanting her tonight and for as long as they were here together was a far cry from wanting a relationship once they were back in the city.

He'd stated very clearly that he wasn't interested in a long-term relationship with any woman. And she wanted the loving husband her mother had never had, wanted to be blessed with children. A close-knit family that was all her own, that no one could ever take away from her. But did that rule out a simple but doubtless glorious fling with Mateo?

A deep sigh left her lungs. Feeling confused and unsettled by the question, she looked up at the stars for guidance. "Star light, star bright, what do you think I should wish for tonight?" she asked aloud.

"If you don't already know, why are you here with my son?"

Startled, Miranda's hand flew to her chest as she swung toward the voice to see Ana walking toward her. "I'm sorry, I didn't know you were out here."

"I'm glad we have this time to talk privately. First, I wish to thank you for your help with my husband tonight."

Relaxing a little, Miranda smiled. "I became an ER doctor to help others, so I'm glad I could be of assistance."

Ana inclined her head, and as she moved closer, Miranda's smile faded. The woman might have slightly thawed with her thanks, and her expression might not be cold any more, but it was weary rather than warm.

"I appreciate it more than I can express. But, despite

that, you must know that neither my husband nor I will ever give our blessing to a wedding between you and our son."

And there it was all over again. It shouldn't feel like she'd been stabbed in the chest with a sharp instrument, since it wasn't exactly news that the Alveses didn't approve of her, but it felt like that anyway. "Why not?"

"I have tried to help you and Mateo understand, but neither of you seem to be listening. With the death of our special Emilio…" Her voice hitched for a moment before she continued, "Mateo must take over his role as the heir to the dukedom. And you cannot fill the role of his wife."

"Why not?" Miranda repeated, somewhat stupidly. Why was she even asking, when their engagement wasn't real anyway? Did she want all the reasons she didn't fit in spelled out in capital letters to make her feel inadequate, like a lesser human being, just like she had thirteen years ago?

"Because you are American, and have an important job there. We are so very afraid that if he marries you, he'll never come back." She reached to clutch Miranda's hands. "We need him to marry a Spaniard, someone who will be content, happy to live here at the Castillo de Adelaide Fernanda. Surely seeing how ill my husband was tonight shows you how much Mateo is needed here, especially since…since Emilio left us. I can't bear to lose both my sons."

Miranda's heart squeezed at the pain and fear in Ana's eyes. "Mateo does understand." Miranda chose her words carefully, not wanting to speak for Mateo but wanting to pass on basically what he'd told her. "Our being together does mean he'll be living in New York part of the time, but he expects to come here several times a year."

"That's not enough. We need him here, which is why

you must let him go." She reached to touch Miranda's arm, an imploring expression on her tired face. "You met my Emilio's wife tonight. You saw what a wonderful woman she is. A woman who adored her husband. My son." She lifted her wrist, encircled with a glittering gold bracelet studded with pearls. "Emilio gave this to me when he first took over running the estate, on my birthday. A gift to show me his commitment to me and our family and his responsibilities. Camilla helped him choose it, I know. She's a woman full of grace and style, loving and giving and from a good family with deep roots here. She has told me she will help find a suitable wife for Mateo."

Astonishment, anger, and hurt burned in Miranda's chest. Even if Mateo hadn't told her the truth about his sister-in-law, she'd have been upset at Ana's utterly rude dismissal of *her* as being worthy in any way of her second son. "What makes you think I don't adore your other son the way you believe Camilla adored Emilio? And why would he want to marry someone who doesn't love him? Perhaps your attitude is why Mateo doesn't want to come back here to live and work full-time."

"What do you mean? I love my son more than anything in the world. A wild boy as a child, we knew the army would bring him focus, and his many medals prove that it did. He's a fine man now, and I have to believe he will step up to his duties as the heir."

"Have you tried to talk to him about all this? About his plans? Maybe his answers would surprise you."

"The only surprise has been his engagement to you, which is the one thing that would keep him away. I would guess that once you found out Mateo wasn't like other emergency medical professionals in the U.S., but, in fact, a wealthy man from a family whose dukedom goes back hundreds of years, you set your net out to snag him as quickly as possible. It's what too many women do."

Miranda gasped in disbelief, anger surging so fast into her skull it made her brain scorch. "I can't believe you would actually say such a thing when you don't know me at all." She wanted to talk about her own family's wealth, her personal hardships, her hard work to prove herself to everyone, but decided she wouldn't stoop to the other woman's arrogant and judgmental depths. But she couldn't keep from telling her, at least when it came to the money, how wrong she was.

"For your information, it's been my experience that fortune hunters impressed by pedigree and money are often represented by the male sex, disguised as appreciative suitors. I've been targeted by fortune hunters interested in everything but me personally since I was in high school. Believe me, the absolutely last reason I'm attracted to Mateo is his money and position here, and the expectations you carry for him as the next Duke. In fact, that's the only thing I can think of that would make me walk away."

She spun away, the woman's words clawing at her gut, her own words disturbing her in a different way.

The only thing that would make her walk away was his parents' attitude?

As she nearly ran back to the house, her breathing went haywire at the realization that, deep inside, she'd meant it. And what did that mean, when all this had begun as a charade? A planned strategy by Mateo, with some pleasant vacation time in the midst of it?

She clutched her coat close to her throat, a stark and scary reality slamming into her, making it hard to breathe.

What had started out as pretence had become horrifyingly real for her. Somehow she'd let herself fall hard for

Mateo Alves. A man who had no interest in a real and lasting relationship with any woman.

She dropped onto one of the outdoor chairs on the loggia and clutched her cold hands together. Mateo had wanted a simple excuse to bide his time taking on his family duties, and have them eventually accept that he wouldn't live here full-time. She'd wanted to help him with that, not fully understanding the difficult dynamics of his family situation after his brother's death.

Now she did. His parents' pain over losing their son was still raw. And even though he hadn't said much about it, she knew Mateo's was, too. No one thought clearly during times of grief. If she was truly a friend to Mateo, she'd help him see that all of them needed more time to process it, to figure out what needed to happen next.

Maybe Mateo really should move back here for a while. Ease his parents' fears. Studying psychology was part of medical school, and she had to assume that the reason Ana had lashed out at her with such harsh words was because, deep inside, she felt scared to death. Her husband was ill, and would slowly get worse with time. She'd lost her beloved son who'd been there to support her. She didn't realize that she'd driven her other son away once, and was doing it again.

As she thought it through, trying hard to see it from Ana's perspective, Miranda's heart felt heavy, hurting for Mateo and for all of them. Because to make one of them happy, the other would be unhappy. So where did that leave them?

She didn't know, but what she did know? She'd lived that quandary herself. Being able to leave behind poverty and an uncertain future to become part of the Davenport family, eventually becoming close to her half-siblings, meant Vanessa had had to endure seeing the physical reminder of her husband's infidelity every single day. Vanessa being happy instead would have left Miranda in a very dark and hopeless place.

A shadowy figure emerged from the garden, and she looked up to see Ana moving up the ancient stone steps to stand next to her, her face now filled with worry instead of hostility.

"I am sorry to have insulted you by assuming you are after money and prestige. Maybe you genuinely care for Mateo. But you must see why we need him here, where he belongs, while you have your work and your own family back where you belong. Do you understand?"

"I believe I do." She rose and let herself really see the pain and anxiety in the woman's eyes. Seeing it there forced her to really look at what a tough situation the Alves family was in. And because she wasn't a part of it, not for real, she suddenly knew it was time for her to go. To let Mateo and his parents work out this problem for themselves, without her being there to muddy everything up with a relationship and engagement that wasn't even real. Her being here, participating in this charade, was just making things worse. Making it impossible for Mateo to stay longer, to deal with the pain of Emilio's death together with his parents. To mend the fences between them.

"I'll be going now," she said quietly. "I'll ask Mateo to cut our trip short so I can go back to New York. Let him decide if he's coming back with me now or staying longer as you...talk more about everything."

A tremulous smile formed on Ana's lips. "Thank you. With you breaking off your engagement, I know Mateo will—"

"Breaking off our engagement?"

Both women swung toward the French doors to see a frowning Mateo striding toward them.

CHAPTER ELEVEN

"WHAT'S GOING ON out here?" Mateo asked. "I was trying to find you, to tell you that Father is feeling much better, only to hear my fiancée is leaving me?" He folded his arms across his chest, giving his mother a sharp look. "What are you talking about? What have you said to her?"

"Merely what you already know, and that she now understands." His mother lifted her chin defiantly. "You must think about your family and why we need you here, without an engagement complicating your thoughts and decisions."

"My decisions are exactly that—mine! Why do you refuse to accept that?"

"Because you know there's more at stake here than selfishly pandering to your own desires! What has happened to you? You spent four years in the army, defending our country and our way of life, always living up to your responsibilities. How has that changed now that you're needed here more than ever?"

"I like my life in New York. I still see no reason why I can't take care of the responsibilities you speak of while living here only part of the year."

"Your brother worked hard here, many hours a week, managing all the business interests of the estate. That's not something that can be done part-time, or from across the ocean." His mother stepped close to him and glared. "You know that Camilla was the perfect wife for Emilio. Glamorous and conscientious, the perfect hostess. You can't choose a mate who has significant work, like being a doctor. A career that would make those other important obligations impossible to meet. Surely you see that!"

"What I see is a woman who refuses to open her eyes to the truth." Mateo's voice vibrated with anger. "Camilla made Emilio miserable! And that's the kind of woman you would choose again for your other son? Camilla hurt my brother over and over again with her infidelity, having numerous affairs with all kinds of men, from politicians to horse trainers to men with trust funds who care only for their jet-setting lifestyle."

Ana gasped. "That is not true!"

"It is true. Why do you think he got so reckless? Began base jumping from places he shouldn't, and went paragliding on a day he *knew* was dangerously windy, only to be killed because of it!"

"It…it was just a terrible accident!"

"Yes, but he knew that mountain like the back of his hand, and I'm as sure as I am of my own name that it was one of Camilla's hurtful affairs that filled him with the desperate need to go out paragliding on a day he knew he shouldn't. He needed the escape from pain that paragliding always gave both of us. You pushed Emilio into a terrible marriage, just as you're trying to push me to be who you want me to be. But I won't accept that. I want the freedom to choose the life I want with the woman I love, and that woman is Miranda!" He moved away from his mother, tugging Miranda up from her seat to hold her close against his side. "We will be leaving tomorrow morning. I'll be in touch from New York."

And with that he marched back into the house, taking

Miranda with him. Her heart pounded hard in her chest from the tense exchange and confusion from his words.

Of course he'd just been angry and upset. He didn't mean what he'd said about her being the woman he loved. She knew that. And yet there'd been something about the way he'd said it—something about the timbre of his voice and the look in his eyes when he'd wrapped his arm around her that seemed to say he had meant it.

Could that be possible? Could he really have come to care for her the way she had for him, even though they'd spent mere days together? Surely that was just wishful thinking on her part.

"I'm so sorry, Miranda," he said through gritted teeth as he led her through the house. "I would never have brought you here if I'd known how bad it would be for you. And even after you diagnosed my father's hypoglycemia and took care of him! My mother should be ashamed."

"She's suffering, Mateo." Miranda wrapped her arm around his waist and gave it a squeeze as they walked side by side toward the stairs leading to the room where she'd changed into her gown. "I've been thinking about how hard all this must be for her, how scary to feel somewhat alone now. Your father is sick and you all know the prognosis for his future is grim. She's lost a son that she loved."

"And I lost a brother that I loved. That's not an excuse to act horribly to someone."

"People do and say things in times of deep stress that they might not otherwise," she said quietly.

He came to a stop. "You amaze me." He grasped her shoulders and pulled her hard against him, his eyes still angry but looking at her searchingly, too. "Another example of how sweet and special and wonderful you are. Trying to understand and forgive someone who's treated you badly, instead of feeling angry and resentful. You did it with Vanessa, too, and your father. It's just one more reason why I've come to love you."

Her heart felt like it stopped beating completely. She stared up at him, trying to see if he truly meant the words that seemed impossible. Impossibly wonderful. Had he said it just because he was feeling emotional? Upset with his mother and with the situation he faced?

"Love me?"

"Yes, love you." He kissed her long and hard, and through it she could feel a passion that made her legs wobble, tightly interwoven with clear anger and distress. "I want our engagement to be real, Miranda. I want to make a life with you in New York, far away from here and my parents."

"Mateo, you…you don't mean that." Miranda's chest constricted so hard she couldn't breathe. "You're just feeling frustrated with everything, and will feel different tomorrow when you've got a little distance from your mother to understand her better."

"I do mean it. And there's something that *you* don't understand." His hands gripped her shoulders. "I told you that my parents never thought highly of me, the way they did Emilio. But now that I'm all they've got, suddenly they want me to come home. If I come back here for good, I'll be surrounded by the knowledge, every day, that I'm not good enough to take his place. I'm just not. I never have been."

"Of course you are," she protested, finding it unimaginable that he seemed to truly believe it. "Why do you say that?"

"Because I've never been the son to them that Emilio was. I wasn't here for my brother when he needed me most." He pressed his mouth to hers for another hard kiss. "I know I don't deserve you, but for the first time in my life I want to share it with someone. Share it with you. Forever."

Oh, God. She wanted to believe it. So much. She searched his eyes, trying to figure out what was really happening here. To see if tomorrow he'd regret his declaration of love, his claim that he wanted a forever-after with her. What she saw in their dark, smoldering depths sent cautious joy surging to her heart.

Heat. Shimmering desire. And the same glow of love that had slowly, insistently crept into every pore, every inch of her being over the past few days.

"I don't know what to think," she whispered. "I don't know what to say."

"Then let me show you how I'm feeling. Let me take you back to the guest house and convince you I mean every word."

He moved toward a side door that led into the dark night, heading quickly toward the small house as the stars twinkled above them.

Gulping in the crisp air, excitement surged through Miranda's veins, and her stomach flipped inside out. "Show" her how he was feeling? That could only mean one thing, couldn't it?

He pushed open the front door and, seeming like he was in a hurry, backed her into the bedroom and kicked the door closed behind them. "I don't expect Paula or anyone to show up, but just in case, hmm?"

The hard edge of anger had left his voice. The low rumble that replaced it was so full of seduction and promise, Miranda trembled in anticipation. He shoved off the coat she hadn't even noticed she was still wearing and tossed it on a chair before turning her around. His warm fingers swept her hair from the back of her neck and she felt his lips follow, pressing tiny kisses to her nape as he unzipped the beautiful dress.

"Mateo…" She had no idea what to say after his name, but even if she had, all ability to speak disappeared as cool air slipped across her bare back inch by inch, his fingers following in a shivery path across her skin. Finally fully unzipped, his hands gently shoved the dress to the floor with a swish. His lips moved to her bare shoulders as he turned her to face him again, his dark eyes glittering as he slowly, excruciatingly ran his finger along the lacy top of her bra.

Part of her wanted him to just keep going, but she didn't want to be the only one standing there in her underwear. She reached for his bow-tie and gave it a tug, sliding it from his collar to drop on the floor before reaching for his shirt. Struggling with the small buttons, she couldn't help making a frustrated noise, and with a heated smile he swept her hands aside.

"Let me."

"All right," she breathed. "That leaves me free to work on the rest of your clothes."

Another chuckle morphed abruptly into a moan as she quickly loosened his belt, undid his pants, pushed them to his ankles, then pressed the palm of her hand to feel the hard erection tenting his underwear.

"*Dio mio.* Slow down." He kicked his pants legs off at the same time he yanked off his shirt. "We have all night."

"I'm feeling in a hurry." And, wow, was that ever true. All worries about how he truly felt about her were forgotten as, with the sexiest smile she'd ever seen, he drew her close and kissed her. First on her mouth then her cheeks and throat then back to her mouth, speaking melodic Spanish words between each one, until she was gasping and clutching his bare shoulders to keep from slithering to the floor.

His hands had tantalizingly stroked and caressed her skin as they'd kissed, exploring her shoulder blades, her hips, her ribs, until one finally moved to unhook her bra, and he drew it off to toss it somewhere. His hands lifted to cup her breasts, his thumbs sliding softly across her nipples.

He lifted his fathomless dark gaze to hers. "You have the most beautiful breasts I've ever seen," he whispered. "Ever touched. Ever kissed." He lowered his hot mouth and slowly ran his tongue over each mound and Miranda held him close, resting her cheek against his soft hair, amazed at the intense connection she felt with this man after mere days spent together.

In a sudden, swift scoop he lifted her against his chest, her breasts being teased this time by the soft rasp of his chest hair as he pressed her against him. He moved to the bed, pulled back the quilt and laid her on the cool sheets, quickly following to lie on her, kiss her and touch her. The heavy weight of him felt so good, so right, and when he slid his fingers down to caress her she gasped into his mouth. He responded with sweet-sounding Spanish words, repeating them over and over as he pushed her thighs farther apart, touching, teasing, until she couldn't bear it any longer.

"I need you inside me now," she gasped.

"I'm here to give you whatever you want, my beautiful one," he whispered. "Always." He rose up to slowly fill her, and her legs wrapped around his back to pull him as close as two people could possibly be.

"Mateo. Mateo. I feel so... It's so..." She found she couldn't say anything more, just moaned at the bliss building inside her as he moved, deep and slow and unbearably delicious.

"I know, *querida*," he said, his gaze locked passionately with hers. "For me, too."

They moved together in a perfect rhythm that built, grew faster and faster until she couldn't hold back the intense pleasure any longer. She cried out as she came, feeling Mateo follow her with a deep groan of his own, until they lay gasping against one another, unable to move.

Long minutes later Mateo lifted his head. The dark eyes staring into hers seemed to hold a deep seriousness, but at the same time a small smile curved his lips. "Miranda Davenport, I love you."

"I love you too," she whispered.

"Finally!" His smile widened. "Hearing you say it back shows me you finally believe I love you. Took you long enough."

Her heart squeezed with an overflowing bubble of happiness. Until something sharply stabbed to deflate that joy.

Disquiet.

Did she believe him? She wanted to. So much. Yet a niggling doubt told her again that it seemed sudden. Too sudden. Right on the heels of the stress of the whole visit, of time spent in the orchards and seeing the horses, of his dad getting ill, of arguing with his mother. Of coping with his brother's death. Of dealing with his obviously deep-rooted feelings of inadequacy when it came to his place in the family.

Spending time together in Catalonia and on the estate had been a pleasant distraction from the weight of all that. Great sex was the perfect way to ease pain, she knew. Was he confusing all those feelings with love?

God, she just didn't know. The chemistry between them from the very beginning, the feelings they'd seemed to share at the dance, wasn't necessarily love on his part. Maybe it was simple chemistry. Lust.

Except surely a man like Mateo knew the difference between lust and love. Much as she wanted to believe with all her heart that he really did love her, she had to question it. Had to wonder.

Did he truly believe it himself?

Mateo held tight to Miranda's gloved hand as they navigated the crowded sidewalks on their way to his apartment. They'd enjoyed another dinner together, talking and laughing and learning about one another, and every hour he spent with her, the more he appreciated her. Her pretty face and beautiful smile, her inquisitive mind, her insight into so many things he didn't usually bother to spend much time thinking about.

He hated that they both had to go back to work the next day, since their vacation time had been far less than satisfying. Had hardly counted as a vacation at all, with all the stress of faking their engagement and dealing with his parents.

She'd protested that he should think about it longer, but he was more than glad they'd left early the next morning. Once they'd arrived back home, they'd spent their last days off going to a few museums he hadn't taken the time to go to recently, to a show, even ice skating at the Rockefeller Center. Laughing as they both fell a few times, enjoying the beauty and magic of Christmastime in New York City.

And making love. Making love with Miranda was like nothing he'd experienced before, probably because he'd never really loved a woman before. How incredible that this woman he'd planned to spend only one week with had sneaked into his heart so completely. Turning upside down his conviction that he never wanted to be committed to one woman, because he knew without a doubt that he wanted to spend his life with her.

He smiled down at her, tugging her away from a gaggle of laughing teenagers dancing along the sidewalk. New York City was always busier this time of year as tourists came to do Christmas shopping or stay for the week to watch the Rockefeller Center Christmas tree be erected, then lit, in all its spectacular glory.

"Oh, my gosh, I haven't told you yet!" Miranda exclaimed, as she hung onto his arm. "Grace wants me to be a bridesmaid at her and Charles's wedding. I guess we'll be going dress shopping soon."

"I'm sure you'll enjoy that. Is there a woman alive who doesn't like shopping?"

"Probably one or two, but I'm not one of them." She grinned up at him. "Do you have any Christmas shopping you want to do while you're still on vacation? It's still early—we have time to look in a few stores."

He looked down at her rosy cheeks and the cute knit hat she had pulled over her soft hair, and realized that Christmas shopping had been off his to-do list for so long, he hadn't even thought about it. He definitely needed to come up with something to give this special woman to show how much she'd brought to his life.

"The only Christmas shopping I need to do is for you, and since I can't do that with you peeking, the answer is no."

"You don't have to get anything for me. I'm still wearing the amazing ring I was supposed to give back to you at the end of this week."

"Except that's changed now. An engagement ring given to my beautiful bride before Christmas can't qualify as a Christmas gift, too."

The eyes lifting to his looked like maybe they were smiling and worried at the same time. "I... Don't you ever buy gifts for your parents?"

His gut tightened, not wanting to think about his parents and their disappointment in him and their nastiness to Miranda. Glad to be far away from that disaster. "Not unless I'm there with them at Christmas, which hasn't happened in a long time. They don't expect me to ship anything from here."

"Do they send you gifts?"

"Usually a basket of fruits and candies that I take to the hospital for the nursing staff or share with other medics. I've told them not to bother, but I guess parents never stop thinking about what their offspring are eating. Or they feel required to make the gesture." He looked down at her again, wondering why she was frowning. "Why?"

"Because I can't help but feel bothered by this... situation. I mean, we're engaged for real now, but you don't seem to want them involved in any way. You haven't called once since we've been back. And now you tell me you don't bother with Christmas gifts. I'm betting not even a card."

"All true. And your point?"

"It's not good. I mean, for better or worse, they're your parents and they love you. I know deep inside you love them too. You can't just shut them out."

"Watch me." He shoved down the uneasy feeling in his chest, the tiny nagging voice that told him Miranda was right. That he shouldn't completely shut out the two people who'd given him life, especially now, when their lives had become so difficult. But both had made unreasonable demands on him. Refused to accept beautiful and special Miranda as his future wife, and if he had to choose her over his parents, he absolutely would.

Miranda opened her mouth then shut it again, obviously deciding not to pursue it. Which he was more than happy about. Talking wasn't going to change a thing, other than to make his stomach hurt and make Miranda worry about it. He'd made his decision about his future, and was more than happy with that.

"Come in here." Miranda took an abrupt left toward a shop doorway, dragging Mateo with her.

He looked around and saw they'd entered a jewelry store. "You have some jewelry you'd like to show me that I can choose from for you for Christmas? A bit of a surprise, but not completely a surprise?" He dropped a kiss to her temple, let it linger there. "I like that idea."

"Not for me. For your mother."

"My mother?" What was she talking about? "First, I haven't given my mother jewelry since I bought her some gaudy fake gold and diamond pin when I was about nine years old. And didn't I just tell you I don't buy her gifts at all? Especially now, considering how upset she is with me."

"All the more reason to buy her something, as a peace offering. A…a really nice bracelet that she could wear and think of you every time she does."

"Miranda." He held her face in his hands, trying to understand why she was so concerned about his relationship with his parents when he wasn't. After all, he'd been more or less estranged from them for years, and this was nothing new. "You need to stop worrying about this. I don't think she needs or wants anything to remind her of me. Especially when every time she thinks of me she concentrates on all the ways I disappoint them. Let's forget all that and enjoy our last night together before work gets hectic again, hmm?"

He read the hesitation in her eyes, then sighed in relief

when she finally smiled and took his hand. "All right. I have to be at the hospital early, so what should we do that won't keep us out late? Enjoy a sweet dessert somewhere?"

"There's one thing I can think of that I'd like to do that won't keep us out late but might keep us up late, and would taste very, very sweet," he said in her ear, glad to be moving to a conversation that involved being alone and kissing and making love. "How about we go to my apartment, and I'll show you what I have?"

"I can't imagine what that would be," she said in faux, wide-eyed innocence. "Did you bake a cake? Buy ice cream?"

He had to laugh, tugging her close and dropping a kiss on her luscious mouth. How had he gotten so lucky as to have the fates throw him and Miranda together in such a surprising way? To meet a woman who was smart and sweet and fun as well, making him feel things, want things he'd never known were missing from his life?

"I think you already know what my very favorite sweet dessert is, and I can't wait to enjoy it all night long."

Miranda grabbed her phone to silence the alarm so as to not awaken the man whose warm, masculine and delicious-feeling body was half-draped over hers. Very gently, she moved his heavy arm from her waist and twisted to look at him. At his chiseled jaw and sensually shaped mouth that had kissed every inch of her body last night. At the dark lashes fanning his cheeks, looking almost boyish in a relaxed sleep. Far different from the fire and passion he'd shown her throughout the night as they'd made love in a way she'd never dreamed possible. In a way that had scorched her body at the same time it reached deeply and tenderly all the way inside her soul.

It was beyond wonderful at the same time it felt awful.

She just couldn't feel truly good about it. Good in a way that told her without a doubt that she was doing the right thing by holding him close and marrying him. Distancing him, both physically and emotionally, from his family. Without their engagement, he might well have stayed in Spain longer. Probably would have. He'd have been there for his father, and maybe even have had honest conversations with his mother that would have brought them closer.

All of them were still grieving Emilio's death, and she knew well that people didn't always think rationally during times of extreme stress and pain and worry. Nearly going off the deep end after her mother had died had shown her that first-hand, but at the time she hadn't even realized she couldn't think straight for a long time.

She reached to tenderly stroke her fingertip across his strong cheekbone, and a sad smile touched her lips as his face twitched in response. Marrying him after such a short time, in the midst of a true-life crisis for him and for his parents, would be wrong. She'd been responsible for ripping a hole in the fabric of the Davenports' lives thirteen years ago, and couldn't allow herself to do that to another family.

Stepping away was the only fair and right thing to do, no matter how much she loved him. Losing his brother and facing responsibilities he wasn't sure he wanted meant that Mateo wasn't in a good place emotionally to make a big, life-changing decision.

No, she had to let Mateo think longer about what he should do. Allowing his family to work together to heal wouldn't happen if she was permanently bound to the man. He'd been so convinced for so long that he never wanted to get married, it seemed impossible that he'd completely changed his mind in one week, much as she'd wanted to believe he could.

If it was meant to be, perhaps someday in the future they'd be together again. But for now, leaving him to figure out what he really wanted, when grief and anger and feelings of inadequacy were clouding his judgement, was her only choice. To know for certain if he really loved her, or if being with her had simply been temporary pain relief.

A lump formed in her throat as she oh-so-gently touched her lips to his forehead. Why did love have to hurt so much? The effort it took to somehow force herself to slip from the bed felt nearly impossible. To dress for work and leave a note for Mateo, explaining why it had to be over between them, at least for now, hoping he'd understand. Hoping he'd be able to look inside his heart and mind more clearly with her gone.

Clicking the door quietly behind her, she crept away with dawn rising between the tall buildings of New York City. The wind that bit her skin and whipped her hair felt colder than it had yesterday. Her chest felt like someone had kicked all the air out of it, knowing that Mateo's arm wouldn't be holding her close, to make her feel safe, to make her feel appreciated, to make her feel loved.

Head down against the wind fighting her progress, she made herself keep going. Hoping that letting him go would truly help him find his way.

CHAPTER TWELVE

FOR AT LEAST the tenth time, Mateo read the note Miranda had left him, and it didn't make any more sense now than it had the first time he'd read it.

Miranda was the most giving, loving, astute woman he'd ever met. A woman anyone could rely on to be honest and trustworthy. A woman who would always be there to help anyone who needed it.

Which meant this staggering news, her breaking off their engagement, breaking off any kind of relationship with him, was clearly all his fault, not hers.

And yet he couldn't figure out how she could be so sure that he only thought he loved her because of the stress he'd been under. That it was all a reaction to his brother dying, to his life changing in ways he wasn't comfortable with. That she was a passing thing to him.

Hadn't he shown her in so many ways how much he loved her? Couldn't she see it in his eyes, feel it in his touch, sense it when they made love?

He crumpled the note in his hand and set it next to the ring she'd left on the table. Yeah, maybe he did have to deal with his grief and guilt, his parents' pain and the situation back home before he could begin to think about another big life change. But they could have stayed together, without setting a date for a wedding yet, right? Spent time learning about one another, loving one another?

But instead she was gone. And he was left trying to cope with the ache in his chest she'd left behind.

He dragged his hand through his hair, forcing himself to face the truth. His insistence that they make their engagement real had come too fast. He saw that now. He'd exposed her to the stress and upheaval back at home and given her a glimpse of the same upheaval he felt in his heart and mind and gut. So, of course, she couldn't believe he really loved her. Wanted her in his life forever. Hadn't he spent half their time together telling her why he never wanted to get married?

Damn it.

He wanted to run after her, somehow convince her that his love for her was real, and not a reaction to everything else going on in his life. But maybe the truth was that Miranda deserved better than him, which he'd thought all along. A man who had the kind of stable family life she craved, that she wanted for herself, that she'd never fully had. God knew, he wasn't that man, the way he'd let his brother down. With his relationship with his parents a complete wreck.

Maybe his attitude about his parents, his avoiding the grief and guilt he felt from Emilio being gone, really was selfish. Maybe he'd been being selfish with Miranda, too.

Not going after her to try to convince her they should be together made his heart feel like a huge hunk of it was being chopped off. She made him feel whole in a way he'd never felt in his life. But would that be what was best for her?

It was time to face the hard truth that it damn well wasn't.

Hadn't she been learning to be the kind of person she

wanted to be? A person who knew her self-worth wasn't tied to her past or her relationship with Vanessa Davenport? She was teaching him that he needed to fix himself first, just like she was doing.

He couldn't give her damaged goods, which was what he was right now. He had to let her go.

He sat quietly, his heart aching as he absorbed the pain of that reality. He'd thought having to live at the Castillo de Adelaide Fernanda would have changed his life in a bad way. After having Miranda in his life for just the briefest time, he knew with certainty his life really had completely changed. Without her in it, he'd have a hole in his world that only she could fill.

The end of a twelve-hour shift always left Miranda exhausted, but today she felt more jittery than tired. All week she'd worked extra hours, trying to keep busy so she had less time to think about Mateo. To wonder what he was doing. If he'd talked with his parents. If he'd thought more about her suggestion to go back home for a while to think things through.

If he missed her as much as she missed him.

Every time an ambulance brought a patient to the ER, she found herself looking to see who the EMT was. Not once all week had it been Mateo, and she'd cautiously hoped he might have gone to Spain. But when she casually asked one of his co-workers, she was shocked to learn he'd asked to be moved to a different precinct.

Guilt clawed at her chest. He hadn't gone home. Her breaking up with him had just pushed him to move on to a different job. He'd talked about how much he enjoyed working as a team with the other EMTs, and now he had to learn to work with new people all over again.

Miranda grabbed her coat from her locker and slowly

headed to the hospital's back door, wondering if she'd made a mistake. Had she abandoned him right when he'd needed her most? Should she have stayed to be there for him, gently encouraging him to talk with his parents? Nudging him to go home again to try to mend the fences that had yawned even wider apart after she'd agreed to fake an engagement?

Feeling too unsettled to think about going to her apartment, she decided she should stop being such a hermit and mingle with the New Yorkers and visitors who were enjoying the Rockefeller Center Christmas tree that had gone up the day before. It would remind her of skating with Mateo on the plaza, but it wasn't as though he wasn't on her mind anyway.

Maybe one good thing could come of this pain and emptiness she felt. Maybe she'd change the way she lived in New York, get out and explore and have adventures like Mateo had encouraged her to. Be bolder and braver. Or would that just make her miss him even more, wishing so much he was there to share it all with her?

Standing in front of the huge pine tree, she hardly noticed the cold wind stinging her cheeks. Dozens of people were there, but somehow she felt more alone than she could remember ever feeling in her life. She took a breath, forcing herself to participate in the cheers as thousands of colorful lights came on and brightened all of Rockefeller Center.

Couples and families stood smiling, holding hands and hugging, and Miranda swallowed back the tears that threatened to spill over. Wishing so much that Mateo was standing there with her, holding her hand, smiling at her. That his mother, who loved Christmas and holiday decorations, could be there too, bringing Ana some happiness in the midst of such a difficult time in her life.

As she stared at the sparkling tree, bringing happiness to so many people, an idea seeped into Miranda's mind, then grew.

She'd been the one to bring chaos and stress to the Davenports' home thirteen years ago. Had made things worse between Mateo and his parents, widening the divide between them. What if it was time for her to be the one to fix things instead? To mend a rift and bring people closer together instead of pulling them apart?

A small smile started to form, banishing her tears. Optimism slowly filled her heart, followed by a conviction that it was the absolute right thing to do. Christmas was about miracles, wasn't it? Maybe, just maybe, she could make a miracle of her own.

Mateo trudged up the stairs to his apartment, wondering when the days might start feeling different from one another. When Saturdays and Mondays and Thursdays wouldn't all blur together into a week of just going through the motions. Taking care of patients, then running errands, then heading back to his apartment, alone. Seeing happy couples hand in hand and kissing, which made him physically ache. Seeing mothers and fathers and children laughing and window-shopping and obviously enjoying the kind of close family bond only parents and siblings were blessed to have.

How had his family gotten it so wrong? How much of it was his fault? The more he thought about what Miranda had said in her note, the more he wondered if he'd blamed his parents when, truthfully, they'd all had a hand in the way their family had fractured over the years.

He'd been more than happy to stay extra time in the army when Emilio had been released early. He was the one who'd left the country and rarely returned for visits. For the first time, he tried to see it from his parents' perspective, and he could understand why they'd been angry—hurt, really—at the distance he'd put between them, both physically and emotionally.

He fingered the box in his pocket that he'd planned to mail home, and suddenly realized that wasn't good enough. That Miranda, as usual, had been right. That he needed to go to Spain and deliver it himself. He had to quit hiding from the guilt and pain about Emilio. Now that Miranda was gone from his life, protecting himself from that pain by living in New York wasn't working anymore.

He'd go home and spend time with his parents. Really spend time with them, and let them know that, despite being gone for so many years, he loved them. Talk about how much he'd loved Emilio, confess the guilt he felt over not being there for him during tough times. Deal with that pain. And once he had, once his family was more together than it was now, he'd come back and find Miranda. Maybe if he had his life together, she'd finally see that he truly loved her.

Yeah, that's what had to happen, and the sooner it happened, the sooner he could come back and see Miranda again. He hurried to his apartment to make a plane reservation to Spain, pronto. He unlocked his door then came to a dead stop. Stunned, because there were three people sitting in his living room.

The three people who meant the most in the world to him.

"Hello, Mateo," Miranda said, her voice sounding a little thin as she stood. "I thought you should have an early Christmas gift. A visit from your parents, so you can talk things through."

"Miranda. Madre. Padre. I can't…believe you're all here."

His mother stood and walked to him, her face anxious and strained and full of something else. Remorse?

"Mateo, I'm so sorry we have been such fools, only expressing anger and disappointment instead of telling you how much we love you."

To his shock, her eyes filled with tears, and he closed the gap between them to take her hands. "Mother, it's all right. I've made mistakes too. Things have been hard for all of us."

"Miranda tells me that you believe we loved Emilio more. That's just not true." She squeezed his hands tightly. "We loved you every bit as much, and were heartbroken when you left."

"I didn't think you needed me there, with Emilio taking care of everything."

"We always needed you, if only to have you close." A tremulous smile touched her lips. "Emilio missed you, too, and I understand now how you tried to protect him. The two of you always had such a special bond, and I know you were a good brother to him."

His throat closed, knowing that wasn't true. And now was the time to confess that. "I let him down. I should have been there for him when things with Camilla got worse. I might have kept him from paragliding that day."

"No." His mother shook her head sadly. "It wasn't your job to ensure that Emilio made good decisions. If anyone must feel guilt, it's your father and me for insisting they marry. For being so blind."

That statement struck Mateo like a hard blow. He realized they all shared the same pain, feelings of guilt they had to let go of to move on.

Mateo's gaze moved to Miranda. Their eyes met, and just seeing that beautiful blue from across the room made his chest ache. Made him want to grab her into his arms and never let her go, no matter if she tried to leave him again or not.

And wouldn't that make him the same, pushy man he'd been last time?

No, what he needed to do was romance her, give her the time he hadn't given her before. Prove to her how much he loved her. How much he needed her. How much he wanted the forever-after with her he'd never thought he'd want with anyone.

"I need to talk to you, Miranda."

"Talking with your parents is more important." She looked down, then away, apparently wanting to look anywhere but at him, which scared the hell out of him. But he had to force himself to breathe and be patient. "I think they have other things they want to say."

"Yes, we do," his mother said.

It was all he could do to turn his attention from the woman he loved to focus on his mother as she continued. "We're very sorry for trying to make you move back home. We'll stop trying to make you step into Emilio's shoes, if only you'll do what you already promised. Which I don't think you'll mind, *si*? That you'll come visit sometimes, and bring Miranda with you. That's all we want."

"Bring Miranda with me?" His heart thumped in his chest as he swung his attention back to her, wondering if for some reason she'd told them they were still engaged. Then again, he hadn't told them they weren't, so who knew what they thought? "I would love to do that, but Miranda broke off our engagement, even though I'm crazy in love with her."

"What?" His mother swung toward Miranda, her eyes wide. "You didn't tell me this! How could you leave my Mateo? He is the best man you could possibly want."

That his mother was saying those words about him were unbelievable enough, and her next words astonished him even more.

"You must convince Miranda to marry you, Mateo," she said in the commanding voice he was used to. Hearing it this time would have made him smile if the stakes weren't so high. "She is wonderful, coming to us and insisting we all get past our frustrations with one another. Talk about Emilio and how much we miss him. If you come to Spain for an extended visit, she could even take over the old doctor's office and see patients there. Locals, and your father and I, would be most grateful not to have to always go to Barcelona to get medical advice and treatment."

"Yes. We need a doctor, and Miranda has already shown how good she is," his father chimed in.

"A very interesting idea, Madre and Padre." He reached for his mother and gave her a hug, wanting to end this particular visit fast so he could get on with the next important reconnection—with his ex-fiancée. "I have to talk with Miranda about all that, but first I do have a gift for you."

"A gift?"

The surprise on his mother's face would have made him feel guilty enough, but when tears swam in her eyes again he thrashed himself for neglecting her for so long. But those days were over.

"Miranda's suggestion. I hope you like it."

He held out the wrapped box, and his mother opened it, then gasped as the tears overflowed. "A bracelet, to go with the one Emilio gave me." She lifted her watery gaze to his. "Does this mean you're coming home for good?"

He glanced at Miranda, and his heart stumbled because, instead of looking like she wanted to run into his arms, she was biting her lip and looking worried, the same way she had before she'd left him. "That has a lot to do with Miranda. Will you leave us alone to talk about it? I'll come to your hotel for breakfast to work out some details."

"Fine. Good." She gave his father the "look", which meant she wanted to give them the privacy he'd asked for. "Here's our hotel information. Let us know what time. Come, Rafael."

Mateo hugged them both, and already the heavy weight that had hung on his shoulders the past six months felt lighter. Except there was another, even bigger weight crushing his chest until he could barely breathe.

Closing the door behind them, he moved toward Miranda, not sure whether he should fold her in his arms and kiss her, or give her space, which he hadn't done enough of before. He pulled in a breath and forged forward with the most critical conversation he'd had in his life.

"Thank you for reaching out to them and bringing them here. You're incredible. The most special woman I've ever known. And now my parents finally realize it, too."

Miranda's heart stuttered at his words before she reminded herself that him saying she was a special woman wasn't a big deal, under the circumstances. "Your situation helped me see things about my own life I hadn't fully realized. That I'd carried the weight of Vanessa's dislike for all these years to the point where I'd let it dictate who I believed I was. That I was the cause of the rift in my family. But I know now that I can't change that situation, that all I have control over is how I react to it. It struck me that you were doing the same thing, and I felt bad about making your family situation worse. So I brought them here to help you all put that baggage behind you. Move toward a better relationship that will make you all happy."

"Miranda." He wrapped his arms around her, bringing her close to the warm body she'd missed so much. "It's terrible that you've believed your family issues were your fault when in truth the problems were caused by your father."

"Hey, I'm not the only one. You were sure your parents thought Emilio was better than you, and you believed it, too. But of course it's not true at all."

"Maybe the reason we fell in love so fast is because we're more alike than we knew. That we were meant to help each other let go of those things. To have wonderful adventures together, bring out the best in each other."

"I don't think you really love me, Mateo," she whispered, wanting so much to be wrong. "It was just the difficulties in your life that made you believe you did."

"Is that why I think about you all day, every day? Why I close my eyes and remember how you looked with the breeze blowing your hair on the funicular? Why I remember how tough you were in the tunnel, and all the ways you're a great doctor? Why I can taste you and feel your soft skin against mine even when I'm sleeping? Why I've been completely miserable without you for the past week? I guess you're right. I guess that's not love."

Her chest expanded with emotion, but she was so afraid to believe it. So afraid he'd regret marrying when he'd never wanted that in his life. She looked up at him, tears stinging the backs of her eyes. "I don't know what to say. What to think."

"Up at Montserrat, you told me you'd had a miracle in your life once, and I said I didn't believe in miracles. But I was wrong." He cupped her face in his hands, and the tender look in his eyes stopped her breath. "You made me believe in miracles, Miranda, and my miracle is you. You've made me see how I shut myself off from being hurt. By my parents, by the guilt I felt over not being there for my brother, by any woman after seeing how much he was hurt by his wife. You've done that, too. Not believed in yourself enough. What do you say we spend our lives believing in each other? Loving each other? Please say yes."

"Yes." She flung her arms around his neck and sniffed back the tears. "I love you so much. I've missed you so much."

He lowered his mouth and kissed her, long and sweet and wonderful. When he pulled back, she felt dazed, even as a happiness bloomed in her chest unlike anything she'd experienced in her life. Then she frowned when his warm body moved away from hers and he went to his bedroom.

"Um, am I supposed to follow you in there?"

"Not quite yet. Soon." He emerged again, smiling, his eyes dark and alive, looking at her with such clear, real love she felt weak all over again. "First, this. Will you marry me, Dr. Davenport? For real, and forever?"

She looked down at the beautiful blue stone winking at her, and held out her hand. "Yes, Mr. Mateo. For real and forever and as soon as possible."

He laughed, sliding the ring on her finger before kissing her senseless.

"So," he said as they came up for breath, "how do you feel about moving to Spain? You can become the region's doctor. But only if you like the idea. We can stay here, and just go a few times a year if you prefer. I'll be happy any place in the world, so long as you're there with me."

"I fell in love with your home almost as fast as I fell in love with you." It was true, and the idea of living in that beautiful place made her chest nearly overflow with the joy of all he was offering her. "Miranda Alves, wife of the future Duke of Pinero, has a nice sound to it, don't you think?"

"Yes." He kissed her again before pressing his forehead to hers. "Almost as wonderful a sound as both of us saying 'I do'."

* * * * *

THE RESCUE DOC'S CHRISTMAS MIRACLE

BY
AMALIE BERLIN

Published in Great Britain 2017
By Mills & Boon, an imprint of HarperCollins*Publishers*
1 London Bridge Street, London, SE1 9GF

© 2017 Harlequin Books S.A.

Special thanks and acknowledgement are given to Amalie Berlin for her contribution to the Christmas in Manhattan series.

ISBN: 978-0-263-92674-3

Printed and bound in Spain
by CPI, Barcelona

Dear Reader,

Every book I write is a new puzzle to figure out—that's part of why I do it. Writing a book in a continuity like this—a miniseries within the line—is the biggest puzzle in the world. If you're unfamiliar with how these book babies are born, this is what happens: our talented editors cook up a bunch of linked characters, do some world-building to craft a community, then put together a project book with outlines and info for the writers who'll be collaborating to write the books.

This is extremely challenging. You have to take someone else's characters, shove them and the outline into your brain, and start running. Because of the nature of the beast, if one story deviates from the plan all the other stories might have to too. It requires a lot of off-the-cuff problem-solving and co-operation. It also requires extremely talented editors to make sure it hangs together at the end.

In short, it's the kind of project that forces you to grow as a writer. It also means the final result is never just due to *your* effort, it's even more of a team effort than usual—and it has to be a great team to work. Writers who'll immediately give feedback on something within minutes, or brainstorm a way to craft an event that has to happen in your book for future books to make sense. It's kind of a miracle, and kind of a nightmare at times, but it turns out some of the best stories.

I really hope you enjoy Gabriel and Penny's story, and I hope you'll pick up the other books in the series to see how the remaining Davenports get their happy-ever-afters.

Amalie xx

First, I must thank Dr Trish Connor from the bottom of my heart for her help figuring out what was wrong with Penny! I knew she had to have had a childhood illness, and had a list of boxes that illness had to tick to make the story work, but no idea what the illness could be. She listened to the list, rapidly spat out several options, and generally was a lifesaver. Without her directing me to juvenile dermatomyositis, which I'd never heard of, Penny might have never come alive to me as fully as she did. Massive thank-you to Dr Connor.

I must also shower love on Robin Gianna, sister-in-law to Dr Connor, who handled the conversation one day over lunch while I was panicking. :)

Finally, I'd like to thank Amy Ruttan, Annie O'Neil and Robin Gianna for the brainstorming and handholding it took to get this crazy book baby born. Love you, ladies!

Amalie Berlin lives with her family and her critters in Southern Ohio, and writes quirky and independent characters for Mills & Boon Medical Romance. She likes to buck expectations with unusual settings and situations, and believes humour can be used powerfully to illuminate the truth—especially when juxtaposed against intense emotions. Love is stronger and more satisfying when your partner can make you laugh through the times when you don't have the luxury of tears.

Books by Amalie Berlin

Mills & Boon Medical Romance

Hot Latin Docs
Dante's Shock Proposal

Desert Prince Docs
Challenging the Doctor Sheikh

The Hollywood Hills Clinic
Taming Hollywood's Ultimate Playboy

Return of Dr Irresistible
Breaking Her No-Dating Rule
Surgeons, Rivals...Lovers
Falling for Her Reluctant Sheikh
The Prince's Cinderella Bride

Visit the Author Profile page
at millsandboon.co.uk for more titles.

PROLOGUE

WERE IT NOT for the strong shopping bags protecting her clanking purchases, Penelope Davenport would never have made the walk back to her darkened motel, if the brisk, sometimes sideways shuffle she'd been doing through the gusting wind and sheets of rain could be called a walk. Whatever it could be called, it was better than her flying had been today.

Deep in the pit of her belly, she still felt the plummeting sensation triggered two hours earlier when the early autumn storm she'd been trying to outrun had caught them despite her best efforts, and a microburst had tried to slam her flying ambulance into the ground.

She still didn't know why they hadn't crashed.

Altitude had been on her side. And the storm's sharp down-blast of wind had probably only caught them at the edge. Luck no doubt could be credited with making her jerk the stick in the correct direction, tilting them out of the wind to where she could level out and avoid killing them all.

The energy, a terrible need to just keep moving, had stayed with her too. If she stopped now, her bones might burst from her skin.

Yes, she'd kept Baby in the air.

Yes, she'd been given clearance to fly between storms.

And they'd gotten their patient to a Schenectady hospital for treatment, even if they'd had to divert an hour's flight north to do it.

But she still felt responsible for such a near miss. Not only had there been almost death, but her partner, Dr. Gabriel Jackson, couldn't even treat their patient at the new hospital, having no privileges there. On top of that, he got a ruined night *not* doing whatever he'd planned on doing, and he was stuck in a powerless motel without supplies.

Precisely how she'd ended up hiking to a strip mall during the height of a line of storm cells for stranded-at-a-lousy-motel-during-a-power-outage supplies.

Anything to make it better. For her. For him…

There had been attraction between them from the jump. A chemical thing that sometimes made them look too long, and sometimes required she remind herself what they were and should be to one another. Professional. Coworkers.

The first week they'd worked together had been peppered with awkwardness only eased when they actively treated a patient. In the confines of the chopper, even though it maintained a mild hospital-like antiseptic scent, she'd babbled her way to every destination because the act of talking helped her keep from thinking too much. To keep from noticing the light cologne he wore with its hints of ginger. To block out that vibrating awareness that filled up the spaces between them.

But with all the crazy bouncing around in her head, none of that would matter tonight. They were just going to hang out, eat some liquor store sausage and cheese sampler, drink wine, play cards, and talk. Him for once, rather than her filling up the space. He knew more about her than she did about him.

A blast of wind flattened her into the side of the

motel just as she'd reached the awning-covered walk that should've gotten her out of the rain. Another ten or so doors, and she'd be inside, and safe, and she could roll up in the bedspread like a burrito to get warm.

Dying of pneumonia from how wet and cold she'd become after all that? Yeah, that'd suck. Gabriel would probably find the biggest horse pills with which to save her life, just to punish her for having gone out in a freaking *monsoon.*

He'd do it all while being sedate and so handsome it was like a big cosmic joke. Of *course* he would have to look like that—jaw that still looked like geometry even with the beard he kept short enough she wasn't sure it was technically a beard, or just some long, perfectly groomed stubble. The best-looking men were always the least attainable.

They'd never spoken about it, never made a move, but there had come to be an understanding between them. Conversations that began with proclamations of the benefit of having such a great partner to work with didn't need many lines to read between. The way he would sit away from her during work meetings, always on the other side of the conference table. She knew what interest looked like in a man's eyes, and she'd seen it there, so his distancing techniques said everything else.

Just as she reached his room, she felt the bag with the wine start to tear, and captured the bottle with her thigh against the hollow metal door. Knocking with her elbow was all she could manage.

"It's me!" A sudden clap of thunder drowned her out. Not exactly the entrance she'd planned. Then again, she hadn't really planned much beyond go to the store and make tonight better. In the back of her mind she held on to *have a great time* as her final objective, because it was at least statistically possible.

If he was moving in there, she couldn't hear anything over the rain.

"Hurry up, I think it's going to rain!" *Ha-ha.* See, she still had a sense of humor, before her untimely passing from hurricane-induced pneumonia.

Another blast of wind smacked her in the back and wrapped her completely saturated hair around her face. It stuck like a furry squid.

She opened her mouth to curse the door down—if she had to dig out her own key for the room next door it was all over. But as she began considering the logistics of juggling her tearing bags, the door opened. Before he could say anything, before he could yell at her for this exercise in ridiculousness, she grabbed her slowly shredding bag of wine by the rip and darted inside, the rest of her loot in swinging bags presently cutting off her circulation at the elbows.

"You think it's going to rain?" he said, like he couldn't tell a joke when he heard one. Because his mood was apparently so foul he couldn't even picture a reason to be in a good one. "Are you nuts? You walked somewhere in this? You look like you just got pulled out of the Hudson."

Laughing a little, she swung the bags up onto his table. "It was only about half a mile. I think. I don't know. I'm better at judging distances from the air, less good at it from the ground. Though since I've only been flying a couple years and been on the ground the rest of my life, you'd think it'd be the opposite."

For a normal person, it probably would've been, but Penny had learned young to judge distance by how far she'd be able to walk or roll her wheelchair. It was more a can-I-make-it-that-far? measuring system than something with math and numbers. Being now able to easily walk a mile, or whatever, in the pounding rain was something to celebrate. Not that he needed to know all that. It certainly wouldn't help put him into a better mood. He might even start fussing over her health—like her family still did on occasion, even though she'd been in remission for years.

"Niagara Falls is coming off the roof." Even though Gabriel's words were complaints, his tone had taken on that sardonic lilt that let her know that even in the dark he was shaking his head and saying words he really didn't expect to mean anything to her. Might even be rolling his pretty brown eyes.

"Yep. But what was I going to do, call a cab to go the equivalent of a few blocks? Rain's not going to kill me." She hoped. But, goodness, she needed to warm up. Which…she didn't have a plan for. No spare clothes.

"Your teeth are chattering," he noted.

"I don't know how you can see anything in here, it's dark."

"I can hear them clacking."

She clamped her mouth shut to control the noise and finished piling her dripping bags on the table so she could dig out the candles she'd purchased. Candles meant fire, meant light, and especially some kind of *heat*.

"I know you're trying to be nice."

"I am," she chirped, felt her voice wobble with her involuntary jaw wobbling, still determined to give Dr. Grouchy a better evening than the universe had conjured for either of them. Finding the matches and grabbing one of the candles, she created fire. And light. "Saw a strip mall on the way here with one of those cheapo general-store places beside a liquor store."

Clack. Clackity. Clack. She gritted her teeth until her jaw tensed and felt more under control. She kept the rest of it short. "Got supplies. You could play along, pretend you're someone who doesn't hate f-fun. M-might s-surprise y-you."

The last several words stuttered out and she gave up trying to pretend. She was cold. During her brisk walk in the downpour she'd stayed more or less warm. Standing around made the chill seep into her, and life become decidedly less livable.

Outside the storm continued to rage, and when a gust blew against the side of the building, she looked over and noticed Gabriel was in his underwear.

Gabriel was in his underwear.

How had she missed that?

Putting the candle down, she smooshed her wet hair back from her face, where it was obviously obstructing her vision, and looked at him. Beneath his carefully zipped flight suit he'd been hiding *all that*?

Even as dark as the room was, she could see the definition of abs in his rich, brown skin. Wide, solid shoulders. Hip flexors. Good God, the man had chiseled hip flexors.

Which would be something she could spend time appreciating as soon as she got warm.

"Did you get something dry to wear in that?"

"Would be wet if I had. But I think you have the right idea."

She fumbled for her zipper, fingers suddenly stiff and wooly, and failed to sufficiently grab the tab to draw it down three times in succession. Her fingers just slid right off the end when she pulled. A mild sound of alarm was all it took to set him into motion, and suddenly he was in front of her, taking over.

Under any other circumstances, she might hesitate to strip down to her undies with the partner she'd been actively trying to ignore her attraction to, but him peeling the sodden, freezing material down her arms at least provided an excuse for the wash of goose-bumps she knew were as much to do with him undressing her as her looming hypothermia. When he knelt to help her with the boots, she put her hands on his shoulders, and immediately wanted to mash her whole body against his. The man was hot, in every sense of the word.

At least that fear that had been pitting through her was gone now. She wasn't feeling…all that hesitant anymore either. "How do you feel about underwear hugging? You, me, mashed together. You're giving off heat like a space heater and I really like that about you right now."

"I'm a normal temperature. You're just cold. It doesn't have to be freezing temperatures to get hypothermia. You know that."

Yes, she did.

Despite the irritation lingering in his voice, his touch was gentle. Large, strong hands cupped the back of each leg as he helped ease her clothing off.

Beneath her suit, she generally dressed for comfort. That meant white cotton bikinis and a snug strappy tank top. Being endowed with modest curves had advantages, one being the ability to skip confining undergarments, especially under such unstructured clothing as a flight suit.

She puffed as he stood back up and she had to clamp her arms to her sides to keep from flinging herself at him. "Yell at me later."

"I will. After you've had a shower and warmed up." And he sounded like he meant it.

Gabriel pulled her back sometimes, providing a special kind of stoicism that balanced her out. She was used to some measure of grumpiness when she did something he found dumb, but after the day they'd had the idea of him yelling at her made her stomach churn.

"Do you hate me?" The words erupted from her mouth before she could give them a proper spin around in her head, and even though she'd just told him to yell at her later.

"Hate you?" He shook her sodden flight suit out and draped it over the other chair, then looked back down at her, his still handsome scowl flickering in the light of the candle. "Why on earth would I hate you?"

"Because I almost crashed us. I couldn't… I couldn't outrun it. I thought… But then the wind…" She faltered around, and suddenly the words caught up with her emotions, and she knew she was crying by the hot rivers on her frigid cheeks.

"You did outrun it," he said, his voice gentle. One strong arm wrapped around her, propelling her toward the bathroom. "You got us here. It was supposed to go south of us. Everyone said so."

Everyone said so. She nodded, squeezing her eyes tightly shut to stop that horrifying leaking. But it wasn't enough. Several big, gulpy breaths later, she gave up and turned to fling her arms around his waist.

Everywhere their skin touched, she grew warmer. The firm wall of his chest under her cheek, the strong arms that immediately came around her wrapped her in heat.

She needed comfort, to know that her partner, a doctor who treated her—the only Davenport at Manhattan Mercy without the title—like an equal, still had faith in her.

"You won't be afraid to fly with me after this?"

Her underthings were wet, she realized as she felt his skin start to cool, or at least stop feeling quite so warm through the soaked material. She was getting him wet.

"I won't. We'll talk about that later, but right now you need to get in the shower," he said, his mouth against the crown of her head. "Who knows if the water will stay hot for long, and you've stopped shaking."

"It wasn't raining that hard when I left," she muttered. The colder she got, the less intelligent her foray into the blistering rain seemed. No matter how good her reasoning at the time.

You've stopped shaking. His words swam up to her as he wrapped his arms around her hips and lifted, then walked into the darkened bathroom to deposit her right in the tub.

People stopped shaking when they warmed up, or when they got too cold and their bodies gave up shaking to get warm.

He adjusted the water quickly, then stepped in with her, positioning her under the spray so that the almost too hot water hit the back of her neck, then her head, and once it had had a few seconds to cascade over her, he turned her by the shoulders so that her back came against his chest, and the water warmed up her front side.

She shivered again for a couple seconds, and then relaxed back against him, her head on his shoulder, and her hands seeking his on her hips to drag his arms back around her waist. Standing under the spray, in their underwear…

"This went a lot different in my head."

"Did you sing and dance your way through the rain in your head?"

"No, the rain didn't factor in. I just thought, get the wine, get some food, get candles, cards, munchies… Talk to Gabriel and give him a good night to make up for whatever you had planned at home."

"I had nothing planned." His mouth was at her ear, and the words should've taken the edge off somehow, but she found herself spinning to face him instead.

Probably her third dumb idea of the day, but, unlike the first two dumb ideas, she just didn't care.

It was dark, the candle left in the other room, but as she pulled the tank top over her head she heard his breathing hitch. He couldn't see anything as with the lights out the small, interior bathroom was little more than a cave, even with the door open to a slightly less dark room beyond. But he felt her skin when she pressed forward. Lifting her arms and rising on tiptoe, she didn't stop, although she satisfied that urge to mash herself against him, and still didn't stop when his head dipped to meet her kiss.

CHAPTER ONE

Two months later...

LOCKED IN A stall in the ladies' room at Manhattan Mercy, Penny leaned against the polished metal separating wall and stared at her watch.

Across from her, perched atop the toilet-paper dispenser, sat a white plastic wand that could change her footloose existence forever.

It seemed emotionally safer to watch the hand on her watch ticking by than to stare at the tiny display for the entire minute it would take for the one line to appear, or two—results on the test she'd put off taking for three weeks.

At first, she'd been unable to accept it was necessary. She'd had condoms. They'd used condoms. They hadn't even been purchased at the cheapo general store, they had just been in her bag in case some kind of life opportunity happened. It was New York City. She could conceivably run into anyone. Like that guy from that movie...the one with the smoldering eyes. And maybe he'd be drunk, bored, or somehow seduced by her ability to walk and chew gum at the same time, and then...*magic would happen.* If she had condoms.

A week later, she'd accepted they may have been old condoms.

Last week she'd known for sure she needed to take a test. It had *really* only taken a week or so to take it…

Still, hoping it was negative felt *wrong*. Because what if it wasn't? She'd already be in the running for Mother of the Year from procrastinating on a pregnancy test without making *disappointment* the first emotion she felt for a tiny life she'd created.

Definitely the sort of thoughts you never ever tell your child. Or anyone else.

Or even better, thoughts to avoid having altogether.

Every second the tiny hand ticked, her stomach grew heavier and more rumbly. When it finally passed the sixty-second mark, she lowered her wrist but still couldn't bring herself to look at the test.

This was not how women took pregnancy tests in commercials. They had pink bathrooms and a partner waiting outside the door, ready to celebrate, with something bubbly but nonalcoholic.

Which she didn't want anyway.

It would be all right. Everything would be all right. Nothing bad would happen just because she looked at the little window…

She closed her eyes and took a deep breath, shoring up her flagging courage that came with a twinge of self-disgust. The fact she even needed to boost her bravery should shame her into looking. Courage was a cornerstone of her entire personality. If something scared her, Penny had a personal maxim to run toward the thing, unless it was a bear.

Another deep breath slowly exhaled didn't help either. *Nope.*

A minute—or even two now—wasn't sufficient time

for this. Why didn't they make *delayed* response pregnancy tests so you could work up to it? It wouldn't have to take that long for the testing, just some kind of delay on the display.

I feel I'll be ready to look at this Thursday. Push the Thursday button. Then take that many days to come up with a plan for how not to freak out.

She couldn't wait for Thursday. She also couldn't look at the thing in a bathroom stall. Leaving aside questions about her emotional maturity, if she wanted to get in the pre-flight and maintenance checks before their shift started, she needed to go now.

She snatched the little wand and stuffed it into the thigh pocket on her flight suit, zipped that pocket closed, and barreled out of the stall to clean up and get upstairs.

The whole not-looking business was even dumber than her hike through a hurricane. She didn't need to look, the answer had burned into her frontal lobe before she'd swiped her debit card at the pharmacy. Regular Rosie didn't miss a single period, let alone two, for no reason. The test was a formality, therefore she was extra-stupid for not just looking at it.

Gabriel would've told her so too, only she'd been unable to tell him about any of this before now. He would've picked her up, and squeezed her like an orange until she tinkled on the damned wand.

The morning after that night, which she still found herself lingering over in quiet moments, he'd suggested the things they'd done never leave the motel room. It became the No-Tell Motel, minus all the sleazy connotations, because he'd declared it and she'd agreed. It was the sensible thing. Gabriel never suggested things that weren't sensible, and sometimes he was the only reason she did things that *were* sensible. She'd seen the sense, despite not really wanting to see it.

When he'd opened the door to leave the room, she'd grabbed his head and kissed the breath out of both of them one last time so she could hold to that agreement. The hedonistic part of her, the part that loved life and experience, hated giving up that experience so quickly.

But? Sensible. She wasn't in the market for a relationship, at least not a *relationship* relationship, even if she could've carried on a little longer. Tried out other rooms and, through trial and arduous study, gathered the data to support the hypothesis their night had borne: sex with Gabriel Jackson was as good as it got.

But so was working with him.

She really had no idea what friendship would be like with him, or anything else outside work and the unspeakable night because, despite her efforts, they hadn't gotten to the cards and friendship-building conversations. They'd showered...vigorously. Then they'd made a mess of the bed even more vigorously. The wine had been drunk in between all that. There had been other pit-stops where they'd consumed cheese and sausage because stamina required fuel, but none of the business their mouths had gotten up to had been in the vicinity of talking.

Unless you counted *that* talk. The sexy smattering of words between lovers.

Just like that.

Don't stop.

Oh, God...

Heaven help her, she was doing it again. Thinking about all *that*, which had caused all *this*. The consequences.

She took the stairs at a run, pounding up the ten flights separating her current floor and the helipad on the roof.

At the top, with blessedly buzzing lungs and legs, she checked her watch on her way to the chopper. Just over two minutes. She'd have to do better if she was going to make it up eighty-six floors at the Empire State Run-Up in the New Year. If she even could do the stair-climbing marathon while pregnant.

She climbed into the thing she'd been calling "Baby" for two years and worked through the checklist to go over gauges and start it up. Only when she'd finished did she sit back and reach into her thigh pocket to pull out the wand. Before giving herself a chance to think anything or to get worked up, she flipped it over and read the display.

Two lines.

Yep.

Out of the corner of her eye she saw movement. A full look tracked Gabriel's long stride eating up the distance between them.

"Dang it." She stuffed the wand back into the pocket and zipped it as fast as she could.

Then the door opened and he gave her a look.

"What?"

"Why aren't you starting it up already? Is there a problem?"

"What problem? There's no problem," she blurted, too fast and too loud, then gestured haplessly at nothing, trying to get back on course. "I've already done the checks. Why are you…?"

He never came up to the roof anymore unless they had a call.

"Did we get a call?" She looked at the radio and her stomach sank. *Off.* She hadn't turned it on during her pre-flight checks.

He said nothing, just turned the radio on while she started the massive rotors spinning.

"Where are we going?" she asked, buckling in, and by the time he'd answered she was ready to lift off. That was part of why she went through the pre-flight checks—it was set up to go from nothing to flight in under a minute.

"Is everything all right?" he asked through the comm once they were in the air. It wasn't concern she heard so much as that hint of frustration that appeared in his voice every time things didn't happen when he expected.

To lie, or not to lie...

"Can't complain."

She really couldn't, at least not right now. And complaining was something she tried to only do inside her head. Complaining about anything could still trigger her loved ones trying to rescue her, which she could appreciate on an intellectual level even if she couldn't abide it anymore. Complaining about anything related to health? That might even bring her whole family out in full flailing fit mode, maybe even with questions about whether she was healthy enough to gestate a human life.

The shape of the test in her thigh pocket stood out, and she prayed Dr. Notices Everything didn't notice until she was ready to share.

"You're pale. Are you sick?"

Gabriel might not understand much about what went on inside Penny's head but he understood her body unfortunately well, beyond just what his training had taught him about her physiological signs of distress.

Pale face and darkness under blue eyes so bright the blackness beneath them seemed blacker. Some kind of unsteadiness in her hands. The silent call radio. No music either during her pre-flight routine, and she always listened to music when on standby. Tight-lipped when normally talkative...

She squinted at him, then adjusted something amid the toggles and switches without answering him. Not right.

Despite the somewhat fumbling quality her hands had taken with switches, on the controls everything went smoothly. The flight was steady, a straight line, something he could appreciate since his life depended on it, but something was wrong. And if she stayed true to form, he was going to have to shake it out of her. Later. They were already in the air, so his chance to swap out a focused pilot had gone.

The two months since their…mistake…hadn't been entirely easy months. The first couple of weeks had been the worst. Awkward enough that she'd barely looked him in the eye any particular day, which had been rougher than he'd have thought. But with a little willpower, and a pact of mutual amnesia, they'd worked through it and things had found a new normal, somewhat off-center from the way things had been before.

Like when they bumped into one another changing in the locker room. She'd been wearing the same kind of simple and somehow ungodly sexy cotton things, and when she'd looked at him, he'd seen his thoughts reflected back at him. The pink that had infused every inch of her pale flesh had backed it up.

Not embarrassed. Aroused. And unhappily so.

Awkward.

Now he changed in the men's room and avoided the locker room unless he had to, or unless she'd gone home for the day. His initial plan had just been to keep everything as low-key and low-stress as he could so that *she* could forget. He knew he couldn't forget, but he wasn't as prone to impetuousness as she was—he could resist. When he found himself watching the way she tapped the end of her pen on her lower lip while filling out paperwork, he could shake himself out of it. Stop thinking about her mouth. Not give in to temptation. But that seemed harder for Penny to do, so he just tried to keep temptation from coming up.

It had worked at first when they'd started working together and just had to ignore a spark, and it had even worked briefly in the middle of the time since their night, but a couple of weeks ago things had started getting tense again. Made no sense, and he didn't know what to do about it. Time was supposed to take care of things like this, but their agreement not to discuss it meant he couldn't even act as he would've in the past. Ask her what was wrong. Offer her an ear for her troubles. Just suss out symptoms and determine whether her oddness was physical or emotional... No easy course of action.

If this was attached to the desire for another night, he couldn't blame her, even if he *would* turn her down.

"How long?" he asked through the comm, since he already had one patient to focus on, righting his thoughts. If she wanted his help, she'd ask for it.

Normally he wouldn't have to ask how long. Normally his chattering partner freely gave information during flight.

She still didn't look at him, but she did let go of the controls with one hand to point. "There. We're landing on the roof next door."

Taciturn. Definitely something wrong. If he didn't expect to need her paramedic skills, he'd put her on light duty for this run. But the patient they were flying to was a steel worker who'd fallen from the beams of a new construction site. Since they'd called for an ambulance rather than a coroner, all he knew for sure was that he'd need her at her best.

"We're bypassing stretcher. I don't know what the site

looks like, the board is the only safe bet. Are you well enough to carry it?"

She did look at him then, her eyes narrowing to slits. "I can do my job. I'm fine."

Gabriel didn't argue with her, but he'd never heard the words "I'm fine" and had it be anything near fine. Even if she put up a fight to stay on the job anytime she was ill, she'd never looked so put out with *him* over asking.

With an easy touch, she put the chopper down atop the neighboring building, and he unstrapped and went to grab bags.

"Get the board," he ordered, wrenching open the sliding door and hopping out to make a run for the roof access door.

It always took her a moment longer to disembark due to having to power down the chopper. Him running ahead to the patient was part of their usual routine as every second mattered and he did whatever he could as she brought up the rear.

He hit the stairs running, and took all eighteen stories down on foot. Waiting for the elevator always slowed them down.

Across the lobby with a nod to Security, he bustled out the door and rounded the building. Just as he reached the construction site, the manager met him, slapped a hard hat onto his head and led the way across the dirt and gravel lot, around piles of construction material, to the concrete pad beneath steel beams, and his patient.

No blood haloing his head, a good sign and something he'd seen enough on the job with jumpers and falls from great height. Heads didn't stand up well to concrete, unless they didn't hit first. The man had landed on his feet, at least briefly, and his head had probably hit last.

Gabriel fell to the man's side.

Unconscious.

Breathing fast.

He felt for a pulse, found a rapid rate to go with the breathing.

"How long ago was it?" He began gathering information as he fished out a penlight to check pupils. One responsive, the other fixed.

"Less than ten minutes."

"How far did he fall?" Gabriel looked up again at the open beams for one that would align with the man's location.

"About thirty feet. That beam there."

Onto concrete.

When he lowered his eyes again, he saw Penny running full tilt across the construction site—without a hard hat but with the backboard held over her head. That would help a little if someone dropped something on her.

"Get her a hat," he said to the manager, then went back to his patient.

When she reached him, she put the board down alongside the patient and then began digging into his bag to help, extracting a neck brace first thing. A hat made it to her head, but didn't slow her down.

"How's he doing? What's his name?"

He hadn't asked.

"Frank," someone answered, and Penny thanked him, then started talking to Unconscious Frank as she fitted the brace around his neck, explaining what she was doing, as was proper.

"He's seen better days. There's some kind of cranial hemorrhage or swelling, one pupil unresponsive. And I think internal bleeding, his heart is going hard. Get a line in him, saline."

He ordered, she complied. That was the one thing unchanged since their unfortunate encounter—she always worked hard and fast. Competent, and something more. She may have been born to society, but she'd managed to become compassionate in a hands-on way, and it made a difference in the way she treated their patients. She might not be one hundred percent today, but she was still fighting for them.

A whole family of doctors, and she'd become a paramedic. He should ask her why sometime, but knowing her adrenaline junkie tendencies, paramedic fit. They were the first on the scene for the big emergencies.

Opening the man's shirt, he looked his belly and chest over, noted bruising on his left rib cage, then began to feel his belly for telltale signs of bleeding.

Like the turgid area on the left upper quadrant. "How's the line?"

She flushed the catheter she'd just inserted into the man's arm, nodded, and then hooked up a saline line to it. "We're good. I'm going to pin it to your suit. It's wide open, do you want it slower?"

"No, his spleen is ruptured, I don't know how badly. Run the drip wide open. We have to get him in the air." He lifted his head out of the way and Penny produced a massive safety pin from somewhere, and clipped the saline line to the shoulder of his suit.

It wasn't exactly the kind of protocol taught in medical training, but she'd done it before. Once they got to the chopper, she'd have to fly them to the hospital, and unclipping it from her own shoulder to free her to fly would slow them down. The first time she'd done it, he'd been surprised, but over their months, working together, her unusual methods had ceased to be strange. She always had a reason for the things she did, and he didn't doubt she had a reason to be so pale and stiff-lipped now. Which was what worried him.

"Get his legs," he ordered once the bag swung from his shoulder, and waited until she was there. On the count of three they lifted, moved, and lowered their patient, then secured straps.

"You and you, help me carry him," he said to the manager and another strong-looking worker watching them. "Let my pilot run ahead and get the chopper running so we don't lose any time."

Penny waited until they'd started moving, then went to take his bag of supplies, swung it over her shoulder, and ran. She would push the button for the elevator and have Security hold it for them while she took the stairs. That was how she worked. She thought ahead, and he was grateful for that.

So, whatever was wrong, she was probably handling it. Maybe he should just let her handle it. The problem was, he had to be the one who forced her home when she *did* get ill, or would admit to being ill. It had become a happily infrequent part of his job description, but a part nevertheless.

By the time they'd reached the chopper, the blades were whirring. They got Frank loaded quickly and he put his headset on.

"They're already prepping an OR." Penny's voice came through the comm. "A surgical team's going to meet us at the roof to type him for transfusion."

"What did you report?" He locked himself into the jump seat over his patient, and while she flew he affixed leads for the portable heart monitor and checked again for pupil dilation.

"Internal bleeding, most likely splenic rupture, irregular pupil reaction, possibly some kind of spinal damage, and unconsciousness."

All that was the most she'd said to him all day.

"Okay." He called in another update, laying on the need for an MRI, then asked over the comm, "Why did you suggest spinal damage?"

"Skydiving. Landing jars badly."

Not his favorite answer, but not wrong either. Leave it to Penny to frame things in terms of extreme sports activities, that was like her. Answering with so few words on a subject she could chatter hours about usually? Again, not like her.

No matter how hard she'd hit the ground running today, something was definitely wrong.

As soon as they'd handed over their patient to the surgical team atop Manhattan Mercy, Gabriel took Penny's elbow to keep her from following the team inside. Not letting himself touch her had been another way to keep temptation at bay, and even this casual, platonic touch to her arm felt exasperatingly intimate to him. But it had a purpose.

She turned to look at him, her elbow held out from her body at an unnatural angle, her brows up in question. On top of the high building, the wind blew loudly enough that talking meant shouting, even with the helicopter blades silent. He jerked his head back toward the chopper.

"You want to go somewhere?" She was nearly shouting over the wind, eyeing his hand on her arm again. It wasn't as though he gripped her in anger, though he'd admit frustration at having to have this conversation again, and his grip wasn't strong enough to hurt. Sometimes he had to grab her to keep her from flitting away.

A quick shake of his head and he answered with one word. "Talk."

The flare of wariness in her blue eyes only firmed his resolve. He released her, went and opened the sliding side door, climbed in, and scooted to make room for her.

If he hadn't suspected anything before, the way she looked at the sky, at her feet, and generally stalled for time would've given it all away.

She had to talk herself into speaking with him.

After about half a minute, she squared her shoulders and marched over to board the helicopter, nearly closing the door behind her. It was enough to dampen the wind and make this conversation less stressful than it would've been if it had to start from a position of yelling, but remained open enough for easy escape.

She perched on the edge of the seat, one hand staying on the door handle, and looked at him. "What do you want to talk about?"

So ready to fly.

"You know what I want to talk about. You shot me a nasty look, but you never actually answered me. Are you ill? Because you look like hell."

Blunt. Maybe a little too blunt, but if that was what it took to get through to her, so be it.

"I'm fine."

"Pale. Black circles. No motormouth. No music before flying. No band radio. You didn't even know we'd been called out. Want to revise your statement?"

"That was a mistake. Normal people do make mistakes sometimes!"

"Fine. If you want to stick to the Not Sick story, then are you hungover? Are you distracted by whatever last night's festivities were?"

"Oh. My. God. You're jealous? That's what this is?"

She couldn't have shocked him more if she'd just decked him.

They'd made an agreement! And the only way to keep up his end was to refuse to rise to the bait.

"I have plans to be alive tomorrow. A distracted pilot is a bad pilot."

"Did I fly badly?" Her voice rose, bringing it right back to near shouting level. "Did I perform badly today?"

"No."

"No. I did my job just fine."

"You're distracted, at the very least, and you're a distraction. Whether or not you're willing to admit it. I can't focus on the patients if I'm constantly checking on you to make sure you're still upright."

"I'm not sick—"

"I don't care." He cut her off. "Do whatever it is you need to do to function at your usual level. Do shifts in Emergency until then, I don't want you on my crew. I'll get another pilot."

A fierce blush washed into her cheeks but didn't detract from her paleness. It actually amplified how very pale she was against that bright red contrast.

"I'm so glad that you don't care."

Still shouting...

"Since you don't care, and I know you don't because we're not friends, this is probably the *perfect* time to put your mind at ease. It's *not* an illness."

She never liked him questioning her over sickness, which had always bugged him, like he should feel guilty for being concerned about her or about their patients. But this was extreme, even for her. His neck prickled and he fought the urge to touch her again, but this time because he wanted the connection that was still there. But her reaction was so far outside the bounds of normal, he couldn't be certain it wouldn't make things worse.

She ripped open the sliding door, climbed out, then

forced her hand into a pocket on her suit. In the next instant she had something in hand, but before he could identify it, the thing bounced off his left cheek and she slammed the door.

She'd *thrown* something at his face.

He didn't know whether to go after her or let her stomp off.

A glance down confirmed the thing had bounced out of his field of vision. With a sigh, he bent forward to look beneath the seats.

There was some stretching and, although he'd spotted it, to reach it he had to smash his face against the front seatback and feel blindly.

As soon as his fingers curled around the length of it, his stomach bottomed out.

He knew very few things that shape.

And only one that could be an answer to what wasn't an illness.

He straightened, pulling his hand from beneath the seat, and looked down as his heart beat louder and louder, like thundering rotors.

Positive.

CHAPTER TWO

No sooner was Penny off the roof than she was jogging for the stairwell. A woman couldn't make an exit like that and then be easy to find...in the extremely unlikely chance that a real, flesh-and-blood man would behave like a movie hero and chase after her. Not that she wanted him to, she'd just bounced a pregnancy test off his face.

She hit the stairs two at a time to head for her supervisor's office. Gabriel had demanded she go home, and she'd take that advice. Not because she was underperforming, she wasn't, but she'd be lying if she pretended she wasn't distracted. She was. And she'd be lying to herself if she tried to pretend she wasn't tired. Emotionally tired or physically, she had no clue, but both should resolve with the same treatment: a nap.

However, there was one accusation she would cop to that had no bearing on the situation—she definitely was behaving differently than normal, and it was hard to be filled with supercharged optimism when you felt like you were in an uncontrollable spin without a fixed point on the horizon to guide you.

Once she'd begged off for the afternoon, she hurried out and summoned a cab. Earbuds and her streaming music service allowed her to shut down for the ride home. It wasn't until she opened the door into her own private space that guilt began to ooze from her chest. She could feel it rising off her like toxic vapor.

She should've told Gabriel more gently and she *really* shouldn't have thrown the test at his head. He hadn't deserved that. But he'd just hit that sore spot, maybe unknowingly, and her knees had jerked. In those few words he'd made her feel she was on the cusp of being rendered helpless again, like a wheelchair waited around the corner, crouched and sinister. Like any second she'd revert to being an observer in her own life.

The flight suit she always changed out of before coming home still hung on her, so she dropped her bag on the way to the stairs to her bedroom loft above to go change into something lounge-worthy, then headed back down to fling herself onto the sofa.

If it was already two months in, she'd have seven, or something, to go. She should make an appointment with a doctor she didn't share genetics with. But how long before she was shuffled off to the side just by virtue of being pregnant, regardless of how healthy she remained during her pregnancy? How long before they took her off the chopper and made her work every rotation on the floor in the emergency department?

How long before she was sidelined by her *baby*?

She stared into the open rafters above, sighing at herself. There was a worse emotion to attach to an innocent baby than disappointment. Resentment.

That word didn't apply yet, but she could see it on the horizon, a black monolith on her own internal skyline. Would that be better or worse than the emotion she couldn't even deny to herself: the fear that her child would be cripplingly sick just like she'd been, but not be one of the lucky twenty percent?

* * *

Darkness fell over the city before Gabriel's day ended. Manhattan was never truly dark, but during the holiday season it was even brighter than normal. Everywhere he looked he saw festive reminders of the holidays, glittering lights, red bows, and jingle bells. In front of Penny's Tribeca building, a leafless tree had been wrapped in tiny blue lights that transitioned to purple and pink. Even the tiniest branches glittered like crystal, but in a funky way that let the outside world know the eclectic apartments they'd find inside the converted factory.

He liked Christmas in a vague sort of way, mostly as a quiet Christmas Day with his parents, but the rest of the season left him flat.

The test felt like an anvil in his pocket, and had all day. From his flight suit to the street clothes he now wore, it had stayed with him. Even now, hours later, he didn't know how to feel about it any more than he could figure out how to get it out of his mind.

He'd had his shot at marriage and a family a decade ago, and had proved insufficient to the task of husband, so he'd never gotten to the father stage of family life. It had been planned—big family, lots of children—but he'd missed important steps somewhere along the way, and hadn't yet figured out where he'd gone wrong. Once marriage had been taken out of his future plans, so had the idea of being a father, one of the many reasons he'd always been meticulous about safe sex.

As he made his way across the lobby, the differences in their lives came into focus. Temperamentally mismatched. Historically mismatched. Socially mismatched. Financially mismatched. He did well, but by Davenport standards...

If she decided to exclude him from his child's life, the attorneys she could hire could see it done.

Her name on the directory pointed him to the top floor. Penthouse, of course. Old wealth.

Which put his next move in a light that people would probably misconstrue, but he'd make it anyway. Even if he'd failed spectacularly as a husband the first time out, even if they were entirely different kinds of people. Marriage before the child came would increase the strength of his rights. He'd like to think he knew Penny well enough to rule out the likelihood she'd bar him from his child's life, but he wasn't willing to bet on it. Look at how wrong he'd gotten things with Nila.

If he and Penny could work things out, it would actually be a good thing. She might be impulsive, but she was also kind, and the days they didn't work together, he missed the optimism that rolled off her for most of the day. He could live with that being part of his daily life. They were extremely sexually compatible. If they could work out some kind of understanding about the rest of it, it could work, at least long enough to provide the kind of stable base their child deserved.

Once outside her door, he rang the bell, and she opened it so quickly she could've been just standing there, waiting for him. Except she was disheveled and had the soft look of sleep about her eyes, along with wearing some rumpled cotton pajamas.

As soon as the door stood fully open, she launched in. "Gabriel, I am so sorry." The words came in a rush and her arms hitched halfway up her chest and back, like she was about to hug him, but wasn't sure he'd let her.

It was the opening he needed. He stepped through the door, closed it and flipped one of the locks before turning back to her.

The stricken look on her face had him reaching for her cheek. It had been in him just to comfort her, let her know he wasn't angry, let her know that things had changed again, but the haunting light of vulnerability in her eyes pulled him in.

Instantly, when his hand cupped her cheek, her eyes fell closed and she tilted her head into the touch, like she'd been just as worried about their fight, like she needed comfort too. Mercy, he wanted to kiss her. And he shouldn't, that would be a jump too far, too soon.

Instead, he gave a little tug to bring her to him. Her arms opened and slid around his ribs and he let himself hold her in an easy, relaxed embrace, his chin resting atop her head as she breathed out so slowly and deeply that he knew she'd needed it.

How do you feel about underwear hugging?

Her question from months before swam back to him, bringing a grin with it. There was something about her that felt great in his arms. Maybe it was her perfect height compared to his, and the way his chin rested on her forehead when she tucked in close, and how he could feel the fan of her eyelashes on the side of his neck. Maybe it was the combination of her slender, feminine frame and the strength he felt in it, or the mop of soft, wavy hair and how, when even slightly ruffled, her delicate scent drifted out, calling to something in his chest.

He just knew he liked it. He liked it enough to force his way through the rest of the questions and worries he'd had all day. Start the conversation. Get it going. Keep things calm. That had been his mistake earlier when she'd grown frustrated and pelted him with a pregnancy test.

"Are you all right?"

"Are *you* all right?" she answered, without moving an inch, but alarm bells sounded in his head. Health con-

versations always set her off, even if this was entirely a
health concern.

"You felt bad earlier." He squeezed her a little tighter as
he spoke, a tool he'd never had the opportunity to use to
calm down these conversations in the past, so who knew
how well it'd work?

"I was shocked. Sort of. I didn't feel sick, I just felt, I
don't know, unsettled? Kind of nervous?"

He simply nodded, still trying so hard to take it slowly.
Not to rush ahead, not to demand answers, not to drag
her off to the court house or frog march her to the altar.

So, today's symptoms weren't directly related to her
pregnancy, not in a physical illness way. That was something. Her pale shakiness was shock. Okay.

Now for the question he'd been dreading. A sinking,
hollow feeling in his stomach made him want to hold
tighter, so he forced himself to relax his hold on her and
lean back so she'd look up at him.

"Are you going to have it? I need to know what you're
intending."

As soon as the words came out, she stepped back from
him, fully back until no longer in arm's reach, her own
arms drawing up like even her appendages couldn't be
within his orbit.

He knew her well enough to know that she'd respond
best to calm discussion, even if he could feel his hackles
rising. He didn't want a repeat of their earlier confron-
tation.

Her eyebrows came together, her eyes went wider, pupils dilating to the point the black overwhelmed the usual
vibrant blue. Mouth open, breathing faster… Fear. Fear
responses. What did that mean?

Tension stole across his shoulders as well, but the emotional landmine between them sat there, both of them frozen, as if even a wrong flick of the eyes could set it off.

Was she afraid of his reaction when she answered, any reaction, or was there a *reason* to be afraid if she responded?

"Penny?"

"What do you want me to say? I don't know what answer you're looking for." She swallowed and her gaze skirted downward, but unfocused, as if searching her own mind for answers. Until the fuzziness lifted, and she focused on his hip.

He followed her gaze to his right front pocket, and the outline of the test there. Maybe it would get her moving again. Ducking his hand in, he withdrew the plastic wand and held it out to her. "I want you to tell me the truth. We made a life, I deserve to know whether or not it gets to come into this world."

Penny felt her throat close as he produced the test, and offered it to her. But it was his words that brought tears. "You want it? You're not trying to tell me you...?"

"I want it. God, of course I want it."

The rasp in his voice echoed the truth she saw in his deep brown eyes. There was even a reverence in the way he held the test out to her she hadn't noticed before. It didn't simply lie on his palm, his fingers curled loosely around it, he cradled it—this nothing piece of plastic.

Whatever else happened, she could count on that. He already loved this child, or at least the idea of it.

She laid her hand over the test and curled her fingers over his hand, then kept right on going until she'd folded her arm back and dragged his around her waist. Her other arm up over his shoulders, she pulled back into the hug she'd escaped when his words had curdled her insides.

"I thought I'd bungled it all up. That you were going

to shout about it, or just…not, you know, because… we weren't…"

Words refused to come into any kind of order, but the feel of his other arm around her waist helped. Made it better. Even after all the torturous hours she'd spent this afternoon practicing the words to use for the Get Out of Jail Free speech she'd been planning to offer. And which she should still give him, even if she was in no way ready to jump into that conversation with both feet when just the merest whiff of discord had almost made her lose her lunch on him moments ago.

"You know, this is all your fault," she half teased instead, but kept her voice light so he'd know she was mostly teasing. "If you hadn't had that rule about not mentioning anything, I could've given you some warning. Like, 'Hey, things are amiss in Uterus Land.' That's part of what I felt so guilty about. I had a little time to work up to taking the test, but you've only had, like…eight hours to get used to this."

"I'm not used to it yet."

"Me either."

"But you want it." He needed to hear it again, and that was okay. That was something easy she could give him.

"I want the baby." She confirmed that part easily enough, but a little rueful chuckle followed. "I *don't* want to be pregnant. At all. I'm trying not to freak out about that part, but I want this child. Really."

The hug started to go past the point where it was probably getting weird for him so, no matter how good he felt, she still felt compelled to try and be sensible. A quick kiss to his cheek, and she stepped back again, snagging the test as she retreated to the sofa to sit.

"Because of work?" he asked, following the conversation, as well as her, to the sofa.

Because it seems too much like sickness.

"Because it seems very restrictive," she said instead, and found herself again looking at the test she'd had so much difficulty looking at earlier. "And uncomfortable. I guess. Plus, there's…you know, figuring things out. I don't even know how to start that conversation, like—"

"We should get married."

He said the words so quickly she had to mentally replay his words to even understand what he'd said. Then came a giggle, which promptly turned to real laughter at the absurdity of the idea. He was playing with her! Joking around! Everything was going to be all right.

"Right? Like that! Because, you know, people are going to ask. I don't know why, but they will. Things at work, I guess that could be weird for you with all the Davenports underfoot. But we should try to be sensible, right? Like—"

"We should get married."

The second time he said it, her laughter was more a confused burst of air. When she looked at him, it stopped cold.

No matter how serious he tended to be, his expression was usually relaxed. At least as long as people were listening to him, and obeying, that was the other one. He was great at his job because the man had a massive brain and cared about people, but also because he projected an aura of confidence and subtle dominance, so people usually did what he said. Except her when she disagreed with him. And sometimes just because she liked to mess with him. Briefly. Playfully.

Which she definitely didn't want to do right now. His narrowed eyes and tilted head gave off a light warning, and killed the relaxed, joking conversation she'd thought they'd been having.

"You're being serious? I thought you were just trying to make like…a tension breaker."

"How many proposals have you ever heard of that were made as a joke?"

"I don't know. I never—" Was she supposed to come up with instances where people fake-proposed as a joke? She didn't have any, but she could identify other jokes that were outlandish and had never happened in real life. "Some days you barely even *like* me. Are you saying you love me now?"

"I'm not saying that. I don't love you, but love isn't a requirement for a successful marriage."

"Yes, it is. Have you ever seen my parents together?"

He skipped her question, and doubled down on his argument, "It's not a requirement. Marriage requires mutual goals, mutual respect, values, and when you add to it a not inconsequential sexual compatibility, it's got all the ingredients. That's before we even consider the child, who deserves the best start we can give it."

"Gabe, the only part of that I agree with is the part about the child." Okay, that was a lie, she agreed with the sex part, but if he was ignoring whatever he wanted to, she could as well. "This baby deserves the very best life we can give it. But the pressure of a home with two people who don't want to be married to one another is not that. This isn't 1960. You don't have to marry me because I'm pregnant."

"If this were 1960, that's not the way this would go between you and me, and you know that."

He'd gone and stiffened up again, and not only did she feel bad for having laughed, she felt bad about her own reaction. Her nerves, usually made of steel, weren't up to another fight today. She tried again. "We don't have to marry to be family to this baby. You're already the father, and I'm already the mother. Rings and empty vows aren't needed to validate biology."

He stood and paced around her coffee table, arms folding in such a way as to draw attention to his shoulders, and the way his long, elegant fingers flexed over his forearms.

Not what she should be paying attention to. She was supposed to be convincing him that it wasn't a good idea rather than just rejecting him, though how this conversation had circled around to marriage, she had no clue.

"I don't want to be married. You don't want it either. You don't want a relationship—you made that very, very clear two months ago. People who don't want to be married have the *worst* marriages. That's a lot to put on kids." Which brought up his point that she didn't want to discuss, but which she now felt compelled to because her mouth had gotten ahead of her to plural it to more than one child. "You know that there would be more than one, because you're right… We have…not inconsequential sexual compatibility. So, you know, this is a bad idea."

For once in her life she didn't want to stand up—she was still tired from her nap—but the way he prowled around made her stand. She put the test on the table, then followed around to his side and promptly wrapped her arms around his shoulders again, over the arms still crossed over his chest.

His already stiff posture turned into granite. She was hugging living rock. What had happened to the relaxed, affectionate man who'd arrived not even half an hour ago?

She squeezed tighter, pulling him down just enough that she could rest her chin on his shoulder and her cheek against the side of his neck.

His arms twitched, and then uncrossed. He placed his hands at her waist, but did not hug back.

"This is the worst hug in history. You did much better

earlier. Remember those hugs? Before and after we got a little panicky? You're supposed to use your arms, not just your big ole man hands."

"Not feeling a lot like hugging."

"You feel like playing some crazy game of hopscotch where you have to hop in every square to get to the next," she said, stepping back again but taking his hands. It felt like tread-lightly territory. "But that square marked marriage is a fake-out. You didn't need to marry me to make me pregnant, that's already been established. Just like I can carry a child to term and push it out of my body without a wedding ring on my finger. You don't have to marry me to be a dad. To share custody of our child with me. We are modern, civilized people. We can make our own family, have like…a parental partnership where we can be friends—which, by the way, it would be good for you to deny you barely like me like you didn't do a minute ago when I gave you the opening to—because we're adults. You don't want an unhappy marriage hanging over this kid's head before she even gets a functioning brainstem."

"You want me to have shared custody?" He cut to that exact part of her speech, once again ignoring the rest.

"Of course I do. I want my baby to know his or her father, to have a real father in her life. You'll be a great dad."

"With paperwork to make it official."

He really thought she was going to screw him over here. He may have skipped the opportunity to reassure her that he liked her, but he *did* like her. Genuinely, not just as his work partner. But he didn't trust her.

She let go and stepped back, her attempts at comfort having served no purpose whatsoever. "With papers to make it official."

They hadn't become friends over sharing their life stories, and they hadn't become friends over this child—

it was far too soon for that kind of friendship to manifest. They'd become friends over work, over mutual respect and trust *on the job*.

They had to figure out how to transform that work partnership to something arguably more important. If he needed paperwork to do that, she could give it to him. And hope trust followed because this suspicion of his made her chest hurt.

The next morning, Gabriel found himself loitering in the staffroom rather than going up to the chopper ahead of receiving a call. He had no reason to stay downstairs, he just needed some space. He had no power over her, outside the ability to send her home from work when she tried to soldier through sickness. He couldn't *make* her marry him, but couldn't make himself give up on the idea either.

He had a living example of the outcome to a kid disadvantaged in the parent department. Plenty of kids came through it fine, but he didn't want to take the risk. He wanted his child to have exactly what he'd had growing up: a mother and a father, both offering stability, love, an atmosphere to flourish in. It was in their power to provide that. Whatever she'd been on about with her parents, it couldn't have been that bad. All their children, except Penny, were doctors. She was successful in her own right, and worked every day to help save lives. She made some other questionable decisions, but nothing malignant.

He should probably go check on her, wade in early, but he just wasn't up to it yet. And she never hung out in the staffroom. Ever in motion, she was always doing something—checking inventory, restocking, performing routine checks on the equipment, or visiting with people in the department so she didn't have far to go when a call came. Her oddest and most recent habit had become running up and down the top three flights of stairs, something he'd taken every opportunity *not* to ask her about. Especially after that night, when he'd decided distance was the only way to get them back to professional-only interactions. Knowing more than she had already just randomly shared would make that harder. But now it was one of a million of questions he should ask.

Not asking had never helped anyway. He still had a bevy of inappropriate thoughts. That was before yesterday had forced their night back to the front and center of his thoughts.

His radio crackled and Dispatch blazed through, announcing their first call of the shift. Time to face the music.

When he reached the chopper, she already had it fired up, ready for him. Only when he climbed in, Penny wasn't at the pilot's controls. It was a man.

Lawson.

They'd flown together a couple times, and he was a competent pilot and paramedic, but he wasn't Penny.

"Where's Penny?"

"Don't know. They just called and asked me to come in and pick up her shift. I guess she's sick."

That sharp pinch at the back of his neck returned.

Sick and called off without a showdown? Was that some kind of carry-over from yesterday's battle, or was she really sick?

Grilling Lawson wouldn't get him answers, and they had a job to do: someone waited for their help. He buckled in and put on his headset. "Go."

Making the decision to focus didn't mean it was so easy to do so.

Penny was stubborn, perhaps the most stubborn person he'd ever met, so it was entirely possible she'd called off to make some kind of point. Last night had started out better than it had ended, but he'd thought the situation at least set to neutral when he'd gone home.

If she called off but didn't call him, did that mean anything? Could she have just called off to go to the doctor?

If she had called off on her own because she was ill, she must be *very* badly off.

"What's wrong, boss?" Lawson's voice cut through his thoughts.

He turned to look at the pilot. "Nothing. Why?"

"You just sighed massively. I didn't just come off shift or anything, I'm not going to be operating at some lower level today than any other shift. Chill."

Chill.

"I know. We're good," he said simply, no desire to engage in further conversation about it. It would be even more futile than the thoughts ricocheting around his cranium.

Whatever was wrong, she should've damned well called to tell him. So much for all her talk last night of wanting him involved.

Soon enough, they arrived at their site and landed, and he had something else to occupy his thoughts.

CHAPTER THREE

SO. MUCH. VOMITING.

Penny's cluttered coffee table practically sagged with barely touched beverages. And two buckets, along with the one she had on her lap. Because nothing stayed down.

It had started around three in the morning, rousing her from a dead sleep, and fifteen hours later showed no signs of letting up.

Electrolyte-enriched sports drinks couldn't help you stay hydrated if they didn't stay down.

Neither would the ones for children, which were honestly more gag-inducing.

Water wouldn't stay down.

Big *no* to milk. No to broth. Juices came straight from the devil. And she still had a crate of untouched other beverages she'd had delivered this morning, and which she'd try to pour down her gullet as soon as she'd got her nerve back up, along with the corresponding energy required to haul herself fifteen feet from her sofa to the kitchen island.

The one bright spot of her day had been not vomiting on the delivery boy. She may have tipped him enough to pay his rent—she couldn't be sure what she'd handed him at this point—but at least she knew he'd come back on future deliveries, rather than avoiding her apartment unless decked out in a hazmat suit.

She knew enough medicine to know dehydration was winking at her from just around the corner, but she didn't know at what point all this would become a danger to the baby.

The doorbell startled her as she reached for the tea she'd yet to sample, and the minuscule amount of fluid her body had been able to replenish in her stomach curdled.

Over her mostly dry heaving, she heard her name shouted through the door.

Oh, it was Gabriel. And he sounded like he was planning to beat the door down.

Would it be easier to let him and just get the door fixed later, or to crawl piteously on her belly across the floor so she could open it first?

As soon as she stopped heaving for a few seconds, she snatched a clean bucket from the table and slogged to the door. If nothing else, he could see what she looked like when *actually* sick, for future reference.

No sooner had she gotten the door open than a fresh round of heaving turned productive and she had to slump on the wall beside the door as she curled over her bucket, and mostly hit her target. Which was at least better than vomiting on Gabriel, the second lucky person she hadn't vomited on today, but who would've at least been less likely to hold it against her than the delivery boy.

"Good God, Pen. Why didn't you call me?" Gabriel ignored the anger that had percolated in him all day and stepped over the tiny puddle that had missed the bucket. Scooping up her, along with her bucket, he carried her to the sofa. Although slender, the boneless drape of her body made her feel even more insubstantial than usual.

He arranged her on the sofa, bucket cradled in her lap, and stood back to get a look at the loft. For perhaps the first time ever when accused of being sick, Penny didn't offer any lip or any resistance. By the look of her, talking might be too much. Every time she opened her mouth, retching sounds followed.

"Okay, maybe not called, but you could've texted." He relented, eyed the full glasses and mugs on her coffee table. "None of these wanted to stay down? Just nod or shake your head."

She shook her head.

Yesterday she'd been pale. Today she almost looked dead—all she was missing was that terrible shade of gray.

"Been going on all day?"

She nodded again.

If she'd looked this bad yesterday, he'd have dragged her into the ED and maybe had her admitted.

"Did it start before you woke up? Did it wake you?"

She nodded again, then did something so uncharacteristic, he felt for the third time in two days that the world had gone off its proper tilt. She started to cry.

"I'm not mad," he said in a rush. Even though he had been angry all day, seeing her like this made his anger feel like something entirely less righteous. And he still had absolutely zero idea how to deal with a crying partner. "Stop that."

Okay, maybe not the right thing to say. Should he hug her?

"It's okay. We can fix this. Just stop crying. I'll get some medication delivered. Concentrate on breathing. Everything's fine. Don't cry."

Fumbling his cell out, he dialed a friend in the hospital. By the time he got the medicine ordered and delivery scheduled, she'd stopped sniffling and started dry heaving again. Which...was a little easier on him, and which he'd feel guilty about later. After he also called a local grocery for ginger and a selection of teas.

"Gabe…"

He turned back to her, stepped over a bucket, and eased himself onto the couch beside her. "It'll be here soon, and will keep you from vomiting, even if it puts you to sleep. I don't work tomorrow. I'll stay. Everything will be okay."

One thing he made himself *not* say again: *Don't cry.* Even if it was right there in his mouth, bashing against his teeth to get out.

The look on her face was one of pure misery, but she nodded.

Seeing her state may have dissipated his irritation, but the frustration still hung around, especially when she weaseled her way under his arm and tucked in beside him so tight he knew she wasn't just physically miserable. She was scared.

"Hey…"

Don't cry…

She tilted her head back to look at him, and he found himself squeezing her a little tighter.

"Don't worry about any of this. I'll get it done. Don't worry about the baby either. It's still early to worry about this becoming a danger."

Her lower lip quivered, but she nodded again.

"Do you trust me to do what's best for you both?"

She nodded again, and the quiver settled down, her eyes becoming more focused, more certain.

"Then don't worry. Stress will just make things worse. It's early days to panic. I know that's easy to say when I'm not the one vomiting, but still true. I'll stick around until you're feeling better. Close your eyes and rest. I'll take care of it."

Still no argument. She couldn't get closer to him with clothes on, but it somehow made him feel better too, even if her slender frame felt fragile to him at that moment.

The antiemetic would help. And if it didn't, they'd visit the ED for IV fluids before dehydration became a massive issue.

"I know you're trying to be nice…" Penny said from the sofa the next morning, watching Gabriel scramble eggs in her kitchen, and alluding to the night they weren't supposed to ever mention, and which they still hadn't really spoken about, even after he'd slung sexual compatibility at her in that long, fraught conversation.

Gabriel dished the eggs onto one plate, but she knew he'd caught the words he'd said to her that night when he lifted his dark brown gaze to hers. She could almost see him silently working through whether or how to respond, and whether their mutual non-conversation treaty had any bearing.

"I'm not trying to be nice," he said finally, quietly, then followed it up with a redirect. "These eggs are for me. I already made you my mom's cinnamon apple tea, which I see is staying down."

Acknowledged, but not deepened. She had no idea what that meant. Was the subject still forbidden? Should it be? She didn't want him getting back on that marriage thing, even if having him there the past day had been nice. Comforting, even. Which was annoying on another level but, still, she didn't want to say anything that made him stiffen up again, or start demanding legal documents.

"It is." She used the cinnamon stick like an inefficient straw to sip the cider and breakfast tea combination. "It's good. Really good. Remind me to send her a thank you for raising such a good man."

The sudden cocking of his head and the surprise she saw all over him surprised her in return. Was it so surprising that she'd say that? She mentally rewound through the past few days, then the past few weeks. When was the last time she'd said something nice to him?

She wasn't mean by nature, but she had to admit that the shock and fear of the past three weeks had perhaps, no, had definitely made her less pleasant than normal. Unless you counted beaning him in the face with a pregnancy test, then it probably had made her completely unpleasant. She just plain hadn't been herself, but if they were going to make this work out well for the three of them, she needed to find her way back to her much-preferred vigorous optimism.

"You're just saying that because I cleaned up so much vomit the past eighteen hours."

"I'm not," she said, then grinned. "I won't lie, that didn't hurt. A good man would do that for an ill friend, right? But, genuinely, it's nice that you're here. Comforting. I don't even really mind having you fuss over me, which is kind of a big deal for me."

"You're a little better today, so I've been expecting my marching papers since you've managed to stay awake for half an hour without trying to turn yourself inside out."

Still deflecting. Did she not sound sincere? Did he just really want to go? The latter thought brought a rush of disappointment that left her staring into her drink for several long seconds.

"If you want to go, I'll probably whine, but I won't stop you." As if she could. Her only superpower right now was regurgitation. "Do you not believe I want you here?"

While eating his eggs, he did the courteous thing and stayed in the kitchen, eating at the snack bar on the rear side of the island—where proximity to eggs was less likely to make her sick. "I think you do now, but tomorrow will probably be a different story."

She took another sip of her non-alcoholic toddy. The

context to her confession mattered, and he should know it. It had been years of work to put that behind her, and she did everything in her power to keep those two versions of herself from intersecting, especially with people she didn't want thinking less of her or diminishing her capabilities, but the introduction of a child changed that equation. He should know, and not just because it would make clear to him how much she appreciated his care. If their child developed the disease, he should know it was possible ahead of it coming to pass.

"What do you know about juvenile dermatomyositis?" She asked this quietly, but knew he'd heard her by the pause of his fork.

After a moment, he went with her direction change. "Rash. Muscle weakness. In adults. Juvenile? I think it starts pretty young. I'd have to refresh my memory for more information. Why do you ask?"

"I had it." She shifted on the sofa to sit up straighter, just to remind herself that she *could* move however she wanted to now. "Autoimmune disease, can be triggered by infection, or not. Usually treated with steroids, but sometimes they don't work and chemotherapy drugs are required."

As she spoke, a frown crept over his handsome face, and although she could still see a pile of eggs on his plate, he put his fork down and swiveled on his stool to look at her. "Do you still require treatment?"

"I'm one of the lucky twenty percent in full remission." She hated putting herself into those memories, because there was no distance. Even after a decade-plus years of remission, if she thought about it, she went right back there and all she felt was confinement. "But it ravaged me before they got it under control."

Ravaged was the only word she could think of to describe the effects and aftermath. Also, because she didn't talk about that part of her life. She'd shut it away behind thirty thousand feet of brick wall, and didn't even like her family to talk about it. That habit left her with a dearth of words to apply, she didn't even know how to start or if she even needed to describe it. She'd much rather gloss over those details, give him the lowlights, as highlights was a word she couldn't apply.

"How bad?"

"I was in a wheelchair for years," she said, because getting this word train going was hard. But it actually got a little easier as she kept on. "I had physical therapy every day from six to thirteen to keep my limbs from withering. If I couldn't get to the rehab center because of vacation or holiday, my parents put me through my paces. As doctors, they knew what could happen and wanted me to have the best shot at a normal body, even without knowing if I would ever recover to use it."

"You resented it?" he asked, but there wasn't any condemnation in his voice. He treated children so he knew how hard it was for them to cope with illness.

"Sometimes," she admitted. "*You're going to be one of the lucky ones*, they liked to say. I kind of resented that. Actually, I hated that. But they didn't give up, and didn't let me give up. I should probably thank them for it every time I see them, now that I fully understand I wasn't just in the midst of a caging illness but an illness that could've been fatal."

That wasn't all of it, that wasn't even the tip of the iceberg, but she could see him starting to put the pieces together. It was more to make him put the *right* pieces together that she kept going. "I'm healthy now, but I've been smothered by loving caretakers so much, I feel like I've used up my lifetime allotment of fuss."

"I had no idea." He abandoned his half-finished plate and came to sit right next to her, his thigh pressed to hers and his arm going immediately around her shoulders.

Would that simple touch from him always be able to push the tension right out of her? She closed her eyes, tried to make herself focus on all those words she'd said, all the reasons she shouldn't take the comfort he gave without hesitation.

"That's why you refuse to call off when you're ill?"

That wasn't one of the threads she'd hoped he'd pick up on, but she nodded, then pressed closer still. "When I say I don't mind you taking care of me, you should know that's a position of dubious honor. I *really* appreciate you coming over to check on me, and staying. No joke. Thank you. I'm sorry I didn't call or text to tell you I was sick. It honestly never occurred to me, but I will. From now on."

His lips on her forehead brought a shock of need bubbling up inside her. Not for sex, though being close to him pretty much meant it was in the back of her mind all the time, but something like sweetness and sadness mixed together. Like homesickness.

"I know I'm weird and sometimes kind of wild in reaction to having spent years living my life on the sidelines, and I don't want that for my...for *our* child. She, or he, should just get to be whoever she would be without leagues of childhood trauma making her into someone who drives everyone bonkers." She felt his arm tighten, his lips still lingering on her skin, relaxed now, but no less sweet.

"You don't make me crazy." His lips feathered against her forehead.

"You're not selling that line in this house, Jackson." She leaned back, breaking the chest-aching touch to look him in the eye. "I could pass it on. I don't know how likely it is, or what it would take. I don't really know anything about the genetics of the disease, just that it is genetic."

"Did they find a cause for your dermatomyositis?"

"At the time they said it was idiopathic. In my adult life, I've done everything possible to not revisit it. I haven't kept up on the latest findings."

He made a sound she couldn't define, and reached over to retrieve her mug and press it back into her hands. Emergency physician, he had to deal with the problem currently on his plate, and her looming dehydration was it. "Drink half and I'll let you sleep. I know the medication makes it impossible to stay awake for long periods."

Another sip and she started to relax again, really feeling better than yesterday—well enough to push liquids a little more vigorously than sips. At least while she had a man with a mop watching over her.

"Will you check your medical journals to see what the latest research on JDM is, like the likelihood of passing it on? Does it require two carriers or one? None of my siblings have it."

"Drink."

She bypassed the cinna-straw and took a big apple-y pull.

"I'll read while you're asleep."

"And see if there's any genetic testing I should have?" Another big drink.

"Okay, drink slower." He urged the mug back down after her second big gulp. "You've finished half. You can stop if you want to."

She relented for the moment, at least on the drinking front. "The testing?"

"I'll see what I can find out. I can always call one of the pediatric specialists at Mercy if I need to."

Satisfied, she went back to the drink. "I think I can finish it."

"Don't make yourself sick, or we'll have to start all over."

"It tastes good."

He stopped arguing, but the softness in his eyes when he looked at her said he wasn't yet unconcerned. "Have you made an appointment with your OB?"

"No, but I only officially knew I needed to for two days, and yesterday I spent the whole day wondering if I should strap the bucket around my neck or install a head-rest on the toilet seat."

That got a little smile from him, and then a little distance. He moved away and sat forward, as if preparing to flee. "Fair enough. Want me to do that while you're asleep?"

Then he was up, and she missed not only the heat of him but the comfort that had seeped into her from the brief cuddle, and especially from that utterly chaste kiss. She couldn't remember the last time anyone had kissed her head like that, like she was the sweetest thing in the world.

Which could've been a trick. It'd be a good one. *Marry me, I'm a forehead-kisser.* Not a bad line of argument, if she didn't have more than a decade of watching her parents implode to know how far from marriage she wanted to stay.

She mumbled the doctor's name and slid down into the nest she'd been living in on the couch since yesterday, when what she really wanted was to ask him to lie down with her. If she closed her eyes, she could still remember the way his strong, steady heart had thudded beneath her cheek when he'd held her as they'd come down from another sweaty tumble.

That wasn't the relationship they had now, though, so

she tugged her blanket over her and didn't stop until it was snugged up to her chin, but the only warmth she felt was in the sofa cushions beneath her where he'd been sitting.

If she wanted more from him, things would get messy. This was probably just a reaction to their situation. She needed something, and he was in White Knight mode. Who knew how far that was from Husband mode?

As she settled, he took her mug and headed for the kitchen, cellphone already out to start making calls.

Probably hadn't even noticed her needy lapse in judgement. Which had to be good. It just didn't feel like it.

"Am I carrying you to bed or are you walking?" Gabriel asked, standing above the Penny-shaped lump burrowed under the blanket on the sofa. Somehow, he was again willing to forgo his rule never to sleep beside any of his lovers. A rule he'd only broken once since his divorce. With her, that night.

With the frown he saw marring her still-pale face, he knew he was testing the boundaries of her gladness at having him around, but after about thirty-six hours of very little sleep he was willing to push a little. That's what he told himself for the thirtieth time, that this was just practical. His decision had nothing to do with the little rush he felt when he considered it. That feeling was worry, not anticipation. Definitely not anticipation.

She rolled her head around dramatically and forward until she cupped one hand over her eyes. "I can sleep on the sofa. It's comfortable."

"But we can't both sleep on the sofa, and I don't want to sleep on the floor."

She squinted at him, starting to catch up. Since she'd downed the first antiemetic, she'd been sleeping so much she barely knew what time it was, let alone how many hours he'd spent hovering. "Did you sleep on the floor last night?"

"Dozed off and on in the chair." Had woken up every time she'd made a sound. And part of that was not wanting her to go through this alone, but another part of it was pure manipulation, something he wasn't sure how to think about. Penny wasn't his enemy, but she could become his enemy if she decided she didn't want him involved with their child after all. Keeping her close, where he could keep an eye on her and pay attention to make sure he spotted it if things suddenly began to go sideways, was the less humanitarian aspect.

"You could've slept in the guest room, still can. It's made up."

"I wouldn't hear you if you woke in distress if I was asleep in another room," he said, and then just confronted the issue. "Do you have a problem with me sleeping in the bed with you?"

"I'm just surprised..."

"Wouldn't be the first time," he reminded her gently.

She looked at him a beat too long. "I know, but are we talking about that now? Obviously, I'm not going to put the moves on you this time, if I put them on you last time. I'm not entirely sure if I did."

"You did."

"Which moves did I make?"

"You went and bought wine to get me drunk and take advantage of me in a seedy motel." The smile blooming on her face made him glad he'd gone with the joke, even if they shouldn't really be trying to make this more comfortable than he already knew it would be.

She picked up her bucket. "That's not how I remember it. But if you want to pretend I stole your virtue..."

It had been hours since she'd needed the bucket, but

it obviously made her feel more secure, so he didn't say anything. Just double-checked the door was locked, and then followed her upstairs. "You were the one to suggest underwear hugging."

"I was freezing to death." She must be feeling better, she was arguing again. "I sleep on the right, which is good for bucket placement. I have nightmares of barfing on you."

"It's high on my list of hellish situations too." All he could think to do was revert back to their between-cases banter, treat everything as business as usual for now. And he kept telling himself that as she crawled into the bed and he stripped down to his boxers and T-shirt.

"If you're staying here in this bed because of obligation…"

"I'm staying because I want to be here. Do you prefer me going to the guest room? I can assure you nothing is going to happen." He sat on the edge of the bed, turned to regard her, and bit the bullet, addressing the elephant in the room directly. "It's pretty impossible not to think about our night together, but a woman who might really vomit if I kissed her makes it easier to ignore those memories right now."

Scarlet stole across her face, briefly giving her cheeks some color. "I didn't mean to insinuate that something was going to happen. I know I'm not in danger, I just didn't want to take bigger advantage of your good nature than I already am. And I really hate feeling like an obligation."

Rolling to his side, he stretched out, put his cell on the bedside table, then opened one arm for her. "You're not an obligation. Didn't we go over this earlier?"

"That was hours ago, and maybe even yesterday."

"It was today."

"And I'm such a mess I had to double-check." She

looked at his outstretched arm. "It's kind of breaking my self-esteem that I'm this wretched at only two months pregnant."

He let his arm drop. Whatever she needed from him, it was possible he'd become too tired to riddle it out. "I want to stay."

As he settled, she switched off the light, and despite her declaration what side she slept on, and despite ignoring his offer of a comforting hug seconds before, as soon as he closed his eyes he felt her shifting toward him on the bed and wriggling under the arm he'd offered. Her cheek pillowed on his chest and she wrapped one arm over his waist.

In moments she was asleep and he drifted off right behind her.

CHAPTER FOUR

GABRIEL HAD AWAKENED the middle of the night because she'd made a noise, only to find her bottom was nestled against his groin and the immediate realization of just how far past businesslike the whole situation had gone.

He'd never spooned with another partner. He hadn't told her no relationships because he didn't specifically want *her*, it had been his basic operating system since Nila. He dated, casually. He had lovers, and did not bring them to his apartment because if he went to their beds, he could leave before things got snuggly. Spooning, like sleeping alongside lovers, had ceased to be part of his life along with Nila. It was too intimate, and felt like promises, or declarations that he felt more than he did, or at least was willing to go further than casual.

And this was intimate. And easy. And felt good. Outside winter winds rattled the windows, but the bed was warm, and her hair smelled like honey with just a hint of something smoky.

Probably the fire they'd enjoyed the previous evening. It would be beyond ridiculous to associate her with smoky hotness. Even if she was.

Sighing, he edged back toward his side of the bed and tried to go back to sleep, but he was decidedly less comfortable there, physically and mentally.

After twenty minutes, languishing in a vicious circle of thoughts that most closely resembled an ouroboros, he eased off the bed, took his phone and clothes, and left the door open so he could hear her from downstairs.

Over the next few hours he read everything he could about juvenile dermatomyositis, the one thing he could control right now, to see if he could find answers that would set both their minds at ease.

At first light she came down the stairs, wrapped in a fluffy bathrobe, and curled right up with him on the couch, where she promptly went back to sleep with her head in his lap.

When he'd read every journal and website he could find about JDM, he slid out from beneath her and headed for the kitchen.

"Did you sleep at all?" She sounded groggy, but when he looked back, she was sitting up.

He slipped his phone into his pocket and stayed at the kitchen island, sitting on a stool there to face her. "I slept fine, but then I woke up and couldn't get back to sleep, so I came downstairs to read."

"Find anything good?" Her sleepy gaze sharpened and she sat up straighter, like it would be better to hear bad news with her best posture employed.

He shook his head in answer.

"You mean you didn't find anything, or what you found wasn't good?"

"I found articles discussing the illness being triggered by viruses and infection, and another stating that it was theorized to have a genetic component, but nothing to suggest the alleles responsible had been identified, only hypothesized about," he explained, and she relaxed back into the sofa cushions again, which seemed like a good reaction. "Which means you might not even be able to pass it on."

"But I still may be able to."

Although still sluggish, she got off the sofa and made her way into the kitchen. "Can you show me the ratios on tea to cider, so you don't have to keep waiting on me for tea? I think I want some toast too. It feels like a day with food in it."

"Take your antiemetic and wait twenty minutes. Just in case?" But what bothered as much as it pleased was the easy domesticity that continued between them. First sleeping. Then spooning. Then breakfast together, sleepy smiles over tea and toast.

He knew what she'd call it, or maybe he didn't know the exact words, but he knew the gist. It was simply them falling into the New Family pattern. He struggled to even wrap his mind around the definition. Family meant something precise to him, and that wasn't this, no matter what he was going along with right now.

Toast and tea went down easily enough, and before the morning was through she was asleep again on the sofa.

Now coming on afternoon, he'd done everything he could think to do to keep from going stir crazy. His research had wandered from diseases to custody, the rights of fathers in New York. That led him to contact a lawyer to arrange a meeting so that he could start the process to draw up papers.

And now he was again out of things to keep busy. The more time he spent in her presence, especially when not busy and unobserved, the more his thoughts strayed into dangerous territory. Like those first awkward days when he couldn't close his eyes without flashes of their night together singeing the pleasure-seeking parts of his brain.

The silken skin he'd become reacquainted with last night.

The remarkable—he now knew—strength in her slender feminine frame. How she'd gripped him with her thighs in the dim candlelit shower. Her heat against him, around him, when the tile wall had been so cold.

He alternated between mindless fantasies and the ones that formed around shared holidays and vacations, with warm-skinned, blue-eyed children running around. It could work, he knew it could. She wanted him physically, she liked him—she hugged him too much to discard the notion that she was actually fond of him.

They needed to talk about this stuff, once she could stay awake long enough for conversation. Until then, he needed something to do. To distract himself, he went to the bookcase lining the far wall of the living area and prowled the shelves.

Organized by color, genres mixed together, she had a little of everything. But there was a shelf in the center that didn't match the others, having spines of every color poking out. Thick spines, leather bound, embossed decoration… Photo albums.

He pulled the first one out and clawed into it, looking for some sort of focus, some sort of decency.

Pictures from last year's work holiday drinks looked like a good place to start.

There would be no pictures from this year's holiday get-together, as Penny hadn't made it to the pub earlier in the week, and he'd pointedly not asked why. Not coming to a pub made more sense now—she'd said she'd suspected for a while. Making understood his unwillingness to speak about their night had been a mistake, and one he wasn't going to make again. They had to talk about this stuff, no matter how worked up either of them got. It was an emotional subject, they were bound to get emotional, but if she wasn't talking to him, he couldn't fix whatever went wrong before it spiraled out of control. He didn't want to miss something like that, like he'd missed with Nila.

Even now, none of that made sense to him. They'd grown up together, became high school sweethearts, dated on and off in college, and then really got back together at the joint barbecue their parents had thrown to celebrate each of them graduating university. Dating exclusively, marriage in medical school, and divorce in residency. Now, having had years to examine it, he still couldn't point to any symptoms of a marriage dying.

Snagging four other albums, he tucked them under his arm and went to sit down to look at something besides the glowing screen giving him a headache since the middle of the night.

The department party photos flowed on to another Christmas scene, and he realized it was moving backward in time. She'd been out of the country last Christmas, so this had to be the year before that.

There organization disappeared after just a few pages. He expected another Christmas, but he got somewhere sunny. Different Davenports graced the pages, and he looked a little closer every time he saw a face he knew. How people spent their holidays said a lot about them. What could these pictures tell him about his child's future family parties?

Were there clues here that he could spot to help him understand Penny better than he already did? Nila's leaving had changed that about him, he paid attention to everything now. Everyone. He examined not just the external but the glimpses he got of the internal. Those glimpses just didn't show enough to make him feel comfortable with any of this.

And the pictures? Well, he could see the Davenports summered in the Hamptons. Fourth of July came with a beach party of some kind. New Year's Eve was always somewhere that glittered. In every picture, the Davenports always appeared perfectly presentable, precisely as he'd have expected.

It was the family Christmas parties he kept stopping at. Something bothered him about those photos. They looked like magazine spreads. Perfectly polished. The trees sparkled but had no personal touches he could see, unless they'd gathered as a family to learn how to blow glass and make ornaments.

It had probably been erected by a hired hand who'd picked every piece for beauty, not for sentimentality. Did the fabulously wealthy decorate their own trees or bake their own Christmas cookies?

He'd liked all the Davenports he'd met, so picking out, or possibly manufacturing flaws for these perfectly good people left a bitter taste in his mouth.

He flipped that album closed and reached for the next in his stack.

This one was both more interesting and more alarming. It looked like Penny's Book of Dangerous Stunts.

Pictures of her racing a horse.

Pictures of her steering a parachute in for a landing.

Pictures of Penny the white-water rafter. The derbycar driver. The hang glider.

Penny caught by the belt by Charles Davenport as she dangled over the safety railing at Niagara Falls, her hands reaching for the water!

That one was older, but no more than a decade, and he could feel his expression mirroring the look he saw on Charles's face—brows down, mouth open and horrified, and *angry*.

He snapped that album closed before his head exploded.

"Hey," she said from the couch, sitting up, her face also mirroring Charles's.

"Are you all right? Did I wake you?"

She ignored his questions, looked at the albums, her head tilted to see the colorful spines, then suddenly catapulted off the sofa to stumble over to snatch up the remaining albums. No words, she just hauled them right back to the shelf where he'd found them.

And didn't even seem to notice that in her haste she'd stepped in one of her buckets and it was still on her foot.

"Glad those are clean," he murmured.

Something she might also be thankful for when she realized her foot was in a pail.

Which hadn't happened yet.

She just turned to look at him. "Don't look at these. Old photo albums are off-limits."

That tranquil bubble that had been making him too comfortable all morning evaporated, which he was thankful for, but not enough to stop himself trying to understand. This was one of those glimpses.

"Why?" He stood up and when she clomped back to him, took her by the hips and lifted her up, booted the bucket out of the way, and set her back on her feet. "You've been wearing your barf bucket like the ugliest shoe in history."

Coming out of a dead sleep and launching herself across the room wasn't great for her powers of perception. But when her feet touched the cool wood floors, the sleepy haze started to lift. "These pills... I don't know what's worse, the nonstop vomiting without them or the nonstop sleep with them."

"You'll get used to them. In a few days you'll be able to stay awake."

She made some disgruntled sound and pulled away so

she could put the remaining albums back, he realized. It was the fastest she'd moved in days, speeding from the chair to the bookshelves.

"What's the point of albums if you don't let people look at them?"

"They're ugly," she argued, then took two specific albums and wedged them behind the others so they were trapped between the books and the wall and not immediately visible, as if he hadn't seen her put them there.

"You don't want anyone seeing your awkward puberty photos?"

She sighed, then sagged against the shelves, but when she looked at him he could see clarity returning to her.

"I don't want *you* to see those pictures. You don't see me like that." She straightened and walked back much more sluggishly, as if all the energy she'd had moments before was gone. "You know I was ill, but when you look at me you don't see that girl. Poor little Penelope. You see Penny, pilot and paramedic, energetic and…maybe sometimes too impulsive. But you don't *pity* me. You don't look at me and think, can she physically do this or that?"

The rawness in her voice gave the words sense they wouldn't have otherwise had.

"You can tell me you were terribly ill, but you don't want me to see it."

"There are very few people in my life I'm close to—you and my sister, Miranda, basically—who don't see the long shadow Penelope casts when looking at me, and I don't want you to see me that way. I want you to see me how I am now, or how I was before all this. Strong. Capable. Healthy. Not perpetually nauseous."

She'd just included him in a small group that consisted of him and her *sister*, the one member of her family who apparently only knew New and Improved Penny.

"Sit down before you fall down." He gestured back to the sofa, then sat back in his chair.

He was in the box of people who saw her as complete. Boxes he could understand. He liked them. If you put people into one box you kind of knew what to expect from them. It kept things neat.

Or it would if he could figure out what box to put her into. She kept moving. Partner. Lover. Possible wife. Mother of his child. The boxes were overlapping, which defeated the whole point of boxes.

But she'd just put him into a box with family. Was that New Family? It couldn't be that easy.

"I feel terrible. I've been letting you take care of me every second of the day so the least I could do is help with dinner." Despite her words, Penny edged onto a stool at her kitchen island and watched Gabriel continue chopping sweet potatoes he'd just peeled. "What is it we're having again?"

"Simple grilled chicken breast, since your kitchen is awesome, and baked sweet potato wedges. Everything I've read said take it easy on vegetables for a few days."

There had even been some kind of marinade for the chicken, which automatically announced that he was a better cook than she was. The very best Penny ever managed in the kitchen when starting from a position of raw food was fondue. She could melt a mean pot of cheese and buy a mean loaf of bread. She also reheated meals from restaurants like a master.

His proficiency shouldn't gall her, but somehow it did. It seemed like he did everything well, except maybe relax. He hadn't relaxed anytime she'd been awake and watching him. Even when he'd said he was tired, he'd still dug into her albums rather than just lean back and have a nap like any sane, overworked New Yorker would.

"I'm feeling better than I did. I'm going to try and go back to work tomorrow."

"Are you sure you're ready?"

"On the floor. The floor is safe. If I'm working in Emergency and I start vomiting, I can just go home. No crash landings to sort out first."

"Sensible," he praised. "Sensible" in Gabrielese was like "awesome" in Penny's world.

She changed the subject before all that praise went to her head. "Did your mom teach you to cook?"

"Grandmother. Mom's mom. My mom's a great cook too, but I learned to cook from my grandma. Spent a lot of time with her in the summer when my parents were still working and we needed minding."

"We?" She didn't have any cozy grandma stories, but that wasn't the part of the statement that interested her. "You have siblings?"

He tossed the potato wedges with oil to coat them, spread them on a baking sheet, salted and peppered, and then shoved them into a pre-heated oven. The show-off.

"No siblings. Cousin. We were as close as siblings but, uh, not now."

She knew next to nothing about his past, and her plan to learn about it two months ago hadn't exactly worked as planned. "Did he move away?"

Everything was on to cook, and Gabriel took his time washing his hands again as they shimmered with oil, and then he turned back to her. "He died a couple of years ago."

The manner of delivery was flat, like he didn't care at all, but that wasn't possible, not when he'd previously referred to him as close as a sibling. That didn't add up.

"I'm sorry."

"Me too."

"Do you want to talk about it?"

He gestured to her untouched cup of apple tea and, before answering, grabbed tongs to flip the chicken breasts over on the grill built into her neglected but terribly fancy range. "There's not much to tell. We weren't close when he died. In junior high, he got involved with the wrong crowd, and it went downhill from there."

The wrong crowd. Downhill. And Gabriel was from New Jersey... "Was he murdered?"

"It was an accident, actually. But he was shot. Wrong place, wrong time."

"Like a store robbery gone wrong?"

He put the tongs down and looked over his shoulder at her. "What made you ask that specifically?"

Penny shrugged, took a sip of her tea so he didn't tell her to drink it again, and it gave her time to work out why she'd chosen that random situation. "You said he went with the wrong people, and then later got accidentally shot because he was in the wrong place, which implies innocence. It was the first thing that popped into my head where an innocent bystander could be shot. You hear about convenience store robberies all the time. Was I right?"

Nodding, and looking a little disconcerted, he came to lean against the other side of the island. "Sometimes your instincts alarm me."

"My gut talks to me. Unfortunately, the past couple days most of what it's been saying has been... 'Let's get all this food out of here.'" She pointed to her belly then her mouth, and when he grinned, she shrugged. "This is why I could never have been a doctor. I like to skip over parts of the whole logical progression of facts. I usually get the right answer, but I also rarely have any real idea how I got there. Whenever they told me to show my work in math classes, I was always in trouble. Got the right answer usually, and never had a complete breakdown of the steps. I could get several of the steps, usually in order, but I always missed writing down some."

"That's why you didn't go to medical school like all your siblings?"

"Nope. I didn't want to go to medical school. Can you imagine me studying that much? I can't. Plus…I had been confined for so long that, once I could, all I wanted to do was keep moving. I didn't even want to go to school as long as it would take to become a physical therapist. I'm not dumb, I just can't sit still that long when I'm not drugged by anti-barf pills. Why did you become a doctor?"

"Because the human organism is fascinating. And it's good to help people when and how you can. And body parts are easier to fix than mental parts. I originally thought I'd go into psychiatry, I wanted to figure out where things went wrong for Kyle." He peeled the chicken off the grill, then went to fetch the potatoes, and when he came back, his brows had come down in such a firm line that she didn't know whether to ask him to expand on his statement.

All she knew was that Kyle was his cousin.

"When did you change track?"

"The first time he went to jail, I went to visit with him to try and tackle this problem, work out some way to get him to change his own track, and he said the best part of his childhood was when we stayed with Grandma in the summer. I knew why, even though he didn't try to explain it, and that I couldn't help him fix it."

She didn't prod at the wound until they'd dished up

plates and relocated to her ever-neglected dining room to eat like civilized people, with her taking a nibble-the-potato-and-see-what-happens approach to eating.

He doled out information slowly, and she was sensitive to making emotional missteps with him, at least outside wrestling her albums away from him. Those were only a fraught subject for her. She waited until dinner was half-over, deciding what and how to ask before she prodded that wound again, gently. "What was wrong with the rest of Kyle's childhood?"

"He didn't have a dad. His mom worked all the time to support them. She loved him and tried to do what was best for him, but he didn't have what I had. A stable home life, the love and support of both parents." He winced a touch, as if knowing how out of step with modern life he sounded, then clarified, "Little boys need fathers to teach them how to be a man. He didn't have that, so he found that instruction from other places. Not good places."

The subject came with gravity, of course it was heavy, but his pauses were just as heavy. There was something else going on in his mind.

Putting down her remaining half a potato wedge, she carefully wiped her fingers, then reached for his hand. "I know I'm not always super-present and good at picking up on social cues, but I'm on the job tonight. There's something you want to say, and you can stop drip-feeding it to me. Just say it. That mutual agreement not to talk about stuff has *got* to go if we're going to have any hope of making this work."

He listened, and she liked the way he paid attention, like every word she said—or sometimes babbled—was important. When she tugged on his thumb, he turned his hand over, fingers opening so she could slide hers into them.

"Whatever is making you retreat into your head, spit it out."

"I'm trying to be careful about all this. You want to know what's going on in my head? We're making another massive mistake."

Her stomach lurched and wobbled, but since nothing immediately rushed up her esophagus, she stayed put and tried to breathe through it. "What mistake?"

"I still want to marry you. I don't understand how this parental partnership will work out."

"I thought it was pretty self-explanatory. We'll be parents, and share stuff. The baby. Responsibilities. Decisions."

"Yes, that's self-explanatory. It's the rest of it."

"What rest?"

He jiggled their intertwined hands.

The relationship stuff. Not the actual parenting. The undefined partnership aspect.

"Oh."

"I only know how to do that one way. The traditional way. Raising children with a wife, making a family."

"We'll still be a type of family."

"No, we won't. We'll be two people who share a family member. At best, we'll be like some kind of in-laws, quasi-related because of another."

"We're going to have legal paperwork for custody."

"Which is what you get after a divorce, when you stop being a family. When you're a *broken* family."

The words sank in slowly, along with the understanding that it meant something to him. The words "broken family" and his tone said enough. There was pain there.

"Did your parents divorce when you were little?"

"They're still happily married."

Which, maybe, provided the blueprint, but didn't explain the pain she saw on his face. Was it to do with Kyle?

"But there's someone who divorced."

"Me." There was a flash of something on his face, but she couldn't name it, only recognized it as a cocktail of something unpleasant, maybe painful, definitely sad. "I'm divorced. A long time now. I wanted kids with her, she said she didn't, then didn't want me either. Smothering her or ignoring her, I never got a good answer—it changed, depending on the day. She left."

He delivered the words simply, even somehow without emotion except for his volume. She knew without him saying so how deeply it had cut him by his volume. His ever-decreasing volume. By the time he'd said "She left," it was almost a whisper.

He'd been hurt, and she hated that this hurt him more. The only parts of this conversation that felt good was the fact that they were talking, and his warm hand linked with hers.

Maybe he was right, maybe it was ridiculous to think they could have a simple partnership, there was too much *something* between them. History? Chemistry? Genuine caring? But the answer to that big riddle wasn't in her gut. The only thing in her gut was the desire to give something back to him that he'd been giving her the past two days—comfort, acceptance.

The day it had all gone down, and he'd come over to find her wallowing in guilt after beaning him with the test, his hand on her cheek had been enough to cleave through the swirling *awfulness* in her heart, and ground her.

Extracting her hand from his, she rose and rounded the corner of the table to stand behind his chair. If those pills hadn't sucked all her energy up, she'd have just muscled his chair back from the table and planted herself in his lap so she could hug him until he felt better. But with her current energy level she might have chicken and sweet potatoes on her plate, but there wasn't any strength there.

"Pen?"

"Shhh," she answered softly, then wrapped both her arms around his shoulders and pressed against the seat-back, until his head rested against her collarbone and her cheek pressed to his head. "I know I can't make that better. If I had a time machine, I would go back in time and stop you from marrying that terrible person."

His chest deflated a little, tension not entirely gone but diminishing. She kissed the top of his head then his temple, letting her lips linger there. Would he feel the same melting sweetness she'd felt when he'd kissed her head?

He breathed out so slowly and deeply she could only tilt her head to try and catch his eye, with no idea what any of it meant.

She'd no sooner stepped from behind his chair than it slid back. His large hands found her cheeks and drew her mouth down to his. Just like the first time in that Schenectady motel room, her whole world narrowed down to just her and Gabriel. Her body moved without conscious thought, bringing her to sit across his lap as he angled his head to accommodate the change in height and keep their mouths from separating.

Nothing about Gabriel's kisses could be called hurried, and he never let her hurry him either. Her whole life was rushing for the finish line, grabbing life and experiences before they could get away from her, but no matter how she clutched at his shoulders, or twisted her hands in his shirt to try and pull closer, he held her still. His hands fisting in her hair held her back enough to force her to focus on the slow, velvety slide of his lips on hers. His tongue in her mouth was a dance, slow and drugging. Smoky and potent, it singed the hard edges of their painful conversation and curled the corners like burnt paper.

She didn't know how long it went on, only that at the last gentle, sweet kisses trailing off, she was breathless and in trouble. Passion was still there, but this was something else entirely. Sweet, exploring, consoling, vulnerable, and all she really wanted was to pull tighter and hold onto him, let whatever wanted to happen happen. Stop trying to force words or expectations onto whatever *this* was.

Only that plan hadn't worked so well for their night together, even less after their night in Schenectady, not knowing what to say. Relationships came with expectations, and expectations came with disappointment, pain.

Asking him to stay another night would be a mistake. Asking him to sleep with her in the bed until morning would be a bigger mistake. Gabriel needed the comfort that his expectations could be satisfied, and she couldn't give him that.

"I think I need to sleep," she said instead, not mentioning the kiss or the way pulling away from him left an ache in her chest. Really not inviting him to stay until he didn't want to stay anymore, be it twenty minutes or twenty years. "It'll be an early morning."

"I'll clean this up."

"No, it's okay. I have someone coming tomorrow. Leave it."

She hurried away from him while trying to seem like she wasn't fazed by what had just happened, then climbed the stairs, leaving the decision to him on how to handle the night.

As she shut off the bedside light to settle into bed, she heard his decision in the closing of her apartment door. He'd left, whatever that meant.

CHAPTER FIVE

"WHAT'S WRONG WITH YOU?"

Penny had just thrown back her head to take her don't-barf-today pill when her brother's voice almost made her choke on the darned thing. Carefully, she swallowed, took another big drink from her tumbler of apple tea, and smiled, probably like she'd just been caught doing something bad, because that was exactly opposite to the kind of smile she was going for.

But, really, what had Zac seen? He'd caught her taking a pill alone in the staffroom. So what?

"Vitamin."

Lying to family was a great way to start your day.

"Really? Have you been grounded because of multi-vitamin dependency?"

Smart-alec brothers were a less great way to start the day. Not having a story primed to tell people she didn't yet want to know she was pregnant? Also a fairly un-great way to start the day.

"I'm not grounded," she denied, tugging at her scrubs, wishing like heck for her comfy flight suit. "I decided to work the floor for a couple days. That's all."

The look he gave her demanded more words, but she couldn't think of any.

"Really." It wasn't even a question. Questions had a

questioning lilt. His word just sat there like a big disbelief log for her to trip over.

"Sometimes I work in the department. You know paramedics are good on the floor." And none of this was making her less guilty, especially since she could feel her cheeks getting hot. "Charles said it was okay."

"Why? Something to do with how pale you are?" Then his brows snapped down like a plank over his eyes. "What's going on?"

"Fine, I got hold of something that made me throw up a lot." Not exactly a lie. Everything made her throw up a lot.

"Are you hungover?"

Hungover. God, why did everyone think she was such a mental case that she'd be drinking heavily when she had to work the next day?

On second thoughts, better that story than the other.

"Not anymore. But you're right, it was tequila. I met this guy, we did some body shots, and then after all the loud, sweaty sex on the jungle gym in his bedroom, then we did some more body... Hey, Zac, where ya goin'? I was just getting to the good part!"

She felt herself grinning at his retreating back, and then chuckling because that look of abject horror? Yeah, that was the stuff littler sisters *lived* for.

But then she remembered Gabriel, and it got a lot less funny. She didn't want to have crazy jungle gym sex with some strange bar guy, but she could easily be talked into that with Gabriel. Though he'd never have a jungle gym. Not that he needed one.

And just like that she felt guilty about the whole thing again. Not just that she'd made up a silly story to Zac, but that she'd lied to him in such a way as to make him as uncomfortable as she was to push him off the subject. She'd never felt bad about messing with him before so she was going to blame this one on the baby. Her judgy, judgy baby.

With a sigh, she stashed her tumbler in a cabinet where it'd stay warm for hours and went to find Zac. It was time for her shift to start anyway.

She buzzed into the department from the east, and after a check of the board headed off in the direction she hoped to find Zac, and nearly ran right into Gabriel with Lawson, wheeling a patient in on their gurney.

"Hey." She scrambled back, but then looked at the patient—a man with a rod of rebar piercing his right shoulder. It took her a moment to get a grip. "Did you call in to get him assigned?"

Gabriel nodded over her shoulder and she turned in time to see Zac and Dr. Ella Lockwood scuttling toward them, along with a team bringing up the rear. She wasn't needed here, so she stepped back out of the way and let them go past.

As they returned to wheeling their obviously pained patient past and Gabriel started reporting the full situation, he locked gazes with her for just a second, but didn't pause either his steps or his words.

He just looked like…

I see you.

I wish you were in the air with me.

Are you okay?

She saw all that, and only had time to smile, and then her own comm was buzzing and it was time for her to go the opposite direction, and babysit a tachycardic patient to Imaging with a cardioversion machine, just in case. Not as dull as being on the floor could be, but subdued enough that she was glad she had this Gabriel business to think about so she wouldn't keep imagining herself yelling "Clear!" and performing chest compressions.

The day dragged on for years, and by the time Penny got home she was only moderately proud of not having vomited at work. Moderately, because she knew she might not have been playing show and tell with the day's menu, but she still wasn't at her best. She was tired. Tired in a way that she'd been hoping would pass. Tired in a way that left her wondering if the wonderful terrible pills were the culprit or if it was just a new fact of life for the next several months.

Her apartment was dark and empty, just as she knew it would be but had still secretly hoped to be surprised about.

But who actually did that kind of thing? Besides some-one who had a key to get in? Even if he had, he couldn't be not only over-the-top romantic but also telepathic enough to know she wanted it when she hadn't told him. If he had been there, without a key, without an invitation, she'd tell anyone else it was time for a restraining order. Instead, she was fantasizing about being stalked.

Because, no matter what she'd been saying about not wanting to be in a relationship, they were already in a relationship. Some kind of relationship. And she liked it. More than that, she looked forward to seeing him in a way that meant every second she spent in a corridor in Emergency was a second she spent looking up and down, hoping to see his broad shoulders and long stride, eating up the floor.

She missed him.

Fishing out her phone, she wavered between calling him and texting.

Texting felt safer.

Again with the courage deficiency. Run toward the scary thing. Run toward it.

She dialed Gabriel's number, and just before hitting the little green button to actually call she lost her nerve.

She texted instead.

You busy tomorrow night? Thought we might do something.

Gabriel rang the bell to Penny's door twenty minutes ahead of when he was due to arrive. It had only been two days since he'd been there, but it felt much longer. At the same time it didn't feel like long enough.

That kiss had crossed a line. At no time since all this had started had he felt like he was in control of anything. And he didn't know what to do with any of it. He also didn't know whether this was a date or just a meeting to discuss responsibilities.

He hoped responsibilities. She already made him feel too good, her apartment felt too good. Too relaxed. Too inattentive.

As unlikely as it was, if she just married him he'd feel so much better. He wouldn't have to doubt her sincerity about the baby. He'd have the law on his side too. Yes, he was rushing things, but as much as he trusted her with his life every day in the chopper, he couldn't find it in himself to trust her with *his child*. Even if his gut told him that fear was somewhat silly.

She wouldn't do anything on purpose to cause it harm, and she'd said she wanted him involved, but…

Nila.

Nila. Nila. Nila.

Where was she?

He pressed the bell again, and seconds later heard thundering feet inside the cavernous loft.

Well enough to run. Good.

"Hey," she greeted him before she even had the door fully open, and her bright smile said she was happy to see him.

"Sorry I'm a bit early." He saw she had on full make-up, which was unusual for her, and didn't seem to be dressed yet. "But I dressed warmly, as you said."

"I see. I need to get dressed still and do something with my hair. Probably braid it so it will go under a knit cap. Otherwise I'll freeze. But I got you something." She gestured him inside, and darted to the kitchen counter to pick up a tiny gift box, which she held out with a smile so wide he could've counted all her teeth.

Outdoors. Probably ice skating or a walk in Central Park… Both of which were *dates*. This was a date.

A date with a gift. After closing the door, he turned back to eye the box and her bright, shining smile, and carefully took the slim, white, bowless box. "Why did you get me a gift? What is it?"

"It's a car," she deadpanned, then just shook her head. "Open it. It's not like I went out and paid a gazillion dollars for something. It's a… Oh, goodness. Do you have an aversion to surprises? I didn't throw it at your face this time."

When he moved his hand, something hard inside the box slid into the side wall with a thunk, and he shrugged through the weirdness to open the lid.

Inside sat a key with a pewter stethoscope keyring. On the inside bottom of the box was a series of numbers written in purple ink.

"It's for the door. I know how close you were to breaking it down that first day I missed work. The code is for the security system. You can change it if you want to, but I just…" She stopped as he pulled the key from the box, brows up, and he could see a shadow of anxiety there in her beautiful blue eyes.

What could he say? The little keyring was thoughtful, but the key? The key was two inches of shining, silvery hope. "I was seconds from putting my shoulder into it, though now that I've seen the thing from the inside, I'm fairly certain all I could've accomplished was hurt my shoulder."

"I probably should've waited until later to give it to you, but we don't always end things on an even keel, do we? I wanted to make sure you knew that my heart was in the right place. I know we both have all this…baggage, and your wife wasn't on the level with you, but I need you to know that I am," she said, her voice softer than before, tentative even when she typically charged forward with such energy, "It's not an engagement ring, but it *is* an invitation."

Now he really didn't know what to say. He looked at the numbers she'd written down. Six digits in sets of two, separated by hyphens. It was a date. Two months ago. His chest tightened as the implication hit him. That was the date they'd spent in the motel. Not just numbers to dial in but an acknowledgement that these particular numbers were important. It was a promise.

"Thank you." His voice sounded creaky to him, and the words wholly inadequate.

He'd taken so long to talk, she'd already reached the stairs to go and finish getting ready, but she stopped with her foot on the first step to look back at him, and held his gaze.

"What do you mean by invitation?"

"To move in."

Three words, and then she left him there with it, jogging up the stairs to get dressed.

Move in.

His heart began to pound, and he walked to the sofa to sit. It wasn't marriage, it wasn't security, it wasn't legally binding, but it was a step. Tonight was a date, but it was also to be a discussion about the future. Not just having fun outdoors. She was trying to meet him halfway.

By the time her feet sounded once again on the stairs, he felt more like himself. He'd threaded the keyring onto his own keys and familiarized himself with the security panel again.

She had braided her hair in pigtails that came from beneath either side of a thick, wooly hat, and had on jeans, boots, a coat, scarf, a bag slung across her torso, and had gloves in her hand. "Are you ready? We have to get a cab to Rockefeller Center, there's a children's choir singing tonight near the tree. Then I thought we could grab something to eat, if all is going well in belly-land."

He should say some words before they left but just didn't know where to begin. To keep her from getting away, he caught her hand before she wiggled it into her glove and stepped closer. The times he'd touched her face, she'd stopped dead in her tracks, so that would have worked, but it also seemed to short-circuit her brain in a way that felt like conniving to abuse, especially right now when it felt like they were suspended over Fifth Avenue on a tightrope.

"Do you want me to move in? Is that what your invitation is, or is that your way of saying I'm welcome, whatever is going on with us?"

His little chatterbox didn't answer for long enough he knew words were as big a struggle for her on this, but she did open her fingers to lace them with his and tilted her head back so she could look him in the eye. When she did speak, her voice was soft. "I think we have to name this *whatever is going on with us* a relationship at this point. I didn't want it, you didn't want it, I get that. But it just is… Isn't it?"

"It does seem that way," Gabriel said, then nodded toward the door. "Children's choir, eh?"

Penny couldn't tell whether that abrupt transition meant anything. There should be a relationship manual for idiots to read.

"Linda's grandson." She went with it, naming one of the women in Dispatch, and tilted her head up to him, still uneasy, hungry for some sign on his face of his thoughts. All she knew for sure was that his hand felt good in hers, she'd missed having him around, and this was the most nervous she'd felt in years. Even more uneasy than she'd been when she'd made the decision and boxed up the key earlier. Now that the words were out there, this all became something that could snap back on her and make her regret. "But we can just stop by there and then go have something to eat. I haven't been to see the tree yet this year, and it's there…"

He shook his head then placed one slow, warm kiss on her lips, just enough to make them tingle, just enough to make her smile, and then pulled the key out of his pocket. "I'll get the door."

"Wait," she said, a playful spark igniting in all the intense tingles. "If we're in a relationship, can I do that anytime I want to?"

The look he gave her was cautiously amused, but he nodded.

Permission given, she reached for his scruffy cheeks and drew him back down for another kiss. This time deeper, mouths open, hungrier. And entirely too short. He lifted his head, smile still in his eyes, emboldening her.

"What about sex? Do I get sex anytime I want it now?"

Then he laughed, "You really are new at this. People usually start out relationships a little slower."

"So that's a no?"

"We're going to be late."

"Fine!" She groaned in melodramatic fashion and armed the security panel, then stepped out of the loft so he could lock it up.

Him with his keys. Did all this mean he was going to move in? Was he thinking about it? The words were already in her mouth, ready to break free, but Gabriel did things at his own pace, and if sex was off the table, that might be too far too. If this was going to work out—if she was going to show him that they could be together, and be a family, and let things flow naturally without labels and flower arrangements in churches—she had to let him get there at his own pace. Even if hers said, *Hurry. Settle it now.*

Like it was even possible to hurry up and make things flow naturally.

Despite sweet kisses, or the hungry kisses they'd shared, neither of them knew what to do when alone together in the back of a cab. Should she offer him her hand? Should she sit near him? People in relationships did that stuff. She did the best she could and scooted closer so that only the width of a skinny thigh separated them, and silently berated herself for this indecision. The other day she'd had no trouble hugging him. She'd had no trouble even cuddling up to him to go to sleep, but that had been before she'd discovered they'd somehow ended up in a relationship. Now everything felt weird. Good, but weird. And something was bugging her, she just couldn't quite put her finger on what it was. Or what they were. It could be many things, for all she knew.

They made small talk about nothing, cases he'd been

on that week without details, and soon enough the car stopped at the corner of Forty-Eighth and Rockefeller Plaza, and they climbed out.

On the way around the block to the tree and ice rink, they stopped at a deli for steaming cups of cider and sandwiches, and finally made it to the plaza just after the children started singing. From their position at the back of a crowd she could see the tree—naturally—but not over the crowd separating them. "Let's sit."

She gestured to a bench close enough to hear the music and far enough they could still speak, and Gabriel went along with it well enough.

"Is it weird for us to eat dinner while kids are singing?" Gabriel asked.

"Not unless they're singing 'Do You Hear What I Hear?' and the answer is *crunching*," Penny answered, mostly because she was actually hungry for the first time in a few days, and her ham and cheese was calling her name.

He grinned, and though it didn't look like he knew how to do this any more than she did, he turned slightly on the round planter benches so he could see her better, and from the return to his sober, thoughtful expression she could see he was chewing on more than his sandwich.

The kids began singing "O Come, All Ye Faithful" and Penny tried to find her way back to banter, that was something they'd always done well before all these *feelings* had got involved. "Have you ever noticed how many Christmas songs start with 'O' something?"

"'O Little Town of Bethlehem'?" Gabriel played along.

"'O Holy Night.'"

"'O...' What else?"

"'O Come Emmanuel...'" That was the last one she could think of.

"Is that it? Four songs is all we could come up with? The way you put it, I thought we'd have some kind of measurable percentage here. There are probably thousands of Christmas songs out there. I bought wholesale into the notion of you being a Christmas carol librarian," he teased, and she could see happiness crinkling the corners of his eyes. Unshielded, uncontrolled, and the sweetness of the sight of him almost choked her up.

"You've got me confused with the internet. But if you get your phone out to check right now, somewhere an angel will…I don't know, fail to get his wings?" With effort, she kept the playful teasing going, wanting things to stay light and happy. Relationships should probably start that way but theirs hadn't, and she truly wanted him to be happy, whatever happened. "Oh, there should be an 'O Gabriel' song. He's an angel, right? I bet he had some job during Christmas night."

"Gabriel was the one who announced the birth," said the man named for an angel, but who was as sexy as the devil…

And who gave her an idea on how to talk to the rest of the world about their new relationship. "Me and God have this in common, I think."

He looked over his sandwich, brows up, definitely not following her clearly insane segue.

"Someone's going to have to announce that this baby thing is happening. Because, oh— *Oh!* That reminds me. Did anything happen the other day when you gave your rebar patient to Zac and Ella Lockwood? They were having a tense discussion later when I stumbled over them, and I think I saw Ella give Zac the stink-eye. Then I felt even more guilty because when he caught me earlier taking my antiemetic I lied about why I needed it." Penny blurted out a bunch of words, and then stopped and made a little circle in the air with her finger. "That started out one place and then kind of came back to that place, which was the place where I don't know what to tell people about being pregnant, but a little more got wedged in there in the middle."

Gabriel could usually keep up with her sudden changes in conversation, though, so he only grinned as the choir drifted into a sober rendition of "What Child is This?" Naturally. "I noticed you went off the rails. One, I'm not announcing this to your family. Two, yes, I did notice something there. Neither of them wanted to give up the patient, so when I left, there seemed to be a showdown brewing. Three, what did you tell him?"

"I told him that I was hungover on tequila after a night of sweaty jungle-gym sex with a guy I picked up at a bar," she answered directly, in one matter-of-fact breath, even though she felt her forehead growing more and more tense and wrinkled as she spoke. "And that's when I knew we were in a relationship, because after I succeeded in driving my brother away so he wouldn't ask more questions, I felt guilty the rest of the day for fake-cheating on you with a pretend person I had just made up."

The seriousness with which he looked at her made her stomach curdle, but just when she thought she was going to have to cry and run away from the plaza in dramatic fashion, he started to laugh. Not a quiet chuckle like she usually got from him either. He opened his mouth and laughed so loudly from their little perch across the plaza, it almost drowned out the singing.

"Shh." She put her sandwich down and her hand over his mouth as he quieted into less raucous laughter, but his eyes twinkled merrily at her as the loudness ebbed and she pulled her hand away. "Come on, now, it's not *that* funny. What are you even laughing at? What I did to Zac, or that I've been feeling guilty? We have to come up with a plan or everyone's going to be squinting at us at work, just like I spent the day squinting at Zac and Ella!"

"If they can handle you trying to throw yourself over Niagara Falls, I think they can handle this."

"I wasn't trying to throw myself over the falls." For some reason, that seemed like the most important part of his statement to address. Or at least the easiest part. "I'd have needed a barrel for that. I just wanted to put my hands in the water. I wasn't going to let go of the railing, I just was doing it from the other side because I didn't think it through very well. Then Charles panicked and dragged me back—almost dumping me into the river in the process, I might add. I had a better grip on the railing than he thought, but no one really trusted in me to not fall on my face every other day at that point."

"My point is the same, this is hardly something that will knock them for a loop." Then he ticked off on his fingers what he'd no doubt learned from her albums before she'd rescued them from him. "Skydiving. Monster trucks. Crash-up derby..."

"My parents are married but they hate each other, because they can't imagine getting a divorce. Does that tell you anything about how traditional they are?"

"Do they really *hate* each other?"

"Yeah, I'm pretty sure."

"Why?"

"You know, Miranda's existence? Dad's affair and whatever? Mom never got over that one." And Miranda was probably who Penny was closest to, but who she absolutely didn't want to tell that she was having a baby outside marriage. Not that Miranda was judgemental, but with the way things had been, growing up—single mom, no father in the picture until her mom had died—it felt like anything even passably resembling the situation had the chance of hurting her only sister. "I guess things were different earlier, back when they trusted one another, but as soon as that trust went, everything went with it."

He finished his sandwich; hers was half-gone, but she'd lost all interest in it. These discussions could probably even sour a stomach completely devoid of pregnancy hormones.

"Trust is important," he agreed.

She couldn't bring herself to ask whether he trusted her. Clearly, he didn't, if he needed a marriage and documentation as much as he'd claimed. "So, I'm just going to say this, because I don't know how to do this relationship thing. All I can think is that being direct is the best way to go."

"Say what you want to say."

"Okay. I can't say I'll ever marry you, but if I can get to this place where I'm even willing to dip a toe into relationship-infested waters, it's possible I could *eventually* come around to the idea of marriage too. If we do this the right way. Like let it unfold naturally. Figure out how to be together as a couple, not just as two people who made a baby. It's not a promise, I literally hate spending time anywhere my parents are in the same room together. Charles's wedding is coming up, which I need a date for, by the way, but also if you come, you'll see them together. You'll understand what I think of when I think marriage. I have some other issues because I'm, you know, a basket case."

He let her go on and on, nodding here and there to show he was still keeping up. Of all the people in her life, Gabriel was the only one who would let her babble on for ages uninterrupted, which was another mark in his pro column.

"That's a bunch of I-don't-knows, but here's what I do know. I can't seem to think of you as just my partner anymore. And, to be honest, I haven't been able to since Schenectady."

His expression closed down, and he'd stopped nodding, but she knew he'd heard her. He'd heard every word, she felt it in the gravity of his gaze and the way he reached over to tuck a flyaway strand of hair into her knit hat. "It sounds like they're winding down."

The singing. She went with the redirect and cocked her head toward the music to listen.

"'Carol of the Bells,'" she murmured, gathering up her dinner refuse to dispose of. "Want to go closer to listen? I can't believe they got a bunch of eleven- and twelve-year-olds to learn this complicated a song."

Trash disposed of, confessions made, she held her hand out to him, needing to test that boundary and know if he'd take her hand in public. When he did, she tucked in close enough to almost lean as they walked back toward the audience to hear the last of the singing.

That first bridge crossed, Gabriel stepped behind her to wrap his arms around her waist, and when she leaned back, she felt pounds lighter. This relationship business was like a dark room and she only had a flickering flashlight. Sometimes she could see a path forward, but then the light went out and left her blindly feeling her way and wondering if she'd just stepped on gum or something worse.

Right now, her flashlight was working. Gabriel stood behind her, his arms around her waist, listening to kids singing Christmas songs while she gazed up at the legendary, glittering tree. In that breath, she could picture it. She could picture glittering Christmas trees in the future, and a chubby-legged toddler with warm brown skin, curly black pigtails and blazing blue eyes. In Gabriel's lap. Not because she wasn't healthy enough to stand on her own but because there was nowhere she'd rather be than on her daddy's knee.

Stinging in her eyes let her know she was going too far into that fantasy, but it was a good step. It was something happy, something *besides* the cold nature Christmases had taken in the Davenport household these past fourteen or so years.

"I ordered a bunch of Christmas decorations for the loft," she said, as much to try and take her mind off that wandering path as to make a sideways approach to including him in it. She'd pretty much used up her daily courage quota, so she couldn't come directly at the question she really wanted to ask. The best she could do was hint and hope he'd just come out and tell her he was going to move in. "Do you think you'd like to come help me decorate this weekend?"

CHAPTER SIX

BY THE TIME Penny got home the next evening, the white sneakers she wore when on the floor scuffed and squeaked across the polished lobby floor, she so failed at lifting her feet fully while walking. Then again off the elevator to her door. Most days in the ER weren't especially exciting for her, but today had been so busy she'd spent the day longing for five minutes just to sit down.

Sliding her key into the lock even felt like a feat of strength. Before she turned the thing, she heard sound through her door. Had she left the television on this morning? Had she even watched television this morning?

That creeping sensation of being watched came up on the back of her neck and stilled her hand. Living alone in New York, she'd developed enough situational awareness to come alert instantly when things seemed out of place. She'd also learned sometimes it was worth looking like a paranoid idiot and getting Security to go into her place with her if she was spooked. Like she suddenly was.

As quietly as she could, she slid the key from the lock and then turned to run for the stairwell, not wanting to wait for the elevator. She could be both brave and *smart* about things like this, which involved running the other way just this once.

Five minutes later, she had the on-site security guard

at her door with her keys, opening it. He had a Taser in hand, and when the door swung open, he dashed in like they were on an episode of *COPS*, yelling that he was armed and if anyone was loitering in the apartment, they should make themselves known.

Basically, her worst nightmare.

But then the nightmare got worse. Her apartment glittered with twinkling white Christmas lights strung up the columns near the door, which she hadn't put up. And then she saw him: Gabriel, rising from the floor in front of a massive, half-decorated Christmas tree, hands in the air, one glittering silver ornament dangling from his thumb over his head. "I'm supposed to be here."

Her stomach sank a good five thousand feet.

Gabriel had come and decorated all by himself. He hadn't said anything other than "Maybe" when she'd invited him to decorate with her, but here he was. She'd caused a Taser to be pointed at him for all his effort.

He caught sight of her peeking around the guard and with hands still in the air, ornament dangling, he shrugged. "Surprise?"

Dammit!

This would be the second time she'd had to apologize to him. But first she should stop the guard from Tasering him—then she'd really have to apologize.

"Don't shoot! I'm sorry. This is my fault." She darted around her escort and moved into the line of fire, her back to Gabriel so she could address the guard. "I didn't expect it, but this is Dr. Gabriel Jackson. He has keys now. I just forgot. And I wasn't expecting him, and then I got all stupid, and then..."

"Everything's okay, Miss Davenport?" the guard double-checked, before putting his Taser away.

"Everything's very okay. Thank you for coming with

me. I'm sorry for...the fuss." She puffed and, after sharing an apologetic look with Gabriel and making a mental note to get the guard something nice for Christmas, she walked him to the door with more apologies.

Gabriel waited patiently until she'd closed the door before he asked, "You thought I was an intruder?"

"A little bit," she admitted, chewing her lip. "I'm sorry. But remember yesterday when I said I'm lousy at knowing how to have a relationship? That's *this*. I definitely want you here, I just... I didn't expect you to come over. Not so quickly. Last night it just seemed like one big question mark, and...then you decorated. Oh, my goodness, Gabriel, you didn't have to do all this by yourself, but it's so beautiful!"

He let it all roll off his back, just nodding and looking wonderfully rumpled but not at all put out by the confusion. Even if he'd had a Taser pointed at him by someone of passing competence. Then he went with the subject he'd probably planned for all day, knowing him, "Don't look on the other side of the loft—that's where the mountain of boxes is living."

She never saw him dressed in casual clothes, not really. Even when he'd been there with her for days, he'd put on slacks every morning. But now he wore jeans. And he wore them fantastically. The white T-shirt he had on was also rumpled, and she could see that he'd had a long day just by the state of his attire. It made him more real. It made him even more attractive, if that was even possible.

Sexy. Right down to the silver glitter that had fallen off the ribbons and ornaments and which would definitely linger in the loft for months, and may need a good scrubbing to get off that rich skin.

Immediately she had mental images of them washing one another, luxuriating in soap-slickened muscles under her hands, and the way his whole body had gone tense when she'd gripped him...

Focus. She looked at the tree, at the fade in and out of the white lights, and tried her best to push memories of their shower out of her head. Even if he needed a shower to get the glitter off him, she couldn't offer to help. She could barely believe he was even there.

"You like it?" He sounded just a little tentative, like she was going to hate it. Like it was even possible that he'd done all this, wasted his whole afternoon. Like he wanted to please her.

"Are you kidding? It's the worst. I mean, I hate it. All the wonderful, glittering lights and big red bows," she said, trying to ignore the warm feelings spreading through her chest, scrambling to find her center, that banter she counted on to help her keep it together. "I love it. Can't believe you did all this. How did you get it done in one day?"

"The tree's not done. But I got here right after you left this morning. Borrowed a ladder from Maintenance." He paused. "You sure you like it? Some things I wasn't even sure what they were, or what to do with them. I improvised. And the tree still needs the rest of the ornaments."

"I love it," she said again, pulling her coat off and dropping it as she jogged straight for him and flung her arms around his shoulders. The man smelled like heaven, if heaven were filled with earthy pleasures. "Thank you. Today was such a dreadful day, I wasn't even sure I had the energy to walk up the stairs to bed. Of course, I was going to detour to the fridge to grab something and stuff in my face as I crawled up the stairs...but all the excitement of you being a possible intruder, and then discovering it's actually *you*, only adorably dusted in silver sparklies? Even better. I love it."

His hands fell onto her hips and then he gave in and

hugged her back. Resting her cheek on his shoulder, she breathed out slowly, instantly relaxing. Then he began to rock, and being too relaxed became a danger to the evening that suddenly had become full of possibilities.

"If you keep this up, I'm going to lose my burst of energy," she murmured. "And possibly sleep standing up."

"Before dinner?"

His voice was like warm honey to her ears, and she grinned against his shoulder, no longer hesitant to ask. "Does this mean you're staying? Tonight? Moving in?"

"I'm staying. We'll call it a trial run. Still think we should take things slow," he confirmed, sounding a little more resolute now, and breaking the spell a little as he let go of her and gestured to something she'd missed entirely in all the awesomeness that had gone on since she'd walked into a magical twinkling wonderland-style living room, complete with sugar-frosted boyfriend. "I just dumped my bags in the guest room and came straight downstairs, haven't unpacked at all. Tomorrow, I guess."

Boyfriend.

The word stuck in the front of her brain, and made her smile. He was her boyfriend. That particular word didn't even scare her right now, not like *relationship* did. It came with images of hand-holding and slow dancing under starry skies. That special time before things inevitably blew up.

"Something smells good, other than the cinnamon. Smells meaty. You cooked?"

"I warmed up a pre-cooked turkey breast, and got stuff for good sandwiches. So, I barely cooked, but I thought you did all right with a sandwich last night." He nodded to the blanket. "It'd be nice to have food that doesn't need utensils by the fire."

Romantic.

"This is a date, isn't it?"

He shook his head, and then gave the kind of half-shrug she knew to be man-speak meaning: *Yes, but I don't want to make a big deal of it or even have it spoken about.*

"Well, let me go get out of my work clothes." She gave him her best, over-the-shoulder sultry voice. "Just so you're aware, I'm going to put on a negligee."

"I thought we agreed to take things slow." Instantly alarmed.

"By negligee you should understand I mean flannel pajamas in cotton-candy pink." She grinned at him as she headed up the stairs, and saw him shake his head, but he was smiling again.

When she returned, she diverted to the stereo to turn on some light mood music. Christmas music, actually. Christmas music was absolutely necessary for a living room Christmas picnic and conversation. And lower lights. And her fireplace all sparked and roaring. She couldn't fully appreciate the twinkling if the overhead lights were canceling out the glow.

By the time they'd settled with their plates on their knees and her with her now usual mug of hot apple cider tea, she began picking his brain about Jackson family Christmas traditions.

This conversation naturally turned back to Davenport traditions, namely her tradition these past few years: Penny's Christmas Adventure.

"I don't know when it started. I guess around twenty-one? I just never really cared about Christmas. It always felt like someone else's holiday, that it was made for the healthy kids—the kids who had a future."

He frowned over his sandwich, so sharply she knew he was taking her literally.

"No one ever said that to me. That's just how I felt. Years of illness takes its toll. I always had very nice gifts, designed to stimulate my mind, and all I wanted was the toys that would stimulate my body. My siblings got bikes and rollerblades, I got a microscope. And then I got a telescope. New computers. Dolls. Good Lord, the dolls. I hated the dolls."

"Didn't they ask what you wanted?"

"Sure. I just didn't have words to tell them, or the heart to say, 'I want to go play in the snow. I want to go sledding. I want to ice skate and trampoline.' Eventually I got better, but Christmas never dazzled me after that. It was tainted with years of heartbreak. I guess that's why I started traveling. Go somewhere new or somewhere I already loved and hadn't fully explored, have some new adventures... I liked it better than sitting with family by the fire, waiting for some present that would disappoint me. Live life, don't just watch from the sidelines."

He looked at the fire, then back at her. "I thought the fire was nice."

"*This* fire is nice. The company is nicer." She tried not to look too wistfully at him. "Really, it's all nice. I wasn't even sure I was going to be able to make myself decorate. Buying things online is a lot easier than putting them up. It even feels different. Maybe it always feels different when it's your own place."

"What's it feel like?"

"Kind of comforting. Kind of exciting? Kind of like a trial run, like you said. Kind of like a last Christmas for just me before I devote the rest of my Christmases to my child. That's not a complaint, just a framework. I should enjoy it so I know what to give her. Or him. And try not to think of it as limiting my adventures, even if sometimes it feels like my adventuring days might be over."

"They're not."

"That's easy to say. They're at least on hold for a long, long time. I've been trying to think of pregnancy-safe adventures to do around the city, and I don't have many ideas at all. Can't go ice skating. Can't go skiing. I've been training for the Empire State Run-Up, where they do this indoor stair-climbing marathon up the Empire State Building. But…I don't know if I can do that while pregnant. Would climbing eighty-six flights of stairs be dangerous? I don't know."

"I don't know why you want to run up eighty-six flights of stairs."

"I don't know why you *don't* want to. Don't you want to find out if you can do it?"

"We climb stairs for work all the time."

"Not that many floors. And not racing other people. Challenging yourself. Seeing if you're as good as they are, or how far you lag behind."

She didn't even realize how she'd said that, putting herself into a position that was inherently *lesser,* until he frowned.

"I doubt you'll lag behind, but you can talk to your doctor about it when you go. You should. If you want to do it, no matter how silly it is."

She nodded, then waved a hand to him. "Do you have any other pregnancy-safe adventure ideas?"

"I guess not shopping."

"Boring."

"Volunteering for a charity? Going to a soup kitchen?"

"That's nice and I should do more of that, but that's not adventurous."

"Dance class?"

She paused. "Dance class? Like, what kind of dance?"

"Interpretive dance."

That made her laugh, and then made her gesture like an idiot for the fruit salad on the other side of him.

He scooted the bowl to her. "Or couples dancing. The classics."

"Ballroom?"

"Or something more fun. Salsa? Swing?"

"That…might not suck. That could be fun," she said, after rolling it around in her head then popping a grape into her mouth. "Go to Georgia and hike the first part of the Appalachian Trail?"

"Camping and hiking? How far is it?"

"I don't know, like a hundred miles or something."

"That's the first segment of the trail?"

"I don't know. I just know that you can do it, and if you do the whole thing, you end up in Maine."

"Scratch that one. You'd give birth in the woods surrounded by elves, and then they'd take our baby away. Elves are like that."

She laughed again at the man, the serious, sober man who was teasing her. "We wouldn't want that."

"Everything I'm coming up with seems results-oriented. But I'm guessing, based on your album, that you're experience-oriented."

She shifted over to him on the blanket and leaned her back against him. "What results?"

"Photography classes, learning to do different things, practical, tangible things." He slid an arm around her, encouraging her to turn in toward him.

"Knitting?"

"For instance."

"Unless it's some kind of knitting marathon where you compete with people while also running around and playing, I don't want to do it. What about that obstacle course television series about being super-fit?"

"You could for a while. I think you've got about three months before your belly will become un-hideable."

"What else?"

"I don't know. Hot air balloons?"

"Oh, piloting?"

"I was thinking riding…"

She tilted her head back to look up at him. "Still, I like that one. I'm keeping it. I'll research online."

In the firelight, she could see at least fifteen specks of silver glitter sparkling on his cheek and forehead, and it tickled her.

He either felt her grinning up at him or she made a sound because he looked down at her, brows raised with unspoken questions.

"You're just sparkly. I'm not sure you haven't already been to the forest with the elves."

"What does that mean?"

"It means you've got more glitter on you than a tarted-up Tinkerbell." She reached up to try and brush it off his cheek, but the glitter didn't budge.

He rubbed his face too. Still it stuck.

"Did you, by chance, take off your shirt while you were dealing with the glittery things?"

"Why?"

"Because if your chest is all glittery, I have to see it. It's really non-negotiable, I'm afraid. I have a rule—if my boyfriend's chest has glitter on it, I get to see it."

She just slipped the B-word right in there.

The disbelieving laugh he gave her emboldened her. Lifting the front of his shirt, she whisked it up so she could peek at the warm brown skin beneath.

"Penny."

"I can't tell. The light's not getting through the cotton. Take your shirt off."

"No…"

She pulled her head back up and lowered his shirt, trying to decide if he was serious or not.

"What if I do a wolf whistle? Men do that all the time on the street, I know it's code for 'Take Off Your Shirt.' Granted, it's dumb code. I could do catcalls!" Which was when it occurred to her. "Wonder why those two different behaviors are attributed to different animals. And wolves don't whistle. Unless they have a sinus condition maybe."

He laughed again then, and didn't even attempt to stop her when she lifted his shirt. His arms went up, he pulled it over his head, and glitter that had been clinging to the cotton fluttered down like little snowy diamonds.

That landed on his chest.

And abs.

And those freaking *hip flexors*…

She slid her hand over his skin, unable to not touch him, just a little mesmerized by the combination of his sparkling flesh and sensation sparking over her own.

It might have started out as playful flirting, but she swung a fuzzy, flannel leg over his lap, getting close, wanting closer. Desperate for his mouth, she'd gotten right up to his, could feel the scruff from his upper lip against hers before she found her willpower. With already accelerated breath, a body aching with anticipation, she leaned back enough to look at him.

Even if he'd played along with the shirt, even if he was going to stay for a trial run, he'd said no sex earlier. And there were things she didn't know, things she needed to understand, and one of them was his boundaries.

As she leaned back, he leaned forward, his gentle hands cupping her cheeks, his wonderful lips brushing hers, beckoning her to forget the words she needed to say. It was the lightest brush, teasing, tempting, and powerful enough to set her heart to hammering.

Nothing could bring her to pull back from him, so it was against his lips, between kisses, that she asked, "What changed your mind?"

The question took his attention and he looked her in the eye. "Changed my mind about what?"

"Between last night and this morning, what made you decide to come for the trial run with me?"

His brows pinched, what she might have called regret in his eyes as he held her gaze. "I knew last night. The instant that key was in my hand. But I wanted to take my time, to think it over."

Did he regret waiting, or was it too soon to regret this? "Were you just trying to be sensible?"

That took him a little longer to put into words, and she saw him look long and hard at her mouth, like he was considering just kissing her again rather than answering.

"It's that bad?"

The quiet ticked on, and whatever words he was running through his mind didn't seem to be lining up the way he wanted. "Because you're—"

A sharp, frosty stab to her chest came with his words.

Criticism was coming. No wonder he couldn't think of the words. She moved back a little further, still on his lap but leaning in the other direction so their torsos made a V. "I'm what? Untrustworthy?"

"I didn't say that."

"You say it all the time. Just not out loud." And she knew it, she heard it every time the thought crossed his mind. Why it hurt so much this time, she couldn't say, but it was there, rotting in her chest. She twisted to the side to climb off his lap.

"You don't trust me explicitly either." His hands

gripped her hips and he pulled her back, not letting her get away that easily. A dissatisfied breath rushed out of him and he grunted, "What I was going to say was you make me want to trust…this. You. Last night, you said a lot of things about what you could and couldn't give, and I'm trying to be that resolute, to find some kind of compromise here when it goes against every instinct I have. Because I don't just want this child, I want you. And I don't."

When he'd pulled her back, his firm hands on her hips had brought her into closer contact with his body in ways she was trying not to make contact with while they negotiated boundaries. He wanted her, and he didn't, which pretty much summed up her feelings on the matter too, only she was trying to confront her own issues on this, to make this work.

"Are we just incompatible? I told you I need time and for this to develop naturally, but my trust issues aren't quite the same as yours. I don't trust *marriage* as a concept more than I don't trust *you*. Sure, I think you're probably going to get to a point where you don't want me to be who I am, but I think that about *everyone*. You seem to think I'm going to lie to you, or trick you until I can one day…run off and take the baby and go somewhere you can never find us."

"I'm not saying I just expect that. I'm saying…it's possible. I don't know."

She grabbed his head to make him look her in the eye. "Tell me what you need. Promises? Do you want to put off the trial period until we've been to lawyers to have custody agreements drawn up? Do you want me to write out a declaration of my intent, of your paternity, in longhand right now and sign it? Would that make this feel… less like you're dangling over Niagara?"

"I don't know." He sighed, reaching for her hands to draw them down from his head, a gentle touch as he continued to hold them in the cradle of their joined laps. "I really don't know. But I'm trying."

He was there, she reminded herself, but he'd dragged it out over a night because he genuinely expected this to backfire.

"I need a promise from you," she said, because all she could do was be blunt and direct in this. Every voice in her head that shouted to retreat was a test of her courage, and she couldn't think of anything more important to be courageous about. "I need you to promise that you won't try to make me into someone else. And the other thing, the promise I make to you—if this isn't working, if I decide you're not the one for me, I promise I'll tell you quickly, end it humanely, not let it drag us to hell to keep up appearances."

"Pen…"

She did climb off his lap then and didn't stop until she was a good foot away, far enough that she felt only the heat of the fireplace at her back, not the warmth of his big body beneath her. "And I promise never to take your child from you unless you do something abusive. If you can put nasty caveats on my future actions—like thinking I'd steal your child from you—I can put caveats on the possibility that you might one day turn into an abusive ass rather than just one unwilling to trust me when I've done nothing to earn that."

His hands flew up and rubbed over his head to the back of his neck. "You went from kissing to angry, and—"

"Yes. I did." She climbed to her feet and began gathering up the remains of their Christmas tree picnic to take to the kitchen, to clean up so she could go to bed alone.

Gabriel rose behind her, disgruntled at himself as much

as he was with her. He'd decorated the apartment on a whim because, no matter how much he tried to rationalize his way out of getting too close, he wanted to be there with her, and he wanted her to see it. See…what was too soon to say. Know that he knew how to make a home. He was husband material, not just parental partnership material, because that was the only thing he could think of to get this point across. Prove this by deeds. His mind was already made up about her, but she needed time and reassurance.

And he'd probably also done it because he didn't know what to tell her.

She clearly didn't want help with the dishes, so Gabriel went to pick up the boxes of ornaments they hadn't hung on the tree yet, clearing up something of the mess. "I only know how to do this one way. I only know how to reason my way through steps to show you that you can trust me. You want promises, fine. I won't stay with you for the baby if—"

"Children. It'll be more than one in a few years if you truly see us being together forever," she cut in, turning back from the sink with a towel to dry her hands. "Because you want me. And I want you. Most of the time. You might be able to hold off, control whether you want me, or how much you want me, but I don't work that way. I don't want to rush you any more than I want you to rush me, but it would probably go a long way toward convincing me that you feel something for me besides attraction and affection if you *stopped* holding yourself back so much."

"What am I holding back?"

"I don't know. I know you take a year to come up with a half-sentence, you hold me back when I want to kiss you. The other day? That kiss was amazing, and I'm sure a lot of that was because you made me slow down enough to really appreciate it, but between your half-finished thoughts and your insane restraint levels, you can tell me you want me until you're out of breath, but it's only words." She tossed the towel on the counter, and as he stood between her and the stairs, she stepped to the side to go round him. "I'm going to bed."

She passed him, having every intention of continuing toward the stairs. Leave him down here with his perfect, glittery chest and his impermeable walls. Let him control the downstairs, she was going up.

She was almost past him when she felt the air stir as he reached for her, one large hand catching her by the back of the neck and the other arm swooping around her waist, spinning her toward him.

Alarm spiked in her belly, but it turned to delight as his mouth came down on hers, tearing from him a groan so loud she'd have thought him in pain. Like steel girders twisting and buckling under the pressure, the sound of Gabriel's control snapping.

Her feet, unprepared, tangled and she grabbed for his shoulders, relying on his strength and the vestiges of his control to keep her upright. It worked as long as she hung there, taking his ravenous kisses, his demanding tongue, his heat and need as she struggled to catch up.

Trying to get her footing, she pulled on his shoulders for support, and just to get closer, and shifted her feet around to find some balance that didn't rely on him, but one of her feet crossed his and he stumbled backward, pulling her with him.

The twinkling Christmas tree broke their fall, and the fall broke their kissing. Gabriel managed to twist them so that she landed on his chest with a grunt on the pillows and comforter they'd picnicked on earlier.

"Are you okay?" she gasped against his lips, lifting

enough to look at him, but he only nodded and rolled them, grabbing the cotton-candy-pink fuzzy pajama bottoms and dragging them off her roughly, panties and all.

CHAPTER SEVEN

PENNY'S TOP FLEW off next, and even though she was naked from the waist down, as soon as Gabriel saw another of those strappy white tanks she liked to wear, as she'd worn in Schenectady, he actually moaned before lunging at her chest. Through the snug, stretchy fabric, he caught her nipple, and every inch of her body sparked.

This was what happened when Gabriel lost control? The material scraped over the stiff peak of her breast, hot and wet from his mouth, and left her too shocked to do anything but grab at his shoulders while his big body pressed her into the pillows.

He finally seemed to realize the tank was there, and let go of her long enough to shove the material up over her breasts, where he could get at the now insanely sensitive flesh.

One hand stroked downward, over her belly, to land between her legs, cupping, warming with his palm, then pressing just firmly enough to part tender flesh and stroke her.

She should be touching him, the thought drifted through her mind. Getting those damned pants off him at least. But she'd never felt so wanted, and it overrode her senses, left her quaking, arching, gasping, full of involuntary movements and sounds. Uncontrolled, desperate, and stunned, she clung to him because her fingers wouldn't stop gripping his shoulders.

They weren't just words, thank the Ghost of Christmas Sexy-Time... He wanted her. He really, really wanted her.

Gabriel closed his eyes and kissed and nibbled up her chest, up the side of her neck, trying to wrest some control back before he accidentally hurt her, went too fast, got too rough.

The taste of her skin and the feel of her writhing made an urgent beast inside him roar to life, but seeing how deeply pink she'd grown and the wild, blank look in her eyes made it too hard to even try to hold back.

The mother of his child, the woman he *wanted* to marry. It wasn't just for the child, God help him.

Her slickness on his hand, the puffy swelling there, it was as long as he could wait. The denim of his jeans already pinched, he'd grown so desperate for her. Wrestling the fasteners open, he shoved the material down, but before he got where he needed to be if he was going to keep breathing, Penny seemed to regain enough of her senses to do something besides squirm and make those pleading little mewls that all but assured he'd never be able to go slowly with her again. She focused enough to grab his head and drag it to hers.

Still no words, but she made her need for his kisses known through a series of throaty cries that only stopped when he covered her mouth with his own, and angled his head to stroke his tongue deeply into her mouth.

But he needed to be inside more than just her mouth.

Condom. The word habit he'd drilled into himself years ago rolled through the fog of need that had become his mind, but there was enough functioning there to discard it. No need.

Self-control slipping, he gripped her hips just to stop her squirming long enough to slide in. First damned night, and he'd said they had to wait...

Looking at her, her swollen lips open for gasping breaths, and feeling her hot around him, it hadn't been like this before. It had been hot and sexy and, God, *fun*, but this ache driving him...he felt it in spiky jabs straight down to the arches of his feet.

"Gabriel?"

She whispered his name and he held himself still, eyes closed, trying to breathe, trying not to buck against her the way he knew would if he didn't get hold of himself.

"Give me a second..." He pulled words together from somewhere.

Something was wrong. Penny searched his pained features, took in the violence of the shaking that had taken hold of him, and began to come back to herself. Yes, something was wrong, and she had no idea what it was.

"Is it too much?" she asked, feeling the need to soothe him, now that she had a second to think without drowning in sensation.

He nodded, eyes still clenched shut, breaths harsh, labored, fighting for something.

"Want me on top?"

The question hung there for several seconds before he nodded, pushed an arm under her back, and rolled them over.

It was her turn to slow them down, for him. Kiss his neck, kiss his face, stroke her hands over his magnificent, glittery chest as she sat up, straddling him.

When he finally opened his eyes again, the look he gave her was full of such longing she couldn't look away. Not even when his hands firmed on her hips, urging her to move. Not even when she grew jerky and uncoordinated from the sizzling jolts of pleasure that pulsed through her. Not even when he sat up, put his strong arms around her, and kissed her.

Not even when she reached that dizzying height and had to fight to keep her eyes open while every other muscle in her body seized and jerked. Or when she felt him pulsing inside her.

He laid them back down among the pillows, hearts thundering, Christmas tree toppled nearby, and a fire beside them.

But the last thing she felt before she closed her eyes was the certainty that she loved this man.

Penny stretched in the big comforter, feeling the crisp cotton slide against her skin, then spiraled through the last things she remembered to decide what was going on.

In her bed. That was wrong. She'd gone to sleep downstairs. With Gabriel.

She didn't even need to look beside her to know he wasn't there. The room felt empty, like always. Just like last time.

She knuckled the sleep from her eyes and sat up, taking further inventory. She was still nude, wrapped in the blanket from downstairs, and she hadn't climbed the stairs swaddled in the thing.

The sinking in her middle set off her inner nausea warning system, but when the retching didn't follow, she made herself examine it. Pounding heart, heightened awareness of every inch of her skin, of the amplified sound of her breathing. More dread. And bigger, sharper than that.

Fear. That was fear…that something bad was going on

with Gabriel and she didn't know enough of how relationships should go to fix it. Or that it was something unfixable.

A look at the other side of the bed confirmed it: blankets entirely unrumpled. Once again, he hadn't wanted to sleep with her. And she didn't know what to do with that.

Right.

She took a breath and dragged herself out of bed. Find him, look for reasons to support this fear, and don't give in to it until there's a good reason to.

Go downstairs, and if he's just somewhere *else* asleep, kick him in the happy place.

Ignoring her shaking insides, she dressed and brushed her hair to look her most presentable, and headed downstairs.

The scent of bacon hit her first, and she found him at the range. To the right, the Christmas tree they'd toppled sat upright again, but looked a little worse for wear, as she was, all evidence of their love nest missing entirely.

Gabriel stood at the range, making breakfast, but at the first sound of her feet on the stairs, what had been hunger gnawing at his belly turned into a slow, uneasy roll.

"Hey," he called, looking over his shoulder at her, silently praying for another calm, easy breakfast together, but knew how useless that prayer was. He'd been downstairs since dawn, having slept in the guest room, fitfully.

With a knot in his gut he scanned her face. The anxious drawing of her mouth confirmed she was upset. That, and her complete lack of greeting in return.

Upset and calm, which made him as uneasy as she looked. Energetic, loud Penny he knew how to deal with, not this version with sad eyes that shot right through his guilt center.

At work he knew how to speak with her, mostly without

things getting fraught. Here, he didn't know which way to step. Apologizing for leaving her, as he truly wanted to do, was the wrong move. Pretending nothing was wrong at least made clear he didn't want to talk about things.

"How are you feeling?"

Her shoulders popped up, and she looked him over in a way that increased the feeling of dread. "You've already had your shower and fixed the tree."

Tree. Quasi-safe subject. As long as he didn't mention how it had got knocked down.

"It still needs ornaments, but no damage done. I thought we could do that after breakfast. Do you think you can handle bacon?"

He could tell by the look of utter bafflement that damage had been done between them. This was a mess. Last night shouldn't have happened, it had been too much too soon. It had changed things too much, too quickly, and he'd already been having a hard time figuring out what was going on. She'd said she wanted to take things slowly too...

"You carried me up to bed last night?"

"Thought it was better than sleeping on the floor."

She was feeling her way too, he could see it in the pauses. Normally she spoke quickly, her excited babbling actually one of the things he enjoyed most about being with her. These heavy pauses made it worse. Not just the lack of excitement, which was the wrong direction for them to be traveling, but the fact that she was so carefully weighing all her words before uttering them.

"Where did you sleep?"

"In my room." He turned off the burner and moved the pan of bacon back so that he could give her all his attention.

"You didn't want to sleep with me?"

Still working through it. He should jump to the explanation, not leave her feeling her way. Wiping his hands, he went to stand across the island counter from her, where she'd eased onto a stool.

He kept his voice gentle and looked her in the eye, though she was having trouble maintaining eye contact with him, which ratcheted up the urge to reach for her. "We were taking things slowly, and then we didn't take things slowly. I was trying to put us back on course."

"What course?"

"Slower, more meaningful intimacy. You wanted it to flow naturally."

She gestured with one hand toward the fireplace, and finally looked him in the eye again. "Sleeping beside me in the bed is more intimate than *that* was?"

"It is, or you wouldn't be upset now."

"I'm upset because I went to sleep in your arms and woke up alone in a different room on a different floor of my home..." She stopped abruptly, holding up her hands and breathing so deeply that dread started to twist at him. Was she going to cry? Not sleeping beside her, not waking up tangled in her sheets with her, was supposed to make this easier.

"We have to stop getting swept up in the physical stuff."

"Why?"

"Because that's just the way it is. Don't you think about how messy this can get if we're not clear and careful about what we're doing?"

"I thought we agreed that this was a relationship."

"We did, and we have very different ideas about relationships and needs. The surest way to make this end in a formal custody battle is to be sloppy and irresponsible now."

Her fists squeezed and released, flexing with the tension she had rolling off her.

"Fine. Rule Number One: if you sleep with a woman, the civil thing to do is wake her up before you leave her."

"Fine."

"Rule Number Two: I'm feeling better, and going back in the air tomorrow."

"That's not a rule." Again it was turning into a fight. "And you're not well enough. You don't even know if it will manifest once you're in the air, like motion sickness."

"I guess we'll find out." She stood up and moved into the kitchen, no longer looking at him, like that could switch off the conversation as easily as she switched on the kettle.

"Penny…"

She rubbed both hands over her face, then waved a hand, like she was trying to dispel the tension. "Tomorrow, at work, if I feel bad I'll go home."

A concession. A compromise of sorts. Except… "You won't. You never admit you're sick until you're forced to."

"I called off the other day."

He took a breath and then nodded. She had him there. "And you know if you don't, I'll send you home."

"I know it if anyone knows it," she muttered, grabbing the cider from the fridge and pouring it into a mug before sticking it in the microwave.

Touching her always helped, she took comfort in it as much as he did when they were at an impasse. He stepped over to her, but didn't touch her until she looked up at him.

Not moving away from him. Gabriel took that as permission, and brushed his hand over her hair and pressed his lips to her forehead.

She leaned in for the barest second, then pulled back. "Don't."

"Don't what?"

"Don't kiss my head."

Head kissing was innocuous. "Why?"

"It makes me feel like you really care."

"I do care."

"Kind of. You proved wanting me, the sexual connection. But you didn't want to sleep with me. That's twice now. First, you wanted to sleep in the same bed as me, and then you left in the night. Then last night I went to sleep with you, after all that, and you left again. Actually, you took me somewhere else and left me there."

"That's stretching what happened. I took you to your bed, not to Dubuque."

"You said it was because of not wanting too much intimacy. That's all I'm asking for. Because as much as you hate that I won't just marry you, I'm the one who keeps ending up being rejected by you. Let's just leave it at that. I won't ask you to sleep in the bed with me, you don't kiss my head like I'm some sweet thing you can't get enough of. Because clearly I'm not."

Denials were rushing to his lips as soon as the words began to make sense to him, but he clamped his mouth shut. She believed that. The only thing clear to him was that his attempt to reset the situation had made things worse, not better.

The next morning was gray and frigid. Overnight, rain had arrived in the city, and then the temperature dropped. She could tell how nasty it was by the coating of ice on her bedroom windows.

A day for thermals beneath her flight suit. Maybe two layers. And two pairs of socks.

Had Gabriel thought to bring a set with him for their temporary trial run? She'd been ignoring the *temporary* part of the arrangement before yesterday, but it truly felt temporary today. Yes, she'd wanted to let things unfold naturally, but nothing, prior to waking up alone, had felt unnatural. She couldn't decide if he was doing this on purpose, or if he truly thought he was helping their situation, and her relationship IQ was practically nil.

Snatching a second set of thermals from her bureau, she stuffed them into the messenger bag she preferred to handbags, then dragged on baggy jeans and sweater to tide her over until she got to the hospital and a fresh, clean flight suit. She'd decide on the commute if she needed the second set, though hers would never fit him anyway.

"Pen?" he called from downstairs, sounding as tense as she'd felt since yesterday.

It was that tension more than anything else that prompted her to hurry. Snatching a brush and hairband on the way out, she went to meet him.

He stood by the door, ready to go, keys and bag in hand. "Everything okay?"

Nope.

"I'm not feeling sick."

He had his keys out, he could lock it up. She stepped on out and went to ring for the elevator, and ignored a disgruntled sigh behind her.

They lapsed into silence for the whole ride to the hospital, with him tucking his nose into his phone and her braiding her hair.

In the locker room, which she realized she hadn't seen him in for weeks, she noted a set of thermals when he changed into his flight suit, and she added her second set because she got colder than he did. But the silence was like a hulking thing in the room with them.

"I'm going to get the pre-flight done."

"I'll come with you."

She knew she winced when he looked at her in a way that said he'd seen it.

With one step, he blocked her exit from the otherwise empty locker room. "We have to get it together. It was a fight. Or a disagreement, or a whatever you want to call it, not the end of the world. If you can't be alone with me in the chopper, we're in serious trouble."

"I can be alone with you in the chopper."

"You wouldn't stay in a room with me yesterday."

"You *hurt* me. Do you get that?"

Just coming out with it seemed to make the situation register with him, she saw it in the way his jaw clenched and he looked away briefly before nodding and looking back to her. One simple acknowledgment shifted what had been feeling like blame to a more neutral footing.

"I know." He said the words she needed to hear, shoving his hands into the pockets of his suit with stiff arms that pulled at the material and showed his discomfort. "I didn't mean to. I'm sorry, and I should've said it yesterday."

An apology was the last thing she'd expected. Acknowledgment would've been enough to satisfy her, but the gruffly spoken apology left her feeling more vulnerable than admitting he'd hurt her. "I get it. It's hard to talk about this stuff, especially if you don't trust me to handle it right."

His silence confirmed the mistrust still there.

"I need to go do the pre-flight before we get any calls. The way things are going out there, you know as soon as we're on duty, calls are coming," she said, letting him off the hook, if for no other reason than because she needed her wits about her if she was going to get through her first day back, without him thinking that she was incapable of performing her duties.

He nodded again, but didn't immediately move out of the doorway. A long silence followed, when he clearly wrestled with whether to say something else, then apparently decided against it as he moved out of the way, then fell into step behind her as she hit the stairs for the roof.

The less he talked, the more certain she got that this wasn't going to work. She should just go to the lawyer tomorrow and have documents started to acknowledge Gabriel as father and begin a joint custody arrangement. It couldn't hurt, and at this point it might be the only thing to save *them*.

CHAPTER EIGHT

As soon as his butt hit the seat, Gabriel switched on the radio. Seconds later, a call came from Dispatch for them.

While Penny went through the pre-flight as fast as she could, he answered.

"I know you're not on shift for another ten, but are you ready to fly yet? Massive pileup on the turnpike at the tunnel toll gates. They're calling in all flight crews."

Gabriel looked at her for confirmation they were ready.

She nodded. "Thirty to flight."

"We're go in thirty."

Grabbing her headset, Penny put it on, buckled in, and he did the same. After she'd checked a couple more things, they lifted off.

"Told you it'd be a busy morning," she said into the comm, "but we're about ten minutes away. I hope they have some ground crews doing triage."

He knew what she was doing, she was trying to make things easier between them, and he appreciated it. Since yesterday morning Penny didn't feel quite so much like the stumbling block to their relationship. He could see she was trying, and the extent of her honesty on any situation cleared up his confusion. He didn't trust her, she said it again and again, but he was starting to wonder if it was her he didn't trust. He trusted her on the job, at least when she wasn't ill as she claimed to not be today, but nothing in their history said he couldn't trust her. Maybe he didn't trust himself.

But he could trust their working relationship, so he leaned on it now.

"Ice and morning rush hour are always bad. I'm going to bet we've got some broken bones, head trauma, maybe stress-induced cardiac events." With any other partner Gabriel wouldn't gamble on the injuries they'd find on accident scenes, it could come off as callous, but no money was ever involved. It had actually turned into a teaching method between them, or more for Penny. She didn't have medical school under her belt, but she had extremely good instincts, and the more she learned, the better at her job she got. She'd already gotten to the point where she could anticipate his needs at least as well as any nurse he'd ever worked with in the ER.

"I'm gonna bet on…some kind of bashing chest injury. Pneumothorax. Hemothorax. Something like that. Flail chest, maybe. Breathing difficulties. Did you double-check inventory on your last shift? What do I need to grab when we jump?"

He went through a list of what he'd grab, confirmed his freshly stocked bag, and told her to grab the board and he'd grab oxygen then run ahead.

"Two minutes," she announced, and then groaned into the headset in a way that set him instantly alert.

"What is it? Are you sick?"

"Look down there." She nodded ahead to the accident scene they were still a good mile away from. Headlights and taillights pointed in all different directions, and there was an overturned tractor trailer blocking two lanes.

"Where are you going to set down?"

"Back of the semi, there's a clear space where cars can't get until that thing is moved…"

"Okay." He unbuckled and climbed into the back to grab his bag and a couple of items, assuming she wasn't ill since she hadn't said, and didn't look it, then held on as she touched down.

The chopper bounced a little and then actually slid, which was new.

"Are we sliding?" he shouted over his shoulder.

"For about a second. Careful when you climb out."

"You too." He looked at the board, considering if it'd be too much for her to carry with the slick conditions, then grabbed the oxygen and went ahead with his original plan.

That was another reason he didn't want her flying right now, because he factored her well-being into every decision, and there wasn't time for that on the ground.

He wrenched open the door and eased out then, with the bags on one shoulder and oxygen on the other, began slipping his way around the semi, and had to grab the hulking metal beast twice to keep from falling down.

Just on the other side of it, one of the cops organizing the scene met him and directed him to his patient's vehicle, an upside-down rust-colored SUV with glass shattered all around.

"My pilot is coming with the board—direct her."

He didn't worry that she'd see the wreck, but there were at least fifteen cars he could see with massive damage and no doubt casualties, and he needed her to find *him*.

He hurried along a path through the wrecks that had been obviously hand-salted, and which provided him better traction. Another NJSP trooper had crawled in through the passenger window. Gabriel could only see legs and feet and so rounded the vehicle to gain access from the other side.

"I'm Dr. Jackson," he said immediately as he looked inside. On the roof, lying over a shattered sun roof, a man lay on his back, white button-down shirt saturated with blood and a tire iron sticking out of his chest.

The officer sat upright, wedged between the seats so she could apply pressure.

"We didn't take it out," she said immediately, "but he's still bleeding. I applied pressure as best I could…"

"Okay, get out and when my partner gets here, direct her in that side," he ordered, and lifted up so he could better examine his patient, almost wishing the man was unconscious. "What's your name?"

"Darren." He said the short first name, and Gabriel could tell he was having trouble breathing. Damn if Penny hadn't nailed it. She hadn't called an open pneumothorax, but she'd called chest damage and difficulty breathing.

"I'm going to get you to Manhattan Mercy, Darren. As soon as I can." He gloved and pulled the compress away from the base of the wound, doing his best not to move the iron, but even a slight touch caused more pain. "I'm sorry about that. I'm trying to decide if we can pull it out."

"I wish you would."

Penny appeared at the other window and crawled in, dragging another bag with her and pulling out oxygen to hook up to the bottle he'd carried.

"His name is Darren." Gabriel filled her in, handing her the bottle. "He needs a line and he needs morphine."

Judging by the usual length of a tire iron, Gabriel estimated that Darren had about four inches of metal jammed into his ribs. The difficulty breathing could be because of the pain—the more it hurt to breathe, the more shallowly people breathed.

Penny didn't waste any time. She tied off his arm and

threaded in a catheter before Gabriel could listen to his chest to decide whether to pull out the iron.

"If we lay the seats down, we can get probably get him out the hatchback," she said, flushing the line. "Darren, I'm going to give you something for pain, and you're going to go to sleep. We're going to take you by air to the hospital, so you will be in the hands of a surgeon within a quarter-hour, okay?"

He nodded, and Penny injected the morphine, flushed the line again, and hooked up a saline drip. Before she was done, Darren was unconscious and Gabriel could listen to natural, painless breathing.

"His lungs are wet," he muttered to Penny. "Okay, lay the seat down there, I'll get mine and go around the back to get the hatchback and pass in the backboard."

She got done first, and he heard her on her radio. "Wet lungs, tire iron protruding. I don't know if we're going to tube him, but he's breathing on his own for now. If we can't get him out of the vehicle with the iron in, we might have to pull it. He doesn't have time to wait for them to cut the doors off."

He hadn't directed her to say that, but she was right. It really was a shame that she hadn't had the patience for medical school.

With the seats were laid back and the hatchback opened, and they managed to get Darren out of the over-turned car. As soon as they had cleared it, Penny hung the saline on Gabriel's shoulder as usual, and they moved as swiftly as they could for the chopper.

While they'd been in the vehicle, someone had thrown down what looked like cat litter on the ice, and around the jack-knifed truck to the chopper, so their path was easier. Barely more than a minute after they'd loaded the stretcher, Penny had them in the air.

* * *

The doorbell had Penny jolting awake on the sofa where she'd fallen asleep. It took her several seconds to ground herself and remember what was going on. Miranda. Visit. Right.

She scrambled upright and smoothed her hands over her hair, praying it wasn't sticking up like crazy. Gabriel had gone out to do Christmas shopping because she'd practically shoved him out the door earlier. This seemed like the kind of visit to not have your significantly strange other hanging around for.

Flinging the door open, she put on her best smile, and waved Miranda in.

"Oh, wow, did you do all this or hire someone?" her sister asked after the hug of welcome, leaving Penny to close the door. "Or is that even a service you can hire, like a Christmas interior decorator?"

Miranda hadn't grown up the same way Penny had, something that Penny often forgot. They'd had Miranda in the family for about half of her life now, long enough for everything to normalize to the point that it felt as if she'd always been there. The only way Miranda was any different from her brothers, aside from being female, was not having had to suffer through the sickness of the baby sister ruining fun things.

"You actually can, but I didn't hire anyone. I bought all the stuff, intending to put it up, but I came home from my shift on the floor the other day and Gabriel had put it all up." Nice lead-in. She was almost proud for just slipping that in there.

"Gabriel Jackson? Your partner? Why?"

"I guess he was being sweet," Penny said, something she'd been quietly smiling about every time she'd looked at the twinkling lights, even while things had been tense between them. "He'd just moved in, which we haven't told anyone yet, and he still has his place for now but, yeah. He's living here. For now. But it's still cone-of-silence stuff because it's a trial run and we're not doing so well with it. Have…things to figure out."

Miranda knew Penny's history, so she looked suitably surprised by the news. "What things do you have to figure out?"

She ushered Miranda to the kitchen and put on the kettle. It was time for tea and another antiemetic. And the part of the conversation she wasn't exactly looking forward to.

"Oh, mostly how to be together without messing everything up. We've got reasons to try and figure it out."

Miranda draped her coat and bag over one stool and sat at the other, amusement in her voice. "You mean like you love him?"

That part of the conversation Penny was not ready for. "Reasons like…I'm pregnant."

Time for Miranda's second shock in as many minutes. "Uh, congratulations?"

Penny nodded, and after getting the mugs ready for when the water was hot, she went to stand on Gabriel's side of the island—in the kitchen, facing her sister on her own usual stool. "Thank you. It is… It's good news. I do want the baby, and so does he, so that's good news. But… um…boy, you know, in my head I didn't just go storming right into the heart of this conversation as soon as you walked through the door."

"There's more to the conversation than you're living with someone and pregnant?"

"Yeah." Penny sighed, leaning her elbows on the counter because if she put her hands on the polished marble, she'd start tapping or fidgeting. "I know we don't talk about, you know, Dad and your mom, and pretty much all that, but even knowing that you're bound for Spain and marriage and duchesshood…duchessdom?… I was a little worried that my deciding to be a single mother could be uncomfortable for you. And I didn't want you to find out from anyone else, or in front of anyone else, which is why I shoved Gabriel out the door about half an hour ago. You can yell at me if you feel…you know, moved to yell at me."

"But you said Gabriel moved in."

"Well, yeah, temporarily. Because we're both hot for each other and too stupid to know how to have a relationship. I'm not ready for marriage, and neither is he, no matter if he's willing to sacrifice himself at the altar for the baby. He's got a bad marriage in his past, and I've got Mom and Dad. I'm pretty much in awe that any of us, let alone all you guys, want to get married. It's fine for you, I mean if you're happy with it, which I assume you are on account of saying yes… I'm just not, which isn't just about them. We're not navigating the obstacles very well."

Miranda nodded like she understood, and Penny didn't explain further. "But you want to be with him?"

"I don't know what I want." She looked at the sparkling tree, then back at Miranda. "No, that's not right. I know I don't want a husband to try and control me, stifle my freedom, grow to hate me, but stay together because of pride and obligation, any of that. But I want to be with him, at least when he's not being an idiot."

She took a moment from her breakdown to pour the hot cider into cups, then followed with the hot water, teabags and cinnamon sticks. Then placed one in front of her sister and went to join her on another stool. "How did you get there? Or were you always hoping to get married?"

"Not always." Miranda answered that first, and then stirred the tea with the cinnamon stick, watching the mug for a long moment. "It's okay, I'm sorry to know that you're struggling, wish I had some advice. We had some obstacles too, but I guess sometimes you have to decide it's worth letting go and just trying. Or that's what it was for us."

"Letting go of what?"

Miranda shrugged. "Fear? Protecting yourself?"

"Oh, is that all?" Penny lifted her mug and took a drink, chuckling over the warm liquid.

"What are you afraid of?"

"Losing myself." The words flew from Penny's mouth before she thought them through, then she shook her head. "That's not exactly it. I'm apparently riddled with issues, but the truth is that I'm willing to try, which is more than I ever thought I would be. It just doesn't seem like he really is willing to try. He has this strange yo-yo thing going on. Sometimes he is so sweet it just about kills me, and then, usually right after he's been amazing, he shoves me so far away that I end up in another room, in another city, on another planet."

Miranda took her hand, and Penny admired the stunning ring on her finger and stopped this pity party.

"Mateo picked a good ring."

It was easy to go with a subject change when there was nothing helpful to say, or when the subject turned to happier news. "It's gorgeous, isn't it?"

"I'd wear it. I mean, not to marry Matteo, obviously. I meant I'd wear it and I hardly ever wear jewelry. So you know I like it." Penny blathered out a bunch of stupid words, grunted at herself and took a sip of her tea. "When's the wedding? Do I need another dress fitting? Because if it's not soon, I'm going to be hard to fit. I know that I'm not going to have a big ole belly by Charles and Grace's wedding, that's right around the corner. The other day when we were doing the dress fitting, that was all that was going through my mind. Not that you don't deserve a big fairy-tale wedding. If anyone does, it's you. Flowers and titles, and all the love. And I'm babbling again."

Soon they were talking all things wedding, from the beautiful dresses Grace had chosen for them and her maid of honor, Dr. Helena Tate, to speculation about when their cousin Jude and Dr. Sarah Grayson were heading for the altar. Penny would admit feeling a little envious about Miranda's coming move to Spain. Maybe next year Penny could take her baby to Spain for Christmas, spend it there if Gabriel wasn't here.

She took another drink of the tea, mostly to mask how her throat had closed up and her eyes watered, and she found herself looking at the single present under her Christmas tree. The gift she'd picked up for Gabriel yesterday and slipped under the tree before he'd gotten home from work.

The kicker of their relationship, and the part of her parents' marriage Penny didn't want to think about, was knowing it was lopsided. She loved him, but he didn't love her, and she didn't know if that also mirrored her parents' relationship. She'd rather think that at this late hour in their union they hated one another equally. It'd be even worse if one of them was still in love, still suffering.

The gift she'd put under the tree was supposed to show Gabe she still planned on him being there when Christmas finally rolled around in a couple of weeks. Sure, she'd gotten a kiss for it—not on the head—and he'd then taken the opportunity to debate whether it was better to open presents on Christmas Eve or Christmas Day, but things were still tense. She couldn't tell if he'd picked up on the subtext of her only gift purchase so far.

His wife had left without warning, though, so maybe

she'd have left a gift for him just to maintain the fantasy of a happy marriage. Or maybe she'd been fooling herself and had then had just snapped one day and gone. All Penny had was Gabriel's words, and he'd been so hurt by it all, she couldn't really count on him having seen it clearly.

"Penny?"

"Sorry, I heard you. It's going to be a month of weddings with Charles's coming up, and you probably before the new year." She heard that much at least and, goodness, she had to pay better attention. She'd invited Miranda here to talk about *her* wedding and shining future, not Perilous Penny's. "Forgive me. I invited you over and I'm terrible company."

"It's okay. Do you want to call him?"

"No. He'll be back in…" Penny looked at the clock "…forty-five minutes, or about that. And considering how punctual he is, probably forty-four minutes."

"Should I be gone before he gets here?"

"Only if you want to flee. If you do, you have forty-three minutes to tell me how to fix this first, because you've obviously got your life together better than I do."

CHAPTER NINE

"GROUNDED," GABRIEL REPEATED, sitting on the bench in front of his locker to tug his boots off and change out of his flight suit, more for Penny than himself. Twice in one week Old Man Winter had invited himself to the city, and while it was possible to fly when the roads were slick, it was something else to fly when the snow fell this heavily.

Penny sat a couple feet down the bench from him, attention focused on her phone, but he knew she'd heard him by the pinching and vigorous pink shade of her lips, still angry that the decision had been made without her. "I'm looking at the radar, and there are gaps in the front. We will probably be able to take runs here and there, just not right now."

"Flying requires visibility." He cringed inwardly at himself. Even to his ears it sounded like he was talking down to her, because he was trying to soften the conflict, where he'd have just been direct before and let her be angry. So much for maintaining their working relationship.

"I know, I'm the pilot. When there are gaps in the cells, I'll be able to see for short runs."

He shook his head, but knew he wasn't going to be able to argue her out of hanging out and hoping. It was the same frustrating battle as sending her home when she was sick. "You're saying you're not going to go to the floor and help out?"

"Storms don't make people not need our services. We're Rescue, we're supposed to be focused on rescuing people whenever we can. They can't get treatment at a hospital if they can't get to a hospital. And the roads…"

"They're terrible, I know." He could agree with her on that part. Things were still tense between them, and every conversation felt like something that could knock them out of the air. "You really hate working on the floor that much?"

"I hate feeling confined. And I do when I'm down there. You might end up doing something exciting, but I usually end up babysitting." The word *babysitting* made her face squinch up, and she puffed. "I think it's time to stop using that word for that, it's increasingly looking like that will be my whole existence in a few months."

"What does that mean?"

"It means I'm not going to be able to do anything but take care of the baby. That sounds selfish, I know. It's not a worry for you because you're not on the verge of being shelved. I know I've had a rough start with the pregnancy, but I feel like other people are taking my choices left and right. Like you telling me to just go home now."

"It's just a better use of your time. Stay here if you want to." He could concentrate on his job better if she went home and didn't hang around the hospital seething because she couldn't do what she wanted or fretting about the people she couldn't help. One boot off, he rose to go peek at her phone and the radar she was currently refreshing. A continuous line of pale blue stretched from New York to West Virginia, and was blowing in such a way that they'd get every mile of that stripe of storms covering several states. "Look at that. You'll be less bored at home."

"There are pockets of flurries, especially here for the next three-ish hours. Then it'll get heavy and stay heavy, but there's people we can help before it gets too bad."

Penny felt her hackles rising again. She knew that Gabriel was being sensible, rational even, but she listened to her gut, and her gut said this wasn't how her day was going to go. "Haven't you ever just felt like something was going to happen, and you want to be there for it?"

"Are you saying you have some kind of inkling you're going to go out there?" he asked, his eyes narrowing a touch, just enough for her to know he wasn't getting it.

What could she say? If she said yes, he'd have a fit and try to force her to go home. "I'm saying I feel like I have something to do today here, not at home. Maybe it's just being with Dispatch in case they need another hand. I don't know, but I'm not going home yet. Even if Dispatch doesn't need help, I can perform some maintenance on the chopper and make sure it's stocked better. I've noticed the supplies haven't been kept up as much as I like while I was gone."

"I'm not going to win this one, am I?"

"I'm pretty sure you have won. You and Charles conspired to entirely shut down flights for the day and I got no input in that. You grounded us. That means you did win. You just aren't winning the ordering Penny home conversation too." Penny tried to soften it with a smile, but she wasn't feeling very smiley.

He shook his head and crammed his boot back on, no longer changing out of his flight suit. "Call me if you get a window and permission to fly."

Fifteen minutes later, Penny was in the chopper with her tumbler of hot apple tea, powering everything up. She stuck her phone into the mount on the dash so she could keep the radar up and running, and the band radio set to listen, then went back to the rear to start her inventory.

She half listened to the radio chatter, just enough to hear her name or their unit number, and to make out the different kinds of calls going out. Bad fall at a museum. The place had slippery steps, and an injured patron.

All their arguments seemed to shadow the marriage argument, even when they had nothing to do with it.

He and Charles agreed there would be no flying, so she was grounded. He hadn't orchestrated it, but she was pregnant, which was kind of like being grounded when it came to doing things she wanted to do. And those were the two unchangeable positions that put her at a starting disadvantage.

"Cardiac arrest at Fifty-Ninth."

He wanted her to go home, and he wanted her to marry him. She'd said no going home, and that she'd work on something else, and she'd also said no to marriage, but she'd work on a relationship.

And they were both unsettled and unhappy.

"ETA Unit 377?"

"ETA Unit 410?"

Maybe she should just marry him. Maybe having that stability would calm him down, nothing else she'd done seemed to. At least he'd sleep in the same bed with her, she could reasonably demand he hug her or comfort her whenever she wanted. But that was part of the problem—she wanted to be fine on her own, without needing that comfort from him. And he seemed to feel more comfortable himself when he was doing something tangible for her.

"ETA Unit 219?"

If she didn't marry him, she might end up having this baby alone. Sure, he'd still be around to be a father, he'd made that completely clear, but she could end up forced to give birth on her own because having Mom there would stress her out, and Miranda was going to be in Spain by then.

She stopped counting and shuffling inventory to look at the radio in the front, and listened to units calling in left and right about the delays, the traffic, and one who was just stuck.

"We're sending a wrecker, 410."

Penny stashed what she'd counted out into her go-bag, and went to check her radar again.

"Any units available? Fire and ambulance needed."

The snow was falling lighter than it had been. Granted, the air had that strange, bluish, foggy quality over the city because of the falling snow, but she could see through it. She could see the roof of the building at the end of the block, which wasn't wonderful but it was something.

"What do you have, Dispatch?"

"Davenport?"

"Yes. Is everyone stranded?"

"It's a mess out there. We've got all units out and are trying to get NYPD to take this call."

"What's going on?"

"Woman in labor, trapped in an elevator."

Her stomach bottomed out and she grabbed the phone to look at the radar. There was a hole. She might not be able to make it *back* to the hospital with the woman, but she could get there. Be there, provide support, and wait for the next ground crew to arrive and take over.

When she'd been so sick, Gabriel showing up and making things better had been like a miracle to her when she had only been vomiting like crazy, not trying to give birth, alone, in a busted elevator.

"What's the address? Is it close enough to go on foot?"

She couldn't just leave her there.

There was a pause, then the answer, and confirmation that she couldn't get there by foot in the snow in less than an hour, even at a run.

She looked at the radar again. Oh, Gabriel would be angry. Charles would be angry. Everyone would be angry, except for the woman and her family. At the least the woman wouldn't be alone, like *she* might still end up.

She could make it there, she knew she could. And then she'd just have to leave the chopper until the storm passed, and come back with the ground crew.

Three switches got the chopper started. She waited until she'd lifted off to call in and let them know she was going.

"Dr. Jackson?" Gabriel turned at the sound of his name from the doorway to see Dr. Miranda Davenport standing there.

"Yes?"

"I'm sorry to interrupt, Dispatch needs you. It's Penny…"

He frowned over his shoulder at Miranda, instantly on alert. Penny wanted to go up. "I'll be right there. We were just finishing up."

It just took a minute to explain the testing he'd ordered to his patient and excuse himself to call upstairs, and about fifteen seconds for his blood pressure shoot into the stratosphere.

Penny had gone out without him. She'd gone out in the storm.

Miranda was at his heels so that when he turned, ready to hit the stairs and get to Dispatch, he nearly ran her over.

"She went out in the snow?"

A nod was all he had time for.

Ninety seconds later he stood in the Dispatch office,

radio open after having called her as calmly as he could, far calmer than his pounding heart wanted.

"I need to do this. I'm almost there," she called back through the radio. "She needs help, Gabe."

Children were always one of Penny's triggers. She'd do anything to get to a child in distress. He'd seen her cow a vicious dog that had stood between them and a child once. Logically, he knew this about her, and she'd been that way as long as he'd known her, long before she'd had her maternal instincts kick into overdrive.

"Ground crews are going to help her. Come back."

"They're at least twenty minutes behind me, and I'm closer to the building than I am to Mercy now. Stop distracting me. I'm flying in snow, I need to concentrate."

She switched off and it felt so final that a swell of premature grief robbed him of words. Swamped with helplessness, rage took control and sent the radio flying into the cinderblock walls of the Dispatch room. It struck hard, then crashed to the floor to clatter across the polished tile, but did little for his state of mind. It was less satisfying to smash unsmashable things against a wall—their radios were built to survive being dropped several stories.

And she was speaking the truth. Distracting her would put her into more danger. All he could do right now was wait.

She'd all but declared earlier that she was going to go out on her own, her gut having told her she was needed today somewhere. Heaven help him, he could barely reason with her under the best circumstances, she listened to her emotions first, reason second. His stomach lurched and he went to pick up the radio to make sure it was on, that he could hear if she called for help.

While waiting, he peppered the staff manning the radio with questions about where the call had come from, then mapped the address. Five minutes of flight, six tops. He looked at the clock. They'd called him as soon as she'd called saying she'd taken off, and he'd run from Emergency to the top of the tower after finishing with his patient, which had taken about three minutes total. Add another minute on the radio with her.

He'd give her two minutes to call in before he lost his mind.

Unable to hold still, he paced the small room until asked to sit. People were there. People had seen him throwing the radio. Would hear everything.

And he didn't give a damn anymore.

Heartbeats thundered in his ears, so loud he wasn't sure he'd hear the radio if she called. It was more that and the fact that he might be having a heart attack that made him sit.

This felt just the same. It wasn't the same, but it felt it. When Nila had gone, he hadn't been able to say anything to change her mind then either. But this was worse. If this was the last time he saw Penny, it wouldn't be by choice. It wouldn't be because she'd remarried and had children with another man, the family she hadn't wanted with him only two years earlier.

He could lose the baby if she crashed. He could lose *her*.

Seconds after he sat, the radio beeped and he heard her.

"I'm down."

He felt eyes on him, but closed his eyes to block them out. Help her. She'd need help.

She was down now, she was safe. Ground crew would come soon.

"What equipment are you taking?" he asked, and waited, willing his voice to be steady and calm.

"Extra blankets. IV, saline. First-aid basics. Rope."

She sounded confident, more than him at least.

"Rope?"

Dammit, he'd forgotten the elevator. "Listen to me, Penny. Do not rappel more than two floors. The shorter the better. If she's between two floors, go to the one directly above it. As close as you can get."

Problem was, he didn't know if the elevator doors on every floor could be forced open. He didn't know why this elevator was stuck. He didn't know anything.

"I'll call building security and tell them to meet you and help. Take a scalpel and clamps. You'll need them."

"Scalpel?" The first hint of hesitation. She didn't treat so much as triage usually.

"It might become necessary. You want to be prepared."

"Yes. Right. Scalpel."

She confirmed with a number from the small selection they had on the chopper.

"Have you delivered a baby before?"

"No…"

He rubbed between his eyes, trying to stop the tension headache he felt coming. "Have you been at a birth before?"

"Yes. I had some training, but I might need a refresher."

Chopper paramedics were usually involved with accidents, not births. If there was trouble, she'd be in over her head.

"What about oxygen?" she asked, breaking into his thoughts. "Should I take the small tank and masks?"

"Yes. And call me the minute you get into the elevator. I'll talk you through it."

As soon as he stopped talking, he remembered another thing and shouted into the radio. "Stethoscope! Take a stethoscope…"

"Dr. Jackson, do you need some help?" one of the dispatchers asked, and he thought a moment and nodded.

"I need an ETA on the crews heading for the building. How are they doing?"

Having them there helped, he'd get as organized as he could. Pulling out his cellphone, he had the other dispatcher read him the number for building security and called to do what he'd promised, but messed up the number three times because of shaking hands.

If he believed in Christmas miracles, he could use one right now. Smooth, easy delivery. Healthy mom and baby. Crew arriving before the action started. That would be the best, if they got into the elevator or got it moving with plenty of time to get them all to the hospital before she had to push or lose it.

Juggling his cell and radio was all he could do, and pray, and the last might be a bad idea until he could control his emotions or he'd just end up screaming at God.

Penny stuffed two large bags with supplies, slung them both ways across her torso, threw the coil of rope over one shoulder, shoved the radio into her pocket, and grabbed the backboard.

She should've asked Gabriel to have them meet her on the roof to haul equipment, she'd be exhausted before she got into the shaft at this rate.

No. Now was not the time for defeatist thinking. She could do this. She'd flown in the snow, landed successfully. And she'd help that woman and baby. Every ounce of her exhaustion tonight would be righteous and hardwon. She'd picked rescue as a career for just this kind of reason.

As needy as she'd been when she'd been vomiting everywhere, Gabriel's arrival couldn't have been more heaven sent if the actual Angel Gabriel had popped into her apartment in her time of need. And she hadn't even been trying to push a baby out of her body in a freaking elevator shaft at the time.

She scooted through the roof access door and inside. A moment to stomp the snow from her boots, and she hit the stairs, bracing the backboard on her head and balancing with one hand so she could get the radio.

"Gabe."

"Are you there?"

"No. What floor? Did Security tell you what floor?"

"Twenty-five." His voice came through the radio, stilted, and measured. She could hear the effort it took him to speak evenly, and it curdled her stomach. "She's just below it."

"Okay." She knew it was a thirty-story building, relatively small by new building standards. Lucky she was close to the top if they had to carry her out. Lucky for *her*, too. Gabriel was too good a doctor and too good a man to leave her hanging on this, even when she could hear his frustration.

She switched off, stashed the radio again, and picked up the pace. Her weeks of stair-marathon conditioning helped and, even heavily laden, she made it there quickly. The elevator was just across from the stairs, and the security officer stood there, working on the doors as she stepped off.

"Do you need help?"

He looked back at her and nodded. "I've never done this before. I think I use this and put it here and turn, and that's supposed to unlock something, and then maybe we shove?"

He was as experienced with elevators as she was with birth.

"I've never done it before but, here, I'll take the crowbar and wedge it in, and as soon as you say, I'll pull it." She ditched her supplies on the floor and braced one foot against the side of the elevator entrance. As soon as he turned something she could only consider a lock and key mechanism, she pulled hard.

The doors popped and he got his hands in there to shove them open. Once it was done, she set the bar on the floor and bent over the edge to peer into the shaft. Maybe ten feet to the top of the box. She could probably dangle over the edge and just drop onto it, but even knowing there were locks to keep elevators from plummeting to the ground, she didn't want to just suddenly drop all her weight, along with the weight of her equipment, onto the elevator and tempt fate.

"Andrea?" She called the name that Dispatch had given her into the shaft, and when she heard a response, she introduced herself. "My name is Penny and I'm a paramedic from Manhattan Mercy air ambulance. There are still ground crews coming, but the roads are terrible. So I'm just going to come on down to you, okay?"

"Please hurry. I think my water broke."

The guard winced, but Penny managed to keep her face placid even if her guts were wincing in tandem with his face. She grabbed the rope and found a nearby pillar to secure it.

"Have you been on the phone with Dr. Jackson?" she asked the guard.

"Yes. I'm supposed to call when we get you in."

Of course he was. Gabriel would be doing all he could to help from his end, even if she was certain there'd be another showdown as soon as they got home later. She'd have rather had him with her, but there hadn't been time. The window would've passed before she could've gotten him to come up from Emergency, and he probably wouldn't have come anyway.

She slung her heavy bag around her again, the one with the oxygen and IV paraphernalia, and took the rope, saying to the guard before she stepped over the edge, "When I get down, I want you to toss me the second bag and hand me the board."

He nodded, and he looked so pale she'd have thought he was the father, but dutifully input numbers into his phone and got ready to hit Send.

It was only about ten feet down, but the rope made her feel more secure, even if she only had to rappel about seven feet before she put her foot down on the top of the elevator.

Which bounced when she stepped onto it.

"Penny?"

"It's okay, that's just me. I'll be right there. If you're feeling like you have to push, try not to… I don't know where you are yet."

And all she remembered from her training involved full dilation being needed before the pushing…but the urge to push often came earlier.

The guard lay on the floor above and stretched the board down, then, when it was still braced against the side of the shaft, dropped the softer bag of first-aid supplies onto it so it slid toward her. Then called down instructions on how to open the top hatch.

She threw the end of the rope through with her heavier bag tied to the end, then dropped in the light bag, and then realized she didn't know how to get the board through.

Dangit.

Planned badly… Assuming she was still a team, that she could slide in and have someone, Gabriel, hand it to her. She grabbed it, turned it diagonally so it would fit through, and then began to lower herself to her knees, and further, and further, until she was lying on her belly, hanging through the top, finally getting it to touch down so she could lever it to the side in a way that wouldn't hit her patient.

Her patient, who was lying on the floor, red faced and breathing heavily. Immediately, she got worried. The elevator still had lights, which was a blessing, but it meant she got to see how terrified Andrea looked, and the amount of pain she was in.

"Tell me how you're doing, Andrea. Have you been timing your contractions? What are you feeling?"

While waiting, she pulled back out of the elevator and climbed in feet first instead of head first.

"Pain," came the woman's one-word answer, and when Penny looked at her, she had rolled onto her side and was obviously trying to breathe through another contraction.

"Everything's going to be okay. You have me, and we have the complete focus of a doctor at the hospital." Which was when she rang Gabriel for help, confirming with the puddle on the floor that the water had gone. "Dr. Jackson, I'm in. She's…mid-contraction, and her water has broken."

Kneeling down, she pressed her fingertips to Andrea's neck and counted, then reported the elevated pulse.

He began asking questions, and as the intermediary she relayed answers and performed different checks. Getting the backboard down, she spread a blanket on it and then helped Andrea onto it, where she'd be a tiny bit more comfortable, but mostly because it would be easier for transport after help came. She rolled another blanket for a pillow before getting gloves on and following Gabriel's instructions to check dilation.

Confirmed: total.

Did she need oxygen?

Wouldn't hurt.

These were things she'd have done, but it was less scary to have someone else backing her on this one. Not because she didn't know the basics, but because his instructions were like a safety net, not for her but for Andrea and mini-Andrea, whenever it came out.

"I'm calling you and putting it on speaker. Get off the phone with anyone else. I can't keep pushing the button on this to talk if I'm gloved for sterility."

"Dialing you now."

She heard her phone ringing, got it out of her pocket, put it on speaker and set it to the side before tossing the radio onto the floor.

With his help, in between calls from the security guard above, they proceeded to deliver that baby.

Every single milestone felt like it was projected on a big screen in front of her and running in slow motion.

Crowning.

Someone called from above, a new voice. A new crew. They were going to try to open the door on floor twenty-four, it might be down enough to crawl through…

The baby spiraled further out, until there was a head visible.

Then there were shoulders, and Penny helped…

Then she was the first person to ever hold that baby.

"Lay the baby on the mother's stomach." Gabriel's voice came through the speaker.

The baby wasn't moving, wasn't crying. Every atom in her body seemed to seize, and it was all she could do to keep from screaming. Not breathing.

"I… Gabe…he's…uh…"

She heard a sound she knew was from the guard getting into the shaft above, someone was opening the doors to the floor below, and it sounded close.

"He'll breathe if you lay him there and get him warm. He's got a few minutes to start breathing on his own. There's oxygen still coming through the cord. It's okay. Get him warm."

She laid the baby on his mother's belly and began rubbing his back with another of her blankets, holding her breath until he started to squirm, and finally let loose a scream that made both her and Andrea start to cry.

"He sounds good." Gabriel's voice had gentled, and just hearing him made her heart soar. He'd be there when their baby was born, he'd be there, and he'd talk just like that, and he'd make this not scary, because it *was* scary. It was scary and not even the kind of scary thing she had always felt compelled to face down.

"He's beautiful," she confirmed, her voice croaking the words out as she wrapped the wonderfully screaming baby in a fresh, dry blanket.

Gabriel talked her through clamping the cord off, cutting it, and she finished by covering Andrea in the final blanket.

The elevator doors opened with about two feet of clearance onto the twenty-fourth floor.

"How are you guys doing in there?" a man's voice called through, and when she looked over, she could see his head.

"We're perfect. So is—"

"Bowie." Andrea filled in the baby's name and Penny smiled.

"She's on the board. Baby Bowie is wrapped up and ready too. If you two can take the bottom of the board and lower her down, I can strap them in and push her through the opening."

The paramedics and firemen—she now saw—on the other side of the elevator all agreed and she began readying her patients for transport.

Which was when she saw the blood.

"Andrea?" She said the woman's name, and noticed the distinct fuzzy quality to her eyes when she opened them at hearing her name.

"Uh, she's bleeding. Gabe? She's bleeding."

"She'll be bleeding…"

"No. She's *bleeding*. There's a lot of blood."

She heard him swear and then picked up Bowie to hand him through the opening to one of the crew, then went back to her patient.

"She needs to get here, honey. I don't want… I don't know if she has… The ground…"

Time. She knew that sound in his voice. He was trying to tell her that Andrea needed to get to the hospital fast. She needed to fly, and he couldn't bring himself to say it.

"Would a line and saline help?"

"Yes."

"On it." Glad she'd passed the baby to the other crew, she dug into her bag and came out with tourniquet, a number twenty catheter, line, saline, a flush, and felt for a vein.

She didn't need to be talked through that. And inside a minute she had a line in, flushed, and hung the saline from her shoulder so she could shove the board toward the opening and they could get her out of the elevator.

A paramedic she recognized helped her out as well, and she transferred the saline to his shoulder as she would've Gabriel.

"Saline buys a few minutes, but we need to get her to the hospital. How do you two feel about flying?"

Neither of them hesitated, just picked up the board. She took Bowie, held him close, left all her junk in the elevator, and gestured to a second elevator beside the malfunctioning one. "That one working?"

"Yes."

The button was pressed, and she went ahead, just like always, hitting the stairs, this time with Bowie in her arms, to get to the chopper and get it ready to take off while they got the patient to the roof.

Once there, she got the chopper started, rotors spinning, and watched from inside where she could keep the baby protected from the cold and wind. If they came out with their gurney, she'd have to dump theirs on the roof.

When they came out, they were still carrying the board, which left her free to settle in. She laid Bowie in the co-pilot's seat, opened the side door, then went to her seat. In a flash, she got the headset on, buckled in, and picked the baby up again while they loaded Andrea. It was when they opened the door again that she fully realized how strong the wind had grown.

Only when the doors were closed did she hand Bowie back to one of them, and skipped the radar. The snow, no longer falling as lightly as it had been when she'd made the flight out, swirled around them. It wasn't as heavy as it could be, but no way would she normally fly in these conditions. Truly, the wind was worse than the snow. She knew the skyline so well she could practically fly it blindfolded, but the wind added a wildcard she didn't want to consider. There was nothing she could do about the wind, and not going would mean Andrea died.

She took a breath and lifted off, calling through the headset to Gabriel that they were airborne, and updates as the paramedics relayed them to her. He'd need two teams on the roof, one for Bowie and the other for Bowie's mother.

It wasn't that far.

She'd be able to see the lights, and she knew the way well enough to fill in any gray areas.

They'd be okay. She wouldn't panic and they'd all be okay. Gabriel would help them once she got them there. They'd be okay...

CHAPTER TEN

LONGER EVEN THAN the three minutes he'd waited to hear from her crawled the five that passed after she lifted off.

He'd assembled two teams in that time and herded them all up to the roof. Obstetrician and team, emergency surgical suite on standby. Neonatologist with team and incubator. He saw the wind blowing in the hair flying from the team members, but he didn't hear it. He felt his own clothing ripple and slap at his body, but it felt like watching the drawn-out roil of the canvas on a sailboat. But the air around him sounded dead.

Falling snow muted the air and the sound of beating blades he waited for, hanging his sanity on. His head fell forward and he took a deep breath, clinging to hope like a tangible thing, fists balled and gripping nothing.

Too much snow. It blew hard enough to sting his cheeks, and he immediately flashed to the storm they'd outrun to Schenectady, where she'd had to fight the wind at times, and flown with it at others. But that had been more or less open terrain, not between buildings. If she'd needed to bank to the left or right to work with the wind, she'd had room. She shouldn't be flying in this, not in the city.

"There they are," someone said, and he didn't even

know who, just looked at the sky to see the lights of the chopper through the gray gloom.

As she started to descend, a powerful wind gust came from the southwest, blasting the chopper off target toward the building.

His heart stopped dead.

"Are they gonna…?" Someone else said the words he couldn't even bear to think, and all he could do was force frigid air in and out. He closed his eyes.

If she hit the building, he couldn't see it. He couldn't see her die.

The snow deadened the air so much he couldn't even hear the blades beating. It took several painful heartbeats to realize he hadn't heard a crash either, and hadn't heard screams from anyone on the teams he'd assembled.

He opened eyes again, noting that she'd pulled the chopper up and now flew above the buildings, circling again.

He didn't have his radio. He hadn't brought it, not that he could distract her, but as much as he struggled to force himself to watch, he needed to hear her voice. Just to know how she was. Was she freaking out like he was? Was she asking for help?

Out of the corner of his eye he saw the neonatologist's nurse cross herself and bow her head, and he was thankful that someone had the peace of mind to pray.

The chopper began to sink again, but at a much faster speed. He watched, horror again shooting up as quickly as the chopper fell. It looked like she intended on slamming the thing into the roof, but now the sight held him gripped and nothing could make him close his eyes.

Close, closer…

Every muscle in his body strained, his lungs growing so tight he could barely breathe, everything else so tight he shook.

She pulled up just in time to soften the landing, and touched down, with only the smallest bounce at the end. He had to clamp his mouth shut to keep a sob of relief from escaping.

The other doctors took the lead, charging out with the incubator and to fetch the woman on the chopper's gurney. He did the only thing he could. He raced with them to help if needed, but his assistance mainly consisted of helping with a tricky latch that locked the stretcher in place, and once they were out, the lot raced back for the building.

Penny was still shutting down. The motor went quiet and he climbed into the chopper and closed the door behind him.

Alive. She was alive, and all right, and when she looked at him, he took in bright, shining eyes and glowing cheeks. The relief he'd briefly experienced fell to his feet. That was excitement, exhilaration, she hadn't been afraid. He had been afraid. He had been petrified—his insides still shook. But she looked rock solid.

When she stepped out of her seat and walked back to him, even as his hands curled over her shoulders, he didn't know whether he was going to shake her, strangle her, or just grab tight.

As soon as he touched her, the need to be closer took over and he pulled her with him to fall into the rear seat. His hands found her face, and he kissed her, every aching inch of his heart needing to feel her life, to taste her sweetness, to blot out the past agonizing hours.

Outside, the wind hit them again and rattled the chopper, chilling the already cold vehicle further, but it wasn't going anywhere now. He angled his head and slid his tongue into her mouth, every second touching her, breathing her in, like a balm, reassurance against what the fear still seeping through him still vibrated with: she was going to die.

"Hey." Something made her pull back, and her own small hands on his face made him open his eyes and look at her. "You're shaking. We can go inside. Are you cold? Are you okay?"

The denseness of the question pulled him out of that need to get closer, like the wind rattling the doors, jarring and cold.

"You damned near died." The words croaked out. But saying them once gave him strength, gave him back the anger that had first seized him. The second time, he shouted it. *"You damned near died!"*

Even shouting, it wasn't enough.

During the hours apart he'd learned what was worse than Nila leaving.

"But I didn't. I'm okay. See? I'm okay." She stroked his face, like she could pet his worry away. The brightness in her eyes dulled a bit, the color faded, like she was just starting to see how horrible the past few hours had been for him.

"You could've died. You had to know how dangerous it was to go. You know better than that. How could you do that?" He pulled her hands from his face, needing her to focus on his words, not soothing him. "How could you put yourself in that much danger?"

The words had no sooner left his mouth than he knew the answer. It didn't matter what she said, this was just how she was. This was what Penny's life was, rolling the dice and always expecting a seven.

She did foolish things, mostly because she wanted to make things better for others, he knew that, had always known that. Even understanding that didn't give him any way to deal with it. All he could do was deal with what was before him right now, and that was a woman who, although he might love her, lived on the edge of disaster.

He put her away from him and climbed out of the chopper, unable to summon any other words. She sat dazed, and he could see her mentally scrambling for the right thing to say, but there was nothing to say.

Penny watched Gabriel climb out of the chopper, senses reeling. The exhilaration of saving a life—of actually knowing this time that she was the one who'd beaten the storm and saved lives, not just luck, faded. She was messing this up with Gabriel. She was messing *them* up.

"I did it because she needed help. If I hadn't gone, she'd have had that baby alone, and probably would have died. They couldn't have ever gotten her back here fast enough."

"Her life is not more valuable than yours. And that baby, that precious baby you helped deliver, is not more precious than our baby."

The wind had rocked her earlier, but Gabriel's words took the wind out of her. And when he slammed the door on the chopper and stalked for the hospital, her chest felt almost caved in from her lack of sufficient breath.

This wasn't going the way she'd pictured. Of course, she'd known he'd be angry, but after she'd—after they'd saved the mother and child, she'd thought he'd calm down. See the earlier small, and admittedly bigger later risk as justified. But when he said it that way…

She scrambled from the back of the chopper to chase him inside. He was getting onto the elevator as she reached him, and she twisted sideways to slip between the doors.

"Wait, please. I'm sorry. It was okay when I went. It was that second line. Snow isn't usually so blustery." She reached for him and he pulled back, shaking his head.

"Don't. I can't do this. I cannot do this again. I can't spend the rest of my life wondering what's the next dangerous, stupid thing you'll do." He swallowed and shook his head. "We can't do this. This isn't going to work."

But he'd kissed her. He'd kissed her the way you kissed someone you loved, or at least felt very deeply for.

"Are you saying you're moving out? You're leaving me?"

"We've never been together. Not really. It was a trial run. Better we learn this early," he said, and the elevator started to go down, and brought a sensation of plummeting in her middle. "I'll move out tonight."

What could she say? There had to be something to say, something that would make it okay for him. "I couldn't let her go through that alone…"

"I told you to go home. I told you to go, you'd have never known."

"You did, but you can't just order me around. If that's your idea of marriage, of a relationship, *that's* why she left."

He flinched, the doors opened, and he walked away again. She didn't even know what floor it was, or where he was aiming. Someone else got on, and she stuck in the corner, unable to bring herself to chase him again.

Go home. Fall apart there. She reached out to press the button for the first floor, but her phone chirruped and she almost lost her mind, fumbling for it, hoping it was him. She wrenched it from her pocket in a heartbeat and looked at the screen.

Text from Charles Davenport. Not Gabriel.

My office.

The new passenger had already pressed the right button, so she slunk back to the corner of the elevator to wait. Like Charles could say anything worse to her than Gabriel had said. If words were teeth, they'd be chewing through her belly, down low where she found her palm pressed and shielding. In that second, she didn't know what to feel worse about.

All the adrenaline she'd been running on was gone, and when the elevator stopped, she had to drag herself out of the back corner and down the hallway to her eldest brother's office. Only he wouldn't be wearing that hat right now, he would be Dr. Charles Davenport, chief of the ER. And she was the pilot who'd violated direct orders.

Charles's secretary waved her through, but the rueful pinch of her mouth said enough. He'd be in a lather, even if it was a Charles special lather, where he'd be too civilized to shove her out of the window even if he really wanted to.

She opened the door to his office and didn't smile, didn't do much of anything except peel her hand away from her womb. She didn't have much emotional currency left to play, but Charles did. He sat behind his desk, hands pressed flat to the desktop, fingers spread out, face red.

Diffusing this situation seemed less important than the situation with Gabriel, so she just held up one hand to signal to him to wait and sat opposite him. Took a breath. Took another. It didn't really help, it gave her oxygen but not words.

As soon as she signaled her readiness, he let loose a stream, echoing the words already seared into her by Gabriel.

Risks. Death. Bad, bad Penny. But it was kind of a blur, right up until the end.

"I asked, do you know what you're doing to the people who love you when you do these things? This isn't new skydiver on a sunny day with a back-up parachute kind of worry, this is watching your sister torment a cobra worry. Do you care that you put your family and friends through that?"

"Yes," she said on reflex, the question so shocked her. Did it really seem like she didn't care about anyone? No other words came. Who knew Charles would be better than Mom with the guilt trip?

Guilt amplified when she remembered the next time she'd see her family. In a few days. At Charles's wedding. These were the last days of work before he married, and things would be stressful enough for him without having to deal with this.

He hadn't even been there to watch her land, or see the wind trying to smash them into the building, but the rant that continued was sharp enough that she'd never have guessed it. It was the end, when he threatened to make funeral arrangements so they'd be prepared, that she just gave up listening and slumped forward in her chair, supporting her head with her palms, elbows on knees.

The day officially crossed over into the territory of Too Much.

"When you have children, maybe you'll understand. Maybe you'll think of family first."

Gabriel's sentiment again, but more pointed. Her direct failure. Her eyes began to well and she could only nod.

He said something about a week-long suspension, and that she'd be fired the next time she violated a no-fly order, like any of that mattered.

Another nod. Her head could move but her mouth could not.

She had to go to Gabriel, that was all she knew, and she stood. She was almost to the door before she realized she probably should ask if he was done. "Am I dismissed?"

He nodded. "Be careful on your way home. The roads are treacherous."

Another nod. She opened the door.

"Pen, I know you went above and beyond for that woman and her baby. I'm proud you have the heart to do things like that. We all need you to be more rational about it."

"I know," she whispered, then, with the tears brimming, she smiled at her brother before leaving. "Thank you."

CHAPTER ELEVEN

PENNY RUSHED THROUGH the door to her apartment and the
only lights in the darkened space came from Gabriel's
room in the open loft above.

The Christmas lights he'd strung sat dark, no twinkling, and she found herself shaking as she sprinted
for the stairs.

After having searched the hospital and called him
twice with no answer, Penny had hoped she'd come up
with the words to make him stay, but she hadn't. The best
she could do was try to explain again, explain better, explain more. Beg.

Up the stairs, she stopped in the doorway of his room
and watched him mechanically moving clothing from the
bureau to an open duffle bag on the bed.

A greeting would be too flippant.

Running to him to throw her arms around him and beg
him to stay would be too much.

"I know I shouldn't have gone," she said, alerting him
to her presence. He looked at her, but his eyes were tired.
He didn't look like a man hoping to be convinced to stay,
but this felt like the most important test of her bravery
since she'd taken those first steps after years in a wheelchair.

"I didn't think about our baby," she said, confirming what both Gabriel and Charles had basically said. "I thought about Andrea and how terrified she must've been. How grateful I was to have you here when I was just throwing up. I thought about how hard I would've been praying for you to drop through the ceiling and make everything okay…if that had been me."

He stuffed shirts into his bag and sat, sighing, his voice soft, even gentle compared to his earlier yelling. "I know all this."

"I still needed to say it. And I have to say this too…" But she needed a breath before she fainted from how fast her heart was pounding. "I love you. I'm… I'm in love with you. So hard I can't… I can't be in a parental partnership either. And I can't have a marriage like my parents', all public face and nothing but bitterness and anger inside. No kind of non-relationship with you is going to work for me. If you don't love me, if you don't think you can be with me and make compromises—both of us—to make this life together work, then you're right to leave."

His dark beautiful eyes left her and fixed on the bureau he'd been working from, no words coming. As the seconds ticked and ticked on, she realized no words were going to come.

It wasn't enough.

"My whole life, my thinking was always, 'Can you do this?'" Her voice went wobbly and she felt burning in her eyes again, but she wouldn't get said what she needed to say if she broke down now. A slow breath was all she allowed herself. "For so long the answer was always no. When the answer finally started becoming yes, I just always did it. Whatever I wondered if I could do, if I could, I did. Tonight there was a lull in the snow, and I confirmed it on radar. Then I asked myself, 'Can you make it there?' I knew I could, and it felt like I should help her if I could. I intended to stay there, not fly back. Leave the chopper, ride in the ambulance and return for it once the storm passed. Then she was bleeding and going by ground would've been a death sentence for her. I admit it, I didn't even look at the radar then. I should've, but I didn't because I didn't want to have to make that call for her. I just took the risk. I can't explain it better than that."

She stepped into the room then, pushing every tattered scrap of courage she had left after the day, and rounded the bed to wrap her arms around his bowed head, and curled her head down to rest her cheek on his hair. This might be the last time she ever got to do it, to touch him close. He didn't push her away as he had, but he didn't reach for her either. He didn't put his arms around her to express his own grief at what felt like something dying.

He didn't move, and said nothing…though she wanted to hear his voice so badly she almost begged him to say something. He wanted her gone, that was all she could surmise.

She kissed his head, lovingly, slowly, breathing him in as much as she could, then let go and reached for the duffle he'd just finished filling, zipped it up, and picked it up. "I'll take this downstairs for you."

"Thank you," he said, and it was something. She'd take anything. She'd even have been grateful for yelling, for more words that would ruin her.

At the door, she stopped and looked back at him. One more time. One more attempt. "I felt like half a person back then. Then I got to be whole, and I…guess I got stuck in that new wholeness where I feel free when I'm not tied to the ground. But I'm not just a whole person now, I'm two. I haven't worked out how to do that yet. I've been focused on getting through the pregnancy and the possible health ramifications of my disease. It's a lot to get my head around but I'm trying."

Tears spilled then, and she knew it was going to turn ugly if she didn't get out of there.

"You should wait until the morning to leave. It's awful out there, especially if you're carrying suitcases. In the morning the roads will be better, you'll be able to trust cabbies and not have to lug this all on the subway."

He stood up and for a second she thought maybe he was coming to her, but he bent and pulled a suitcase from under the bed.

Right.

"I'm going to bed. You won't see me. I'll stay out of the way," she said.

She might not be as sensible as everyone wanted, but she was sensible enough to not stay there and wait for an answer. She hitched the bag higher and immediately carried it downstairs, leaving him to pack and leave, or pack and loiter until morning.

Downstairs, she eyed the bookcase and the albums she'd hidden from him. Words hadn't worked. Maybe pictures. Maybe if he knew what she was struggling against. For all she'd been trying to be open and honest, she'd still kept that part of herself hidden from him, protected this vulnerable spot.

She felt sick, but while he packed, she slipped albums into his duffle, then covered them all up with clothes and zipped it up to put by the sofa.

If he was going to reject her forever, it would be for the whole her, not just the parts she'd let him see.

After Penny's living space, which had been bright and colorful even before he'd strung thousands of twinkling lights, his apartment couldn't compare. It had never felt flat and cold before, but now the neutral colors irritated him. Looked lifeless. Like he couldn't pick a color if he had to. It was supposed to be tasteful, but it was just bland.

He dropped his bags on his brown sofa and sat, using the duffle like an armrest.

He'd stayed until first light, and leaving still didn't feel right. Even after an afternoon in hell, which had hurt even more than when Nila had left. Being the one to leave didn't feel any better.

She'd said love, and he knew it was true just as sharply as he knew it wouldn't work. But he still hated knowing what she was going through too. He'd stayed until morning to keep from giving her worry in return, sitting among the Christmas decorations he'd put up, in a place that now felt more like home to him than his own home.

Over the past two weeks she'd kept hammering about how he didn't trust her, and there couldn't be any question now about whether or not he could trust her to stick around. She might love him, but there would never be stability with her.

He scrubbed his hands over his face and forced himself to get up. Sitting here feeling sorry for himself wouldn't make anything better. He should put up some decorations, try to make his apartment feel like home again. Unpack. Get in some groceries…

Not sit on the couch and mope.

He grabbed the bags and hauled them to his bedroom. Do the things that needed to be done. Keep moving. Don't think about the way she'd kissed his head, hugged it, and he hadn't even put his hands on her in return.

Don't think about how it felt like abandonment and rejection to leave her like that.

He unzipped the duffle and dug his hands into the top

layer of shirts, but his knuckles struck something hard. Had he put shoes in there?

Lifting the clothes away, the bottom fell out of his guts. Photo albums sat in his clothes. The albums she'd taken away. Not just taken, the ones she'd hidden behind the others.

His first instinct was to step back from them, ignore them, even put the shirts back and cover them up. A smart man would send them back to her and be done with it.

Hands shaking, he pulled them from the bag. A slip of paper fluttered to the floor.

If this is it, if you're going, I want you to understand. You seeing these still scares me. I'm still working this out. But this fear feels like one of the things that scare me and I should still run toward it.

Strong, hastily scribbled words, devoid of the usual hallmarks of her notes. No smiley faces anywhere either—even if they were her usual method of punctuation. She hadn't even signed it. And he hadn't left her with enough courage to give them to him directly.

Which meant he had to look. She was far from a bad person, and he owed it to her to see what she now wanted him to see. Even if it couldn't change anything. She was like lightning across a dark sky, beautiful to watch but scarring or deadly if you got too close.

Tucking them under his arm, he headed for the living room, stopping at the fridge to get a beer.

Blue album: *Penny's Birthdays*.

Red album: *Penny's Progress*.

Progress? A strangely detached way to chronicle your child's life…

He opened the blue album. It started with the first

birthday. His first time seeing baby Penny. She was all eyes, those dazzling blue eyes, and smiles. Ribbons in her baby curls. Pushing a bear-themed walker around and honking the horn while laughing. People in the background winced.

He felt a small smile. How much would their child look like her? Would his dark brown eyes overwhelm those dazzling blues? His mother had hazel eyes, and her father's eyes had been green. There was a chance for blue.

Two. Favorite gift, tiny tricycle. No horn, had a bell this time. Chubby toddler legs. Bunnies to pet or chase while laughing, if that picture was anything to go by. Then half-naked and running from Mom, cake and frosting covering her face and mashing her hair up at an insane angle on one side.

He couldn't help his smile then. That was his girl. Half-naked, running around laughing, covered in cake.

The smile faltered. Was his. Not is.

Three. Small trampoline with safety bars. Pigtails. Skinned knee. Always running.

When had she started to get ill? He felt it lurking, like some hulking monster, ready to take away those rosy cheeks.

He sped through four, through five, six… More of the same, happy, bright, lively.

Seven. The seventh birthday was different. Indoors. At a table. Dressed in ruffles and ribbons. An angry red rash cascaded down her right cheek, around her eyes. Her swollen eyes. So red on her pale skin. She sat behind a cake burning seven candles but didn't smile for the camera.

Other pictures followed, showing her opening gifts. He could see the rash on her knuckles and marked the ones that had cracked to bleed by the bandages covering them.

Then a picture of a box someone else had to open. Too heavy, he realized, or she'd simply grown too tired. It was a disease that sapped strength. Mom posed for the picture that followed, showing the gift. Telescope.

The gifts on the first six birthdays had been the kind to encourage play, physical toys. But this toy was sedate for the little girl who'd been so active.

His chest burned sharper but hadn't really stopped since yesterday.

He put the book down and leaned back, just to get his breath. And to guzzle his beer. To remind himself that she'd gotten better. She was better now.

But when had she gotten better?

Dropping the empty bottle on the table, he picked up the album again and flipped the page.

Eight. Birthday in a pool. Water wings on her arms and Mom behind her, holding her for safety. Scrawny little body.

Nine. On the back of a pony with Dad holding her.

Ten. In a wheelchair.

No smiles. No smiles anymore. Never smiles. It was like looking at the embodiment of suffering. Her family loved her and the weaker she got the closer they held her, but her eyes were just dead. None of that Penny spark shone there.

He put the birthday album back down and reached for the other. He'd spent a half hour watching her deteriorate. He needed to see some progress.

But that's not what it showed. The first fifteen or so sheets of images showed progression, not progress. Small, fragile, but trying so hard to do what the therapists told her. Tears. So many tears.

God, this wasn't any better.

He skipped chunks he simply couldn't bear to see, and

didn't stop turning pages until he saw a twelve- or thirteen-year-old Penny in a safety harness, gripping parallel bars and walking. Supported, but walking. And smiling. With no fresh redness on her face, just a lingering pink shadow of it around her eyes, those brilliant, shining, hope-filled blue eyes.

Progression became progress. She worked the bars, bearing more weight in every picture as her cheeks and arms filled out.

She used weight machines, and her legs grew thicker, took on definition. Grew strong.

Braces became crutches, became a cane, became nothing. And her smile, God, her smile…

My whole life, my thinking was always, "Can you do this?" And for so long the answer was always no. When the answer finally started becoming yes, I just always did it.

He picked up the first album and flipped to those teen-aged birthday parties.

Thirteen. Go-karts.

Fourteen. Horseback riding without someone holding her.

Fifteen. He couldn't tell what was going on, just that there were girls and boys in bathing suits, running amok in the surf at the beach, and probably some kind of wet sand fight? There was sand flinging, which wasn't entirely safe without protective eyewear…

Sixteen. Dancing with friends and live music in the background. Who knew where…?

Always outside. So happy. So alive.

They'd had to hold her up, and then it became holding her back from all the things she wanted to do, and she'd pushed back against it. She hadn't sought out dangerous things because of some kind of desire for an adrenaline high, she'd wanted to do things that celebrated that freedom she'd fought so hard for. And to help others who were hurting. She understood suffering.

He didn't want to be someone who held her back. He wanted to celebrate with her, to see that sparkle in her eyes.

The sparkle that hadn't been there last night.

She'd gotten used to fighting for her freedom, and he'd gotten used to protecting himself. It couched all his decisions—that need to be safe.

Until that night…

CHAPTER TWELVE

PENNY CHECKED THE GPS as she turned down the drive where it told her, into trees, somewhere on the outskirts of Gabriel's hometown in New Jersey.

She hadn't heard from him the day he'd left, hadn't seen him that morning. She'd promised to stay out of his way and she had.

But she *had* heard the moment he'd gone, and even if she hadn't heard the door closing, she still would've known. A whole night awake fantasizing that he'd find her albums and change his mind had made her even more hypersensitive to his presence than usual. The moment he'd stepped out, all the hope had left her, had left with him.

Then she'd cried.

The next day had passed the same way—not knowing if he'd found them, if they'd made any difference. If he'd cared. If he even still wanted to be part of their child's life or if she'd ruined that too.

By the time his text had come late last night—We need to talk—along with some coordinates and a time, her hopes had fallen too far to even speculate about his thoughts.

On the drive, she'd conjured two options: meet his parents because he did still want the baby. Or meet at a lawyer's office because he did still want the baby, as in sole custody.

The long, private drive said *parents*. Which was good. She'd take it—she'd take whatever she could get.

Through the thick line of trees running along the drive she saw a field of white, and then color. Red and white checks like a massive gingham picnic blanket.

And then the trees opened out and she saw a big gingham hot-air balloon.

Her heart stuttered.

She sped up to get to the end of the road, wherever the heck it was, and around the bend came to a parking area before a massive red horse barn. Gabriel was there, leaning against the front fender of his car, arms crossed, knit cap and coat to warm him in the frosty but bright, sunny day.

She parked right beside him and got out, going a bit snow blind with the early afternoon rays bouncing off the snow. Snatching her glasses, she put them on and closed the car door.

The hot-air balloon could just be there by some coincidence. Maybe. She was afraid to get her hopes up or even to look at him, though the glasses made it a little easier as she could hide it if she got weepy again.

He didn't say anything but she could feel him watching as she pulled her gloves on and went to lean on his car beside him.

"Is that balloon for you?"

"Yes."

"I thought they only flew them when it was warm?"

"They usually do," he said softly, "but I begged."

Pregnancy-safe adventure. They'd even talked about this as a possibility. Oh, her hopes, they were climbing.

"It's not dangerous?"

"It's cold. People don't do it because it's very cold." His arms uncrossed and he slid one down her arm to take her gloved hand in his own. "Want to try it?"

She nodded, smiling even as she felt sneaky tears trying to leak out and had to dip her free hand up to swipe under her glasses before he saw them. "Even if you planned on chucking me out of the basket at ten thousand feet."

"You know better than that," he said softly, but let go of her hand and rounded to the trunk of his car. He soon returned with the largest parka she'd ever seen, and a thick, wooly beanie too. He pulled the hat onto her head, mashing her hair down, and she didn't care at all.

Standing so close and not touching him when her arms ached to wrap around him took strength of will she'd have doubted she possessed, but this felt like something that had to happen at his pace. The man liked to take his time in things...

"You only brought one big coat? That's not going to fit either of us." She tilted her head back so he could adjust her hat, and closed her eyes against the blinding afternoon sun.

"Trust me, I have a plan," he said, then, with her eyes to the sun, face lifted, she felt the brush of something cold and firm on her lips. It took a second, but she identified it.

Lip balm.

He did have a plan. Keep her warm, protect her lips from the wind. She smiled.

"Perfect. That makes it easier," he said, and finished. Then, before she could open her eyes, he pressed his lips to her newly moisturized mouth.

It was probably supposed to be a sweet little smooch, but the second she felt his warm lips against hers, her restraint evaporated. All the hurt of the past—Lord, she'd lost count how many days, it felt like years—evaporated with it.

This time, when her arms whipped around his shoulders, his came around her too, and he didn't kiss her back in the way of a man suffering her touch or indifferent to it. He angled his head, held her tighter, kissed deeper, until it was clumsy and wet, teeth, tongues, tears, and skewed sunglasses.

"This isn't the plan, baby." He panted more than spoke, his lips brushing hers with every syllable. Then lifted his head and pulled the glove off one hand so he could wipe the tears on her cheeks. "These will freeze up there."

She sniffed, then laughed a little and eased her hands back down. "I think I need more lip balm…"

He presented the tube, winked, and while she reapplied it, he put on the massive parka.

"Doors locked?"

She stuck the balm into her pocket, pulled out her key fob, and locked the door. With the keys stashed again, and her hands back in gloves, he put his arm around her waist and led, their steps crunching across the snowy field.

Two people waited at the balloon—the captain she could identify because he climbed into the basket, and a man at the moorings to knock off the anchor ropes when they were ready.

She didn't know how high they were going to go, but they couldn't reach her hopes and the burst of joy that had her just a little terrified she was getting too far ahead of herself.

The prospect of how much colder she knew it would be even a few hundred feet off the ground should probably factor into that fear, but it didn't. Gabriel would always try to keep her and the baby safe, and he was too sensible to go up for any other reason but to show her something. He loved her. He had to.

"Think you have room in there for me to huddle in? I'm not sure my wool coat is going to be warm enough. Also, I'm hoping to force you to hug me for a long stretch of time. It's my clever plan that I'm telling you like the villain at the end of a movie when they think they have the hero in the right place and…" She stopped, chuckling at herself. "Those thoughts started out from a much funnier place than they became as I kept explaining."

"They didn't have any parkas in your size, so I got the big one to share. It was my plan all along. My improvised romantic plan when they didn't have your size."

She smiled then and stepped in front of him, pressed her back to his front, and clamped her arms at her sides to keep them out of the way.

"Sleeves."

"Really?" She looked at the sleeves and then back at him. "Are you going to have one and me the other?"

"We could do that, but you'll probably be warmer if my arm is there too. The sleeves are big."

Penny wasn't about to put up a fuss about anything. She eyed the sleeves to make sure they were roomy enough, then just shrugged and went with it. It'd be better if her coat were off so she could actually feel him without the layers between them, but maybe that would come later. He had said *romantic*.

When it was done, and only her fingertips poked out of the wrists, making her hands utterly useless, he stiffly zipped them in. He was right, it was warm, and nice with him behind her, around her. To smell him, even among all this new-coat smell. Made the hard days blur about the edges.

Below, the land fell away as they rose. Gabriel lifted

their arms together so he could pull up the hood, then rested his chin on her shoulder so they were both protected from the wind.

"How did you set this up so fast? Or did you do it when we talked about it?"

"I did it yesterday. Their schedule was totally open," he said, and then added in a softer voice, "It was easier to arrange than the mental stuff."

"The not wanting to be anywhere near me bit?"

"That wasn't it. It was more being afraid to be with you." His mouth stayed at her ear, making it easy to hear over the wind. "Actually, that's not it. You kept saying I didn't trust you, and you were right. After Nila left, I always held part of myself back, and when I realized what you and the baby mean to me, I was in some broken pattern of trying to protect you both, or trying to protect myself. You humbled me. I know what it took for you to show me those albums, the albums that almost killed me."

She closed her eyes and let those words wash over her. Then turned her head toward him so the crosswinds wouldn't eat her words. "It was easier than you think, when it became necessary. If you were going to leave me, I wanted you to leave the real me. I should've let you see them before."

"You were protecting yourself. I get it. Neither of us were ready. If I'd looked then, I might not have seen it. Especially after having just looked at your Adventure album."

"Seen what?"

"What really drives you."

She hadn't really ever thought about her motivators aside from the excitement of *doing stuff*. "What do you think drives me?"

"Life. You just want to experience what life has to

offer. You don't do things that people frequently die doing. You use safety equipment. You always buckle in when you fly. You don't *chase* death. You chase experiences," he explained, shaking his head. "Did you just want me to say it, or do you not really know this?"

She shrugged He'd feel her shoulders creep up his chest, and no doubt saw her brows moving her knit cap.

"You told me you need *adventures*. That was your word, so on some level you know your motives. You didn't say you wanted thrills, stunts, or even fun. You said adventure."

"Yeah, okay. I guess that's right." She straightened and looked out over the sea, only realizing then that they were drifting out over the bay to the Atlantic. The gray winter water below still sparkled under the sun, and toward the northwest she could see the city skyline in the distance.

"I want to have adventures with you. I don't want to watch and worry. If you storm the gates of hell, I need to be storming them with you."

She smiled, and even her lip balm felt like it was stiffening from the cold, but she didn't want to cut their time short. "I promise not to storm the gates of hell. Or exclude you."

"I promise to work every day not to hold back from you, even if you're the one person in the world with the power to destroy me."

His words bounced around in her heart and she tried to turn to him, but her arms were stuffed in the sleeves and he'd wrapped their arms around her, which made it impossible. "I wouldn't... I wouldn't ever destroy you."

"I know. In my heart I know you would never do anything to hurt me, not on purpose. Logically, I know that it's going to be a struggle, me wanting to hold back. But you have a way of breaking through those barriers. I need that." He held her gaze as she twisted as best she could to look at him. "I need you. I asked you to marry me, and I told myself it was just for the well-being of the baby, but I need you. And I can give you however long you need, as long as you keep fighting for me too."

Her lower lip quivered and her throat had closed up again, so she nodded with as much vigor as she could manage tucked against him like that.

"Do you know the best adventure for us?"

She did. Oh, she did. But she needed to hear him say it, even if it would just be whispered in her ear.

"A life together. Laughing, fighting, driving each other crazy, knocking over Christmas trees because we can't stop touching long enough to lie down sensibly." He said the words she'd been waiting for. "Never giving up on one another. Raising our kids. Going on vacations to…scuba dive in the Keys or…to Iceland for the Northern Lights…"

It all sounded perfect, even before he said the thing that was sure to rip her guts out.

"Doing with them all the things Penelope didn't get to do."

Tears on her cheeks would freeze so she turned her head to him so he could see her cheeks. He was the one mostly in control of their hands right now.

"None of that," he said, reaching up to rub them away with his gloved hand, and then brought their arms together so he could cuff the left sleeve enough to expose her hand. Then took off her glove.

She started to pull the shared-sleeve arm to her face to get to her cheeks, but he already had them bending down and in.

"Pocket," he said.

She slipped her hand into the pocket, confused. Pockets were warm…

Except this one had a small velvet box in it.

"No balling my fist up for warmth with this thing in there," she said, closing her fingers over the box, and they pulled it from the pocket in tandem.

Gabriel stuffed her glove into the other pocket, then removed his own on the right, and stashed it too. Right hand his, left hand hers, he reached for the box. "Hold tight."

She nodded, and watched as he raised the lid. A glittering diamond winked at her from the black interior. "Man, I never thought I'd be excited to get an engagement ring, but if you don't hurry up I'm gonna die."

She'd have to tell him later that she didn't need a long engagement. He'd gone to such lengths to plan this, and he'd said even more than her heart had been aching to hear for what felt like years.

He plucked the ring from the velvet perch and she flipped her hand over to flex her fingers out to receive it. And dropped the box right over the edge, into the sea.

"Oh, no… Oh, *no*! You got it? You got it, right?" she babbled, until he showed it to her. "Hurry, before we drop it too! Hot-air balloons are dangerous if you've got butter fingers. Maybe we should step back from the edge of the basket."

In answer, he slipped the ring onto her finger.

"You know, in my head, I was going to kiss the ring, it was going to be extremely romantic. But now I'm thinking gloves."

"Yes. Yes, gloves." She laughed, and between the two of them wrestled her left glove on over the ring, and his right one back on.

As soon as the maneuver was complete, Penny wiggled and turned, pulling her arms from the sleeves.

"Pen?" Despite his confusion, he held still, didn't try to stop her.

She didn't stop, even to explain, until she'd gotten her arms free and spun inside the oversized coat to get her arms around him.

His smile was beautiful, and short-lived. She tugged on him and leaned up on her toes, mouth presented for kissing. That was all it took to convince him to kiss her again. Kiss for real. Kiss enough to make the balloon captain feel awkward, probably.

When he lifted his head, she felt words bubbling out. "When you said to meet you in New Jersey, I joked to Miranda in my best mafia talk, 'He's gonna make me an offer I can't refuse.' But I really thought maybe you wanted me to meet your parents, or maybe you'd told them about me and they wanted to meet me and asked. But you really did ask me to New Jersey to make me an offer I couldn't refuse."

"I did." He laughed again, "But that's not New Jersey. *The Godfather* was set in New York."

"It was?"

He nodded.

"I've never watched it. I only know that line. I just thought it was Jersey, for some reason."

"You never watched *The Godfather*?"

She shook her head again and teased, "Is the wedding off now?"

His disapproving squint was beautiful, and full of charm. "No. It just means we have to watch some movies before we get married. Or on our honeymoon. However, to answer your other question, my parents do want to meet you. Just not today. I want you to myself today."

"Me too. Let's go home."

"You're done with the balloon flight adventure?"

"It's cold," she whispered, then gave him her best sexy

eyebrow wiggle over the top of her glasses. "I have another adventure in mind."

"Do you?"

"Mmm-hmm. A sexy adventure. Then a nap."

There her stomach pitted a little and she knew she lost the flirty glint in her eyes, but still kept looking over the top edge so he could see her. "And you stay. You're there…"

"When you wake up?"

She nodded.

"I can guarantee it."

"Even if you need to go to the bathroom."

"Is that a question?"

"No. I mean I need you to be there when I wake up, so wake me up first. Or put a sign on the pillow that says 'Be Right Back.'"

"We might need to talk about this later."

"*Humor* me."

"We'll have a neon sign made up, and I'll flip the switch so that it says: 'Gabriel has Gone to the Bathroom. Don't Go Looking for Him.'"

Satisfied, she nodded, grinning and raising her face for another kiss. But he took her cheeks in both hands and pushed the brim of her hat up with his thumbs to bare the space between her brows, then pressed his lips to her forehead and lingered there. A feeling she could only call relief started where his lips touched her head and then seeped into the rest of her body, down to her toes. The need for hungry kisses faded back for the moment, and as the soft, loving kiss faded, she rested her cheek against his shoulder and let that sweetness fill her.

They stayed like that a long time, paying no attention to the views or the cold. It was the lump on her left ring finger stretching her gloves tight that made her think about weddings. "Oh—ah—are you going to be my date tomorrow?"

"You can assume I'm going to be your date for everything."

His words made her smile, and she had to drag herself away from drifting right back into that happy place again. "Charles's wedding... I don't think we should tell the family about our engagement or the baby tomorrow. It's their special day and I don't want to stomp all over it. So I'll need you to put the ring back on me tomorrow when we get home."

"And not mention the suspension?"

Oh, yeah, the suspension. And her father, Chief of the ER before Charles had ascended to his position. "Yeah, let's leave that out too. I don't want to...make a scene when Dad decides to drown me in the chocolate fountain."

He laughed and made all the right sounds of agreement, then directed her to look toward the other side of the balloon, at the skyline in the distance.

The captain had turned them back toward land. Bless him.

"I think we owe him a good tip," she murmured against his neck.

"A better tip than 'Don't take lovestruck idiots up in the middle of winter'?"

"I'm pretty sure he's got that one already."

EPILOGUE

Seven months later...

THE CAB PULLED up outside the emergency doors of Manhattan Mercy, and Gabriel breathed a sigh of relief to see his brother-in-law, Zac, waiting there with a wheelchair.

In the backseat beside him, Penny held his hand but said nothing. She'd taken up meditation as a way to get through the last few months of pregnancy, when she truly had felt restricted, and now sat with her eyes closed, practicing deep, mindful breathing. It might not be Lamaze exactly, but whatever worked for her, he was happy to support. Especially since one of them needed to be calm for this, and he'd passed calm ten blocks back.

The hold she had on his hand tightened, clueing him in on the approaching contraction. She squeezed hard enough that he could feel her racing heart.

"We're here," he said gently, then opened the door with his free hand.

She opened her eyes to the sight of Zac rolling the wheelchair toward the cab, and her heart rate kicked up higher. "Who does he think is sitting in that?"

No sooner had the words flown than the contraction crested and she squeezed his hand hard enough to pop his knuckles. He sat with her, waiting, breathing, for it to pass. "It's just until we get upstairs."

"I can walk," she panted, then nudged him so that he took the hint and got out. A short time later he had her out and paid the cabbie, but when he turned back, he found her arguing with Zac about the chair.

"You're in labor."

"I figured that out when it was my womb that started seizing up."

"You know hospital policy."

"I don't care about hospital policy. Let's just walk in quickly. You can roll behind us and if I have to sit down, if another one comes...before we get upstairs...we'll cross that bridge..." Obviously it was his turn to be the calmer one. Luckily, he'd planned for this.

He took her hand again and didn't even attempt to drag her the remaining two feet to the chair. Wheelchairs were emotional landmines for Penny. Before they'd decided it was time to come to the hospital, she'd even suggested they should call an ambulance when they still had time, because gurneys were better than wheelchairs.

He sat in the chair, then gestured to his lap with his free hand. "I'm sitting in the chair, you're sitting on me."

It stopped the argument, and when she looked at him, he saw her eyes soften, and she even smiled.

"That's against policy too," Zac said, but his heart didn't sound in it.

"I don't care about hospital policy." This time the words came out of Gabriel's mouth. He simply locked the wheels, then helped ease his waddling wife onto his lap. When they were settled, he unlocked the wheels.

Zac's lip service to policy became evident when he fell in behind them and began pushing them toward the sliding double doors and into the hospital.

* * *

Nearly twelve hours later, in the middle of the night, Mia Jackson came into the world. Penny handled birth far better than she had handled the last month of pregnancy, when she'd repeatedly insisted she was so large, the baby had invited over friends to have a "pool party" in her womb.

Now, as Gabriel sat by his sleeping wife, holding his baby girl, throat so full of happiness and gratitude, he half feared he'd drown on the thick, syrupy sweetness filling him if he breathed too deeply. And he couldn't take his eyes off the little sleeping face, or the tiny hand wrapped around his fingertip.

"Penny for your thoughts."

He smiled at his wife's sleepy, quiet, exhausted voice.

"Penny's always in my thoughts," he whispered, not wanting to wake Mia as she'd had just as hard a day. Catching sight of Penny over the head of their sleeping newborn, he asked, "How are you feeling?"

"Tired. Sore. *Wonderful,*" she said. Then she added, "You didn't answer."

He didn't answer because his heart was too full to translate any of it into words. Instead, he handled what was before him. "Do you want to hold her?"

In answer, and with the help of the bed controls, she sat up and held her arms out. "Still not what you were thinking."

Slowly, he rose and transferred the warm little bundle into her arms, then stood back to take them both in. Penny had held Mia briefly right after she'd been cleaned up, but a long labor had left her too exhausted to really *meet* their daughter before. The grin that split her face flashed like a tropical sunrise, and he knew what she was smiling at before she lifted a hand to stroke through the fullest head of downy black hair he'd ever seen on such a tiny baby.

"I was thinking how much she looks like Baby Penny, but with more enviable locks." He murmured one of a thousand wondrous thoughts that had filled his mind the past few hours.

With soft laugh and the misty eyes, she nodded, clearly as overcome as he'd spent the hours being.

"And that we're going to teach her to crawl, to walk, and to run. And how to know what things she should always run toward."

The family motto, and they still occasionally debated the list of *things*.

A tear fell onto one tiny hand, and she smoothed it away just as he reached out to do the same to her cheeks. "Think we'll have it figured out by the time she's running?" she asked.

He knew her way of loving teasing, always sunshine on his days. "We have a good start on it. Always run toward us. That should buy us some time."

"Always run toward each other," she said, lifting her eyes again to him, and that playful light he loved had been replaced by such devoted reverence he almost lost it. It was a promise, one she silently made every day.

Once again speech left him. All he could do was nod, his life so full of goodness and beauty he couldn't believe it, but knew he'd never let it go.

"Hey."

He looked up again.

She slowly shifted to the side to make room in her bed, and looked down at the space she'd made.

"What about hospital policy?"

"I don't care about hospital policy," she dutifully murmured.

Moments later, he reclined with her, holding his whole

family in his arms. As they looked down at her, Mia quietly opened her eyes.

"They're blue," Penny whispered.

Gabriel kissed her temple. "I told you they would be."

* * * * *

Welcome to the
CHRISTMAS IN MANHATTAN
six-book series

Available now:

SLEIGH RIDE WITH THE SINGLE DAD
by Alison Roberts
A FIREFIGHTER IN HER STOCKING
by Janice Lynn
THE SPANISH DUKE'S HOLIDAY PROPOSAL
by Robin Gianna
THE RESCUE DOC'S CHRISTMAS MIRACLE
by Amalie Berlin

Coming soon:

CHRISTMAS WITH THE BEST MAN
by Susan Carlisle
NAVY DOC ON HER CHRISTMAS LIST
by Amy Ruttan

MILLS & BOON®

EXCLUSIVE EXTRACT

He enticed her into one sizzling night… Now notorious sheikh Hazin al-Razim is desperate to claim midwife Flo as his bride!

Read on for a sneak preview of
CHRISTMAS BRIDE FOR THE SHEIKH
the second book in Carol Marinelli's
RUTHLESS ROYAL SHEIHKS *duet*

Hazin lowered his head and their mouths met before he was even fully seated. His lips were warm and Flo's pouted to his.

Soft and sensual, his mouth claimed hers.

She had never known a kiss like it, for it sent a river of shivers through her and the brief bliss of relief faded for she *had* to taste his tongue, yet Hazin made her wait. His hands came to her upper arms and he held her steady when she ached to lean into him.

Then his mouth left hers and she felt its warm drag against her cheek and the scratch of his jaw as his lips found her ear. His breath was warm and he told her his truth. 'I want you so badly.'

For a second she sat, his cheek pressed to hers, his ragged sexy breathing in her ear and his hands firm on her arms and Flo closed her eyes in a vague prayer for common sense to prevail.

It didn't.

Fired on by one kiss, her body crackled like a chip in hot oil and she offered her response to his indecent request. 'Take me to bed.'

Don't miss the scorching duet from Carol Marinelli:

RUTHLESS ROYAL SHEIKHS
Two royal brothers – bound by duty,
but driven by desire!

A born leader and a playboy prince… But *nothing* is
more important to Ilyas and Hazin al-Razim than
honouring their royal birth right!

Until their searing passion for two beautiful, fiery women
challenges everything they've ever known – and these
sheikhs won't rest until they've claimed them…

Discover the first part, Ilyas's story
CAPTIVE FOR THE SHEIKH'S PLEASURE

Sheikh Ilyas al-Razim won't let *anything* stand in his
way, especially not the waitress daring to think she can
blackmail him! He'll take the impossibly stunning
Maggie Delaney as his hostage… But once her
innocence is proven, dare she surrender to the pleasure
this desert prince promises?

Available from Mills & Boon Modern

And read the second part, Hazin's story
CHRISTMAS BRIDE FOR THE SHEIKH
Available from Mills & Boon Medical Romance
Both available December 2017!
www.millsandboon.co.uk

Join Britain's BIGGEST Romance Book Club

- **EXCLUSIVE offers every month**

- **FREE delivery direc** to your door

- **NEVER MISS a title**

Call Customer Services
0844 844 1358*

or visit
millsandboon.co.uk/bookclub